Mrs. Christie
at the
Mystery
Guild
Library

Mrs. Christie

at the

Mystery

Guild

Library

AMANDA CHAPMAN

BERKLEY PRIME CRIME

NEW YORK

BERKLEY PRIME CRIME
Published by Berkley
An imprint of Penguin Random House LLC
1745 Broadway, New York, NY 10019
penguinrandomhouse.com

Book design by George Towne
Interior art: Vintage Objects Collection © Marish / Shutterstock

Library of Congress Cataloging-in-Publication Data

Names: Chapman, Amanda author
Title: Mrs. Christie at the mystery guild library / Amanda Chapman.
Description: First edition. | New York: Berkley Prime Crime, 2025.
Identifiers: LCCN 2025003617 (print) | LCCN 2025003618 (ebook) |
ISBN 9780593818817 hardcover | ISBN 9780593818831 epub
Subjects: LCGFT: Detective and mystery fiction | Novels
Classification: LCC PS3603.H3595 M77 2025 (print) |
LCC PS3603.H3595 (ebook) | DDC 813/.6—dc23/eng/20250417
LC record available at https://lccn.loc.gov/2025003617
LC ebook record available at https://lccn.loc.gov/2025003618

Printed in the United States of America
1st Printing

The authorized representative in the EU for product safety and compliance is
Penguin Random House Ireland, Morrison Chambers, 32 Nassau Street,
Dublin D02 YH68, Ireland, https://eu-contact.penguin.ie.

For my grandmother

What a very extraordinary person you are.

What sort of a woman are you?

Why are you talking like this?

Who are you?

—Clotilde Bradbury-Scott to

Miss Jane Marple, *Nemesis*

Mrs.
Christie
at the
Mystery
Guild
Library

Prologue

◇◇◇◇◇◇◇◇◇◇◇◇◇◇

"DO YOU KNOW, WHEN I WAS A CHILD, IT WAS THE LAVATORY TO which I retired for quiet meditation."

I froze. The voice behind me, British and unmistakably posh, had come out of nowhere. But this was impossible. There had been no one in the library when I'd locked up. And surely no one upstairs in the Christie Room when I'd hurried in, grabbed my book from its shelf, kicked off my shoes and thrown myself full length on the nice cozy couch for a little me time.

"I would close the heavy, mahogany, shelflike cover and sit on it," the voice—high and fluting, slightly breathless—continued, "giving myself up to reflection. I think Mr. Wright catches that sense of retreat rather well."

When this remarkable statement had concluded, I sat up, carefully closed the volume I'd been perusing (which, yes, just happened to be Lawrence Wright's charming *Clean & Decent: The*

Fascinating History of the Bathroom and the Water-Closet) and turned my head toward the speaker.

It was a woman. A woman sitting a bit behind me and to my left in the alcove of the Mystery Guild Library's Agatha Christie Room, entirely at home on its gold velvet–upholstered armchair. I supposed that I must have missed her in my beeline for the couch, though there was something about her that was, well, unmissable. Not to look at, exactly. She was fairly unremarkable in appearance and could have been any one of the interchangeable New York matriarchs who so generously fund the library. A woman of late middle age with what might be described as an interesting face— a mouth that looked quick to smile and a long nose below heavy-lidded eyes that nonetheless sparked with humor. A hat like a deflated velvet soufflé was perched on her waved grey hair, and sensible, well-polished brogues encased her feet. She was wearing the kind of boxy tweed suit that had gone out of favor at least three-quarters of a century ago, though the cut and the material told me it was bespoke. On the floor next to her, waiting like a patient puppy, was a black patent leather handbag that I immediately pegged as by Launer, handbag makers to the late Queen Elizabeth II. Also, I was quite sure the five strands of pearls around the woman's neck were the real deal.

My guest looked familiar. Was she one of the library's patrons? Someone I'd met only briefly? But those eyes—from which shone an unmistakable intelligence—also held a hint of mischief, and I had never sensed even a glimmer of wit in any of those pillars of our institution. This woman was different. She had real presence. There was something, well, irresistible about her. Not that I didn't try to resist. She might well be contemplating a nice fat donation to the library, but that didn't mean she could make herself at home after hours in the Christie Room. I stood, and using my sternest *I am the librarian* (which I am not) tone of voice, said, "I'm very sorry, but the library is closed for the day."

"Lovely," my visitor responded, waving one beringed hand gaily. "I've always been a bit shy. Especially when I'm on the lam, so to speak."

Oh, good lord, I thought, *the woman's made a break from whatever loony bin her family has convinced her is just a "rest home."* Probably the same one where my great-aunt Doris, who has frequent spells where she imagines herself to be a goldfish, sometimes "rests."

"I'm leaving now myself," I lied. "But I'm happy to walk you out, Mrs. . . . ?"

"Mallowan," the woman replied. "Mrs. Max Mallowan."

I froze again. *Mrs. Max Mallowan.*

"Although you probably know me as Agatha Christie."

One

"Do you think it might be beyond the realms of possibility that I might get a drink?"

—Mr. Venables, *The Pale Horse*

MY NAME IS TORY VAN DYNE. I AM A BOOK CONSERVATOR AT New York's Mystery Guild Library, and until that rainy late-September evening when a woman claiming to be the Queen of Crime first materialized in the library's Christie Room, I'd been working very hard at living a safe, sane, sensible life. A life shielded from the eccentricities of my Old New York family (including a grandfather given to penning naughty limericks and the aforementioned great-aunt), the antics of my socialite/actor cousin Nicola (popularly known as one of the three Belles of Broadway), and my own particular brand of crazy (about which, I'd always felt, the least said the better). I lived instead a quiet life. A safe, sane, sensible life.

Later, when I'd had a chance to process our little encounter, I realized it made a kind of weird sense that if my guest was indeed Agatha Christie (*which I did not believe for a minute*), and if she had

indeed decided to visit New York City some fifty years after she'd
been airlifted to the Great Beyond (*which I also did not believe for a
minute*), she might indeed choose New York's Mystery Guild Library as a home base. Even in the After Life, she would surely have
heard about the library's Agatha Christie Room, a very close replica of British mystery novelist Agatha Christie's personal library
in Greenway House, her holiday home in Devon, England.

The Christie Room had been a labor of love masterminded by
my grandmother Margaret Jane Van Dyne in what was at the
time her home on Washington Square North and which now
houses the Mystery Guild Library on the first two floors and Yours
Truly on the two floors above. The house is one of the dozen or so
remaining Greek Revival redbrick, marble-trimmed town houses
in what is known as "The Row" overlooking Greenwich Village's
Washington Square Park, and it is still as covetable an address as
it was in 1880 when Henry James limned the life of the wealthy in
his masterpiece, *Washington Square*. I had always loved the park. It
is small, no more than a few square city blocks, and I loved its in-
timacy, its shaded benches, its great round fountain in the central
plaza. And, like all good New Yorkers, I loved its monumental
Washington Arch, the park's official entrance at the foot of Fifth
Avenue. Grandmother's house on Washington Square North was
a mere half block to the west of Fifth, and from my tiny Juliet balcony on the third floor, I had enviable views across to the park and
the arch.

Grandmother, one of the last of the New York Montagues
(railroads and coal), had brought the house to her marriage to Ty-
ler Anson Van Dyne (finance and real estate) in 1947. But Margaret Jane had been a smart cookie. She knew whom and what she
was marrying ("a Van Dyne, yes, but a devil with women and a
damn fool with money"). And so she had held on to her girlhood

home as her plan B, leasing it at an exorbitant rent to "the right sort of people." By which she meant her sort of people.

Her foresight paid off. When my grandfather finally chased one extramarital skirt too many, she'd shocked her social circle by divorcing him. "I could overlook it in his younger days," Grandmother had sniffed. "But in a man of sixty, what had been merely a failing now began to look like bad taste." She'd then given her bewildered tenants exactly thirty days to remove themselves from her house and betook herself from the Van Dyne mansion on Upper Fifth Avenue all the way downtown to Washington Square. There she lived quite happily with her extensive collection of Agatha Christie first editions, spending the last twenty years of her life absorbed in re-creating as closely as possible Mrs. Christie's library at Greenway House.

And when I say as closely as possible, I am not kidding.

The Christie Room had been carved out of Grandmother's second-floor drawing room overlooking the park. It was not only an architectural replica of the Greenway library—including faithful reproductions of its wonderfully eclectic furnishings—it also housed copies—hunted down over years by my grandmother—of many of the more than four thousand volumes on the Greenway library shelves. These, of course, included Dame Agatha's own sixty-six mystery novels (every one of which I had read, and in many cases reread, much to Grandmother's delight), nineteen plays and two memoirs.

The room itself was a comfortable space, large but quietly informal, with cream walls and white bookshelves and a down-filled blue damask couch facing the fireplace. That couch fairly begged you to pick up one of Mrs. Christie's mysteries (maybe *The Body in the Library*) and curl up for a good read. Or you could browse the offerings in its cozy alcove, where a collection of bargeware teapots shared space with a well-stocked bar cart, an armchair upholstered in dull gold velvet with an intricate design recalling Egyptian hieroglyphics, and a navy velvet settee edged with gold-embroidered trim. There you might want to pick up one of the six romance novels the author had also written under the pen name Mary Westmacott.

But the most interesting volumes, at least to Grandmother—whose goal was to plumb Mrs. Christie's very mind—were the books used by the writer in her work, including, of course, Martindale's *Extra Pharmacopoeia*, with its vast compendium of poisons. Or you could while away an hour or two with some other delight from Mrs. Christie's rather eclectic collection. Perhaps a treatise on Buddhism or D. M. C. Prichard's *Commentary on the Laws of Croquet*. Or, if you were one of the library's younger readers—and we have a surprisingly large number of them—a copy of one of the many books Mrs. Christie had read herself as a child and lovingly saved. Perhaps Frances Browne's *Granny's Wonderful Chair and Its Tales of Fairy Times*, which had been given to the young Agatha Miller by her own grandmother. I, though, was partial to ephemera like the first edition of Robert Vermeire's 1922 classic *Cocktails: How to Mix Them*, which I happened to know had cost Grandmother a cool couple grand.

I loved the Christie Room. The truth is, over the past several years I'd become out of necessity a fairly solitary creature, and I often retreated to its soothing quiet when unwelcome memories invaded. On those days, after I'd finished my work and ensured that all of the library's patrons had left for the day—or, as on that evening, after an interminable Sunday-afternoon dinner with the family—I would lock the heavy oak front door and take shelter in the Christie Room. There I would pull out a volume at random from the shelves and, with a grateful sigh, sink into the soft cushions of the couch and lose myself in whatever subject had once caught Mrs. Christie's attention. Like water closets.

Now, looking back to that night—that rainy Sunday night in late September when a woman wearing well-polished brogues, sensible tweeds, five strands of big, fat pearls and a hat like a deflated soufflé introduced herself as Agatha Christie—I wonder if I somehow knew then that my safe, sane, sensible life was as dead as a body with a knife in its back in one of Dame Agatha's own mysteries.

WHAT I CERTAINLY DID KNOW AT THE TIME WAS THAT I WAS SIT-ting in the same room with a woman who *thought* she was Agatha Christie. *Tread carefully here, Tory.*

What really worried me was that my guest knew enough about her alter ego to be aware that after Agatha Christie's divorce from her first husband, Archie Christie, the author had continued to write mysteries under her married name—even after her later marriage to archaeologist Max Mallowan in 1930. This knowledge on the part of my visitor argued for a certain amount of obsessiveness on her part.

Oh well, I comforted myself, *at least she doesn't think she's a goldfish.*

I took a deep, calming breath. Which never works. "Yes, well, the fact remains that the library is closed, Mrs., um, Mallowan."

"Why don't you just call me Mrs. Christie?" the woman said, with a smile of considerable charm. "Everyone did." *Was it weird that this woman was referring to herself in the past tense?* "Except my dear friends, of course, who simply called me Agatha in the modern style, and my household staff and local tradesmen, to whom I was, of course, Lady Mallowan."

She said the title—which the real Agatha Christie had acquired not when she herself had been made a Dame Commander of the Order of the British Empire by Queen Elizabeth in 1971 but three years earlier, when her archaeologist husband had been awarded *his* OBE—with a kind of childlike pride. I was reminded of the author's rather sweet admission in her autobiography that her childhood dream was to be "Lady Agatha" one day. But this, I reminded myself, was no time for reflections on Agatha Christie's childhood. Particularly when Agatha Christie's childhood was *not* the childhood of the woman sitting in the Christie Room at the moment.

I attempted to stem the flow. "Yes, certainly. Whatever you'd like, Mrs., um, Christie."

I also tried for a sympathetic and trustworthy smile but was pretty sure that I just ended up looking as peculiar as I felt. "Maybe there's somebody I could call?" *Like your keeper?*

Because it was obvious that this lady wasn't going anywhere without a lot of encouragement. She'd settled back in her armchair and was gazing around her with unconcealed delight. "Oh no, I don't think so, Miss . . . ?"

"Van Dyne. Victoria Van Dyne."

"Ah," the woman murmured, almost to herself. "After the great queen." *Well, no, after my great-grandmother, but fine.* "I was only eleven when the Queen died, you know. It made a very great impression on me. It was the same year that my beloved father died. Life took on a completely different complexion after my father's death . . ." Her voice trailed away.

I wasn't sure how to respond. There was real grief here, I was sure of it. But before I could say anything, she shook her head slightly, as if to bring herself back from her memories.

"How do you do, Miss Van Dyne," she said, holding out a gracious hand.

I crossed to the woman seated in the armchair and took the offered hand. Her grip was firm and warm. *Real.* Firm and warm and *real.* "How do you do," I said.

It was then that my eye was caught by the black-and-white photograph on the small round table next to the room's fireplace. I'd seen the photo so many times that I'd stopped really seeing it. It was that famous image of Agatha Christie seated at a desk signing copies of her latest whodunit and looking a bit worriedly at two crooked stacks of books piled perilously high on either side of her.

The same woman who is now sitting in the Christie Room of the Mystery Guild Library talking to you, Tory Van Dyne, about water closets.

It took me a second to get a grip. If anyone had a genetic predisposition to, shall we say, over-imagination, it was probably Yours Truly. I needed to watch out. *So this woman is a dead ringer for Agatha Christie,* I told myself, hardly registering my unfortunate choice of words. *That doesn't mean she is Agatha Christie. You shook her hand. It was warm. The woman is real.*

I reminded myself of the thousands of Elvis impersonators out there. A lot of them probably got their start because they *looked* like Elvis. Why couldn't there be some Agatha Christie wannabes? God knows the woman has fans. She was and still is the most widely read author of all time, outsold only by the Bible and Shakespeare. Indeed, her books continue to sell in the millions some fifty years after her death.

So what we probably have here, I told myself, *is a slightly nutty Christie fangirl. You should appreciate that, Tory. After all, it was your grandmother who obsessively re-created Mrs. Christie's library to "understand how her mind worked." Just be polite. The lady will leave once she's had her thrill.*

But the lady clearly wasn't ready to leave quite yet. She gave a little sideways tilt of her head toward the room's bar cart with its silver cocktail shaker, cut-glass siphon and bottles of various spirits and liqueurs. Grandmother had always insisted that the cart be fully stocked, and had often taken an evening cocktail there. The tradition continued under the library's board of directors, who liked to use the room for fundraisers featuring drinks with ridiculous names like Pretty Poison and Deadly Doornails.

"Perhaps," she said, "you'd be so kind as to mix me a cocktail."

Aha! Gotcha, Mrs. So-Called Christie! You only had to read one biography of Agatha Christie to know that the bar cart in her library was a concession to her friends and family. The woman herself did not drink.

With the relish of a poker player whose opponent has just betrayed their hand, I said sweetly (for me), "But you don't drink, Mrs. Christie."

Mrs. So-Called Christie smiled and corrected me gently. "I *didn't* drink, Miss Van Dyne. But I have never been an advocate of teetotalism. A little strong drink is always advisable on the premises in case there is a shock or an accident."

I had to smile. "Or, of course, if a gentleman should arrive suddenly," I said, completing the quote. "Miss Jane Marple, *The Mirror Crack'd from Side to Side.*"

She matched my smile with one of her own. "Well done, Miss Van Dyne."

"That being said," I pointed out, "the fact remains that you yourself don't drink."

"That certainly *was* true," my guest acknowledged, "but no longer. I now abide where ambrosia was invented, and I quickly developed a taste for a well-made aperitif. The beauty of it is that, in the Eternity, ambrosia stimulates, warms and inspires, but never inebriates."

I thought about that for a moment. I'd had a classical education. I knew that in Greek mythology ambrosia was the drink served to the gods on Mount Olympus to confer immortality.

Well played, Mrs. So-Called Christie.

I found myself moving obediently toward the bar cart. The truth was, by that point I needed a good stiff drink myself. "What can I get you?"

"Perhaps a Satan's Whisker?"

I stared at her blankly. *A Satan's Whisker?* Why did that sound familiar?

My guest took pity on me. "It's quite simple to make. You'll find the recipe in Mr. Vermeire's invaluable compendium, though I believe he calls it a Devil's Cocktail."

Then she pointed to the very shelf that I knew held *Cocktails: How to Mix Them.* I'd put it back there myself after looking up how to make a gin gimlet last week. Which I'd desperately needed after one of my cousin Nic's escapades had required a trip uptown to bail her out before word got back to the family.

"Not that you will need to look up the recipe," Mrs. So-Called Christie added. "It's merely equal parts of brandy and crème de menthe, but you mustn't forget a shake of red pepper. That's most important. It's absolutely super, and guaranteed to put some pep into you."

Super? Pep? That didn't sound like Mrs. So-Called Christie. And then it came to me. In Agatha Christie's first play, *Black Coffee,* these were the words said by the murdered scientist's niece, Barbara Amory. Who had been hankering for a cocktail called a Satan's Whisker.

I had to admit Mrs. So-Called Christie was good at this game.

But then she really unnerved me. "You'll find the ground red pepper in the silver shaker next to the Cointreau."

I noticed that she hadn't even glanced at the bar cart, as if she'd simply known that there would be a silver shaker next to the

Cointreau. Which there was. I'd always assumed that it held something like nutmeg. I'd never actually checked it out. I loathe nutmeg. But now I was fairly certain that the shaker held ground red pepper. Which, after an exploratory tap into my hand, I saw that indeed it did.

"And do please join me," Mrs. So-Called Christie added, for all the world as if she were the hostess and I her guest.

"I think maybe I will," I said. "Do you want yours straight up or on the rocks?"

"Rocks?"

"I'm sorry," I said. "Over ice."

"Ice would be lovely," Mrs. So-Called Christie said. "I got rather in the habit of cold drinks with ice during a trip to America in, when was it . . . ?"

"1966," I supplied hopelessly.

"Yes! How clever of you to know that!" she cried delightedly.

I didn't know how to tell her that I'd devoured every biography of her ever written, as well as her own autobiography. Somehow it seemed rude to mention it, as if I'd gone rooting through her underwear drawer. Then I remembered that this woman *wasn't actually Agatha Christie.*

Nonetheless, I dutifully went to get ice from my grandmother's one concession to modernity in the Christie Room, a small kitchenette hidden behind a door cleverly disguised as a bookshelf. A newcomer would never guess what lay behind its rows of Christie novels in all their various international translations unless they happened to notice a volume entitled *Eepingslay Urdermay* (*Sleeping Murder* in pig Latin, which as kids Nic and I had considered hilarious). If said visitor happened to try to pull the book out, the camouflaged door would swing open, revealing the small but very efficient kitchenette.

"How terribly clever!" she said, rising from her seat to peek in at the little room, complete with its sink, minifridge and all the fixings for tea and coffee. And cocktails.

I dumped a tray of ice into a silver ice bucket and took it out to the library. I mixed our drinks in the silver cocktail shaker, then poured them into highball glasses piled high with ice, dutifully adding a shake of ground red pepper to each. I handed one to my guest and raised my glass to her. Then I took a slug of my first-ever Satan's Whisker.

"Whew," I said when I'd recovered. "You're right. It certainly does have pep."

Mrs. So-Called Christie laughed, a lovely musical laugh, like water spilling over a creek bed, and I was absurdly pleased that I'd amused her.

She then leaned toward me. "I do realize, you know, that this is not actually *my* library."

Well, hallelujah, I thought. *Not totally crackers anyway.*

"No?" I said neutrally.

"Of course not, my dear Miss Van Dyne," she said. "This is merely a remarkably good approximation of my library at Greenway House."

But still pretty crackers. We needed to move on. I was ready to get off the bus to Bonkersville. "Excuse me if this seems rude, Mrs., um, Christie," I said, "but why are you here?"

"Not rude at all, my dear," Mrs. So-Called Christie responded graciously. "I'm here, of course, to help you solve a mystery." *So definitely still on the Bonkersville bus.*

I took a deep, calming breath. Which again totally did not help. I had to ask. "What kind of mystery, Mrs. Christie?"

She didn't miss a beat.

"Why, my dear Miss Van Dyne, a murder mystery, of course."

Two

"Everything that has existed, lingers in the Eternity."
—Miss Jane Marple, *Miss Marple: The*
Complete Short Stories

HELP ME SOLVE A MURDER MYSTERY?

Given the Van Dyne family history of what could politely be called eccentrics, it generally takes a lot of loony to rock me. I come from what those who still care about such things call "old money." This is snob code for wealthy families with a long pedigree. ("New money" being snob code for wealthy families with limited pedigree.) The term, however, can be misleading. Like many of New York's old-money families these days, the money part is not what it used to be. Except, of course, for Nic's father, my uncle Rupert, who makes pots of dollars at one of those newfangled (at least from the family's point of view) hedge funds. But the rest of our clan has been clinging to shrinking trust funds that—after four generations of profligacy—barely keep them in the style to which their forebears had been accustomed.

Also, as is so often the case in old families, successive generations had gone a little doolally. There was, for example, Great-

Aunt Doris, she of the goldfish delusion, and my grandfather Percival Van Dyne, he of the racy limericks. Both of these ancient ones still made their home at the family pile on Upper Fifth Avenue, as did my father as well as Nic's parents and Nic herself. It's a big family pile.

More recently, my father, after he'd run through his own much-diminished trust fund, had gone completely off the rails, siphoning the capital from mine into an infamous Ponzi scheme (yes, that one), where it poofed away like water on a hot griddle. To this day, I bless him for his cluelessness. It was the making of me. I had been terrible in the role of trust fund kid, which I could never quite get the hang of, but was quite good at my work, which I loved.

My mother, a solid New England Yankee and easily the most sensible of the Van Dyne bunch (perhaps because she was not actually a Van Dyne), had also benefited from the Ponzi fiasco, using it as the perfect excuse to "take some time off" at her family's compound on Cape Cod with her "best friend," Marjorie Harcourt. Fifteen years later, Mom and Marj were still living on the Cape, happy as the proverbial clams. My annual August vacation with them was something I looked forward to all year, and Mom's biweekly Sunday-night calls meant I always had someone who understood the clan and could put their nuttiness in perspective.

And then there was my younger cousin Nic, whose "reality mirrors fiction" debut as Christine in Broadway's *Phantom of the Opera* was theater lore. Here was a girl stepping in at the last minute to replace the lead in a play about a girl stepping in at the last minute to replace the lead in a play. And the crowd had loved it. From the moment Nic began to sing her little heart out with a ringing "Think of Me," the audience was hers. And for the next two years, she was theirs. Nic absolutely blossomed in the limelight, whether onstage or off.

Onstage was better, of course, but off was fun, too. As a card-carrying member of New York's charity gala brigade, Nic was a photographer's dream, and her wide, delighted smile and outré fashions often spiced up the staid society columns of *Town & Country* and *Avenue Magazine*. Besides being, in Nic's view, "super fun," this ubiquity on the red carpet ensured that she remained in the public eye when she was "resting between roles." And if there was no red carpet available, she thought nothing of shimmying out of the latest Alexander McQueen confection to frolic with her two best friends in Central Park's *Three Dancing Maidens* fountain wearing only her teeny, tiny silk La Perlas. A photo of which escapade, when posted online by the *New York Post*, absolutely blew up the internet.

And so—what with Nic frolicking half-naked in fountains; Great-Aunt Doris circling her imaginary fishbowl; my ninety-something grandfather beavering away at *Racy Rhymes, Vol. 2*; my father dreaming up ever-more-outlandish schemes to remake his fortune; and, let's be honest, my own considerable peculiarities—yes, I thought I knew crazy.

But this lady was definitely raising the bar. *Help me solve a murder mystery?*

I just nodded at her. I just nodded because for the moment I had no words.

"You see," she continued in what she seemed to think was an explanation, "despite the ambrosia and being together with my darling Max, I have found the Eternity to be a tad dull. I was accustomed to solving complex, if fictional, murders. Truth be told, in many of my books I was not at all certain when I began them who had committed the crime. Oh, how I *loved* working it all out in my little exercise books. I have missed that dreadfully."

She sighed and added, "Fortunately—as I suppose a kind of

reward for some hard work I'd been asked to do on a few of my Earthly failings—I've been granted a short holiday from the Eternity to allow myself the thrill of solving a complex murder again. Although this time not fictional, of course."

This explanation, if you could call it that, had given me time to catch my breath. "But if in the Eternity everything is known," I countered, "then surely you'll know who the evildoer is."

I said this for all the world as if we were having some kind of intelligent, sensible conversation. As if I really believed the woman in front of me was Agatha Christie reincarnated or whatever. I honestly couldn't think of any other way to handle it.

"Not at all," she responded briskly. "The rules are that once I set foot back in the land of the living, I am as ill-informed of whodunit as you are. I know nothing more than what you share with me in this room."

"Okay," I conceded. "But the fact is, I don't *have* a complex murder for you to solve."

I very carefully did not say "help me solve." If she wanted to solve a murder mystery, fine. But leave me out of it.

"Oh, but you will," Mrs. So-Called Christie returned. "That much I do know. You most certainly will."

She was so calmly convinced of what she was saying that I almost believed her. But before I could ask what kind of complex murder could await a book restorer leading a safe, sane, sensible life, the front doorbell pealed like Gideon's trumpet.

"I wonder who that could be," I said brightly, hoping the relief didn't sound in my voice. With any luck, it was Mrs. So-Called Christie's keeper. Or at least someone who could call her keeper.

"I'll be right back," I said, and scurried out of the room.

The reading rooms on the second floor of the Mystery Guild Library are dedicated to specific mystery and crime collections. As

I trotted down the hall toward the staircase to the ground floor, I stopped briefly to lock the doors of the Edgar Award Winners Room, the Dashiell Hammett Room, and the Golden Age Room. I wasn't taking any chances that my visitor would take my brief departure as an opportunity to explore, or worse, hide.

Confident that there was nowhere for Mrs. So-Called Christie to hole up, I hurried down the wide marble staircase and across the black-and-white-checkered floor of the foyer to the front door. But when I pulled it open, any hope I'd had that help was at hand was short-lived.

In front of me, huddled under the ionic-columned portico to avoid the rain, was my cousin Nic. If a photographer had snapped our picture at that moment, they would have captured two almost identical young women—short-waisted, long-legged, glossy brown hair, clear olive skin, hazel eyes, high cheekbones—but with almost diametrically opposed "looks." I preferred the classic, Nic the current.

That day, she was all Cool Cinderella in a blue satin Fendi jacket, white Rag & Bone jeans and red Doc Martens. She'd accessorized her look with a pair of chandelier earrings made of some hippie-looking red beads that matched the boots perfectly. She'd clearly rushed out without an umbrella, but even dripping wet, she looked great.

I, in contrast, was clad in a vintage House of Chanel day dress of fine black wool jersey bought in Paris in 1927 by my great-grandmother Victoria Van Dyne. My Ferragamo kitten-heel pumps were an eBay find. My earrings were gold studs from Tiffany's given to me by my parents on my sixteenth birthday. My hair—the same deep brown as Nic's but lacking the artfully placed golden highlights—was brushed up into a French twist. So I looked pretty good myself, but, I suspected, about ten years older than my cousin (as opposed to my actual two-year advantage) and infinitely less interesting.

And compared to the girl standing next to her, I was sure I looked positively middle-aged. I sighed. Nic's friends tended to be an eclectic bunch, ranging from debutantes to Goths to avant-garde artistes, most of whom I liked a lot. But I had never warmed to the Queen of the Upper East Side Debs herself, Sailor Savoie, who was easily the most entitled girl I had ever met.

Sailor was a stick-skinny blond creature who favored twee fashion along the lines of that day's black minidress complete with white collar and cuffs à la Wednesday Addams. As usual, she was also wearing her *I'm so bored I could just expire* expression on her face, which, as usual, annoyed the hell out of me. We nodded coldly to each other, which sufficed for both of us.

I held the door open, saying to Nic, "And where were you today, cuz?"

Sunday for the Van Dynes means not church, which is pretty much reserved for Christmas and Easter, but the obligatory Sunday dinner at three p.m. sharp at the family pile. That particular Sunday, Nic, contrary to all tradition, had not only not appeared, she had not called to explain her absence. Shock all around, of course. One did not fail to appear at Van Dyne Sunday dinner without explanation. Now it seemed the explanation was forthcoming.

"I have a problem," Nic said.

Before I asked what the problem might be—because with Nic there is always a problem—I felt obliged to point out the perils of going out on a rainy evening without an umbrella. "You know, Nic, you've pretty much ruined that Fendi jacket."

"Oh, Tory," Nic wailed, "who cares about a stupid jacket?" *Well*, you *would usually*. "This is an *emergency*."

Even then, I wasn't particularly worried. All of Nic's little problems tended to be emergencies.

I glanced back at the staircase, nervous about leaving my visitor alone for too long. "Can it wait?" I asked. "I'm a little busy at the moment."

"No, it can't wait," Nic keened. "Oh, Tory, somebody's poisoned Bertram!"

Three

◇◇◇◇◇◇◇◇◇◇

"I'll have your liver and your lights!" he snarled. "I'll tear you limb from limb!"

> —Bob the Dog, "The Incident of the
> Dog's Ball," *Agatha Christie's Secret
> Notebooks: Fifty Years of Mysteries in
> the Making*

YOU HAVE TO UNDERSTAND. BERTRAM WAS A DOG. NOT EVEN Nic's dog. Bertram was Howard Calhoun's dog. Howard was Nic's theatrical agent. Howard had arrived in New York about ten years earlier from LA, where apparently he'd been "consulting" for the West Coast talent agency International Artists. Once in the Big Apple, though, he'd ditched that gig in favor of using the charm that he was perfectly capable of employing when the rewards were sufficient to worm his way into the hearts of several lonely society matrons—most notably, Brooke Sinclair.

Brooke, a widow of long standing, was a very active committee member for a select group of charities. Her specialty was fund-raising events, particularly the galas so beloved by her circle. And she found in Howard, though twenty years her junior, a socially acceptable and, let's face it, very flattering escort to these high-lights of the social calendar. That he might also occasionally warm her bed was generally assumed, though never, of course, mentioned aloud. The other lonely ladies soon realized that Howard belonged to Brooke and Brooke only. In return for his exclusivity, she taught him everything he needed to know about New York society and the life to which he wished to become accustomed.

But even seemingly rich boys need a job or risk becoming known as freeloaders. Unless they are gay, of course, in which case they are known as best friends. Howard, therefore, convinced his previous employer that what IA really needed was a New York–based agent for rich-kid actors whose parents were happy to agree to an exorbitant 20 percent agent commission. IA was quick to agree to this scheme.

I first met Howard at Nic's college showcase, the capstone of her four-year pursuit of a BFA in musical theater at the Manhattan School of Music. Howard was there to scout prospective clients; I was there to loudly applaud Nic along with her two besties, Wren Madison and, yes, Sailor Savoie, in their joint showcase.

The three girls had been friends since their years together at the Spence School, that Upper East Side educational bastion of the daughters of the rich and/or powerful and/or socially prominent. Sailor and Wren were each striking in their own way—Sailor whip-thin and all blond-and-blue-eyed innocence but with a chilling intensity beneath the girly surface, and Wren all dark and Gothy but with a hypnotic, languid grace to her long limbs and a sincerity that belied the witchy look. Both, in my opinion, were the exact opposite of their looks—Sailor hard as flint, Wren a big old softy. And both had been as theater mad as Nic.

The night of the showcase, the threesome had blown the doors off the joint with their hilarious take on *Kiss Me Kate*, and Howard had immediately zoomed in. Before the evening was over, he'd found out that Wren, easily the most talented of the three, already had an agent. And the real prize, that Savoie girl, had briskly informed him that she did not need an agent, thank you. This was because Sailor was theater royalty by birth. Her grandfather, as Howard well knew, was Moncreiff Savoie, founder of the Savoie Theatre chain, and her grandmother was the onetime movie star Clara Connolley, who'd given it all up to play the much more lucrative role of Mrs. Moncreiff Savoie. Sailor was a Savoie. Sailor didn't need no stinkin' agent.

But Nic did. Nic had about as much street smarts as a housebound Persian kitten. Howard glommed on to her that night, and I had to admit, over the next few years did very well by her. It was Howard who'd engineered Nic's big Broadway break in *The Phantom of the Opera* as understudy to the then-current Christine, knowing full well that the lead was so close to rehab it was only a matter of time until Nic would need to step in. Of course, as a newbie she wasn't making big bucks, and as one of the thirty-six actresses who played Christine over *Phantom*'s thirty-five years, she was only on that stage for a couple of years, but it was enough to establish her as a rising talent.

Anyway, Bertram was Howard's dog, a pug of illustrious descent and much given to snapping and yapping at visitors. Bertram had been given to Howard "to look after" by Brooke Sinclair. The general opinion was that Brooke had simply tired of the pup's bad manners and pawning him off on Howard was an acceptable way to park the dog until the time came when she might want to breed him. My view, though, was that Brooke, whose possessiveness of Howard was an open secret among her set, had also wanted a way to tie them more closely together.

Bertram soon became notorious among Howard's crowd when Howard—who, to give him credit, was a fabulous cook—took up the fashion of insisting that his dinner guests leave their shoes at the door in exchange for slippers that had been worn by god knows how many other people. This, in Bertram's view, was a heaven-sent opportunity to savage the various Blahniks and Stan Smiths left behind in the foyer.

So pretty much nobody loved poor Bertram except Howard's personal assistant, Rachel Featherstonhaugh (whose name nobody could pronounce or, for that matter, remember). It was Rachel who oversaw Bertram's daily life because even Howard didn't love Bertram. But he valued the canine highly. You didn't refuse a present from Brooke Sinclair and you certainly weren't careless with it. Unless you wanted to be cut off from her guest list forever. Me, I couldn't have cared less, but Howard cared *a lot*. So Bertram stayed.

And now someone had apparently poisoned the pup. Which seemed to me not only overly aggressive but just plain mean.

I needed more facts. Nic was prone to exaggeration. "Poisoned as in dead?" I asked.

"Well, no. But almost," she said, and promptly burst into tears.

This struck me as something of an overreaction. "What?" I said. "I mean, it's not like you and Bertram were, um, close . . ."

"But he was my responsibility!" she wailed. "I was dog-sitting him this weekend while Howard was staying at his fancy guest house in the Hamptons stalking Grant Neuman, you know, the guy who's producing *BB the Movie*, about nailing me down as Mrs. Potts."

Everyone who followed theater knew about *BB the Movie*, the planned film version of the off-Broadway cult musical simply known as *BB*. The play had been a modern take on the "Beauty and the Beast" fairy tale, employing the conceit that Belle and Beast were two sides of the same person—the vain, self-absorbed Belle and (in a trouser role) the macho, mansplaining Beast.

"It's about learning to love your whole self," Nic had explained to me two years earlier when she'd been chosen—along with Sailor and Wren—to play Belle, Beast *and* (in this version) the housekeeper-cum-therapist, Mrs. Potts, on a revolving basis. Thus, for one month Nic played Belle, Sailor played Beast and Wren played Mrs. Potts. The next month, the roles shifted, with Wren as Belle, Nic as Beast and Sailor as Mrs. Potts. The month after that it was Sailor as Belle, Wren as Beast and Nic as Mrs. Potts. And so on.

"It's about the actors understanding the whole character," Nic had continued, faithfully parroting the play's director, Jonathan Schifrin, darling of the avant-garde. "You have to play all the parts to do that." I thought (but did not say) that it was more probably Schifrin's way of encouraging his fans—and the director had *a lot* of fans—to see the play three times so they could discuss the pros and cons of each actor's "interpretation" of the roles. But I have to say the press loved the concept, with *Variety* rather unimaginatively dubbing Nic, Sailor and Wren "the Belles (and Beasts) of Broadway."

The play itself had closed a few months earlier, which had been "super sad," as Nic put it. But then came the news that indie film producer Grant Neuman had picked up the movie rights, which was "super exciting." The casting for the film version was under way, but of course each role would be played by only one actor. Nic, Wren and Sailor were the obvious possibilities for the three leads. Neuman had recently announced that Wren Madison would take the role of Belle.

Nic had desperately wanted the part ("I mean, if anyone can play self-involved, it's me, right?") but she was also the first to understand the producer's call. ("We're all good, you know? But Wren's the best of us.") She wasn't wrong there. When Wren had belted out "Defying Gravity" during her stint as Elphaba in *Wicked*, she'd reinvented the term "showstopper."

But Howard, who'd been lobbying madly for Nic as Belle, took it all pretty badly and was even more put out when Sailor was confirmed in the Beast role. Nic, on the other hand, agreed with this choice, too. "I was never any good as Beast. I don't have that edge, you know?" she'd admitted. "And Sailor's, well, Sailor."

She would never say it, but we all knew that once again the Savoie name had worked its magic. After MSM, all three girls had gone on to good, solid careers in Broadway musicals, but Sailor, it always seemed to me, simply assumed that choice roles were hers by divine right. And apparently most of the theater world agreed with her. Her name alone guaranteed publicity.

Nic was a realist. Nic understood Grant Neuman's choices. And despite her disappointment, she seemed honestly pleased for her BFFs, and had cheerfully transferred her hopes to playing the third lead, Mrs. Potts. "Mrs. Potts is funny like me," she'd explained, "but smart, too. Howard says it's time for me to play against type." I'd felt that Howard had been less than kind to put it that way but was probably right. Howard's instincts were actually pretty good.

Except when it came to dogs, I thought, bringing myself back to the matter at hand.

"So anyway," Nic was saying as she peeled off the Fendi and dropped it carelessly on the high-backed bench by the front door, "I was staying in Howard's place and taking care of Bertram while he was away."

Well, I wanted to say, *then this is Howard's fault*. You gave Nic many things—introductions to filmmakers, three-figure bottles of vintage tequila, sparkly jewelry—but you *didn't* give her responsibility. Howard, of all people, knew that. Howard didn't even give Nic responsibility for showing up to auditions on time. That kind of thing was Rachel's responsibility. As was playing babysitter to Bertram. Usually Rachel took Bertram to her Lower East Side apartment when Howard was in the Hamptons. Howard must have been in desperate straits to leave Nic in charge of the dog.

But before I could make this argument, Nic, with Sailor trailing behind her, headed across the hall to the staircase, saying, "I totally need a drink." Even though the first two floors of the house had been leased by the Mystery Guild Library for the past five years, Nic still considered the whole place ours. And she knew exactly where the bar cart was.

"Whoa, Nic!" I shouted after her, "Don't go in the Christie Room!"

"What, are you crazy?" she flung back over one shoulder and, if anything, increased her pace.

I gave up. Everything was out of my control. Which didn't mean I liked it. What I like is everything *in* my control.

I skidded in behind Nic as she threw open the door to the Christie Room and flung herself down on the blue couch. Sailor followed suit and immediately whipped out her iPhone to check the hits on her latest TikTok reel or whatever. Both had moved so quickly that, just as I'd done earlier, they'd completely missed the woman sitting slightly behind them next to the alcove's bar cart, quietly sipping her cocktail. *Good. One crazy at a time, please.*

"Make me a drink, would you, cuz?" Nic moaned.

"What do you want?" I asked helplessly.

"Whatever you've got," she said. "Something strong, though."

You want something strong? Here's something strong. I dumped a handful of ice into a glass and emptied the rest of the cocktail shaker over it. Mrs. So-Called Christie, with just a ghost of a smile, reached over to the bar cart to pick up the red pepper shaker and quietly handed it to me. I put a hefty shake of the stuff in the drink and handed it to my cousin.

"Here," I said. "This'll give you some pep."

Nic took a mighty swig of the concoction. If I was hoping for a sputtering explosion (and I confess I was), I was sorely disappointed. I'd forgotten that Nic had never met a cocktail she couldn't swill. She was impressive that way.

"Ooh, that's the stuff," she said. "What is it?"

"That, my dear, is a Satan's Whisker," Mrs. So-Called Christie said from behind her.

Nic froze in a kind of weird replay of my own response to that voice coming seemingly out of nowhere. Then, ever so slowly, she turned her head to look toward the alcove. I stood back so she could get the full effect of the squashy hat, the upscale handbag, the good pearls and the utter confidence of the woman sitting in the Christie Room as if she had every right to be there. Which, apparently, she thought she did.

"Well, hello!" Nic said, surprised out of her drama. "Who are you?"

Before Mrs. So-Called Christie could begin her whole rigmarole again, I jumped in. I decided to ignore Sailor, given that she was determined to ignore us, but Nic needed an introduction. And even Nic, who read about one book a year, would recognize the name Christie, seeing as we were actually *in* the Christie Room.

"Mrs., um, Mallowan," I said, "this is my cousin Nicola Van Dyne. Nic, this is my, um, friend Mrs. Mallowan."

To my enormous relief, Mrs. So-Called Christie did not go into her but-you-probably-know-me-as-Agatha-Christie routine. In fact, I could have sworn the woman gave me a little half nod of understanding.

"How do you do, Miss Nicola," she said. It was like something out of Jane Austen. I, as the elder of the two, was Miss Van Dyne. Nic, as the younger, was Miss Nicola.

Nic put down her drink, stood and came over to shake my, um, friend's hand.

"How do you do," she responded politely. "I'm sorry, I didn't see you there."

"Well, you were upset, my dear," Mrs. So-Called Christie said mildly. "Did I hear you say that a friend had been poisoned? How very dreadful."

To give her credit, Nic looked a little embarrassed. "Well, not a friend, exactly. A dog. A friend's dog. And not poisoned to death. Just super sick."

"I see," Mrs. So-Called Christie said. "How distressing."

She got up from her armchair and moved over to the alcove's settee, patting the cushion next to her in invitation. Nic promptly came over for a nice friendly chat.

I give up, I thought, *I just give up.*

"I was devoted to my dog Tony," Mrs. So-Called Christie said. "He was a Yorkshire terrier given to me on my fifth birthday." This I knew to be true. Tony features prominently in the real Agatha Christie's autobiography. "Within a week we were inseparable. He was good-natured, affectionate and lent himself to all my fancies. I often called him Lord Tony."

"Well," I felt obliged to put in, "Bertram has pretty much never lent himself to anybody's fancies. He's a bit of a curmudgeon." Somebody had to add a dose of reality here.

"I see," Mrs. So-Called Christie said again, acknowledging my contribution but never taking her eyes off Nic's face. "And how, my dear, was the dog poisoned and by whom?"

"Well, that's just it," my cousin said. "I *think* he was poisoned, but I don't know who—whom?—did it or how. I was, you know, apartment-sitting for Howard, Howard Calhoun, my agent, you know? Howard lives around the corner at One Fifth, so when he goes out of town, I usually stay in his place to let the cleaning service in and to take deliveries and stuff. Plus, it's close to Tory so she has someone to go out with and doesn't get nervous."

I glanced quickly at Mrs. So-Called Christie to see if she'd noticed that last little bit, but she had either missed the reference or was too polite to show that she'd found anything odd in what Nic had said.

"I get tired of living uptown with the 'rents and the olds," Nic continued blithely. "But Daddy says he won't get me my own place until I turn thirty and have some sense. So that's, like"—Nic paused to count on her fingers—"another eight months I have to wait."

Mrs. So-Called Christie made a sympathetic noise, though whether the sympathy was with Nicola or with long-suffering Uncle Rupert was unclear. I personally did not expect that Nic would find some sense in the space of eight months. Nor did I want her to. I liked Nic just as she was.

"So anyway," Nic hurried on, "Howard was going out to the Hamptons to try to talk to Grant Neuman, the guy who's producing *BB the Movie*, to get him to confirm me for Mrs. Potts, you know?"

"Mrs. Potts?" Mrs. So-Called Christie inquired politely. Which Nic immediately took as permission to go through the whole *BB the Movie* saga for her listener's edification.

To her credit, Mrs. So-Called Christie listened as if the digression was of great importance, but then gently prompted Nic back to the subject at hand. "So, you offered to take care of the dog in Mr. Calhoun's absence?"

"Not really," Nic said. "I mean, he, Howard that is, asked me to stay at his place and his assistant, Rachel Whatshername, would take Bertram like usual. But Friday afternoon, like, fifteen minutes after I get there and Howard leaves, Rachel calls and asks me to keep Bertram because she's having a kidney stone blown up with a laser." Mrs. So-Called Christie looked rather startled at this. "I said okay because I didn't really mind. Some people don't like Bertram but I'm okay with him. I mean, I couldn't refuse, could I?"

"Not possibly," Mrs. So-Called Christie agreed. "A very sensible decision, I think."

Nic gave Mrs. So-Called Christie one of her 200-watt Nicola Van Dyne smiles. It is not every day that someone calls Nic sensible.

"So anyway, last night I had my besties Wren and Sailor . . ." Here Nic nodded over to Sailor, who looked up from her phone long enough to give an obligatory "Hi" to the room at large. ". . . over to Howard's place for a little, um, drink, you know, before a party we were going to later? We're all between roles at the moment, so we can play a little."

Uh-oh. Sailor *and* Wren. The last time I'd partied with Sailor and Wren was almost eight years ago at the girls' joint twenty-first-birthday blowout at the then very trendy NoMad Hotel. Nic had been a little tipsy, but Sailor and Wren had been high as kites—Sailor on tequila, Wren from a little pre-party nose candy. From the stories Nic had told me since, nothing much had changed there. The Belles of Broadway still did what they wanted, how they wanted, and their triplet antics had garnered them a devoted online fandom.

"So," Nic was continuing, "the three of us were hanging out at Howard's sipping a little Siete Leguas that Sailor had brought. Sailor adores a good tequila. I mean, who doesn't, right?"

Mrs. So-Called Christie merely nodded, understanding that the question was rhetorical.

"And I thought we were good with just the Patrón, you know. I mean, Wren likes a little cocaine—it perks her up—but she does it at home before she goes out. She says it's 'undignified' for people to see you with a tiny spoon up your nose." I had to agree with Wren there. "But Sailor, she has this, like, *hoard* of leftover oxys from back when doctors were prescribing opioids like candy, you know?"

To my amazement, the woman in the sensible tweeds nodded. "There seems to be a kind of fashion in drugs like everything else," she said. "Doctors seem to follow one another in prescribing like a lot of sheep."

A little flag went up in my brain. The words were familiar. Ah, yes. Inspector Sharpe in *Hickory Dickory Death*. I had to admit, the woman knew her stuff.

Nic gave Mrs. So-Called Christie a grateful smile. "Exactly," she said, nodding madly. "So I'm thinking maybe one of Sailor's old oxys fell out of her bag and maybe Bertram maybe snapped it up?"

Sailor looked up at that. "I bet that's not what you thought," she said bluntly. "I bet you thought I gave him one *on purpose* just to watch the mutt trip out. *Jeez*. Like I would waste good oxy for that." She glared at Nic. "You know, Nic, I could have told you that on the phone, but you just kept yelling 'Meet me at Tory's' like it was something *important*."

And with that, Sailor Savoie stood up, tucked her iPhone back into her baby blue crossbody Kate Spade bag, said an automatic "Nice to have met you" to Mrs. So-Called Christie (which I thought was hilarious) and made her escape from the nuthouse. I didn't bother to do the polite thing and see her out. Except during library hours, the front door locks automatically behind anyone leaving. And since good manners were lost on Sailor Savoie, seeing her out of the building would have been wasted effort.

I looked at Nic. "You don't believe Sailor, do you?"

"No, yeah, I do kind of in a way," Nic said. "I mean, Sailor doesn't lie. Not because she's honest or anything but because she doesn't have to. She's Sailor Savoie." I nodded. Nic had always been ridiculously loyal to her friends, but she had no illusions about them. "So if she says she didn't give Bertram an oxy for fun, she didn't." Here she looked truly distraught again. "The thing is, though, I keep thinking that maybe Sailor gave Bertram one not for fun but because she's always been really mad at him for destroying her best Tory Burch flats and maybe she wanted to . . . I don't know . . . kill him?" She trailed off miserably.

"Ah," Mrs. So-Called Christie said, her voice heavy with significance. She looked directly at me. "A mystery. Perhaps even a murder mystery."

Four

◇◇◇◇◇◇◇

"Women observe subconsciously a thousand little details..."
—Hercule Poirot, *The Murder of Roger
Ackroyd*

*REALLY? I WANTED TO SAY TO MRS. SO-CALLED CHRISTIE. THIS IS
your big mystery that you came all the way from the Elysian Fields to
solve? The Mystery of the Super Sick Dog?*

What I actually said was, "Bertram didn't die, so he wasn't,
technically, murdered."

Mrs. So-Called Christie ignored my sally. Turning back to Nic
she said, "I admire your earrings, Miss Nicola."

Which was random. But older ladies were random sometimes,
as I knew very well. And granted, it was kind of hard to miss Nic's
earrings with their three dangling tiers of bright red beads, each
topped with a little black spot. Like Nic herself, the earrings were
charming in a free-spirited kind of way but I wouldn't have thought
they were Mrs. So-Called Christie's style.

"I know," Nic said. "They're cute, right?" She stood and wandered over to the Venetian etched-glass mirror above the room's

fireplace, turning her head from side to side so that the earrings clattered softly against her long, graceful neck. "I forgot to take them off last night."

"Were you in India recently?" Mrs. So-Called Christie asked.

"Wow, like, no," Nic said, returning to the settee. "But Howard was. That's awesome that you figured that out. He and Brooke, that's Brooke Sinclair, you know, got back two weeks ago from some fancy package tour there. So last night I saw these and a matching necklace on his bureau because his apartment is only a one-bedroom so I'm sleeping in there while he's gone and anyway I saw them and I had a kind of boho chic look going on, you know, a long floaty Alice + Olivia maxi dress with chunky platform boots to add a little contrast. I skipped the necklace because it didn't go with the dress's neckline, but I knew the earrings would be perfect with the look so I borrowed them. I figured he'd brought them back for me anyway."

I thought Nic was probably right about Howard meaning to give the earrings to her in the first place. When wooing prospective clients like Sailor and Wren or keeping a current one like Nic happy, Howard had a penchant for giving expensive gifts (tequila, coke and jewelry, respectively), though these hippie earrings didn't strike me as being his usual over-the-top offering.

"Was there always a bead missing from the left earring?" Mrs. So-Called Christie asked.

Oh, I get it, I thought. *Another mystery for you to solve. We're going to be here all night at this rate.*

Nic looked just slightly uncomfortable at the question.

"No," she admitted. "So I was putting them on in the bathroom after I did my face and I dropped one on the floor and kind of stepped on it and one of the beads got smushed and I figured nobody would notice it was missing. But you did. You don't miss a trick, do you?" Nic may talk like a teenager on speed, but she's no dummy.

"I am a noticing kind of person," Mrs. So-Called Christie said quietly. I had to think for a minute. Ah, yes. Miss Jane Marple, *The Murder at the Vicarage.*

"Anyway," Nic said, getting back to the Mystery of the Super Sick Dog, "then Wren and Sailor rang the doorbell and we loosened up a little like I told you and then we went to the party. But before we left, I put Bertram in the utility room where his bed and pee pads are."

"Oh, yuk," I muttered.

"I know, right?" Nic said. "And when I got back at, I don't know, around four in the morning or something, I looked in to check on him and he was all wheezy and when I picked him up to try to comfort him, he was, like, soaked with sweat and, oh jeez, it was horrible." Nic shook her head, as if to rid herself of the memory, which I happen to know doesn't work.

"My goodness," Mrs. So-Called Christie said, patting Nic's hand in sympathy. "How very unpleasant."

"And then he just kind of went still and I thought he was dead, but it turned out he just fainted or something, so I took him into bed with me, and when we woke up today, he was tired but okay and I felt a lot better."

Sometimes I just loved my cousin. She took *a sick dog covered with sweat* to bed with her.

"So then I took him to the vet," she continued. "And I got all upset again, because the vet said the symptoms sounded like Bertram ate something, like, poisonous. He said Bertram should stay until tomorrow just for observation, though. And then I called Rachel Whatshername's cell to tell her about Bertram being sick but not the poison part, just how I tried to take care of him and that he, the vet that is, said he thought he, Bertram that is, would be okay so she shouldn't worry and just go pick him up tomorrow morning. And then I called Sailor and then we came here."

"And what was Mr. Calhoun's reaction when you told him about Bertram?" Mrs. So-Called Christie asked mildly. Nic squirmed in her seat. "I haven't exactly told him yet. I mean, I wrote him a text that said Bertram had had a little tummy upset and was at the vet's but was okay." Nic turned to me. "I thought I'd just check with you first, Tory, before telling him the whole story because I'm super scared I'll get blamed if that vet opens the whole poison can of worms. I don't know what to say to Howard. But you always know what to do."

Which is not true, but Nic believes it to be so. Which is why every time she turns to me to get her out of one of her scrapes, my heart softens, and I do what I can to help.

"Don't worry, Nic," I said, as I always did. "Everything will be all right."

Much cheered at the shifting of her problem onto my shoulders, Nic said, "Good, because I asked Howard to meet us here for a drink once he got home from the Hamptons."

"Whoa," I said, raising a hand like a traffic cop. "Howard is coming *here*? Why here?"

"Neutral territory," Nic said. "Here he has to behave himself. If I told him at his apartment, he'd totally scream the place down. You know what he's like."

I did. Howard in full angry spate was a force of nature.

"But how did you know I'd even be here?" I asked.

"C'mon, Tory," Nic sighed. "You're always here."

Which, I realized with a jolt, was true. Too true. I was always there.

———

AT HER DEATH SOME FIVE YEARS BEFORE, GRANDMOTHER HAD willed the house on Washington Square North to me with the proviso that the Mystery Guild Library—a wonderful resource for mystery and crime fiction fans and scholars that had until then been jammed into four cramped rooms on the Upper West Side—would be given a twenty-year lease on the first two floors of the house. Her one condition was that the Christie Room remain unchanged. The Guild was delighted to comply, given that the room would be the crown jewel of the library's collection.

I loved the place, not only because my apartment on the top two floors had long been my refuge but also because it was in New York's Greenwich Village, which is exactly that—a village. A walkable neighborhood of unassuming brick row houses, small cafés, bistros, basement comedy clubs and quirky vintage clothing shops, not to mention New York University, which adds a certain intellectual atmosphere to the conversations in those small cafés and bistros. For me, the Village was safe and familiar and usually blessedly uncrowded.

But mostly I loved the house for the basement laboratory that Grandmother had installed for her great friend, the book conservator Abraham Plum, who introduced me to my life's work.

Abe was a good man. In Grandmother's workshop he'd patiently restored and helped conserve priceless volumes from collectors and museums and libraries around the globe, volumes I would never have dreamed of touching. But noticing the odd, awkward teenager's fascination with the miracles he wrought, Abe kindly took me on as an apprentice when he made small repairs on the books destined for Grandmother's Christie Room. Neither rare nor priceless, but precious nonetheless.

Working alongside Abe on Grandmother's collection, I painstakingly patched broken hinges, repaired torn pages, relined flapping spines and restored covers. In later years, as Abe's sight began
to fail and his limbs to tremble, I became his eyes and hands, following his careful instructions as we worked together on the actually rare and priceless.

"The successful restoration of a book," he would say to me in
his precise, donnish voice, "depends not only on period-appropriate
materials and an accurate measure of the repairs to be done but
also, and perhaps most importantly, on the spirit of the book and
how best to preserve that spirit."

And then I, who really had no idea in my callow youth what he
was talking about, would try to impress my mentor by saying, "But
preservation of the original binding is always the first consider-
ation."

At which he would smile and say, "Ah, if only one could do the
same for people," glancing at his age-spotted hands and exaggerat-
ing the curve of his back, now permanently bent from decades of
close work.

And I would reply, "But, as we both know, age is just another
name for patina, and what really matters is what lies between the
covers of the book."

And then he would smile at me, and we would continue our
labors.

This happy state of affairs continued for several years, until five
years ago when, quite suddenly, Abe and my grandmother both
died within months of each other. In the fog of my grief, I barely
registered the lawyer's exhaustive recitation of the terms of Grandmother's will. It seemed the house on Washington Square North
now belonged to me as both a home and as a place of work. However, Grandmother hoped—which in Grandmother-ese meant

that even from beyond the grave, she would brook no argument—
that I would continue to help with the preservation of the library's
books gratis.

Of course I would offer my services to the library gratis. I had
by this point a good number of clients of my own, mostly private
collectors, but I was honored to resew the library's first edition
of Agatha Christie's *A Murder Is Announced* for free. For me the
work was my tribute to Miss Jane Marple, who, along with Doro-
thy L. Sayers's redoubtable Harriet Vane, was one of my favorite
Golden Age amateur sleuths.

Gradually my aching heart began to heal. And when my work-
day was done, most evenings I would retreat to my rooms upstairs,
where I would fix myself a bit of dinner and read the next Richard
Osman or Tana French or an old Christiana Brand hardcover that
I'd found at some dusty secondhand bookstore and would later
donate to the library proper.

So Nic was right. I was always there. I lived on the top two
floors and did my conservation work in the building's basement
laboratory. I had friends, but most were clients or work colleagues.
And though I'd had a few boyfriends since college, none had lasted
more than a couple of months. I was nobody's idea of a good-time
gal. Unless your idea of a good-time gal was someone who thought
a big Saturday night was one spent binge-watching *Foyle's War*.
Again.

"SO," NIC SAID, "I NEED YOU TO EXPLAIN TO HOWARD WHAT
happened."

"Nic, I don't *know* what happened," I said, and took a nice big
slug of my Satan's Whisker. I needed the pep.

But she wasn't listening to me. "I mean, I know Howard is

going to say that Bertram was my responsibility even if he was supposed to be Rachel's and she wimped out and why was I having friends over to his apartment anyway."

"Well, if Howard does think that someone did maybe poison his dog accidentally on purpose," I pointed out, "he's also going to know it wasn't you because he knows Sailor loves pills and he knows you can't take drugs."

Which was true. Nic was one of those rare souls whose reaction to drugs was often the exact opposite of their intended effect. Once when we were teenagers, she'd been prescribed Percocet after she'd had "just a teeny, weensy bit of work" done on her already-perfect nose. She took exactly one tablet and spent the next eight hours clinging to me and crying inconsolably about "the sadness of life." Ever since, her self-medication of choice has been a good stiff drink.

At this point Mrs. Christie seemed compelled to chime in with a question that once again seemed totally off topic. Which alerted me. I was beginning to suspect that nothing she asked was totally off topic.

"And what do you think Mr. Calhoun will say about you stepping on the earring?" she asked.

"Oh, I hadn't even thought about that," Nic said, wide-eyed. "Do you think I should tell him?"

I almost laughed at that point. I wasn't sure how Mrs. Christie had done it, but Nic now seemed to consider this deceptively mild-mannered lady with her deceptively aimless questions her new BFF. Like Jane Marple, Mrs. Christie was of an age for others to accept her snoopy nature as natural.

"Well, that, my dear, is up to you," Mrs. Christie responded. "Do you want Mr. Calhoun to know that you poisoned Bertram?"

Five

◇◇◇◇◇◇

Mrs. Oliver was asking Major Despard if he knew of any unheard-of, out-of-the-way poisons. "The people who read my books like untraceable poisons!"

—*Cards on the Table*

NIC LOOKED AT THE WOMAN SHE'D MISTAKEN FOR A FRIEND with a kind of horrified dismay.

"What are you talking about?" she cried. "Tory just told you I don't do drugs. And for sure I wouldn't want to poison Bertram. The last thing I need now is Howard mad at me, not when I'm this close"—she held her thumb and forefinger about a half inch apart—"to getting Mrs. Potts. Brooke Sinclair gave that dog to Howard. Which means that Howard would totally freak out. And I don't want to miss my big break just because you think I poisoned Bertram."

Mrs. Christie shook her head. "Do not mistake me, my dear. I don't think you *intended* to poison Bertram, but poison Bertram you did."

"But how?" Nic wailed, running a neon green gel-tipped hand through her hair in her distress.

I stepped in. "You think the earring and Bertram's illness are connected, don't you, Mrs. um, Mallowan?"

"But it was just a little bead," Nic protested. Like *I* was the crazy one there.

"Not really a bead, Miss Nicola," Mrs. Christie corrected. "The beads on those earrings are actually seeds. The seeds of *Abrus precatorius*, in fact, although they are sometimes known as rosary peas or rosary beads because of their long history of use in saying the rosary."

Nic looked at her blankly. What Nic knew about saying the rosary was exactly nothing. We came from not particularly observant Episcopalian stock, and I doubted very much that she had many devout Catholics among her friends. Any devout anythings, for that matter. Unless you counted vegans.

"Whatever," Nic said, then paused as if she'd just thought of something. Thinking always caught Nic by surprise. "How did you know these whatchamacallits were from India?"

"*Abrus precatorius* grows only in tropical climates, and most jewelry incorporating the seeds is made in India," Mrs. Christie explained.

"That's interesting," Nic said in all sincerity. Nic was deeply interested in accessories.

Mrs. Christie, it turned out, was not. "Do you recall if the seed you stepped on was crushed?"

"Yeah, it was," Nic said, almost proudly. "Not the red shell, that was just kind of in little pieces, but I was wearing my platform boots that weigh, like, a ton, and the insides were totally smushed into a kind of powder."

"And did you tidy the lavatory after you stepped on the seed?"

Again Nic looked proud of herself. "I did. I wiped the mess up with a piece of wet toilet paper and flushed it down the john." This actually surprised me. Nic is not the kind of person who tidies up a bathroom. Nic is the kind of person who turns a bathroom into a tornado of spilled makeup, used tissues and half-empty jars of La Mer moisturizer.

"I didn't want Howard to know I broke his earring," she added. *Ah, that explains it.*

"And was the dog ever in that lavatory after the incident with the seed?" Mrs. Christie asked in another of her quick swerves. "My Tony was insatiably curious about what, ahem, went on in the water closet."

Nic grinned. "Oh yeah, Bertram was always whining outside the bathroom door. So I just started leaving it open, you know. I mean, who cares what a dog sees you doing, right?"

Mrs. Christie looked just a little shocked at that but soldiered on. "And was Bertram in there last night?"

Nic thought for a minute. "I'm not sure," she said. And then her face lit up. "Yeah, he was!" she announced. "I remember because when I threw the TP into the john, I almost stepped on Bertram snuffling around me. He's a pug, you know, and that's what pugs do. They snuffle."

"I see," Mrs. Christie said thoughtfully. "So any of the powdered seed that you may have missed"—*probably missed*, I thought to myself—"might have been inhaled by your sniffing canine friend?"

Nic blinked. "Well, yeah, sure. Is that a problem?"

"Well, apparently it was for Bertram," I said, trying to push Nic along. I turned to Mrs. So-Called Christie. "I'm guessing the seed is toxic to animals?"

"Not just to animals, Miss Van Dyne," Mrs. Christie said. "The dried seed of *Abrus precatorius*—known, by the way, as *kundumani* in Tamil—contains abrin, which is closely related to ricin and is one of the most toxic substances found in nature."

"Why haven't I heard of it then?" I asked. I mean, I'd read literally hundreds of murder mysteries and not one of them had mentioned this very scary little poison.

"Fortunately, deaths from abrin are rare because the seeds, if swallowed whole, pass through the body essentially intact because of their hard shell. But one ground seed swallowed or inhaled can easily kill a grown man. A mere pinch would be fatal to a small dog and a few grains would certainly cause the symptoms Miss Nicola described."

It was a testament to the effect of this little bombshell that Nic was, for once, struck dumb. I swear her mouth literally dropped open. To be fair, I'm pretty sure mine did, too.

"You can see for yourself in Martindale's," Mrs. Christie added, pointing unerringly to the bookshelf where, as I knew very well, a copy of Martindale's *Extra Pharmacopoeia* held pride of place.

"That's okay," I said. "I'll take your word for it."

"Oh shit, shit, shit," Nic moaned, holding her head in her hands and rocking back and forth. "Shit, shit, shit, shit, shit."

"Indeed," Mrs. Christie said, all business now. "The classic feature of ingested abrin poisoning is diarrhea. But *inhaled* abrin presents differently, with difficulty breathing, fever and sweating, and with a full dose, fluid buildup in the lungs leading to low blood pressure and respiratory failure. There is no antidote, although rapid administration of oxygen and treatment of the pulmonary edema can be effective in preventing death."

I, for one, was very impressed by the woman's expertise, but

Nic was no longer listening. She had moved in an instant from moaning back to wailing. "Oh no, no, no! Are you saying that Bertram almost died from snorting abrawhachamacallit?"

"It is highly likely," Mrs. Christie said.

"Oh god, oh god, oh god," Nic said, looking over at me. "What if Howard gets that vet to do some tests on Bertram? If he finds out that I almost killed Brooke's dog, I am so dead." Which, given the circumstances, I thought was a poor choice of words.

"Not at all, my dear," Mrs. Christie said, patting Nic's hand. "Abrin poisoning is virtually undetectable after death. In fact, in India, *Abrus precatorius* was used for centuries by the Chamar in a clever scheme for illegally and undetectably killing cattle for their hides."

Nic raised her head and stared wild-eyed at Mrs. Christie. "Why are we talking about *cows?*"

"She's trying to tell you that nobody is going to find this abrin stuff in Bertram," I explained patiently. I actually thought Mrs. Christie's little aside was pretty fascinating, but maybe that's just me.

Nic clutched Mrs. Christie's hand. "Seriously? So you think I'm safe?"

"Unless, of course, you choose to tell Mr. Calhoun of your suspicions."

"My suspicions," Nic said thoughtfully. "I mean, that's all they really are, right? I can't *prove* Bertram snorted the stuff, right? Nobody can prove it?"

"It's unlikely," Mrs. Christie agreed.

"But do you think I should tell him what we think?"

I liked the royal "we." Like Nic had done any of the thinking.

"That depends on if you believe in the value of truth." As Mrs.

Oliver explained to Rhoda in *Cards on the Table*, I wanted to say but didn't. This was not the time for Name That Quote.

"Of course I believe in the value of the truth," Nic said, raising her chin defiantly. "And of course I'm going to tell him."

Sometimes I truly admire my cousin. If I'd been her, I would *never* have considered telling Howard the truth. The Mrs. Potts role meant a lot to Nic, and I didn't want Howard crossing her off his list just because she'd almost accidentally killed Bertram and pissed off Brooke Sinclair.

I took a moment to express my doubts to Mrs. Christie about the virtue of honesty in this case. "Howard has a tendency toward vindictiveness," I said. "I don't think Nic should tell Howard the truth."

Mrs. Christie calmed my fears by quoting from Jane Wilkinson's letter to Hercule Poirot in *Lord Edgware Dies*. "I've always noticed," she said, "that if you speak the truth in a rather silly way nobody believes you."

I had to laugh. "Well, then, Nic's out of danger."

Even Nic smiled at that. "I say everything in a silly way," she agreed cheerfully. "I can't help it. It's just how I talk."

At which point she leaned over and gave Mrs. Christie an enormous Nic hug. "Oh jeez, I *love* you, Mrs. . . . what did you say your name was?"

"Mallowan," I said quickly. "Her name is Mrs., um, Mallowan."

"Well, I *love* you, Mrs. Mallowan," Nic said. She then cocked her head and added, "How do you know all this stuff, anyway?"

"Well, during the first war I worked in a hospital dispensary, which was an education in itself," our guest explained. "And then later, of course, I did a great deal of research on poisons for my books."

For a moment, I thought the game was up. Nic was looking a

little confused by the "*first war*" and "*my books*" references. But we were literally saved by the front doorbell announcing that a visitor had arrived.

"No doubt," Mrs. So-Called Christie said, "that will be your Mr. Calhoun."

Indeed, there was Howard standing at the door looking as Waspy as they come—chino pants, blue Brooks Brothers button-down-collar shirt, navy blue blazer, brown Sperry top-siders on his feet. I wanted to die of boredom just looking at him. Howard, who was only just tall enough to avoid being called "short," made up for his lack of stature by being exceedingly well-groomed—hair cleverly styled to disguise the receding hairline, teeth as blindingly white as bleaching could make them, a chin so closely shaved the term "baby's behind" came to mind.

Presentation aside, if I had to describe the guy in two words, it would be "social climber." Howard's origins were shrouded in mystery. No prestigious prep school, no Ivy League college, no family that anyone knew, and when he'd first landed in our fair city, no discernable source of income. He would occasionally make vague references to "coming into my money," which everyone understood as code for *trust fund*. But whatever the source, it had to be considerable judging by the apartment around the corner in the venerable One Fifth Avenue, by his elaborate dinner parties and by his gift-giving to his favored few.

And then there were his rare books. I'd worked on a few volumes in his collection, though I use the term "collection" loosely. In my opinion, a book collection should be books acquired over time because you have a strong affinity for a particular writer or writers or are fascinated by a certain historical period or subject. Or, better yet, you just love books. Howard's was not that kind of collection. Howard's was a collection of rare books you could boast about at dinner parties because they cost so much. Which he did with every new acquisition. After which he moved on to the next prize without so much as a backward glance.

So Howard's collection tended to be all over the place, from a first edition of Charles Darwin's *On the Origin of Species* (roughly $50,000) to a first edition, first printing of *Harry Potter and the Philosopher's Stone* with "1 wand" printed twice on Harry's shopping list for Diagon Alley (roughly $70,000). *Fine. Whatever.* He paid well and some of his books needed my help. It wasn't their fault they belonged to Howard Calhoun.

Who was now standing impatiently at my door waiting for me to let him in.

"Howard," I said, stepping back and trying to sound welcoming, "please come in."

But Howard was already through the door, doing that in-and-out flapping thing with his umbrella so that it sprayed water all over the floor of the foyer. I took it from him and placed it, pointedly I hoped, in the foyer's brass umbrella stand.

"How are you?" I asked automatically.

"Wet," Howard snapped. Howard had never understood that "How are you" is a purely rhetorical question to which the answer should be "fine." The last time I'd asked Howard how he was he'd said he was constipated. Howard husbanded his "charm" carefully, spending it only on those who had something he wanted.

"Come up and have a drink," I said. "We're all in the Christie Room."

"All?" Howard asked as he pushed past me toward the staircase, not so much because he really needed a drink but because Howard's default mode was to push past people. Howard, like a dog that had never learned to heel, liked to lead the way.

"Nic and I and a, um, friend of mine. Mrs. Mallowan." I really,

really hoped Howard didn't recognize the name. I had no idea if he was a Christie fan.

I needn't have worried. Howard had other things on his mind. "Why am I even here?" he asked when we'd reached the hallway at the top of the stairs.

"Nic wanted to see you," I hedged. "She feels terrible about Bertram."

Howard tossed this off. "No need," he said. "Dogs get sick. It happens." Which was not what I would have expected, but I'd take it. This was going to be easy.

And at first it was.

WHILE HOWARD AND I HAD BEEN CHATTING, NIC HAD MIXED another batch of cocktails under Mrs. So-Called Christie's tutelage and had started in on her second drinkypoo. This might explain why when Howard walked into the Christie Room, she rushed over to him and threw her arms around his neck, saying, "Oh, Howard, I am so, so sorry about Bertram."

Howard went all noble, patting her back and assuring her that the fault was not hers but, if anybody's, Rachel Whatshername's. "Bertram was Rachel's responsibility," he said. "She never should have left him with you. You were supposed to be house-sitting, not dog-sitting."

"But it wasn't her fault she got a rock in her kidney or whatever," Nic protested.

I had to give Nic credit. She wasn't going to let Rachel take the fall. I sat myself back down on the couch and picked up my drink. Suddenly I had a feeling I was going to need it.

"Let's just call it one of those things that happen," Howard said, dismissing her concern. "Dogs get sick. It's nobody's fault."

If Nic had stopped there, we might have got through this thing without fallout, but she was in full principled form now.

"And it wasn't Sailor's fault, either," she said.

I swear I saw Howard go a little pale. He took a step back from Nic. "*Sailor?*"

"Yeah," Nic said, standing there shamefaced but determined. "I asked her and Wren over, you know, before a party we were going to and I kind of wondered if maybe Bertram had found a dropped oxy or something, but . . ."

Before she could finish, Howard interrupted, now sounding kind of intrigued. "You're saying Sailor gave Bertram oxy?"

"*No*," Nic said. "That's what I'm trying to tell you. It was the earrings."

Howard looked at her blankly. "The earrings?"

"Well, one of the earrings you brought me back from India," Nic said. "The ones on your bureau. I'm wearing them now." She shook her head, and the red beads clattered gently. "They were for me, right?"

"Yeah," Howard said. "But I don't get the connection."

"Well, I kind of stepped on a bead—actually it's not a bead, you know, it's a seed—when I dropped one of the earrings and, like I said, when I stepped on it, it was smushed into a kind of like a powder, and my friend Mrs. Mallowan . . ." Here Nic gestured toward Mrs. So-Called Christie, to whom Howard had given barely a second glance. ". . . she thought maybe Bertram snuffled up a little bit of it and it made him really sick."

I could see that, in spite of himself, Howard was intrigued. "He sniffed one of those crushed seeds from your earring and it, what, almost killed him?"

"Yeah," Nic said resolutely. "Because they have this, um, untraceable stuff in them called Advil or something."

"Abrin," Mrs. So-Called Christie supplied.

"Yeah, abrin."

Howard thought about this for a minute and then seemed to come to a conclusion. "Well, I'm sure Bertram did not almost die from a *seed*," he said in a firm, I'm-going-to-set-these-silly-women-straight kind of way. "I mean, do you really believe this old lady's fairy tale?"

Well, *that* got Nic's hackles up. As it turned out, being taken for a fool was insulting. Not so much to her—she was used to being taken for a fool—but to her new friend. She straightened and used every inch of her height advantage to face down the agent she'd so hoped would help fulfill her dreams.

"I do, Howard," she said. "She's a smart lady, and if she says it's poison, I believe her."

You go, girl. Sisters before misters.

And suddenly if a person could be said to look murderous, it was Howard at that moment.

"This poison talk is ridiculous," he snapped, his face red with bluster. "If anything made that stupid animal sick it was some kind of party drug courtesy of Sailor."

"I don't think so, Howard," Nic said stubbornly. "I think it was the poison bead."

"Fine," Howard hissed, his eyes narrowed. "Believe whatever stupid thing you want. But you keep quiet about this poison bullshit, right?"

And with that, Howard Calhoun turned on his heel and left the room.

Nic semi-collapsed onto the settee next to Mrs. So-Called Christie. For a moment we sat stunned, not saying a word. Or Nic and I sat stunned anyway. Mrs. So-Called Christie was clearly invigorated by the whole scene. "Interesting," she remarked with what I thought was inappropriate relish. "*Very* interesting."

"I call it crazy," Nic said. "One minute he's all 'it's okay, it's not your fault that my dog got sick,' and the next he's mad at me because maybe I almost accidentally poisoned his dog?"

"It is weird," I agreed. "I mean, what's the difference between you poisoning Bertram and Sailor poisoning him? It's got to be that if it was you, it was in a way Howard's fault since he brought the seeds back from India. He really, really doesn't want Brooke to blame him for any part of this."

Mrs. So-Called Christie looked unconvinced, but simply said, "Perhaps."

"He'll come around, though," Nic said confidently. "He's my plus-one for Lizzie Mellon's wedding, and no way is he going to take any chances with *that* networking opp." Sometimes my cousin's insight into people's motivations was a little alarming. "Actually, the Mellons are coming for drinks with the 'rents tomorrow. Maybe I'll ask Howard over for that." She nodded, delighted with her little plan. "If I know him, he'll be all forgive and forget. Lizzie's mom has almost as much clout as Brooke Sinclair."

It sounded like a good plan to me, but it seemed that Mrs. So-Called Christie had concerns. "Do be careful, Miss Van Dyne," she said. "One knows so little. And when one knows more it is too late." As Mr. Satterthwaite advised "Egg" Lytton Gore in *Murder in Three Acts*.

Nic, however, was no longer interested in what Mrs. Mallowan had to say since, as far as she was concerned, she was going to solve her little Howard problem with some deft social bribery.

She jumped up and, leaning down to give our visitor another one of her enormous Nic hugs, said, "Gotta go, Mrs. M! Thanks a mil for your help!"

"It was my pleasure, Miss Nicola," Mrs. So-Called Christie said, politely disentangling herself.

I followed Nic downstairs and found her an umbrella from the vast selection in the library's lost and found, which is a virtual treasure trove of forgotten umbrellas. I have never understood why people who presumably have the brains to puzzle out the solution to a Josephine Tey or a Ngaio Marsh don't have the wits to remember their rain gear.

After getting my very own Nic hug, I ushered my cousin out the door. As I activated the alarm system behind her, I felt the way I always did after a visit from my cousin—that all the fun had left the building. Nic was gone.

And so, when I made my way back upstairs, was Mrs. So-Called Christie.

I didn't know whether to be relieved or worried. *Or even a little disappointed, Tory?* I shook my head to clear it. It was true that I'd rather enjoyed my mystery guest's visit. That had been one impressive feat of deduction—and impersonation. But the fact remained that she had now wandered out of the Christie Room and was either roaming the library or, worse, had found the door to the stairs leading up to my apartment, which I was pretty sure I'd locked as usual when I'd come down to work in the morning. Nonetheless, I went with worried.

I decided to start at the top and work my way down. A quick survey showed that I had indeed locked my apartment door when leaving that morning. But I still went up to make sure it held no uninvited caller. After all, the woman had managed to sneak into the Christie Room somehow. Empty. Good. I then went down and scoured the library's first-floor reading room and restrooms and double-checked that the doors to the library office, the staff room, the storage room and my basement laboratory were securely locked. And then opened and checked the rooms anyway. Nothing. No one.

Mrs. So-Called Christie had vanished.

Six

"I told you there was nothing to it. But you know what it is—
early hours of the morning—everything very still—the thing
had a sinister look—like a detective story. All nonsense, really."

—Colonel Arbuthnot, *Murder on the*
Orient Express

I AWOKE THE NEXT MORNING AFTER A NIGHT OF SPLINTERED dreams featuring Mrs. So-Called You Know Who. The last thing she said before I woke up was to quote Tommy Beresford in Christie's short story "The Man in the Mist": "Very few of us are what we seem to be."

Well, if that wasn't ambiguous, I didn't know what was. Was she trying to tell me that she *seemed* like a ghostly manifestation but was *actually* a real person? Or *seemed* like a real person but was *actually* a ghostly manifestation?

It took a minute for the dream shadows to clear. It was a relief to realize I was snug in my own attic bedroom, luminous with skylights and made cozy by its sloped ceiling. I was safe in my space, my retreat when I needed a break from my own sometimes unruly thoughts. Which, that morning, were particularly so.

How had my mystery guest escaped my notice when I went into the Christie Room? Granted, she hadn't been in my direct line of sight, but I didn't think I'd been *that* distracted. And how could she know where even the most obscure books lived on the room's shelves? Or that the bar cart held red pepper? And how had she managed to slip out of the building while my back was turned?

The questions buzzed in my head like persistent flies. I knew there was only one way to calm them. I needed to lose myself in my work. I crawled out of bed, and after a shower, spent some quality time debating what to wear. Nic's visit the day before had made me feel positively middle-aged. Today, I decided, called for the mint green Courrèges A-line "Space Age" minidress from the 1960s that I'd scored at a thrift shop that didn't know what it had. I'd never really had the nerve to wear it before, but just pulling up its oversize white zipper made me feel, well, young.

I clattered downstairs to my combined kitchen/dining/living area on the third floor to gather myself for the coming day. My spirits lifted a tiny bit as, coffee mug in hand, I stepped through the room's French doors onto the narrow wrought iron balcony overlooking the quiet street below and the park opposite.

The morning was as glorious as only a crisp fall morning can be in New York. Yesterday's rain had washed the sky a clean, clear blue, and the sun as I stood on my tiny balcony was warm on my face. The park—framed by my own rather sleepy Washington Square North and its fellows, Washington Square South, East and West—was spread out in front of me, the trees still leafy green with barely a touch of autumn's golds and reds. The Washington Arch was a half block to my left, and from where I stood, I could see just beyond it to the heart of the park, the central plaza, which is mostly just used for hanging out, arguing politics, listening to whatever jazz trio has set up that day and, weather permitting, wading in the shallow basin of its fifty-foot-wide fountain or, should you not be so inclined, simply watching those who do.

On a whim, I decided to go out for a few minutes of my version of meditation, which was to sit on one of the benches circling the fountain, staring mindlessly at its jets of water rising and falling and rising and falling until guilt about missing valuable lab time would send me scurrying back across the street. I figured I could put in maybe fifteen minutes of zoning-out time before getting started with the day's work.

I trotted over the half block to the corner of Washington Square North and Fifth Avenue, then crossed to the park's entrance, pausing for a moment in front of the curved frame of the arch to admire the ongoing spectacle that is and always has been the tradition of Washington Square Park. Milling around the fountain was a flock of NYU students fist-bumping one another on the way to their first classes of the week, the daily convocation of older men and women doing their slow-motion morning tai chi, and the steady parade of canines taking their humans with them on their morning walk so that the human could pick up their poop.

"G'mornin', Ms. Van Dyne! Remember me?"

Truthfully, the kid waylaying me would be difficult to forget. It wasn't so much the mane of carrot curls or the wide grin that seemed to split the freckled face in half as it was her clear confidence that all the world was her friend and would, of course, remember her. Which, of course, I did.

She had been one of a half-dozen fifth-grade students from PS 41 who had visited my lab a few weeks earlier for Career Day. The teacher had asked each child to introduce themselves and say why they wanted to learn about "fixing books." I'd been kind of curious about that myself. I mean, what kind of eleven-year-old chooses a visit to a book conservation laboratory over the firehouse or the veterinarian's office? Except, of course, a kid like I'd been. Who are few and far between. In fact, I did get a few mumbled complaints that "there wasn't any more room on the vet trip." But not from the little redheaded girl wearing faded jeans with rolled-up cuffs, faded red Vans, a faded U2 T-shirt and toting a faded crossbody book bag with a battered laptop peeking out of it.

"I'm Mairead Butler," she'd said as introduction. "M-A-I-R-E-A-D. Mairead. Rhymes with 'parade.' I'm Irish, y'see." As if I couldn't tell by her soft lilt. "My da, he's a visiting professor of Celtic history at NYU from Trinity College in Dublin. My mam is dead. But she told me the story of how the book doctors at Trinity patched up a copy of the Book of Kells. Are you not a book doctor, too?"

I had been so busy trying to process her matter-of-fact announcement of her mother's decease that I only managed to stammer out, "Well, I hadn't thought of it in quite that light, but, yes, I guess I am." Having regained some of my composure, I added, "Although the technical term is 'book conservator.'"

"Brilliant," she'd said, her little freckled face lighting up. "I want to be a book conservator, then." At which point she'd pulled the laptop out of her book bag and proceeded to take copious notes on my presentation.

Abe, I thought, *would have loved this kid.*

And now here was this raggedy mini-me in Washington Square Park walking a raggedy little dog at the end of an equally raggedy leash and carrying a carefully knotted poop bag.

"Of course I remember you," I said. "Mairead. Rhymes with 'parade.'"

If it was possible, the girl's grin got wider.

"Where's your dad, Mairead?" I asked. Although it wasn't unheard of to see a child of her age out and about alone on the quiet streets of Greenwich Village, it was unusual.

"He's up there," she said, pointing up at what I thought at first was heaven—*surely she'd said it was the mother who'd died?*—and then realized was the top story of NYU's Kimmel Center looming over the south side of the park. "It's my job to walk Tony here in the morning," she continued. "'Course I know Da's watching me with his binocs from the top floor of Kimmel and that he has a tracker on my mobile, but it's independence of a sort and I intend to encourage it." I blinked at her. *Okay.* "And besides, I've got Tony with me, and if anyone gives me any bother, he'll fix 'em. He knows who the villains are. I don't know how he knows, but know he does. And they'd best look sharp. Tony's wee but he's fierce."

"And this, I assume, is Tony?" I asked, bending down to pet the scruffy little black-and-brown dog whose head had been swiveling back and forth from speaker to speaker like an umpire at a tennis match.

"Aye, this is Tony," Mairead said proudly. "He's a Yorkie."

A Yorkie. A Yorkshire terrier. A Yorkshire terrier named Tony.

Suddenly I couldn't get away fast enough. "Well, gotta go, Mairead," I said, standing up so quickly I felt lightheaded. Or at least I told myself that was why I felt lightheaded.

The girl's face fell at my dismissal, and I felt like a total grinch.

"I tell you what," I said, relenting, "I've got to get to work now, but how about you ask your father to call me about setting up a time for you to come by one day soon, and I can show you what I'm working on."

"That would be grand," Mairead said with another face-splitting smile. "Bye for now." And off she trotted with Tony the Yorkshire terrier.

Don't even go there, Tory.

In something of a daze, I made my way back across the street, pushing through the gate in the black wrought iron fence surrounding the small front garden and trotting up the twelve rather grand limestone steps to the front door. Checking my watch, I was almost amused at my own unconscious internal clock. Somehow I had managed to arrange this morning so that I would enter my basement workroom, as I did every weekday morning, at precisely eight a.m. When you make your own hours, it is essential to keep to a schedule, at least it is for me. Otherwise, I'd probably spend the day reading the latest Deborah Crombie while devouring an entire bag of Trader Joe's chocolate-covered pretzels.

Once in the lab, I arranged the tools I would be needing that day on my workbench and lost myself re-backing a beautiful, if fragile, Cobden-Sanderson binding on *The Harbours of England*. T. J. Cobden-Sanderson was a revered nineteenth-century book-binder of the British Arts and Crafts movement, and the volume I was restoring had boasted a beautiful leather-bound Cobden-Sanderson cover when it was published in 1856 but was now suffering from an immobile spine. Its thick cover boards were barely held on by a few frayed slips, some very thin leather and, inside the cover, single sheets of marbled endpaper. The day before, I had removed the old spine and used my lifting knife to gently pry up the sides of the leather holding the boards. It was the kind of exacting work that I loved. I was looking forward to spending the day removing the excess spine linings and relining the volume with paste and tissue.

Sure enough, the job was immediately and totally absorbing. I was only dimly aware of the footsteps above my head that meant that Adrian Gooding, the Guild's head librarian and my best friend in the world, had arrived in the library proper. Adrian and I often went out for a quick bite at noon, but that day I decided to skip lunch and sent him a "drowning in work" text. I didn't look up from my labors until I heard the library chimes gently reminding our patrons that the library would be closing in fifteen minutes, at five p.m. sharp. It took me another half hour or so, but finally *Harbours* was done. I gazed with satisfaction at the finished product. It was, to my eyes, simply beautiful, the repairs virtually indistinguishable from the original.

I tidied the workbench and hurried up to the library proper, where I knew Adrian would be waiting for me in the front hall to lock up behind him. With any luck he'd have a few minutes to help me swat away that morning's questions, which had come buzzing back like the proverbial flies the minute I'd put my tools down.

Adrian Gooding is the most sensible person I've ever met. Adrian believes in exactly nothing. Not a higher power, not love at first sight, not even the keto diet. I needed someone to tell me that the lady in the pearls and the squashy hat was just a real live human being with a few marbles missing, not some kind of Other Worldly manifestation of the Queen of Crime. I was convinced that if anyone could help me see who Mrs. So-Called Christie *was* as opposed to who she *seemed to be*, it would be Adrian.

Sure enough, there he was, waiting impatiently by the front door when I came up into the hall. As usual, he was dressed immaculately—a perfectly tailored navy Ralph Lauren suit, crisp Canali dress shirt blindingly white against his ebony skin and, in the perfect Adrian touch, a Ferragamo tie sporting what at first appeared to be a fairly standard floral print but on closer examination revealed tiny bunnies peeking out of the vegetation.

"Love the bunnies," I said by way of hello.

"Love the groovy outfit," Adrian said. "Ever so mod."

Greetings dispensed with, I got down to business. "I need to talk to you."

But Adrian had no time for fly-swatting. "Sorry, girl, it'll have

64   AMANDA CHAPMAN

to wait for tomorrow. Hot date waiting. And he is not somebody you keep waiting."

I sighed. "Okay, but just tell me this. You didn't have any troublesome lady visitor in the library today, did you?"

"Not unless she was disguised as an elderly gentleman who took it into his head to reshelve the Campion novels in order of his preference rather than alphabetically by title."

"Probably not her, then," I said, much relieved.

"Let's do lunch tomorrow, and you can tell me all your troubles."

"Honey," I said, as I waved him out the door, "you have no idea what a boatload of crazy you're in for."

The news that Mrs. So-Called Christie had not visited us that day was encouraging, but I was nonetheless determined to do a thorough check of the building. After locking the front door and setting the alarm system, I began as I usually did, with a check of the reading room to ensure no one had fallen asleep in one of its all-too-comfy wingback chairs. This time, though, I also looked behind the circulation desk and even kneeled down to peer beneath the reading tables, which made me feel like an idiot. The very idea of that dignified lady on her hands and knees under a library reading table was ludicrous. But I peered beneath them nonetheless. Nothing. No one. I then trotted upstairs to inspect and lock the special collections rooms. All good. Finally, holding my breath, I peered into the Christie Room.

This time you couldn't miss her.

Because this time Mrs. So-Called Christie, in a dark blue silk dress with a jaunty sequined bow appliqued on one shoulder, had really made herself at home. She was, it seemed, preparing to host a tea party. On the coffee table in front of the blue couch she'd set out a teapot, two teacups, a cream pitcher and sugar bowl, all from the bargeware collection in the alcove. She'd pulled the gold velvet armchair she'd used the day before from its usual spot next to the bar cart forward to the coffee table and was placing a small wooden chair opposite it. *Who did she think she was?*

As I marched into the room, Mrs. So-Called Christie straightened up from her task and gave me one of her warm, disarming smiles. But I was determined not to be warmed or disarmed. This had gone far enough. I'm not sure what I would have said at that moment had the front doorbell not started pealing like the end of the world had arrived.

"I'll be back," I warned, hoping I sounded like Arnold Schwarzenegger.

As I ran down the stairs, the bell continued to ring insistently, which ticked me off. *Who rings a doorbell like that?* And then I remembered. *Nic rings a doorbell like that.*

Supremely annoyed, I pulled the door open.

Surprise. Nic it was. Nic in a fairly conservative, for her, grey houndstooth Jill St. John sheath dress. Which barely registered with me because standing next to her was a man wearing a truly ugly brown suit. Which is redundant, since virtually all brown suits are truly ugly. Nonetheless, I was transfixed.

But it was not the suit that transfixed me.

What transfixed me was the man who wore it.

Tall, with that perfect slim ratio of shoulder to hips. Hair the glossy black of a raven's wing. Not that I had ever seen a raven's wing, but that was the phrase that sprang to mind. A high, intelligent forehead that was, at the moment, creased with a frown. Dark eyes fringed with eyelashes so thick they made me jealous. The face was too long and thin to be called conventionally handsome, but the slightly aquiline nose was noble, and the mouth—*oh my god, that mouth.* That mouth was what they'd had in mind when they invented the word "sensual." Wide, with a full lower lip that made me want to bite it. *Good lord, girl, calm yourself.*

I forced my gaze away from that mouth only to be caught again by the man's eyes. Not sexy, not sensual. And suddenly, I was ashamed of my flight of fancy. Because in those eyes I thought I recognized someone who had also seen more than their fair share of the world's tragedy. I wondered briefly (and insanely) if he was some kind of priest.

"Ms. Van Dyne?" the man asked. "Tory Van Dyne?" His voice was low and quiet but something about it demanded your full attention.

I just nodded, as it seemed I was temporarily bereft of speech.

"Your cousin," the man continued, "has had a shock. She asked me to bring her here."

Well, that knocked a little sense into me. I turned my gaze back to Nic. She looked like she'd had more than a shock. She looked like she'd lost her wits—lips pale, skin the color of parchment, tears streaking her cheeks. She also seemed bereft of speech, which was truly alarming. I'd never known Nic to be at a loss for words. Words generally spilled out of Nic like champagne from a magnum. *What was going on? What was wrong with Nic? And who was this man who was very clearly calling the shots?*

"What's going on? Who *are* you?" I asked. Well, demanded really.

"Detective Sebastian Mendez-Cruz," he said. "I'm with the Sixth Precinct." *This man, this man with the eyes of a sad saint, was a cop?*

"*Detective* Mendez-Cruz?" I repeated idiotically.

And then the detective did what I thought they did only on TV. He pulled a leather folder out of the inside breast pocket of the disaster that was his suit and flipped the case open. Inside was one of those could-be-anybody headshot IDs and a gold-and-blue honest-to-god shield emblazoned with the words *City of New York Police Detective*. Well, no arguing with that.

"Maybe we should come in," he suggested, giving a slight sideways nod at the passersby on the sidewalk behind them, some already stopping to wonder why that pretty girl on the steps of that big house was crying. *And why that other girl was just standing there like an idiot staring at that tall guy in the ugly suit.*

"Yes, of course," I gabbled, holding the door wide. "Of course you should come in."

Nic walked past me like an automaton and folded herself onto the bench in the foyer, dropping her head into her hands. I sat down beside her and put an arm around her shaking shoulders. I looked up at the detective.

"What's going on?" I asked him again. This time more politely.

"I was called to the incident," he sort-of-but-not-really explained.

"The incident?" I was beginning to sound like a brainless wonder.

Nic raised her head from her hands. "Oh, Tory!" she wailed. "Somebody's killed Howard!"

Seven

◇◇◇◇◇◇◇◇◇

"What are you doing this afternoon, Griselda?"

"My duty," said Griselda. "My duty as the Vicaress. Tea and scandal at four-thirty."

—The Murder at the Vicarage

I COULDN'T TAKE IT IN. IT WAS LIKE SOME KIND OF WEIRD RE-peat of the night before. Except infinitely worse. Because Howard was not a dog. Howard was a real person. A real person who had been standing in the Christie Room not twenty-four hours earlier.

I looked to Detective Mendez-Cruz for clarification. "The incident?" I repeated.

Before he could answer, Nic clarified the situation herself.

"The *incident*," she said with a little hiccup, "where somebody killed Howard by pushing him under the No. 6 train."

"Somebody *pushed* Howard under a subway?" *Are you just going to repeat everything everyone says to you, Tory?*

"Yes," Nic moaned. "And I saw it."

Again, I looked helplessly at the detective. "She saw it?" *Again with the repeating.*

He nodded. "Is there somewhere we could talk?"

"Of course," I said, shaking my head a little to clear it. "We can use the Christie Room."

By the time I remembered, it was too late.

Mrs. So-Called Christie was sitting in the gold velvet armchair sipping a cup of tea when we walked in. I couldn't help but notice that she'd already also set out two more teacups on the coffee table. She leaned forward to set down her own cup, looking at us gravely. And it seemed to me that in that single glance she absorbed every detail of the scene. Nic's shock. Detective Mendez-Cruz's poker face, just doing his job, nicely but officially. My dismay, not only at what Nic had told me but at Mrs. So-Called Christie's presence at a drama that had nothing to do with her. Nic, on the other hand, was clearly relieved and comforted by the sight of her new friend.

"Oh, Mrs. M!" she cried, "I'm so glad you're here! You won't believe what's happened."

Mrs. So-Called Christie shook her grey head slightly. "At my time of life, my dear," she said (causing me to wonder briefly how someone who claimed to be dead could have *any* time of life), "one knows that the worst is usually true." To quote Miss Marple in *Murder at the Vicarage*. "But do have a seat on the sofa. A nice cup of tea will put you right."

Nic looked less than convinced and gazed longingly at the bar cart, but nonetheless sat down on the couch.

"Cream?" her hostess asked politely.

Nic looked at her blankly. I don't think Nic had had a cup of tea since our annual tea parties as very small girls with our other grandmother, Nana Pat, at her summer "cottage" on Cape Cod.

"I think a little cream and four lumps of sugar," Mrs. So-Called Christie decided for her, choosing Hercule Poirot's pick-me-up preference in *Dead Man's Folly*.

Once she had Nic nicely settled and sipping the traditional British panacea for shock, our hostess turned to her other guests. I had been standing next to the couch, arms folded across my chest, trying to figure out if I was angry at Mrs. So-Called Christie for making free with the library's premises or grateful that she was there to handle the situation. Mendez-Cruz was standing seemingly at ease just inside the door to the room, his face revealing nothing, but clearly taking it all in. Each blink of his eyes was like another photograph of the scene. Click, click, click.

"Miss Van Dyne, perhaps you'd like to introduce your cousin's friend?"

Honest to god, the woman was Grandmother all over again. The rules are the rules.

"Mrs., um, Mallowan, I'd like you to meet Detective Mendez-Cruz." I looked over at the man and immediately lost my train of thought. "He's, um, a detective." *Idiot. You are an idiot, Tory.* I trailed off, and Mendez-Cruz took up the social reins gracefully.

"Detective Sebastian Mendez-Cruz of the Sixth Precinct, ma'am," he said. "I'm sorry to have interrupted your evening, but Miss Van Dyne's cousin has had a shock."

"Yes, I think I heard her say downstairs that Mr. Calhoun has met with an accident?" It would have been hard *not* to hear Nic's keening from the floor below.

Mendez-Cruz nodded, but Nic was having no truck with euphemisms. It seemed the tea was having its effect. "Accident *nothing,*" she said. "Howard has been *murdered,* Mrs. M, and you're the only one who can figure out who did it!"

I glanced over at Mendez-Cruz, whose job it presumably was to figure out who did it. But if he was annoyed at Nic's passing of the baton to this rather unprepossessing middle-aged lady, his face did not show it. He was just taking it all in. Click, click, click.

"Well, in that case, Miss Nicola," our hostess said mildly, "why don't we ask Detective Mendez-Cruz to join us for a cup of tea, and we will see what we can do to help him with this sad business."

She leaned over and patted the couch next to Nic, saying to me, "You sit here next to your cousin, Miss Van Dyne." So I sat. "And Detective Mendez-Cruz, I'm sure you'll find the chair across from my own more comfortable than it appears." So Detective Mendez-Cruz sat in the small wooden chair that I certainly hoped was more comfortable than it appeared.

"I'll pour, shall I?" Mrs. So-Called Christie asked. The question was clearly rhetorical. We all nodded in unison.

Once the formalities of who wanted what in their tea (Mendez-Cruz and I nothing, and Mrs. So-Called Christie mostly cream with just enough actual tea to still be called a cup of tea), our hostess really got to work. Her face was alive with barely contained curiosity, and I realized that she truly did not know what had happened. It seemed, as she'd advised me, that the Eternity was not providing her with inside information.

"Now, Miss Nicola," she said. "Why don't you tell me what happened."

Again, I looked over at the representative of New York's Finest to see how he was taking this usurpation of his role, but the detective's focus never wavered. How unusual. A man who valued results more than his own ego.

Nic got a kind of panicked look on her face. "I don't know, really," she said. "It all happened so fast. Howard and I met at his place at One Fifth before going uptown for drinks at the parents' with the Mellons." Which explained tonight's primly proper dress. The Mellons were nothing if not proper. "Howard wanted a little pre-drink celebration."

"Celebration? Celebration of what?" I asked.

"He told me that Sailor was going to sign with him now that she's going all Hollywood and all." I nodded. Yes, that would have been cause for celebration for Howard. "So that was the good news." *Uh-oh.*

"What was the bad news?" I asked.

"It seems wrong to be upset about this now, I mean after what's happened to Howard and all, but he told me when I got to his place that the Mrs. Potts thing isn't gonna happen because Grant Neuman thinks I'm not mature enough or something and that kind of bummed me out."

"I'm so, so sorry, Nic," I said, meaning it. "I know how important it was to you."

Nic smiled wanly. "Well, yeah, it is, but Howard said he wanted me to come out to the Hamptons this coming weekend anyway and we'd both stay at this guest house he likes . . . liked . . . and maybe I could talk to Grant Neuman myself, so maybe it's not a done deal, and he promised to take me to that international film festival in the Hamptons in a few weeks to network there so that was nice because it's the weekend of the library gala so I can get out of that, but still I cried a little and didn't really want to do the drinkypoo thing with the olds, but not to go would be rude and embarrass the 'rents . . ." Only Nic would put aside a major career disappointment to avoid embarrassing her mother and father. ". . . so we tried for a cab or an Uber, but you can't get them at rush hour, you know, so we decided to take the subway from Union Square."

Nic paused for a moment, and I could see her steeling herself. *All you want to do is forget.* I put down my teacup and took her hand in mine. She stared into my eyes, but I knew she wasn't seeing me. She was back there. In the horror.

"So we're on the uptown platform at rush hour and it's mobbed like always," she began, and I flinched involuntarily. "You can hear the train coming into the station through the tunnel so Howard pushes forward to the edge of the platform like he always does, you know, because he likes to get into the car before the passengers even get off even though it's not polite so he can grab a seat. But that was just Howard, you know?"

I patted her hand with my free one. The prohibition against speaking ill of the dead is still strong in all of us. Nic swallowed hard, and the rest came out in a rush, as if she couldn't wait to be free of the words. And the memory.

"So anyway, I'm trying to follow him so I don't lose him in the crowd and then I see the train coming in and he's in front of me right at the edge of the platform and all of a sudden this guy in one of those surgical masks like everybody wore in the pandemic and a scarf tied around the neck of one of those black designer hoodies, you know . . ."

I knew. I knew because Nic had once bored me to tears about a Prada hoodie that Howard wanted her to wear during New York Fashion Week, but she had refused because it didn't fit her "brand." (Whatever that might be.) But Mrs. So-Called Christie wanted some clarification. "Excuse me, Miss Nicola. What is a *hoodie*, exactly?"

"Well, it's a sweatshirt, like, with a hood attached to it."

"I see. Do go on."

Nic steeled herself. "So all of a sudden this guy comes out of nowhere and, and, and pushes Howard down on the tracks *right in front of the train*."

At this Nic turned to me, her face a mask of horror. "Oh, Tory, it was horrible. I don't think I can ever unsee it. Now I know how it must be for you."

I felt rather than saw Mendez-Cruz look at me sharply. But

this wasn't the time to worry about that. I took my cousin in my arms and let her sob it out on my shoulder.

"Don't worry, Nic," I said, rubbing her back in comfort circles. "Everything's going to be all right."

Which I didn't believe for one minute.

IT TOOK A LOT MORE THAN COMFORT CIRCLES TO BRING NIC back. Mrs. So-Called Christie poured Nic another cup of tea, which revived her somewhat. Blowing her nose loudly on a clean handkerchief passed to her by Mendez-Cruz also seemed to help. *Were all NYPD detectives required to carry clean handkerchiefs in the event of damsels in distress?*

Finally restored to us, the old Nic carried on. "You know, it could have been me that lunatic was after," she said wonderingly. "I've had to block some real weirdos with Beast and Belle fantasies from my 'Gram feed sometimes." She shuddered, and I remembered why I really didn't much like social media.

Mendez-Cruz's brow furrowed, and he shook his head. "I doubt the attack was premeditated or aimed at any particular person, Ms. Van Dyne." I confess I liked the man's formality. "These things tend to be random acts by someone who's mentally unstable, usually on drugs, and Mr. Calhoun"—again, that careful formality—"standing at the edge of the platform would be an easy target. But we'll take a close look at the station's security footage, of course. And at any suspicious characters following you online."

Mrs. Christie, who had been in strictly listening mode up to this point, nodded thoughtfully. "It might also be interesting to know who benefits from Mr. Calhoun's death."

And there she goes, I thought, *still looking for her murder mystery.*

"We will, of course, look into anything that might be relevant,"

Mendez-Cruz responded politely, as if the woman hadn't just tried, ever so gently, to tell him how to do his job.

"Howard told me once that his only family was a cousin in Cincinnati," Nic chimed in. "A fat cousin, he actually said. Which wasn't very body positive, I thought."

Mendez-Cruz merely nodded. "My sergeant is at Mr. Calhoun's apartment now. Once we know who his lawyer is we can look into any significant bequests."

Mrs. Christie shared what could only be called a knowing look with the detective. "Yes, greed is often the motivation for murder," she said, and gave a little cough. "But not, of course, the only one."

Mendez-Cruz nodded but appeared to feel that this was not the time for a listing of all the possible reasons why one person would choose to do away with another. Instead he turned to Nic and asked, "Can I give you a ride home?"

This, of course, would have been the time for Nic to say thank you to the handsome detective for his thoughtfulness but that rather than take up any more of his valuable time, she'd ask her father to send his driver down with the car to pick her up. What she actually said to the handsome detective was, "That would be super nice."

Before I walked them downstairs, I made a half-hearted attempt to include Mrs. So-Called Christie in the exodus, but she shooed us all out of the room, saying she'd "tidy up" a bit.

At the front door, I hugged my cousin once more and then stood for a moment watching as she and Mendez-Cruz walked up the street to an unprepossessing grey sedan parked in front of a fire hydrant. Presumably there was something that indicated to the parking police that the car belonged to New York's Finest, but if so, it was nothing that I could see. What I *could* see was that Nic seemed to be recovering nicely in the detective's company. Which was good. Anything that might lessen the trauma, that might make my cousin feel that life was safe, that things could somehow get back to normal, was very, very good. As Mendez-Cruz held the passenger door open for his charge, I turned away, closed and locked the door, set the alarm and made my way back upstairs to my other guest.

Who had, of course, vanished.

Eight

"The impossible cannot have happened, therefore the impossible must be possible in spite of appearances."

—Hercule Poirot, *Murder on the Orient Express*

NORMALLY, I START MY DAY NEATLY WRITING AN EXTENSIVE to-do list on a fresh page of my official to-do list notebook. The day after Howard was killed I had exactly two items on that list: CHECK ON NIC and TALK TO ADRIAN ABOUT MRS. C.

My call to Nic went immediately to voice mail, which I hoped meant she was sleeping. Sleep was good. I moved on to my second to-do. Adrian's office is at the rear of the library's ground-floor hall. He usually leaves the office door open to allow him to "keep an eye out for the Groupies." The Groupies are our handful of fanatical mystery buffs who think nothing of having long and loud debates about such divisive topics as the traditional locked-room mysteries pioneered by grandmaster John Dickson Carr versus the contemporary practitioner—and to my mind equally talented—Seishi Yokomizo. This ruckus, though, tends to annoy the other patrons, much as they may enjoy both authors. From his vantage point behind Grandmother's enormous walnut desk, Adrian could note any of the usual suspects coming in the front entrance. Then he would text assistant librarian Susie Sabatini, who manned the checkout desk in the reading room proper, so she could anticipate and head off any disruptions.

I took the stairs up to the ground floor from my work room at eight thirty to meet Adrian as he came in the door. As head librarian, Adrian worked Monday through Friday, leaving Saturdays, with their three p.m. close, to Susie. Sundays were a day of rest for all. During the week, his rule was to arrive precisely at eight thirty, then open the front door to Derek Collins, our cleaner, at nine and finally, once Derek had finished his daily rounds, unlock the library's front door for business at ten, when Susie would more or less wander in. At the end of the day, he was responsible for locking the front door at five fifteen behind the last of the stragglers. His other firm deadline was his own five thirty departure. As he was fond of reminding me, he had a life. I didn't mind; I was happy for him. One of us should. I also liked his punctuality. Sure enough, the minute I came up from the lab to the front hall at eight thirty, he was just walking in the door.

"I need to talk to you," I said. It was a measure of how distressed I was that I did not notice or comment on what he was wearing.

"Yeah, I bet you do," Adrian said. "I saw in the *Post* this morning that Howard Calhoun got pushed under the No. 6 train last night."

"True," I said. "And Nic was there." My voice shook a little, and I felt like I always do when my voice shakes a little. Like I didn't want to put the terrible thing into words.

"She was *there*?" Adrian said, almost in a whisper. "She saw it *happen*?"

I nodded.

"That's so incredibly shitty."

I just nodded again.

"How's she doing?"

"Better now, I think," I said. "Nic's pretty resilient." *Unlike Yours Truly.*

"Was it some crazy person?"

"The cop who brought her here said it was probably something like that. Drugs maybe. But they're going to look into it." I took a deep breath and shook my head like a horse trying to shoo off a fly. "But that's not what I wanted to talk to you about."

"You have something more important to talk to me about than your cousin seeing her agent getting pushed under a subway," Adrian said flatly.

"Well, not more important," I admitted, "but more . . . immediate."

"Can it wait until lunch?"

Adrian, like me, loves routine. Unless one of us was slammed by work, we usually ate a takeout lunch together in his office, where first we would discuss any pro bono work I was doing for the library, then move on to any new and relevant *CrimeReads* articles one or the other of us needed to know about. Adrian was gradually building the library's contemporary crime fiction list, especially works by people of color or LGBTQ authors, and I was always on the lookout for reissues of long-out-of-print classics.

We occasionally discussed world events, but found that, unlike our sometimes widely divergent opinions on crime fiction, we were boringly in line with each other on politics, so that topic really wasn't much fun. On the other hand, Walter Mosley versus Eleanor Taylor Bland? Now, *that* was something you could really sink your teeth into. But not today, alas.

"No, it can't wait until lunch," I said. "It's a long story and I'm only going to be able to get through it with a Caffè Reggio cappuccino."

Adrian still looked undecided.

"C'mon," I urged him. "Derek's off today and Susie has a key. She can open up."

"No way," Adrian said. "I'll come back to half the returns shelved upside down." Susie is as laid-back as Adrian is buttoned-up.

"She'll be fine," I said, adding as incentive, "and I'll fill you in on what we know about Howard."

Adrian's need for bookshelf order was no match for the very human urge to rubberneck the accident on the side of the road. "If I must, I must," he said.

I pulled the door closed behind us, and we headed down to the southwest corner of the park where the usual mixed group of chess enthusiasts—old, middle-aged and young; clearly well-to-do and clearly not doing so well—were setting up their chessmen for the first games of the day. As we walked, I steeled myself and told Adrian what Nic and Mendez-Cruz had said about Howard's death, leaving out Mrs. So-Called Christie for the moment. By the end of it, Adrian was visibly shaken. Sometimes it's better not to look too closely at the accident on the side of the road.

"Poor, poor Nic," Adrian said, then caught himself. "And poor Howard, too, of course."

At MacDougal we turned left and walked the half a block south to Caffè Reggio. While we waited at our little wrought iron table for the caffè's splendid chrome-and-bronze espresso machine to hiss out its magic elixir, I wondered why I didn't come to this warm, ocher-walled, welcoming spot every morning. Was it possible that I was slightly too focused on my work?

"Do you think it's possible that I am slightly too focused on my work?"

"Oh, good lord," Adrian said. "Please tell me we're not here to talk about work-life balance. There is no such thing as work-life balance. It's just something those 'life coaches' made up to take your money." *Yup, this was the Adrian I needed.*

Once our server had brought us our coffee and croissants, I jumped into the fray.

"Is it possible that a dead person can come back to Earth?"

Adrian rolled his eyes. "No."

I wasn't sure that was good news. If Adrian was right, it meant one of four things about Yours Truly. As the dapper Belgian detective put it in *Third Girl*, "Eh bien, then, you are crazy, or appear crazy or you think you are crazy, and possibly you may be crazy."

I wanted a fifth option—none of the above.

And so I told Adrian about our mystery visitor.

"I'M TELLING YOU, ADRIAN, MRS. SO-CALLED CHRISTIE JUST vanishes."

"First of all," Adrian broke in, "enough of this 'Mrs. So-Called Christie' nonsense. I mean, I get it, she's not really Agatha Christie. But can we just call her Mrs. Christie for simplicity's sake?"

"Okay," I said. "But not in front of anyone else like Nic. She's Mrs. Mallowan to her. And the truth is, sometimes I'm convinced that she *is* Agatha Christie. I mean, both times, it really was like she just apparated and then disapparated."

Adrian snorted. "Get a grip, girl. We're talking about the Mystery Guild Library here, not Hogwarts."

"Then *you* explain it," I snapped.

"Okay, let's start at the beginning. Think about the first time you found her in the Christie Room. You open the door. The alcove is slightly behind and to the left as you walk in and the open door itself now actually *blocks* the view into the alcove unless you take a few steps in and look around it. Did you do that?"

I shook my head. "No, I was heading straight for that book in the bookshelves to my right. The one I told you about the other day."

"Ah, yes," Adrian said. "A history of toilets, as I recall. Nothing odd about that."

"A history of *bathrooms*," I objected, with all the dignity I could muster. Which is never a lot. "Or, more specifically, British water closets."

"And again I repeat, nothing odd about that."

This from a man who was wearing a silver skull ring on his right forefinger. Which, if you think about it, probably isn't so very odd in a librarian at a library devoted to murder.

"Anyway, no, I didn't look over at the alcove. I just went and pulled the book off one of those low shelves to the right, where I'd put it back yesterday."

"And then you hurried over to the big comfy couch facing the fireplace with the alcove to your left and slightly behind you. It wasn't until the woman spoke that you turned around. So the sensible conclusion is that the woman sat very still as you walked into the room and you didn't notice her."

"But that doesn't explain how she knew where the Vermeire and the Martindale were or that there was red pepper on the bar cart."

"Unless, you dope, she's been in the Christie Room before. Or even been a regular visitor to the *real* library in the *real* Greenway House."

Of course. Agatha Christie's house in Devon had been open to the public since 2005. My own grandmother had visited it countless times over the years she'd spent re-creating her version of Mrs. Christie's library. Of course this woman—whose voice alone marked her as British—would have haunted (oops, bad choice of words) the real Greenway library.

"Okay," I said, "I'll give you that one. But it doesn't explain how she managed to vanish while I was letting Nic out the front door that first night or Nic and that detective last night."

"Again," Adrian said with a sigh, "one step at a time. When you locked the front door after you let your cousin *in* on both nights, did you set the alarm system?"

The house has an alarm system wired to both the front door and the back door to the alley leading to a mews behind the house. When switched on, the thing clangs incredibly loudly if either door is opened from the outside or the inside.

"No," I said. "You know I usually only set it just before I go upstairs for the night or, if I have an after-hours visitor, after they leave." *As if crowds of people were dropping by in the evenings on a regular basis.*

"Now, tell me, Tory," Adrian asked, still in professor mode, "what would happen if someone were to leave the premises by, say, the back door before you set the alarm?"

The question was rhetorical. Adrian knew as well as I did that exactly nothing would happen. Nothing at all.

"Okay, I get it," I muttered. "I guess Mrs. Christie could have left by the back door while I was letting Nic out the front. But she would have been working against a pretty tight time frame. Both times I activated the alarm the minute the front door was shut behind my visitors."

"But how long was it from the time you left the Christie Room, said goodbye to your visitors, closed and locked the door and activated the alarm?"

I thought about that. "Ten minutes, I guess."

"So, if your ghostly visitor were to leave the premises by, let us say, earthly means, she would have had a good ten minutes to make her escape through the back door."

"Yes," I admitted reluctantly. *Why are you hoping for a less prosaic explanation, Tory?*

"Well, then, there you have it," Adrian said triumphantly. "You see, my dear Victoria, you have made the unforgivable error . . ."

I knew exactly what was coming. Adrian and I had been playing Name That Quote for years. "'. . . of overlooking the obvious,'" we chanted in tandem. "Poirot to Hastings. *The A.B.C. Murders.*"

MAYBE IT WAS THE CAFFEINE KICKING IN OR MAYBE IT WAS the reassuring effect of Adrian's common sense, but as we strolled back across the park toward the library, I basked in a kind of glow of normality. I liked normal. I'd been chasing normal all my life.

Adrian left me at the arch, saying, "While I'm out, I think I'll go check the Strand for anything new. You want to come?"

By "new," Adrian meant "secondhand." The Strand is The Best Bookstore in the World. (Caps mine.) A New York landmark, it was founded in 1927 on Fourth Avenue, which was then known as Book Row. In the late '50s it moved to its current location on the corner of Broadway and 12th Street. It carries more than two and a half million new, used and rare volumes in what it proudly claims to be eighteen miles of books. The place is total catnip to book lovers. I can't tell you how many of the library's crime offerings have come from Adrian's visits to the Strand.

I, on the other hand, am addicted to the store's sidewalk $2 bin, where I once found a first Scottish edition (go figure) of Washington Irving's *A History of New York*, which I promptly took home and rehabilitated for my own small collection.

"I'd love to go," I said, "but I'm already way behind. That first edition of *The Moonstone* that I froze yesterday needs to be vacuumed." Freezing is the best way to kill any paper-loving insects that think they have found their forever home in an old book. I'm talking about icky things like silverfish and book lice and bookworms. And, yes, bookworms are a real thing, not just little kids reading under the covers with a flashlight.

Adrian wrinkled his nose in distaste. "Better you than me."

"I'll buzz your cell if Mrs. Christie shows up while you're out."

"Sounds to me like the lady only comes by at the shining hour, though."

"True," I said thoughtfully.

"And what are you going to do if she does show up again after work?" Adrian asked. "Make her another cocktail?"

"I haven't thought that far ahead," I admitted.

"Better start," he said.

Nine

"One needs some really good food and drink after all the magnificent blood and gloom of Macbeth.*"*

—Mark Easterbrook, *The Pale Horse*

BUT MRS. CHRISTIE DIDN'T SHOW UP THAT NIGHT. OR THE NEXT. Or the next. I was unaccountably disappointed and told myself it was because I didn't like to drink alone. Which wasn't true. I was perfectly fine with drinking alone.

Also unaccountably disappointing was the radio silence from Detective Mendez-Cruz, who was presumably busy chasing down Howard's killer. I checked with Nic, who hadn't seen or heard from him, either.

On Wednesday, I got a call from Brooke Sinclair informing me that there was to be a "celebration of Howard's life" in the New York Public Library's Trustees Room the coming Saturday. Now, I, like all right-thinking New Yorkers, love the public library's main branch on 42nd and Fifth. But I had been to events in the Trustees Room years before, and my recollection was that its dark wood-paneled walls, dreary hanging tapestries and heavily ornate plaster ceiling were hardly conducive to a "celebration." Although pretty much perfect for a funeral.

But you don't say that to Brooke Sinclair. What you say is, "Of course I'll be there." So that is what I said. Even though I knew there was every chance that I wouldn't be. This, when I admitted it to Nic, was unacceptable to my cousin.

"The man practically died in your house," she protested.

"No," I corrected her, "he did not. The Union Square subway station is *not* my house."

"Whatever," Nic said. "Dr. Cynthia says I should go. She says it will be cathartic, whatever that is. And I can't face it without you."

Dr. Cynthia is Dr. Cynthia Moore, my onetime therapist. She is also a very good person and had agreed to fit Nic in daily until she'd dealt with the immediate aftershocks of Howard's death. I was concerned about Nic attending the memorial service. But I trusted Dr. Cynthia, and if she thought it was a good idea, then it was a good idea. Nic should go. And apparently she wasn't going without me.

"We can be each other's emotional support dog," she added. She's brave, Nic is. Unlike Yours Truly. But I reminded myself that in this instance the venue was familiar to me and Brooke had said that the gathering would be a small one. I told myself I would try. Baby steps. Dr. Cynthia would be pleased. She'd been encouraging me to take baby steps for years. Fruitlessly.

NIC AND I AGREED TO MEET FOR LUNCH AT THE MINETTA TAV-ern before the memorial service. The Minetta serves *the best* hamburgers in New York. "We're gonna need our strength," Nic had

pointed out, and I agreed. Plus, for me there was something wonderfully comforting and old-school about the eatery, with its red
leather banquettes and black-and-white photographs of the writers
(including Ernest Hemingway and Eugene O'Neill) who had
haunted the place in its heyday.

We'd only just ordered our burgers and beers, when Nic spotted a familiar brown-clad back on a stool at the bar. "Detective
Mendez-Cruz!" she shouted across the room. "Yoo-hoo! Detective! Over here!"

Literally every person in the room turned to look at us. Including, yes, Detective Sebastian Mendez-Cruz. I felt my face flame.

"*Yoo-hoo*, Nic?" I hissed. "Who says 'yoo-hoo' anymore?"

"People who want to get the attention of other people in a noisy
restaurant."

"People could just go over and say hello," I muttered, but Nic
was already on her way.

Within minutes she was headed back to our table with Mendez-
Cruz, a busboy following behind them like a supplicant, a plate of
half-eaten burger in one hand and a half-empty beer in the other.
The detective walked with a loose, easy grace that even today's terrible brown suit (*did the man have a closet full of them?*) couldn't
disguise. His smile when he saw me at the table made the breath
catch in my throat.

I raised my hand feebly and said, *idiotically*, "Small world."

"I live around the corner," Mendez-Cruz said, then handed the
busboy a few dollars and thanked him politely in Spanish before
taking his seat. "I thought I'd grab a bite before heading over to
the service for Mr. Calhoun."

Now, my impression from the bazillions of police procedurals
I'd read over the years was that the reason homicide detectives go
to the victim's funeral is to suss out possible suspects in said vic-

tim's death. So *that* was interesting. Maybe Detective Mendez-Cruz wasn't so sure Howard's death had been random after all.

Once Nic had us all arranged around the table the way she wanted—Mendez-Cruz next to her on the cozy banquette, me on a hard wooden dining chair across from the happy couple—she proceeded to grill our guest as to the progress on what she called "my case."

In between bites of burger, Mendez-Cruz did his best to answer her questions.

Yes, they had reviewed the security tape. Yes, it had happened just as she'd said. The person who'd sent Howard to his death (now, I noticed, called "the suspect") did seem to be focused on Mr. Calhoun and had shouldered several people out of their way as they moved toward "the victim."

I shuddered involuntarily at the word. *Victim.* A word I'd read a million times in hundreds of books. A word that was suddenly much too real. Howard had been the killer's *victim.* Whatever Howard's shortcomings, whoever he had crossed, he certainly had not deserved this horrible death.

Mendez-Cruz seemed to sense the direction of my thoughts and tried, gently, I thought, to redirect them. "Of course," he said, "that doesn't mean the suspect knew or was targeting him. There's every possibility that they chose Mr. Calhoun at random. That it wasn't personal."

Which was some comfort. But not a lot.

"So you haven't found this person?" Nic asked.

For the first time, Mendez-Cruz looked uncomfortable. "Actually, no," he said. "They were wearing a loose hoodie and, given the angle of the camera, were mostly hidden by the crowd on the platform, so we can't even be sure if they're male or female. Sometimes the hands give them away, but in this case, the hands were pretty much covered by the long sleeves. They're maybe five foot ten or so, average frame, maybe youngish, but hard to tell. And there's no point in trying to do facial recognition, not with the surgical mask and the hood. The clothes are all black, so nothing to go on there."

Nic looked perplexed for a moment, but I had to agree with the detective. Given that everyone in New York under the age of thirty pretty much wears all black all the time, I could see how he wouldn't get very far with that. Anyway, the man was still talking, so both of us put that aside for the moment.

"We've checked out the usual shelters and encampments," Mendez-Cruz continued, "but nobody seems to know anything, not the street people we usually count on for info or the volunteers who work with them. We're asking for help from other precincts now, but usually these guys don't stray far from their territory."

In my head I could hear Mrs. Christie's voice as clearly as if she were sitting at the table with us. *It might also be interesting to know who benefits from Mr. Calhoun's death.*

"So maybe it wasn't a mentally ill person," I said. "At least not someone random. Maybe it was someone who knew Howard, had some reason to want him, um, out of the way."

"Yeah," Nic chimed in. "How about the cousin, the one who maybe inherits his money?"

Again Mendez-Cruz looked uncomfortable. "Look," he said, "I can't go into the details of an ongoing investigation, but I can tell you nobody pushed Mr. Calhoun under a subway for his money. The guy was stone broke."

Nic and I looked at each other. *The apartment in One Fifth? The weekends at the fancy guest house in the Hamptons? The rare book collection?* Then, simultaneously, we both shrugged. Nobody knows better than a Van Dyne how easy it is to spend or borrow your way into a hole. And, it now occurred to me, Howard's collecting phase seemed to have stopped at least a year ago. It also explained his decidedly downscale choice of jewelry for Nic after his latest trip.

So Detective Mendez-Cruz didn't think Howard was killed for his money. But the fact remained that the detective was going to Howard Calhoun's memorial service for some reason, and I really doubted that it was to pay his respects.

Ten

◇◇◇◇◇◇

*"I admit," I said, "that a second murder in a book often cheers
things up."*

—Arthur Hastings, *The A.B.C. Murders*

ATTENDANCE AT HOWARD CALHOUN'S MEMORIAL SERVICE
was sparse. Which was just fine by me. The Trustees Room was no
place for a crowd, not with only one exit. A few rows of folding
bamboo chairs on each side of a wide aisle faced the room's magnificent marble fireplace, where a highly colored photograph of
Howard in an ornate gilt frame held pride of place on the mantel-
piece, flanked on either side by a tasteful arrangement of white
lilies.

Nic waited with me just inside the door to the room while I
tried to calm my very rapid heartbeat and look like I was simply
choosing where to sit. Mendez-Cruz had walked in with us and
now stood next to Nic, quietly surveying the three dozen or so
people who had come to mourn Howard's passing. Click, click,
click.

A heavyset middle-aged woman in tan slacks and a brown

sweater sat in the front row accompanied by a silver-haired gentle-man in a well-cut grey suit. This had to be Howard's cousin and Howard's lawyer, respectively, given their looks of personal and professional boredom, respectively.

In the row behind the family, such as it was, sat Brooke Sin-clair, dressed in a black Chanel suit and dabbing delicately at her eyes with a tiny square of Irish linen. A Pomeranian puff ball (Ber-tram's successor?) sat on her lap, its fur almost exactly matching Brooke's helmet of expertly tinted ash-blond hair. Howard's posse of rich widows and divorcées were taking their places next to and behind their leader.

"See that pancake makeup Brooke is wearing?" Nic whispered to me. "She had her sunspots from that India trip lasered off about a week ago. She's been in hiding at her house in the Hamptons until the scabs fell off. You can see the skin is still kind of pinkish. So the timing wasn't great but how was she supposed to know she was going to have to show up covered with concealer in front of all her friends?"

Behind said friends sat Howard's assistant, Rachel of the Un-pronounceable Last Name, a tall, thin young woman probably on the cusp of thirty with curiously colorless skin and hair. Like Brooke, she was dressed in unrelieved black. Unlike Brooke, she was dry-eyed. I didn't blame her. Howard couldn't have been an easy guy to work for.

On the other side of the aisle were a few corporate types with very tan faces who I assumed were West Coast colleagues from International Artists. Next to them sat a flock of actors, among them Wren Madison wearing a tasteful grey wool dress and a suit-ably somber expression. To her right was her erstwhile director, Jonathan Schifrin, whom I'd met a few times before. Schifrin was

a small man with an unnaturally large head and a face that registered his every emotion, which in my view made him exhausting
to be around.

"Schifrin looks pretty upset," I whispered to Nic. Which was
true; today's face was doing outrage in spades.

"Yeah, well, not about Howard," Nic responded with her usual
devastating accuracy. "He's just, like, so furious that he wasn't
asked to direct that movie, and I bet Wren, who's mega clueless
and nice, sat down next to him, not getting that he hates her just
for being in it."

Which didn't surprise me. Schifrin had always struck me as
one of those the-friend-of-my-enemy-is-my-enemy types. He was,
I now realized, pointedly ignoring Wren in favor of the occasional
comment out of the side of his mouth to the much younger and
very fit man seated on his other side.

"I'm surprised he even made it," Nic continued. "He's supposed
to be in rehab, which is like a big secret except everybody knows
it. I wonder, who's the beefcake next to him? I mean, who brings
a date to a funeral?" I snorted at that and noticed even Mendez-
Cruz cracked a small smile.

I looked over the rest of the theater gang for Sailor Savoie, but
it seemed she was missing in action. I suspected that she had not
been invited to Howard's "celebration." Brooke had taken against
Sailor early on in Howard's pursuit of the girl as a client, which
had involved, of course, much escorting of Ms. Savoie to parties
and giving of expensive presents. His recent increased attentions
had, by all accounts, only increased Brooke's animus.

Bringing up the rear and representing Howard's literary interests were a handful of rare book dealers. Many of them I knew
through my work, innocent-eyed men and women whose distracted air belied the dollars they could pluck out of the wallets of

fanatical collectors. My old pal Graham Nickerson, the rare book expert at the Atheneum Book Store, had reportedly managed to pry something like eighty thousand from Howard for a rare first edition of Hemingway's *The Sun Also Rises* with—among other errata—the misprint on page 181 of "stoppped" for "stopped." No wonder Howard had died broke. Who pays $80,000 for three p's?

By this point, Mendez-Cruz wandered off to stand very, very still at the back of the room and Nic, having grown tired of waiting for me to decide if I was going to have a panic attack—which, I realized with a start, I'd completely forgotten to have, so interested had I been in parsing the crowd—grabbed my hand and started pulling me over to her actor friends. "Come on," she said. "Wren promised to save us seats because she knows I'm gonna need all the support I can get at this shindig."

I'd always liked Wren Madison. She came from stolid banking stock and had never even been to a Broadway play until Nic and Sailor dragged her to *A Chorus Line* on her twelfth birthday, after which she pursued theater with the single-minded determination of the truly talented. And despite her successes, including a critically acclaimed one-woman show as Edith Piaf, I'd never known her to be anything less than modest about her accomplishments.

When she saw us coming, Wren waved and gathered up the purse and sweater she'd been using to reserve the two chairs next to her. Nic and I slipped into our seats, and, amazingly, I found that the gabble of greetings and chitchat around us calmed me considerably. Also, I was impressed by the sensitivity of Nic's peeps, not one of whom brought up Nic's trauma, choosing instead to smooth things over with the usual benign gossip.

"You can't be serious, Wren?" a girl with a beautiful shaved head and cheekbones that could cut glass was saying. "You and Sailor *always* have a joint birthday party." Which was true. Sailor's and Wren's birthdays were only a few weeks apart and their annual joint birthday bash had become a fixture of their crowd's party scene.

"Yeah, well, not this year, Logan," Wren said. "This year's the big three-oh for both of us, and Sailor's taking it hard. It was her actual birthday yesterday, so she decided to fly off to that fancy resort in Cancún she likes where, she said, she didn't know anybody and nobody knew her and she could drink tequila in peace thank you very much."

"I get it," Nic put in. "I mean, who wants to celebrate getting old?" *Howard probably would*, I thought but didn't say.

"I sent out a group text weeks ago canceling the annual bash," Wren continued. "I must have missed you, Logan."

"Well, just so long as I wasn't disinvited," Logan said. Better her friend was doing the lonely sulks on the Mexican Riviera than that Logan had been ghosted from a party.

"But what about you, Wren?" Nic asked. "You could still play."

"Nope. This year, in honor of my advanced age, I'm going all traditional. On my birthday, I'll be back here at the main branch for the Library Lions Gala."

Logan mimed falling asleep, and Wren grinned at her. "I know, I know, everybody's on their best behavior there. But that's good. I figure they'll all wish me a happy birthday but be much too polite to ask which one it actually is."

I suspected this rationale to be a fiction. The New York Public Library's annual Library Lions Gala is a glittering society event honoring arts royalty like the novelist Margaret Atwood and film director Martin Scorsese. I hadn't been able to attend for years, though I had loved it once. Aunt Bunny was a bigwig on the gala committee as was Wren's mother, and I suspected Mrs. Madison, not Wren's advancing decrepitude, was the reason for her daughter's attendance. Mrs. Madison had been recently widowed, and I knew that Wren had been doing everything she could to keep her mother from sinking below the waves of her grief. No way was she going to let her mom miss that gala, not even if she had to go to it herself. On her thirtieth birthday no less. *She's a good egg, that Wren*, I thought.

"Well, at least I'll have you to hang out with there," Nic said with a sigh. "I was supposed to go with Howard to the Hamptons that weekend for that film festival, so that got me off the hook with my mother. But that's off now."

Which brought her back to the reality of where she was and why.

"I mean," she added, stricken, "obviously."

At that point, all conversation ceased as Brooke Sinclair rose from her seat of honor and went to the podium at the front of the room.

"Ladies and gentlemen, friends and family," she began, "I welcome you to this celebration of the life of our dear friend Howard Calhoun . . ."

THE CELEBRATION WAS BRIEF. BROOKE SINCLAIR'S OVER-wrought eulogy had me twitching almost immediately at platitudes like "our world will never be the same" only to wish moments later that she'd stuck to well-worn clichés. I was at a loss as to how to make sense of lines like "those who did not pay due credit to Howard's genius in his lifetime now have a lifetime of their own to pay that debt." The mood was then lightened a bit by one of Howard's foodie friends extolling his prowess in the kitchen ("the

man was master of the mortar and pestle and never met a reduction he couldn't add more butter to"), but then took another nose-
dive with some anodyne remarks ("Howard will be much missed")
by the silver-haired gentleman, who was indeed Howard's lawyer.
Finally, after thanking those attending on behalf of Howard's
cousin, Zella Emory (who managed nothing but a sour smile), the
lawyer concluded the formalities.

The rush to the temporary bar set up in the back of the room
confirmed what I already suspected—that this event was less a
celebration of Howard's life than an opportunity to gossip about
it. I was also confirmed in my suspicion that Mendez-Cruz—who
had taken a seat in the back row at the start of the proceedings and
was still there doing that click, click, click thing with those eyes—
was here to suss out the crowd for a possible killer. Or at least to
confirm the improbability of that line of inquiry.

Either way, it occurred to me that this might be a chance to help
him in his information gathering and thus redeem my earlier rep-
utation for idiot-speak. I knew these people. He didn't. Snagging
two glasses of wine from the bar, I took one over to the detective.

"Here," I said, shoving the glass in his hand. "You pretend to
drink this while we wander around listening in on the conversation
of our fellow mourners."

He didn't even pretend not to understand me. "Eavesdropping," he said with a grin. "Good plan." I'd never seen him grin
before. I liked it.

I grinned back at him. "Thank you. I am in full agreement with
Miss Jane Marple that if people do not choose to lower their voices,
one must assume that they are prepared to be overheard."

Then he surprised me. "And will you also be doing your best
dithery Miss Marple imitation?"

The hot detective knew Jane Marple! I was delighted with this discovery. "Of course," I said. "And thus lull the suspects into damaging admissions."

Mendez-Cruz laughed. I hadn't heard him laugh before, either. I liked that, too.

"Which will ultimately prove to be critical to cracking the case," he said.

"No doubt," I said, and then, reverting back to boring-old-Tory mode, admitted, "Not that anyone here looks like they make a habit of pushing people under subway trains."

"Agreed," said Mendez-Cruz, reverting to boring-old-detective mode, "but it's my job to at least consider that possibility." *I knew it.*

And so we set off on our voyage of discovery.

IT HAD TAKEN BARELY ONE GLASS OF LUKEWARM CHARDON-nay to start the tongues wagging.

"Candice, is it true?" one society matron was asking breathlessly. "I heard poor Howard was absolutely penniless."

"It *is*. My friend Marla, you know, the real estate broker with Sotheby's, told me he'd put that lovely apartment of his on the market *weeks* ago. After re-mortgaging it *twice*."

"So the cousin gets nothing?"

"Just his debts." A superior smile here.

"No wonder she looks like if he wasn't dead already, she'd murder him."

Much tittering from women who had more money than God.

Spying Brooke Sinclair heading their way, though, they almost instantaneously replaced the laughter with suitably somber faces.

"Brooke, darling," the one named Candice exclaimed, her voice dripping with sympathy, "how good of you to organize this lovely service. There must be so much to do after Howard's passing."

"Well, I could hardly leave it to that cousin of his," Brooke said acidly. *Now there's the Brooke we all know and dislike.* "Although I must admit his assistant, Rachel whatever her name is, has been quite efficient in tying up various loose ends. She's even agreed to take on darling Bertram."

"You gave Bertram to that girl?"

I could tell that even Candice thought this was a little heartless. After all, the dog was Brooke's closest link to Howard. Brooke, however, took her friend's surprise as a nod to her boundless generosity.

"One wanted to keep him, of course. But Bertram never got on as I would have liked with my sweet Poppy." Here Brooke paused to acknowledge the toy Pomeranian now peeking out of the handbag hanging from her elbow. "And that Rachel girl is besotted with the dog. I felt she would take the best care of him." She then rather spoiled the boundless-generosity effect by adding, "Though I will of course hold his papers in the event that I choose to breed him." The brief mental image of Bertram at stud was so awful I had to turn away from the conversation.

Next stop, Howard's cousin Zella, standing quite alone in one corner of the room with a completely drained wineglass, her face an absolute thundercloud. I felt sorry for the woman, all plain and plump and beige in that glittering crowd. But I decided to put away any scruples about making the day any more unpleasant for her than it already was in favor of doing my bit toward Mendez-Cruz's investigation. Presumably he had already talked with her officially, but it couldn't hurt to try my luck. Even if she hadn't actually inherited anything, maybe Zella had had expectations.

I went over to the bar, snagged two more glasses of wine and approached Howard's onetime heir apparent. Mendez-Cruz immediately understood my plan and wandered over to stand just behind my quarry.

"Ms. Emory," I said, pressing one of the wineglasses into her hand, "I'm Tory Van Dyne. I was a friend of Howard's. I'm so sorry for your loss."

Grandmother had drummed it into me that this phrase and *only* this phrase is appropriate for the bereaved. Anything more or less and one risked venturing into uncharted emotional waters.

"Thanks," Zella said, taking a hefty slug from her glass. I got the feeling it wasn't so much the condolences as the wine that she was thanking me for. "But I gotta say, I didn't really know Howard all that well, you know?"

I didn't know, but, taking a page out of Mrs. Christie's playbook, I nodded as if I did.

"He left Jersey a long time ago for Hollywood." *Howard came from New Jersey?* "And after he married that rich old lady in Cincinnati, we never really heard much from him. Not even when he came back east after she died."

Howard had been married? To a rich old lady? I glanced over Zella's shoulder at Mendez-Cruz, who clearly didn't share my surprise. *Well, of course, Tory. It's the guy's* job *to look into the background of murder victims.*

Channeling Mrs. Christie again, I smiled at Zella and murmured, "I see."

This was all the encouragement Zella appeared to need. "We heard she left him a boatload, but I guess it didn't last because there's nothing left now but a bunch of old books. The guy was a total fraud. I wish I'd known." Ah, I thought, so the cousin *did* have expectations.

Zella's voice had gotten increasingly strident as our conversation progressed and was now loud enough to alert Howard's lawyer, who had been chatting nearby. He walked over and, snatching the wineglass from her hand, said, "Ms. Emory, if you're going to make your train back to Millburn, we should probably put you in a taxi to the station now." And so saying, he put a firm hand on Zella's elbow and steered her out of the room.

Well, *that* was interesting. And Zella's dismissive reference to a bunch of old books was curious. Surely she'd been given some approximation of the value of Howard's collection, which had to be worth a smile or two. And so Tory Van Dyne, girl sleuth, toddled off to join the little circle of rare-book sellers where my friend Graham was holding court.

"Follow me," I said all Sam Spade out of the side of my mouth as I passed Mendez-Cruz.

"Roger that," he said out of the side of his.

He's having fun, I realized with amazement. Even more amazing, so was I.

I'd known Graham Nickerson for years. He was all absent-minded professor sartorially (*so many* shabby tweed blazers with leather patches on the elbows) and positively Victorian in speech, and I liked him a lot.

As I approached, one dealer was saying, "So, Graham, I hear you managed to grab the gold ring."

"If by that you mean that I have been asked to handle the sale of Mr. Calhoun's library," Graham replied with much wounded dignity, "then yes. In fact, I had already been in highly confidential discussions with Mr. Calhoun himself about a possible sale of the collection." Much raising of eyebrows at that little gossipy nugget. "So, very appropriately, his cousin has agreed that I am ideally positioned for its dispersal, as I had advised Mr. Calhoun on much of what was best in it."

"Well, you're sure to get a good price on that first edition, first printing of the Potter book with the double wands in the shopping list," his rival said, adding waspishly, "which, of course, *I* advised him to bid on."

"Actually, Mr. Calhoun's Potter volume is *not* one of those with that misprint," Graham said with just a trace of satisfaction. "A first edition, of course, but not the first printing. I've already checked it."

"That's odd. He seemed desperate to get his hands on the rare one."

Odd, indeed, I thought, since the book that I had worked on for Howard *was* one with the misprint. Odd but not, I concluded, particularly useful. Time to move on.

I spotted Howard's assistant, Rachel, standing by herself and pretending to be absorbed in one of the seventeenth-century Flem-ish tapestries decorating (and I use the word loosely) the room's walls. I wandered over and Mendez-Cruz, who no longer needed stage directions, followed behind at a discreet distance.

"Who's that lady supposed to be?" I asked Rachel, pointing to a tapestry of a plump damsel in flowing robes who appeared, weirdly, to be riding a tiger.

Rachel turned to me, startled out of her reverie. "What lady?" she asked.

"That one," I said, pointing again to the tapestry she'd been staring at for the past ten minutes.

"No idea," she said, her voice expressionless.

I'd noticed before that Rachel had a curious flattened quality to her, more like a life-size cardboard cutout than a three-dimensional person. It was as if every emotion had been tamped down to dull embers. I'd only ever seen her truly alive when I met her happily walking Bertram in the park.

I tried again to engage her. "I'm afraid it's been a tough time for you," I offered.

"Well, yes," Rachel said, reviving a bit. "But he's going to be fine." *What was this, some kind of weird denial going on? Did the girl not accept that Howard was dead?* "But it was touch and go for a while for the little guy," she added.

The little guy. She was talking about *Bertram.* Bertram the dog, who was very much alive. Not her boss, Howard the man, who was very much dead.

"It would be such a *wicked* thing to do," she suddenly blurted out, two angry spots of color appearing in her pale cheeks. "To try to kill a defenseless little dog. Wicked, wicked, *wicked.*"

To *try* to kill? Apparently Howard had decided against sharing the theory of Nic's *accidental* poisoning of the dog, preferring to accuse Sailor of deliberately slipping Bertram a mickey. The guy really hadn't wanted any hint of his involvement in Bertram's near demise reaching Brooke.

But again, none of this was anything I didn't already suspect. And Rachel all worked up was even harder going than Rachel all blank. I took the coward's way out, ostentatiously checking my watch. "Oh, Rachel, I'm sorry, I've got to go. I'm late for an appointment," I lied.

Mendez-Cruz and I wandered over to the relative quiet near the room's door. "What was that about killing a defenseless little dog?" he asked.

And so I went through the whole Bertram-poisoning drama for his benefit, only to get a studiously neutral "Duly noted" in return. Honest to god, the guy gave nothing away.

Defeated at this sudden return to our official relationship, I said wearily, "I'm sorry but I really do have to find Nic and take off. I'm totally done in." Which was true. I was utterly exhausted by my efforts at socializing (if you could call it that). Introvert that I am, my batteries had been completely drained. On the plus side, I reminded myself, I hadn't freaked out in a semicrowded public space.

Mendez-Cruz nodded briskly. "Yeah, I need to get going, too. Thanks for your help."

And with that he left the room. And all I could think was, *I want to go home.* Straight home and straight up to the Christie Room. Where, with any luck, Mrs. Christie would be waiting with a shaker of Satan's Whiskers in hand. *Dream on, Tory.*

I scanned the room for Nic to let her know I was leaving. I expected to see her chatting with her acting peeps, but there was no sign of her. I was about to give up when a tap on my shoulder almost gave me a heart attack. I whirled around and there was Nic framed in the doorway, white-faced, a glass of wine in one hand and cell phone in the other. I *knew* coming to this service had been a bad idea. I put an arm around her shoulders and led her back out to the relative quiet of the hallway.

"Hey, Nic, it's all right," I said. "Everything's going to be all right."

Nic looked at me, her eyes filled with unshed tears. "No, it's not going to be all right," she almost whispered. "Not for Sailor."

I stared at her. "What are you talking about? Not for Sailor why?"

"Because she's dead," Nic said, the tears flowing freely now. "Oh, Tory, Sailor's dead."

Eleven

◇◇◇◇◇◇◇◇◇◇

*"I'm perfectly well provided for. Reams of paper, oceans of ink
and I'm sure Robin has gin. What else does a girl need?"*
                                    —Ariadne Oliver, *Mrs. McGinty's Dead*

SEVERAL TISSUES AND A GOOD NOSE BLOW LATER, NIC WAS FI-
nally able to choke out her news. "Sailor's sister Aspen just called
me. She said Sailor died of food poisoning last night at that resort
in Cancún. Housekeeping found her this morning in her bungalow's bathroom."

I shuddered. What a way to go. All alone in a hotel bathroom.
On her birthday, no less. It didn't bear thinking about.

"I mean, I didn't, like, *love*, Sailor, you know?" Nic blurted out.
"She was, too, you know, prickly for that. But she was fun and she
was my friend for, like, forever and I really, really wish I could talk
to Mrs. M. I'm so confused and she helps me think."

You and me both, girl, I thought. And suddenly realized, almost
begrudgingly, that this was true. I wasn't hoping Mrs. Christie
would be in the Christie Room when we got home because she
knew how to make a Satan's Whisker. I wanted her to be there
because the woman helped me think. Was helping me—helping

all of us, actually—solve a murder. Just as she'd promised. *Don't go there, Tory.*

"Could you call her?" Nic asked plaintively. "Ask her to meet us for a drink?"

"I don't, um, have her number," I said. Which was true. Sort of. "But, yeah, let's go have a drink in the Christie Room." I glanced at my watch. "The library closed at three and it's three thirty now. Adrian's filling in for Susie today and I know he wanted to get some paperwork done, so he'll probably still be around. So that's something."

Nic did not look like she thought Adrian was a proper substitute for Mrs. M.

"And with any luck," I added lamely, "Mrs. M will be there, too."

I sent a heartfelt *Please let Mrs. Christie be there* to the Universe before I realized what I was doing. *Your Mrs. Christie does* not *live in the Eternity, Tory,* I reminded myself—and promptly canceled the order.

Nic frowned. "But the library's closed," she pointed out. "How could she be there?"

I gave up. "I don't know, Nic," I said helplessly. "She has her ways."

IT SEEMED AT FIRST THAT MY TELEGRAM TO THE UNIVERSE HAD indeed been canceled, because when we trudged up the front steps and opened the door, we were greeted not by a slightly loony middle-aged lady offering us a Satan's Whisker but by a volley of barking from a small dog attached by a leash to a little redheaded girl, both of them attended by a more-than-slightly-annoyed head librarian.

Uh-oh. I'd completely forgotten about my phone conversation

with Mairead's father in which we'd settled on that Saturday for
the girl's first visit to my lab. The plan had been for her to arrive
just after the library closed at three and I would take it from there.

Instead, Adrian had taken it from there. He'd clearly been
waiting with Mairead and the pup on the hallway bench for about
twenty-nine minutes longer than he thought reasonable. And he
was not happy about it. I could tell because today's neckwear, a
fuchsia bow tie, was slightly askew, as if he'd tugged at it in frus-
tration. Kids were *so* not Adrian's thing. Or barking dogs.

Fortunately, Mairead quickly got things under control. "Shut
your bake, Tony!" she commanded. And Tony shut his bake.

Adrian took advantage of the silence to point his phone at me
accusingly. "Where have you been?" he demanded. "And why
didn't you answer my texts?"

"I'm so, so sorry, Adrian," I said. "I was at Howard's memorial
service so I had my phone on mute and I stayed longer than I had
planned because I wanted to . . ." *find some clues to impress the swoony
detective* ". . . talk to a few people, and then Nic got some bad
news and we had to get a taxi and I didn't check my messages and
I forgot all about Mairead coming or I would have called you."
Good lord, I was talking just like Nic.

Adrian looked closely at my face, then at Nic's.

"Okay," he said in his nice normal Good Adrian voice. "I get
it. Well, I don't get it, but it's okay. What's going on?"

"I need a drink," Nic said.

"Yes, I get that, Nic," Adrian said patiently. "But why?"

"Sailor is dead," Nic said flatly.

Shocked, Adrian looked to me for clarity. "Sailor is dead?" he
asked. "Nic's friend Sailor?"

"I *really* need a drink," Nic said.

"Let's go upstairs, Adrian," I said. "And we'll tell you what we know, which isn't much."

"What about . . . ?" He cocked his head toward Mairead, her face alight with curiosity, following every word of our conversation. "Apparently the father's at some lecture by some visiting bigwig."

"She can come up, I guess," I said. "I'm not going to leave her down here by herself."

I turned to the girl. "Listen, Mairead. The grown-ups have to discuss some bad news we just got. You can come upstairs with us but maybe you could do homework or something and be very, very quiet while we talk."

"Sure thing, Ms. Van Dyne," the girl said, pulling the battered laptop out of her bag. "I'll just work on this mystery I'm writing. I'm at the scene where the villain is sneaking up on the victim so he can strangle her."

Well, I thought, *that ought to keep you busy.*

APPARENTLY THE UNIVERSE HAD RECEIVED MY MISSIVE AFTER all, because as Nic, Adrian, Mairead, Tony and I marched into the Christie Room, Mrs. Christie was there. *Of course.* Sitting in the gold velvet armchair I was beginning to think of as hers.

"Am I ever glad to see you, Mrs. M," Nic said, rushing over to give her a big Nic hug.

My reaction, however, was mixed. When I'd hoped earlier that Mrs. Christie might be available for consultation, I hadn't planned on Adrian being part of the gathering. Adrian, who knew all about "Mrs. Christie" and considered her a confirmed nutcase. Nor had I anticipated Mairead being there. The kid was sharp. She clearly knew something about the real Agatha Christie. That she'd named her Yorkshire terrier Tony couldn't be coincidence. She could easily make some kind of connection if we weren't careful.

"Ahem," a small voice at my elbow said. Never in my life had I heard a kid say "ahem." But what did I know? Maybe Irish kids said "ahem" all the time. And maybe they were accustomed to telling grown-ups to mind their manners. Anyway, it worked.

"Mrs., um, Mallowan," I said to Mrs. Christie, "this is Mairead Butler. Mairead, Mrs., um, Mallowan." *Honest to god, Tory, if you say Mrs., um, Mallowan one more time . . .*

Mairead, like the well-brought-up little girl she clearly was, walked over to Mrs. Christie and politely shook her hand. "Sure it's a pleasure to meet you, Mrs. O'Mallowan."

"Sorry, Mairead," I said. "It's just Mallowan. Mrs. Mallowan."

The little girl gave me a sharp look, but simply said, "Of course. Mrs. Mallowan."

I turned to Adrian, who was standing stock-still just inside the door, his eyes darting back and forth from our visitor to the framed photograph of Dame Agatha Christie on the small round table next to the fireplace. As nonchalantly as I was able, I walked over and casually placed it facedown. Then I said, very deliberately, "Mrs. *Mallowan*, I'd like you to meet our head librarian, Adrian Gooding."

"How do you do, Mrs. Mallowan," Adrian said equally deliberately.

"How do you do, Mr. Gooding," Mrs. Christie said, also deliberately.

Good. Two hurdles met and leaped.

"And who is this charming fellow?" Mrs. Christie asked, looking down at the little black-and-brown dog waiting politely to be introduced.

"This is Tony," Mairead said. "He's a Yorkshire terrier."

For the very first time since I'd met her, Mrs. Christie seemed at a loss for words. After a pause, she repeated quietly, "Tony. A Yorkshire terrier. How very . . . unexpected."

"Mrs. Mallowan had a Yorkshire terrier named Tony, too," Nic explained to Mairead, whose eyes widened a bit but who then nodded sagely as if to say of course anybody with any sense would name their Yorkshire terrier Tony.

With this third hurdle behind us, I managed to get Mairead settled at the table behind the couch so she could go to work getting that victim strangled.

"You're going to be very, very quiet, right?" I reminded her.

"Of course," she agreed. And like the fool that I am, I believed her.

Twelve

◇◇◇◇◇◇◇◇◇◇

"Poison has a certain appeal . . . It has not the crudeness of the revolver bullet or the blunt weapon."

—Inspector Curry, *They Do It with Mirrors*

DRINKS WERE SIMPLER THIS TIME, WITH NIC TAKING MATTERS into her own hands and pouring all the adults two fingers of twelve-year-old Macallan.

"Yessss," she said, sinking into the blue sofa with a sigh. "This is exactly what I need."

While Nic took a moment to pull herself together—well, several moments actually and two more fingers of Macallan—I updated Adrian and Mrs. Christie on Howard's memorial service while Mairead listened avidly to every word. This took longer than I expected due to several interruptions on the part of Mrs. Christie asking for the precise words used by Rachel or Brooke or whoever and homing in on the varied emotions on display—Schifrin's resentment at being passed over for *BB the Movie*, Brooke's ire at those who hadn't sufficiently appreciated her protégé, the cousin's disappointment at her unmet expectations. When I finally got to the moment of Nic's dramatic revelation about Sailor's death, I was more than happy to hand the narration over to my cousin.

"I'm just so confused," Nic began.

"You're not the only one, honey," Adrian said, looking at Mrs. Christie and then me with one perfect eyebrow raised significantly. I shook my head no. Now was not the time.

"And what is confusing you, Miss Nicola?" Mrs. Christie asked.

"My friend Sailor, the one you met last Sunday, remember? Well, at the memorial service, I got this call from Sailor's sister, Aspen, and she said she, Sailor, that is, was in Mexico last night and ate something bad and died. I mean it's super sad, but mostly it seems weird, right? First Howard, then Sailor? Both friends of mine? That's a big coincidence. I mean, maybe I'm some kind of a jinx?"

Her voice had gone all high and shaky by this point, and Mrs. Christie hastened to reassure her. "No, Miss Nicola, I do not think you are, as you put it, a jinx. Though it is true that any coincidence is always worth noticing. You can throw it away later if it is only a coincidence."

Adrian looked up sharply from his drink, then at me. *Yes, Adrian, that was Miss Marple in* Nemesis. Again I shook my head in a silent no.

"But perhaps," Mrs. Christie added calmly, "it would help to tell me more about how your friend died."

Unconsciously adopting this unemotional approach, Nic was able to go on. "Well, her sister said she died of traveler's tummy."

I was fairly sure Mrs. Christie had no idea what traveler's tummy was, but she merely murmured a quiet "I see" and allowed Nic to continue with her story.

"She said that Sailor had texted her saying she was celebrating her birthday or really more like trying to forget her birthday in her room with some tequila and, like, really fast, it made her feel sick to her stomach but she was drunk so Aspen wasn't really worried and figured she'd sleep it off but when she didn't answer her texts, Aspen's that is, this morning she called the hotel and the concierge went to her bungalow and found Sailor dead in the bathroom with all the signs of food poisoning. Whatever they are."

I guess I shouldn't have been surprised when Mairead, who had clearly been taking in every word being said by her elders and betters, tapped a few keys on her laptop, then looked up and chimed in with, "It says here that the symptoms of severe food poisoning are"—she looked down at the screen again—"nausea, intense gastrointestinal pain, vomiting and diarrhea."

So much for being very, very quiet.

"Eeuw," said Nic. "Kind of wish I didn't know that. But, I mean, who dies of food poisoning these days?"

Mairead obligingly clicked a few more keys. "'Out of 1.35 million cases of food poisoning in the US yearly,'" she read out, "'only about 250 people die of it.'"

She looked up at the rest of us, her face alight. "So maybe it wasn't food poisoning," she said with relish. "Maybe it was real poison! Like in an Agatha Christie novel!"

Mrs. Christie looked straight at me and took a small sip of her scotch.

Oh no no no. We are not going into Agatha Christie land. I'd changed my mind. I didn't want Mrs. Christie helping us think this through. One murder was scary enough.

"Mairead," I said firmly, "we are not in some kind of Golden Age mystery."

Mairead shot me a glance and murmured, "But does it not sometimes feel that we are?" Which I chose to ignore.

Mrs. Christie took another delicate sip and said mildly, "That is as may be, but Miss Savoie has certainly died of poisoning, whether by tainted food or . . . otherwise."

Oh no no no. We are not going into abrin-land, either. Already been there. Before Mrs. Christie could mention the a-word, I said warningly, "But Sailor's symptoms were nothing like Bertram's."

"Who's Bertram?" Mairead asked, prompting a long and typically rambling report from Nic as to Bertram's near demise.

"Ach," Mairead said at the conclusion, "poor wee pup."

I could see that Mrs. Christie was itching to get back to the matter at hand, so I tried again to preempt her. "Given the different symptoms," I pointed out, "it couldn't have been abrin in Sailor's case."

"Actually," Mrs. Christie began, "that poor dog's symptoms indicated *inhaled* abrin. But the symptoms of *ingested* abrin, that is, through food or drink, are very much like those of food poisoning." *Oh no no no. You want to* connect *the two deaths?*

Fortunately, Mrs. Christie was quick to put me out of my misery. "However, with ingested abrin there is also a long lag, sometimes of many hours, between the ingestion and symptoms. And it appears Miss Savoie's symptoms began almost immediately after drinking this tequila she mentioned to her sister."

Yessss. For a moment, I thought we were safe from further speculation. I should have known better.

"But, of course, there is another possibility . . ."

I gave up. All I could do was nod and motion to her to go on. We all knew who was in charge here.

"The symptoms of food poisoning," she said, "are virtually

identical to another poison which generally manifests in under an hour. I'm speaking, of course, of arsenic."

Arsenic. *First abrin, now arsenic.* That was just too much for me. We were not here to provide this woman with another murder to solve. Particularly since she hadn't even solved the first one.

"The days of convenient cans of rat poisons are long gone," I responded acidly. "It is virtually impossible to get your hands on anything containing arsenic in the twenty-first century."

"Then, my dear Miss Van Dyne," Mrs. Christie said, smiling at me benignly, "one would do well to look for sources of arsenic from other centuries."

I rolled my eyes at Adrian, hoping for at least one person on my team. But no. Adrian, it appeared, had gone to the dark side, too. "Maybe a source of arsenic," he said, gazing down modestly at the skull ring on his right forefinger, "like emerald green dye."

I blanched.

"Do please go on, Mr. Gooding," Mrs. Christie said. "It appears you have some fascinating expertise to share."

Adrian, trying hard not to look flattered, cleared his throat.

"Well, as you know, Tory," he said pointedly, "in the nineteenth century, middle-class Victorians were particularly fond of a pigment known as emerald green dye, which was used to color everything from wallpaper to the fabric used on book covers. The dye was exceptionally vivid. It was also, as book conservators have recently discovered, exceptionally toxic."

Mairead's eyes grew round. "How toxic is toxic?"

I sighed. "The average emerald green book cover can contain as much as 750 milligrams of arsenic."

Mairead's fingers flew over the keyboard. "It says here that without medical care, just 100 milligrams of arsenic is enough to kill a full-grown man."

To which Mrs. Christie for some reason felt compelled to add, "Yes, that was always my calculation. About the mass of a few grains of rice."

Mairead looked up sharply at that, and I had a terrible feeling she was going to ask this woman *why* she had calculated the volume of arsenic required to kill a full-grown man.

I tried to temper the drama a little.

"However, as *you* know, Adrian," I said warningly, "nobody died from the arsenic in emerald green book cloth, except, we now suspect, those who produced it or worked with it."

"True," Adrian said, "but also true, as *you* know, Tory, old books covered in emerald green book cloth *do* pose a danger today to collectors, librarians and book conservators, especially if the cover is flaking."

"Which is why, as *you* know, Adrian," I shot back, "most librarians and book conservators wear gloves when handling those books."

I turned to Mrs. Christie. "I've got some clients with books in emerald green covers in their collections—I've even got one myself upstairs—and I always caution them that even though opening a volume a few times isn't a problem, they should be careful not to overhandle them, particularly if the cover is flaking. A few flakes won't kill you, but they could make you sick."

I hoped that that would put an end to the discussion, but Nic, who had been listening with, for her, unusual concentration, had a question. "So the only way you could poison somebody to death with an emerald green book cover is if they ate it?"

I started to roll my eyes again but stopped when I realized that Mrs. Christie was looking at Nic with something very like respect. "To every problem," she murmured, almost to herself, "there is a most simple solution."

Adrian glanced at me and mouthed, "Hercule Poirot in *The Clocks*," hoping, I knew, for a confirmation from the expert. But I was otherwise engaged. I was thinking.

If they ate it.

A simple solution.

And suddenly I was pretty sure I knew how you could indeed poison a full-grown man—or woman—to death with an emerald green book cover.

Thirteen

◇◇◇◇◇◇◇◇◇◇◇◇◇◇

"How wonderful science is nowadays."

—Miss Jane Marple to Dr. Graham,
A Caribbean Mystery

OUR CONFAB BROKE UP SHORTLY AFTER THAT, THOUGH NOT before I, under the influence of my little brainstorm, suggested a second meeting of those present. "Not that I believe for a minute that Sailor died of arsenic poisoning," I'd said, "but I do think I know how, hypothetically, it could be done."

The reaction to this statement varied from skeptical (Adrian) to amazed (Nic) to serene (Mrs. Christie) to delighted (Mairead). Tony, it appeared, was unfazed, though he had pricked up his ears briefly when his human had clapped her hands excitedly before he settled back to chewing one of her shoelaces.

"I have to do some research," I continued, "but I can probably confirm my theory in the lab tomorrow. If you want, we could meet here again on Monday after the library closes, and I'll let you know what I've learned."

"Super," Mairead said, her eyes shining. "I'm sure my da will let me come."

I was trying to figure out how to say she wasn't actually invited when Nic broke in. "Sorry, but I've got a dinner date with Seb on Monday." Like I was supposed to know who Seb was. I looked at her blankly.

"Seb," she said, "Sebastian."

I shook my head.

"Sebastian Mendez-Cruz," she said. "*Seb.*"

Seb. You call Detective Mendez-Cruz *Seb.* And you have a dinner date with him on Monday.

I tried very hard not to show what I was feeling, but a quick glance at Adrian's face told me I'd failed miserably. The guy could read me like a book. Which was annoying.

"But I could bring him along for a drink first," Nic offered helpfully.

No. Just no.

"I mean, he's a detective, right? He might be helpful."

"He might indeed be very helpful," Mrs. Christie agreed.

Thank you very much for nothing, Mrs. C.

"All in favor of inviting Detective Mendez-Cruz, raise your hand," Mairead chimed in.

Needless to say, the measure passed unanimously. I was tempted to abstain, but what was I going to say? I don't want to see Detective Mendez-Cruz and my cousin making eyes at each other in the Christie Room? But I did notice that Adrian, bless his cranky heart, didn't raise his hand until he'd seen mine go up.

With that settled, Nic left to break the news to Wren about Sailor, saying, "I don't want her to hear it over the phone like I did."

A glance at my watch informed me that I was already late in returning Mairead to her da, and Mrs. Christie very considerately offered to "tidy up" while I walked the girl home. I knew that was just an excuse to disappear mysteriously while I was gone, but frankly, I was too exhausted by my day to care. I went up to my apartment briefly to get a jacket to ward off the evening chill, and as I came back down into the hallway, Adrian, before rushing off to meet whatever hot date he didn't want to keep waiting that night, pulled me aside and said in a low voice, "You realize now you'll never get rid of the brat?"

"I like the brat," I said. "She reminds me of myself at that age."

"The last thing I would want is to be reminded of myself at that age," Adrian said.

"Oh, come on," I said. "What could be cuter than a miniature Adrian with a miniature bunny bow tie?"

"I agree," Adrian said. "But somehow the kids on my block didn't see it that way."

This was about as close as Adrian ever got to talking about growing up a little gay kid from Barbados on a very tough street in Brooklyn's Bed-Stuy neighborhood. I leaned against him for a moment, my shoulder bumping his softly. This was about as close as I ever got to expressing my understanding. But it seemed to be enough.

Adrian smiled ruefully, and then added, almost in a whisper, "You also realize that we need to talk about *her*," cocking his head toward the door to the Christie Room.

"Yeah," I said. "I guess we do."

"She's not really *her*, you know, right? I mean, she's really smart and she knows her stuff and she looks like *her*, but you know she's not *her*, right?"

It sounded to me like he was trying to convince himself more than me, but I let it ride.

"I know that, Adrian," I whispered back.

"Good," he said. "Right. Well, I'm glad you see it my way."

I did see it Adrian's way. I wasn't given to flights of fancy any more than he was. Maybe our Mrs. Christie was simply an enthusiast with an intimate knowledge of both her heroine and the building that housed the Mystery Guild Library. After all, it was common knowledge that many of the houses on Washington Square North had once had a network of attic passageways leading from one to another.

On the other hand, I reminded myself, Agatha Christie had also loved writing what were essentially ghost stories and often left the door open to speculation, as she did in the short story "The Hound of Death," writing, "The supernatural is only the natural of which the laws are not yet understood."

So, yes, there was a lot I didn't know about our Mrs. Christie. But I was damned if I was going to start trying to prove my new friend's true identity or trap her into acknowledging it. What I did know was that she was there to help me. And that was all I needed to know.

"We should probably talk more about this," I said, still whispering, "but now is not the time. *She* is waiting for me in there"— a quick nod of my own toward the Christie Room—"with Mairead, probably discussing how best to get that victim strangled."

Adrian laughed and, with another glance at his wrist and a quick wave, he was gone.

"DID YOU TEXT YOUR DAD THAT WE'RE ON OUR WAY?" I ASKED Mairead as she, Tony and I made our way across the park, skirting laughing groups of college kids under the soft glow of streetlights and buskers playing everything from electric saxophone to the accordion.

"Aye, I did," she assured me. "He says there's no rush."

"I'm sorry we didn't have a chance to get down to the lab."

"Don't be sorry," the girl said. "This was the best night of my life."

"I'm not sure your dad will think so," I said. "I mean, it's not exactly what we agreed to."

"Not to worry," she reassured me. "Da's happy if I'm happy." She glanced up at me, then looked away and added quietly, "Because sometimes I'm not."

Of course you're not, I wanted to say. *You've lost your mother and you're in a strange land and it appears your only friend is a dog.* But I contented myself with patting her shoulder, and given the shy smile she gave me, that seemed, as with Adrian, to be enough.

Mairead and her father lived in what is now NYU faculty housing, just a few short blocks south of the park. Their building, one of three enormous apartment blocks built in the 1950s, had all the charm of any apartment block built in the 1950s. Which is to say, not a lot. But the complex, encompassing a treed courtyard the size of two city blocks complete with a playground, was a cozy, welcoming haven. As we made our way across the quad, Mairead and Tony stopped frequently to chat with and sniff at, respectively, their neighbors and their pooches, respectively. Well, I thought, I was probably wrong about no friends. The kid was a people magnet. She liked them, and they liked her.

Once in the lobby of her building, Mairead exchanged greetings with the cheerful, white-haired security guard behind the front desk, who promptly rang up to Mairead's father to announce us. Putting the house phone down, he said, "Your dad's coming down. In the meantime, how about a dog biscuit for the mutt?"

At the word "biscuit," Tony immediately sat and lifted one paw, looking about as adorable as a dog can look. Which is a lot. Which is also why, when a man who could have been mistaken for the Irish actor Colin Farrell stepped out of the elevator into the lobby, there I was grinning like a madwoman. Which made me feel pretty silly. My preferred look when meeting a man who could be mistaken for a famous movie star is what Grandmother would have called "a dignified self-possession."

Fortunately there was no dignified anything required with Mairead's da. Bounding out of the elevator, he lifted his squealing daughter into the air, planted a loud kiss on each cheek and demanded, "So, lass, what's the story? Have you come back wiser than when you left?"

"So much wiser," Mairead said. "I'm now knowing how many grams of arsenic can kill a full-grown man."

"Ach, well, then, I'll be on my guard," he said.

He then turned to me with an enormous, face-splitting smile that would have immediately pegged him as Mairead's father even if I'd met him as a stranger. "Cormac," he said. "Cormac Butler. And you must be Ms. Van Dyne. It's a great pleasure to meet you in person. And I do thank you for your kindness to my daughter." The words were spoken lightly, but I suspected the emotion behind them wasn't.

"Tory, please," I said. "And no need to thank me. She's a great kid. Smart. I enjoy her company."

"Well, Tory," he said, ruffling his daughter's red curls with one hand, "as long as she's not a bother to you."

"Not at all. Although I should tell you, this evening's tutorial didn't go exactly as planned."

"It was grand, Da!" Mairead interrupted. "Someone Tory knows died in Mexico and they said it was food poisoning, but *I* think it was *real* poison. Just like in an Agatha Christie mystery! And Tory's going to figure out how it was done." Apparently, she'd

decided that the permission to call me Tory was family-wide.
Which was fine by me. What did worry me, though, was how her
father was going to take all this talk about poisoning.

To his credit, all Cormac Butler did was raise one amused eyebrow at me.

"It's a long story," I said, "and I'm afraid I have to get back. I
have a, um, friend waiting for me."

"Not to worry," he said. "It sounds like it was right up the wee
one's alley. She loves her Agatha."

"I do," Mairead said happily. "And on Monday, we're going to
have another gathering and Tory's going to tell everybody how it
was done!"

"How it *might* have been done," I corrected her. "It's all speculation, remember?"

"Well, anyway, I can't wait," Mairead said.

"I'm so sorry, Mairead," I said, once again feeling like a total
grinch, "but it's really a grown-up thing."

The kid was not to be dissuaded. "But I'm the tech guy," she
argued. "I do the real-time online research. And I'm the clever
clogs who came up with the poison theory in the first place. We're
a team." Her face lit up as another thought hit her. "We can call
ourselves Agatha Incorporated!"

I looked at her father for help but all I got was a rueful grin. "I
gave up arguing with the lass long ago," he said.

And then I remembered. *Da's happy if I'm happy. Because sometimes I'm not.*

"It's a deal, then," I said. "Why don't you come by after school
on Monday to shadow me in the lab and if your da can spare you
that evening for an hour or so, we'd love to have your help."

Her da nodded his agreement, and Mairead gave me a swift
and unexpected—at least by me—hug.

"I promise to be very, very quiet while the grown-ups talk," she said.

Yeah, right.

DESPITE WHAT I'D SAID TO CORMAC BUTLER ABOUT RUSHING back to my, um, friend, I had absolutely no expectation that Mrs. Christie would be waiting for me when I returned. So it was no surprise when she was nowhere to be found, though she had tidied up according to her lights, which meant putting the glasses next to the kitchenette's sink for someone—*some maid named Gladys maybe?*—to wash up. I shook my head and headed upstairs to my apartment. The washing-up could wait.

What I was rushing back to was the glass-fronted bookcase in my living room where I kept my personal book collection, a fairly random assortment of old volumes, some rare, some not so rare, but all with a story behind them. The one I wanted was on the bottom shelf: *Ten Nights in a Bar-Room, and What I Saw There.*

Ten Nights is what is known as a temperance novel. It was penned in 1855 by a certain T. S. Arthur to impress the wives of America with their duty to safeguard their menfolk from the dangers of drink. It was an instant bestseller, quickly becoming the second-most-popular novel in Victorian America after *Uncle Tom's Cabin.* I'd found it in the Strand in my college years and had fallen in love with the book's title (because who could resist?) and its gold-embossed, yes, emerald green cover. Not that I'd known about the risks of emerald green at the time. It was only years later that I, like most conservators, learned about the issue when the Winterthur Museum published their researches in what they called, alarmingly, the Poison Book Project.

I'd immediately sent *Ten Nights in a Bar-Room* for testing, which it passed—or failed, depending on your point of view—with flying colors, dooming it to spend the rest of its days lying flat in a zip-top polyethylene bag on the bottom shelf of my bookcase. Mentally apologizing to Mr. Arthur for the indignity of what I was planning to inflict on his magnum opus—not to mention how happily I had knocked back my Macallan earlier—I took the book down to the lab for a little experiment.

Suitably gloved, gowned and masked, I removed *Ten Days in a Bar-Room* from its polyethylene coffin and put it on my worktable. As I intended to re-back the book with pigmented muslin at a later date, I painstakingly detached the glued book cloth with a lifting knife so as not to harm the boards beneath. Then, using round-tipped tweezers, I dropped the fabric into a half-gallon glass beaker of boiling water. Fifteen minutes later, I fished the fabric, now a pallid light olive, out of its bath. The water was a very unattractive greeny grey, which I took as a good sign. I boiled off most of it, reducing it to about a half cup of deep green and rather muddy liquid. This reduction I poured into another beaker through a Japanese horsehair strainer, which helped considerably with the muddiness. I raised the final reduction—now a few tablespoons of a deep greenish-brown, viscous solution—up to the bright fluorescent light above the worktable.

Yessss. In my hands, I felt sure, was *a simple solution* that could kill a full-grown man—or, as the case might be, woman—*if they ate it* or—as the case might be—drank it.

Not, I reminded myself, that I believed for a minute that Sailor Savoie had died from drinking tequila adulterated with an arsenic reduction. But it was nice to know it was possible.

Fourteen

*"Children feel things, you know . . . They feel things more than
the people around them ever imagine."*

—Miss Jane Marple, *The Mirror Crack'd
from Side to Side*

IT WAS A MEASURE OF HOW MUCH I HAD LOOKED FORWARD TO
my researches that I'd completely forgotten how much I *wasn't*
looking forward to the next day. Because the next day was Sunday.
And Sunday for Yours Truly is not a day of rest. Sunday is a pretty
heavy lift. Sunday means Sunday afternoon dinner at 999 Fifth
Avenue with "the whole famdamnily" as my grandfather invariably
calls the Van Dyne clan. This was funny when I was ten.

Not that I don't love my relatives. But their ability to walk the
fine line between maintaining the conventions of their class while
simultaneously breaking them was a skill that I'd never mastered.
When I was a child, my father liked to joke that I was the cuckoo
in the nest. For the longest time I thought that he meant *I* was
cuckoo, which made me think I was doomed to be the next Great-
Aunt Doris. And when I later discovered that it meant that I, the
awkward, grumpy bookworm, wasn't upholding the image of the
Van Dynes as charming eccentrics, it made me even sadder. If only

I could be like Nic, who managed to flaunt society's expectations in a completely delightful and acceptable manner.

Nic was a true Van Dyne in a way that I could never be. I had always been an observer of life rather than a participant. In fifth grade, while Nic was rehearsing her starring role as Maria in the Spence School production of *The Sound of Music*, I was diligently scribbling away at my book report on *Murder on the Orient Express*. In high school, while Nic devoured *Teen Vogue*'s advice on "50 Ways to Rock Your Own Look," I was researching my senior paper on "Costume as Character in Golden Age Mysteries."

Nic lived her life out loud. I lived mine at a whisper. I was, much like Agatha Christie herself, inherently shy. It could have been me in *Murder in Mesopotamia* rather than the awkward Mr. Reiter saying, "You see, I am not very good in company. I am clumsy. I am shy. I always say the wrong thing. I upset water jugs. I am unlucky." I read those words for the first time when I was all of twelve, and I despaired. I should instead have taken comfort from the wise counsel of Hercule Poirot. "We all do these things when we are young," he reassures Mr. Reiter. "The poise, the savoir faire, comes later." Though I have to admit, the poise, the savoir faire was a long time coming for Yours Truly.

Because it was Sunday, the uptown M1 bus was almost empty, so I had no trouble snagging one of the coveted single seats in the front. For reasons of my own, I hadn't taken a subway for years and I'd grown to like the slower, more civilized pace of the MTA's buses. It took about twenty minutes to get to my stop at Madison and 80th and then only a minute or two to walk one block over to the family pile on Fifth, so I was slightly early for my two p.m. arrival.

Pile is perhaps misleading. I suppose it could be better described as the "family seat." My great-great-grandfather, Melville

Van Dyne, had been one of the very few stockbrokers to see the Crash of '29 barreling down like a freight train and had sold out his substantial holdings just in time. He then proceeded to buy up bunches of New York real estate going for peanuts during the Great Depression. This included the ten-thousand-square-foot manse on Upper Fifth Avenue that became the family home. Over time, Melville's feckless descendants, few of whom had his financial acumen, sold off various other properties in the portfolio when the need for ready cash was pressing, but never the family home.

Both my father and Uncle Rupert had grown up there, and neither had seen fit to leave, even after marrying and begetting a daughter each. My father stayed put because he had no money of his own. Uncle Rupert remained because—as a reward for turning a portion of his hedge-fund millions toward the homestead's considerable property taxes—the family had rewarded him, my aunt Bunny and my cousin Nicola with the entire top floor of the house, including its private elevator and rooftop terrace.

Even I will admit the limestone and brick Beaux Arts town house topped by its fourth-floor terrace is lovely. Looking up at it from the sidewalk, I tried to see its charming bowed-front façade looking out across Fifth Avenue to the Metropolitan Museum of Art opposite and Central Park beyond with fresh eyes. With appreciation. Nope. Never works. The family home, no matter how grand, is still the family home. With the operative word being "family."

I was expected to arrive at precisely two o'clock, and, as usual, at precisely two o'clock I took a deep calming breath (*as if*) and, obligatory bunch of flowers in hand, rang the doorbell. The front door was immediately answered by our housekeeper, Mrs. Johnson. Mrs. Johnson—who in looks could double for the Wicked

Witch of the West, except not green—was not someone you wanted to keep waiting or otherwise mess with. It was as if she'd walked into the House of Van Dyne some forty years ago and said to herself, "Well, somebody has to be the adult here."

"Victoria," she said, her thin lips almost smiling. I have always suspected that Mrs. Johnson has a soft spot in her heart for me. There are very few others in my family she almost smiles at. "Do come in."

"Hello, Mrs. Johnson. How are you?" I asked, as I always did.

"As well as can be expected," Mrs. Johnson answered, as she always did. Sometimes I wondered what was to be expected, but I'd never had the nerve to ask.

I handed her the flowers, as I always did, and she said, as she always did, "Very nice. I'll just put them in some water and bring them up to your aunt."

Mrs. Johnson left me to make my way up the curving staircase to what my family insists on calling the "music room," even though not one of them can play the massive grand piano that dominates the space. My father, Grandfather and Great-Aunt Doris were already ensconced in their usual armchairs, usual gin and tonics in hand, in front of the room's heavily draped and swagged floor-to-ceiling windows. Uncle Rupert was at the drinks cabinet making Aunt Bunny her martini. In our house, ladies do not mix their own cocktails. This is men's work, like killing spiders when opening the summer "cottage" and hailing taxis when unexpected weather threatens their wife's coiffure.

After air kisses all around, Aunt Bunny thanked me nicely for the flowers that Mrs. Johnson had obligingly brought up in the usual Czechoslovakian cut-glass vase and my father—fit and dapper as usual in a double-breasted navy blazer with an ascot, no less—offered me my usual glass of sherry. In our house, young ladies do not drink spirits. So far I hadn't had the nerve to point out that I was no longer young (or at least I didn't feel that way) and had never been much of a lady.

Nic, I knew, would slide in just before dinner was served, but I, as the one that got away, was expected to sit and chat until we all trooped into the dining room at three o'clock precisely. Sure enough, just as Mrs. Johnson was herding us in to eat, Nic clattered downstairs from her rooms. As always, we exchanged air kisses. Air kisses were not something we did outside of the confines of the family home, but the Sunday niceties must be observed.

I took my usual seat at the long mahogany table next to Great-Aunt Doris, who promptly engaged me in an in-depth discussion about *Finding Nemo*, which she seemed to regard as a documentary based on fact rather than a children's cartoon movie based on an imaginary fish. That part I didn't mind. I was actually quite fond of Great-Aunt Doris. Tall and thin, with a long, horsey face, she had never married and retained a kind of girlish innocence that never failed to charm me. And I was always interested to see what she might be wearing from her extensive piscine-adjacent wardrobe. That day it was a pair of pink inflatable children's swimmies tucked up high on her skinny arms over an otherwise unremarkable cashmere cardigan.

Grandfather, tall and thin like his sister but with a devilish twinkle in his faded blue eyes, recited his usual grace at his usual top speed ("forwhatweareabouttorecievemaythelordmakeustrulythankfulamen"), after which we tucked into our meal with varying degrees of enthusiasm. At chez Van Dyne, the food was generally as dull as the company was odd, and I honestly cannot remember what it was we ate. Overcooked roast chicken, probably.

Or overcooked roast beef. One or the other. Somehow, Aunt Bunny, once she'd taken over the reins of the house from my runaway mother, had managed to find a cook whose interest in food was even less than her own. And yet she'd retained her plump, well-upholstered figure, the result of the generally known but never acknowledged addiction to chocolate in literally any form.

Aside from chocolate, what Aunt Bunny really liked was remodeling—repeatedly—her house in the Hamptons, about which that day she talked at me for a mind-numbing fifteen minutes. Which was better than Uncle Rupert's rant about how the contractor was bleeding him dry. (This from a zillionaire.) So it was a great relief when Grandfather interrupted the program by reciting his latest spicy—and actually pretty funny—limerick ("There once was a lady from Kansas . . ."). This was followed by my father's usual complaint about my mother still trying to "find herself" by building boats on Cape Cod "with a bunch of lesbians." I'd often wondered when he would awake to the fact that his absentee wife *was* a lesbian. Probably never, I decided.

Not surprisingly, given the incredible speed with which news travels between the ladies who lunch, Aunt Bunny had already heard about Sailor. The unpleasant details of her death were suitably glossed over (we were, after all, at the dinner table) but everyone agreed that it was a "terrible shame and so difficult for her family." Everyone but Great-Aunt Doris.

"Terrible tragedy aside," she remarked airily, "I never liked how that Savoie girl always got all the best parts. So it's very good news for you, Nicola dear."

This was greeted with shocked looks from the rest of the table. Even Nic seemed at a loss for words. Fortunately, the arrival of a truly amazing chocolate ganache pie allowed a smooth pivot away from awkward truths.

Nonetheless, and despite the almost farcical nature of our little gathering, it was with real affection that I kissed every one of these lunatics goodbye—actual kisses, not the air kind. But it was not until I was back on the M1 safely heading downtown that I felt like I could breathe again.

Fifteen

◇◇◇◇◇◇◇◇◇◇◇◇

"You have a tendency, Hastings, to prefer the least likely. That, no doubt, is from reading too many detective stories."

—Hercule Poirot, *Peril at End House*

MONDAY DAWNED CRISP AND COOL. I WISHED THAT I COULD say the same about myself. I'd had a good chat with my mom the night before, who'd been properly shocked and dismayed at the news about Howard and Sailor. But Mom was not someone to whom one confided about one's love life. And it was my love life—if you could call it that—that was on my mind that morning. The fact was, as eager as I was to share the results of my experiment, I was also absolutely dreading seeing Detective Mendez-Cruz later that day. Or rather, Detective Mendez-Cruz on a date with Nic. I told myself I was being ridiculous. I reminded myself of the man's terrible taste in clothing. Nothing worked.

And then it hit me. Adrian. Adrian could snap me out of this. That would work.

I was waiting in the front hall when he walked in at precisely eight thirty, as crisp and cool as the day in a Ralph Lauren blue plaid sport coat, a pale blue dress shirt open at the collar and navy slacks. I, in contrast, was wearing what could only be called funereal black. Granted, it was a vintage Dior velvet shirtwaist. But still . . . black.

"I thought it wasn't done to wear velvet before four," Adrian said by way of hello.

"Maybe back in 1955 when this dress was made," I countered. "You need to keep up with the times, Adrian."

"Well, no one's going to see it under your lab coat anyway," he said. And then the penny dropped. "Oooh, I get it. You're all dolled up for tonight's drinkypoos with the hot detective."

I could feel my face flooding. "Yeah, well, I kind of wanted to talk to you about that . . ."

"The doctor is in," Adrian said, leading me back to his office and closing the door behind us. "Take a seat and tell me all about it."

Adrian's office is not the office of your average librarian. (Of course, Adrian is not your average librarian, either.) No manila file folders slipping off the ancient rosewood desk, no coffee mug reading "Rock Star Cleverly Disguised as a Librarian," no books piled haphazardly on the shelves. In Adrian's office the books—mostly reference works like Stephen Soitos's *The Blues Detective* or anthologies like Eleanor Taylor Bland's *Shades of Black*—were lined up neatly on the bookshelves, all the spines exactly one inch from the edge. Files were nonexistent, as Adrian did most of the library's paperwork online, using the cloud as his professional filing cabinet. Coffee was taken from a spotless porcelain cup in a spotless porcelain saucer. The only artwork on the walls was a black-and-white photograph taken in the 1940s of Bridgetown Harbour in Barbados. The overall effect, given my emotional chaos, was incredibly soothing.

Adrian, however, was not.

We'd barely made it into our respective chairs—Adrian behind the desk looking very, very stern; me facing it looking, no doubt, like a kid who's been caught smoking in the girls' room—before he said, "What on earth do you think you're doing?"

"I know, I know," I gabbled. "He likes her, she likes him. I'm an idiot. I need to back off."

Adrian shook his head, clearly exasperated. "Once again, my dear Tory," he said, "you're all backasswards."

I blinked. "I don't get it."

"That's just it," he said. "You don't get it. Did Nic back off? No, she did not. Nic knows a smart, hot guy when she sees one."

That stung. "I know he's smart and hot," I protested, then felt compelled to add, "except for his suits."

Adrian nodded. "Yeah, the suits are unfortunate."

"So what do you want me to do, Adrian?" I asked. Okay, whined. "I can't *make* the smart, hot guy in the ugly suit like me. He likes my cousin. He asked her out."

"Well, if you'd bothered talking to your cousin *like I did*, you would know that Nic asked *him* out."

"Oh," I said.

"Yeah, oh."

"How did she even know he was . . . um . . . available?"

"She asked him that, too."

"Oh," I said.

"Yeah, oh."

"Anyway," I countered feebly, "it's too late. She got there first."

"Oh lordy, girl," Adrian said. "You and Nic aren't six. It's not like whoever says 'I call, I claim' first wins the smart, hot guy. You need to step up."

I knew he was right. I knew I was making excuses. Excuses not to open myself—my weird, wounded self—up to a man who, if he was as smart as he seemed, would then run for the hills from my weird, wounded self. And I wasn't sure I could face that.

"I'm sorry, Adrian," I said, standing up from my chair. "I'm just not there yet."

"Tory," Adrian said, gentle now. "It's been seven years. You *are* there. Or you could be if you let yourself take a chance."

I opened the door to the office. "Thanks, Adrian," I said, looking back over my shoulder. "But I'm gonna pass."

BUT THAT NIGHT'S GATHERING WASN'T AS BAD AS I'D FEARED. Mairead came by that afternoon as planned to shadow me in the lab, and I'd been pleased to find that it was actually fun to have her there in one of my old lab coats with the sleeves rolled up and the hem almost to her ankles, so interested and eager to learn. I was under deadline for a series of inner-hinge repairs for Graham on a leather-bound, five-volume translation of *Plutarch's Lives*, first published in 1683 and now, understandably, a little worse for wear. It soon became clear that I was going to be a little late for the meeting of "Agatha Incorporated," so I sent the girl on ahead at five to make my apologies. When I finally hung my lab coat on its hook a half hour later and trotted upstairs, the festivities were already under way.

I stood in the doorway for a minute or two unremarked. Nic was mixing drinks and Adrian was happily discussing *The Westing Game* with Mairead. Detective Mendez-Cruz—outfitted in a horrendously rumpled navy (for a change) suit—was standing with his back to me, deep in conversation with Mrs. Christie, seated in her gold velvet armchair.

Nic quietly handed me something called a Bronx Cocktail (named, I later learned, after the Bronx Zoo), and I stood by the door sipping my drink and eavesdropping on Mrs. Christie quickly and efficiently bringing Mendez-Cruz up to speed on the probable cause of Bertram's narrow escape as well as the case for Sailor's death by poisoned tequila.

"Miss Van Dyne thought it might have been abrin poisoning"— *I did not!*—"which was understandable given that Mr. Calhoun's dog had almost certainly nearly met his end by inhaling a minute trace of crushed *Abrus precatorius*. But given the rapid onset of Miss Savoie's symptoms, abrin poisoning was unlikely to be the cause of her death."

Mendez-Cruz, his back to me, nodded. "But you have another possibility in mind, Mrs. Mallowan?" he asked, and it seemed to me that his voice held a great deal of respect for the mild-mannered British lady sitting there talking calmly about poisons and their effects.

"Well, of course, the obvious answer is that Miss Savoie was poisoned with arsenic, whose symptoms are identical but take effect far more quickly."

There was a short pause. "Arsenic," Mendez-Cruz finally repeated. "Is that possible?"

"Well, that is what Miss Van Dyne is going to tell us here tonight, I believe," Mrs. Christie said, nodding to where I was standing behind the detective.

Mendez-Cruz turned abruptly, and I don't think it was my imagination that he seemed relieved to see me. This Mrs. Mallowan could be pretty overwhelming when you weren't used to her.

"Miss Van Dyne," Mrs. Christie said. "I was just telling Detective Mendez-Cruz that you perhaps have an interesting update for us."

It seemed the meeting was being called to order.

"Would you be wanting me to take minutes?" Mairead asked,

pulling her laptop out of her bag with the speed of an old West gunslinger.

Mendez-Cruz looked at me quizzically. "Is it all right for her to be here?" he said sotto voce.

"Well, her dad is all right with it," I whispered back. "And if nothing else it might actually keep her very, very quiet."

And, as it turned out, the kid was a whiz at taking minutes.

AGATHA INCORPORATED
MEETING MINUTES, OCTOBER 7

Members present: Mrs. Mallowan (hereafter Mrs. M), Victoria Van Dyne (hereafter Tory), Nicola Van Dyne (hereafter Nic), Adrian Gooding (hereafter Mr. G), Detective Sebastian Mendez-Cruz (hereafter Det. M-C), Mairead Butler, Secretary (hereafter MB)

First order of business: Drinks all round, secretary excepted

Second order of business: Discussion, death of Sailor Savoie

Q1: How did Sailor Savoie die? Possibilities:

    A) Food poisoning (very rarely causes death in young healthy person) or

    B) Arsenical poisoning

Q2: If B, how could arsenic be obtained?

Tory: Boiling of emerald green book cloth containing arsenic to a liquid reduction. Could be done in anyone's kitchen. Ensuing fascinating discussion of extraction.

Q3: How could poison be ingested without being noticed by victim?

Mrs. M: Arsenic is tasteless, though reduction might well create a rather musty flavor from old book cloth.

Tory: Also reduction is greenish-brown.

Mr. G: So reduction would need to be added to a strongly flavored drink that comes in a bottle that won't show the color.

Nic: Tequila, Sailor's fave, has a super-strong taste, and there are fancy tequilas that come in ceramic bottles. And even in her glass probably wouldn't pay attention to the color anyway because there are aged tequilas in weird colors like brown and gold and even blue.

Q4: How do you test a body for arsenic?

Det. M-C: Standard test for arsenic used to be the Marsh test but now use the Reinsch test for heavy metals like arsenic. But not a test run in standard tox screens.

Next steps: Det. M-C to call in a favor (given that all is theoretical and unofficial) and ask Mexican authorities to check for arsenic with Reinsch test. Further next steps to depend on results of test.

Later, looking over Mairead's meeting minutes that Adrian had printed out in his office and handed to the rest of us, I was pretty impressed by their accuracy (including the correct spelling of Reinsch, which I had to look up). What they did not cover, thank god, was Nic and Detective Mendez-Cruz (*Seb*) sitting next to each other on the cozy couch all, well, cozy together. Or at least Nic was cozy, her ballet flats kicked aside and her legs tucked up under her in a way that made her lean ever so slightly into her date.

Mendez-Cruz, though, had been all business, sitting quietly, taking everything in. Click, click, click. But when he'd finally spoken to say that he would consult with the detective in charge of the case, his was the voice of authority. And suddenly, our little parlor game had become very, very real.

NONETHELESS, YOU WOULD HAVE THOUGHT THAT, HAVING
provided the detective with a good lead on the suspicious death of
Sailor Savoie, we would be entitled to hear back from the man on
the forensic results. But no, two days went by with Mendez-Cruz
all radio silent again—even with Nic, despite what she called a
"super nice dinner" at the Gotham. Instead, we had to wait until
Thursday to learn about the results secondhand from Sailor's sister,
Aspen. Who is nobody's idea of a reliable narrator. But you take
what you can get.

I was in the middle of repairing a split hinge on a signed first
edition, first printing of Walter Mosley's *Down the River unto the
Sea* for the Edgar Award Winners Room when Nic called me with
what she said was "a great lead on the Sailor Savoie homicide." I
put down the gluing brush that I'd inherited from Abe and
punched the phone to speaker.

"You need to stop talking like someone on *Law & Order*, Nic,"
I said. "And to stop interrupting me when I'm working."

"Yeah, yeah, I know," Nic said, "but I was checking in with
Aspen on if there was going to be some sort of service or something for Sailor and she said not until they know more about how
she died and that made me sad, but then you won't believe what
else she told me . . ."

I actually did want to know what else Aspen had told her, but
the PVA glue on that new hinge was going to dry out fast. "Listen,
Nic, how about we meet after I'm done here?"

"Okay," she said. "I'm heading down to Fifth and 29th for an
Alice + Olivia sample sale. You want to meet there?"

It's not that Nic needed to buy her designer clothes at a discount,
but like all good New Yorkers, she wasn't about to pass up a bar-

gain. But the last thing I wanted to do was meet Nic while she slapped the racks at a sample sale.

"Not really," I said, "but we could meet at that rooftop bar on 230 Fifth when you're done. It's still warm enough, right? And if not, they'll have the space heaters going."

"Oooh, yeah, great idea! I absolutely love love love that place."

I snorted with laughter. How many times had Nic and I read *Eloise* together as kids, delighting in the poor little rich girl's noisy, anarchic life at the Plaza Hotel ("I absolutely love love love the Plaza")? Come to think of it, Nic was exactly what you would imagine a grown-up Eloise would be like. Except a better dresser.

"Okay," I said. "I'll meet you there at, say, five thirty?"

Nic, of course, did not meet me there at five thirty. Nic did not even meet me there at six. But I was happy enough on the open-air terrace nursing my glass of pinot grigio and surrounded by young wannabe investment bankers drinking violently colored cocktails and madly swiping right. I, in contrast, was gazing out at the sleek Art Deco lines of the Empire State Building looming over us, its spire glowing silver against the darkening sky. I absolutely love love love the Empire State Building.

Nic finally dashed through the glass doors to the terrace at six fifteen enveloped in what had to be her bargain find, a full-length, bright red leather cloak complete with cowl. It looked like something a slightly kinky Little Red Riding Hood might wear.

"You like?" she asked, twirling to give me—and, let's face it, the bros in their Bonobos suits at the next table—the full effect. "It's vegan leather." This from a woman who would eat a medium-rare steak every night of her life if she could.

"What does that even mean?"

"It means it's polyester," she said with a grin. "But 'vegan leather' sounds better."

"I'm not sure it does," I said. "But anyway, sit down, order a drink and tell me about your great lead."

At a crowded rooftop bar full of thirtysomethings on expense accounts, it had taken me at least fifteen minutes to wave down a server. Nic didn't even need to try. One had followed her directly from door to table and now stood waiting next to her like a love-sick puppy. She sat herself down and asked him for "a *really* dirty martini," at which I thought the poor guy was going to pass out. I calmed him down by ordering another glass of pinot grigio. There is nothing even remotely sexy about ordering a glass of pinot grigio.

"So here's the scoop," Nic said, once she had her martini in hand. "Aspen called me to say that Sailor's service will be next week but it will be private because they don't want any publicity, her being a Savoie and all, and then, get this, she tells me that the police did a search of Sailor's hotel room and they found some Dos Artes tequila, you know, the super fancy blue agave kind that comes in that hand-painted ceramic bottle . . ." Which I didn't know since I almost never drink super fancy artisanal tequila. ". . . that had been FedExed overnight to the resort the night before to be delivered to Sailor Savoie's bungalow with a card saying happy birthday, too special to share."

This did not sound particularly ominous to me. "And?"

"And guess what? Some New York cop who shall remain name-less suggested that they do that whatchamacallit test and *it had arsenic in it.*"

I choked on my wine. "You're kidding me."

"Not kidding," Nic replied solemnly. "And then—and I warn you, this is pretty gross—they did that same test on her urine. Well, the urine in her body, I guess."

"I get it, Nic," I broke in hastily.

"And it was. Arsenic, I mean. Sailor died from arsenic poisoning."

We were both quiet for a moment, remembering Sailor alone in her hotel bathroom.

As if to break the gloom, Nic said, "But here's something I guess you could call good news. The bottle was sent by your friend and mine, Rachel Whatshername."

This time the wine went right out my nose.

"*Howard's* Rachel?" I gasped when I'd recovered. "Rachel *Featherstonhaugh*?"

"Yup," Nic said. "Rachel Whatshername."

"Rachel is the last person I would have suspected," I said, almost to myself.

"Which is exactly why it had to be her!" Nic said triumphantly. "I mean, in those movies with that little French detective with the crazy moustache . . ."

"Belgian," I corrected her.

"Okay, whatever," Nic conceded. "But in those movies, the bad guy's always the last person you'd suspect, right?"

Sixteen

◇◇◇◇◇◇◇◇◇◇

She had poise and efficiency . . . But she was, he decided, just a little too efficient to be what he called "jolie femme."
—Hercule Poirot describing Miss
Debenham, *Murder on the Orient
Express*

EXCEPT FOR MY CHECK-IN CALL WITH MY MOM, WHO HAD LIS-
tened with only half an ear to the Sailor Savoie saga and then bent
mine talking about the new catboat design she and Marj were
working on, the rest of my week had been disappointingly solitary.
I have to admit I was hoping that Mrs. Christie would see her way
to dropping by the Mystery Guild Library at some point so I could
tell her the news, but days went by and there were no sightings.
Maybe now that she'd solved the "how" of Sailor's death (with, I
might add, some expert help), she'd decided not to be on holiday
from the Eternity anymore. Not to mention that the "who" was
still out there. And what about Howard? I mean, was one mystery
her earthly limit? And what if the two murders were somehow
connected? Which was pretty unlikely, but wouldn't that make it
one mystery for her to solve? Couldn't she get some kind of divine
extension?

It was when I caught myself thinking like this—thinking that *my* Mrs. Christie was *the* Agatha Christie—that I knew it was time to get back to my old life. My safe, sane, sensible life. This did not cheer me as much as I'd hoped. I would miss my brilliantly bonkers friend.

The following Monday, after one of Mairead's now regularly scheduled book-doctoring sessions, Adrian, Mairead and I—and Tony, trailing his raggedy red leash—stuck our heads into the room to check for Mrs. Christie just in case.

And there she was in her armchair, discreetly checking the slender gold watch on her wrist to determine just how late we were for the tea for four she'd already set out. Including, I saw, dog biscuits for Tony. In fact, it soon became abundantly clear that she'd shown up not for an update on the death of Sailor Savoie but to spend some quality time with the pooch.

Nonetheless, once the tea had been poured and Tony had very politely begged for his biscuit, I told her what I'd learned from Nic about the arsenic-laced tequila. None of it seemed to come as any great surprise to her.

"Tell me, my dear. Had you made Mr. Calhoun aware of the dangers of emerald green?"

I thought back. "Yes, I did, actually. Maybe a few months ago when Nic had dragged me along for drinks and 'nibbles' at his place, I noticed a book on his shelves that I knew was on the database of the Poison Book Project."

"Not to put too fine a point on it," Adrian said to no one.

I ignored him and continued. "It was called *Angel Whispers: or The Echo of Spirit Voices Designed to Comfort those who Mourn.*"

"Catchy title," Adrian said, again to no one.

"Which is why I remembered it," I snapped, maybe just a tad annoyed at all the editorial comments.

Mrs. Christie chose to ignore the children's squabbling. "And did Miss Featherstonhaugh also know about the arsenic in emerald green covers?" she asked me. I loved the way Rachel's last name just rolled off her tongue: *Fether-stin-aw.* Like it wasn't tricky at all.

"Well, Rachel helped with the business side of Howard's collecting and was around a lot . . ." I paused, thinking back, but couldn't be sure. "Nic, do you remember if Rachel was still around that night?"

"I think she left not too long after we got there," she said uncertainly. Then inspiration seemed to hit. "But yeah, she was still around when you started talking about the book with a creepy name. I remember because I said one of those scary 'ooo eee ooo' sounds like you do, and she just sniffed at me like I was being silly."

I smiled and turned to Mrs. Christie. "In short, yes. Rachel was there when I cautioned Howard."

"So there you have it," Adrian announced triumphantly. "Rachel knew about emerald green *and* she sent the spiked tequila. That's means and opportunity. What more do you want?"

"A motive," Mairead the Mystery Expert said. "Traditionally you need means, opportunity *and* motive."

"Traditionally," Adrian shot back (at an eleven-year-old, I might add), "the motive becomes clear after the fact."

More to stop the bickering than anything else, I offered, "You know, Rachel seemed very upset about Bertram at Howard's memorial service. She said Howard told her that Sailor had slipped the dog an oxy. Maybe she wanted revenge."

Adrian rolled his eyes. "Poison someone for making a dog sick? A dog that doesn't even belong to you? Seems a little extreme to me. There's got to be more to it than that." But Mrs. Christie, perhaps thinking of her beloved Tony, took the opportunity to channel Hercule Poirot in *Death on the Nile* by saying, "Motives for murder are sometimes very trivial, of course."

"So *in conclusion*," I said, hoping to call an end to all this fruit-less speculation, "what we can all agree on is that Adrian is prob-ably right. Whatever her motive, it looks like Rachel deliberately poisoned Sailor."

To which Mrs. Christie replied rather enigmatically, "It is al-ways wise to suspect everybody until you can prove logically, and to your own satisfaction, that they are innocent." In the words of Hercule Poirot in *The Mysterious Affair at Styles*.

With that we had to be satisfied, and the rest of the tea party was spent applauding Tony's mastery of several rather unusual tricks taught to him by his person. These included a version of "play dead" in which Mairead would make a gun with her thumb and forefinger, point it at the pooch and say, "Bang!" At which Tony would drop to the floor, roll onto his back, all four legs to the sky, and, now motionless, *close his eyes*.

It was very clear that with this stunt, Tony had made Mrs. Christie his devoted follower.

"How utterly charming!" she exclaimed. Turning to Mairead, she added, "He so reminds me of my own Tony. You know, his original name, given to him by my father, was George Washing-ton. I called him Tony for short."

"Why didn't you just call him George?" Mairead asked.

Mrs. Christie looked shocked. "Because, my dear, it would never have done, of course, to give a dog the name of the reigning king."

Mairead looked a bit confused, as well she might, since the only reigning king she knew was Britain's current king, Charles III. Whereas I understood that Mrs. Christie was referencing George V, who had, in fact, died in 1936.

Well, time to nip this little conversation in the bud.

"I should get you home, Mairead," I said briskly.

No one could have been more surprised than I was to hear Mrs. Christie say, "I do hope to see you and Tony back here next Monday, Miss Butler." Such is the power of doggy charm.

NATURALLY, I AWOKE THE NEXT MORNING FACED, AS THEY SAY, with a conundrum. On the one hand, I wanted to tell Detective Mendez-Cruz that Rachel had known about the arsenic in emerald green book covers. On the other, I didn't want it to seem like I was looking for excuses to talk to him. Because, let's face it, I probably was.

The truth was I missed the guy. Nic had said very little about him, perhaps sensing a certain awkwardness between us when his name came up, for which I was grateful. I assumed he was still pursuing her—men seldom gave up pursuing Nic—but was also consumed by work. He now had two unsolved murders on his plate. And though Mrs. Christie and I had provided the detective with the means of Sailor's death, the clues pointing to Rachel as the killer, while damning, were only circumstantial. Mendez-Cruz would now, through painstaking police work, be looking for evidence to confirm Rachel's guilt—or innocence.

Which is why it came as something of a shock when, a few days after that last Mrs. Christie sighting—and while I was still dithering about calling him—he called to ask if he could meet with me "to discuss the Sailor Savoie case."

Well, not with *me* exactly.

That day Adrian had been deep into preparing his fourth-quarter report for the library's board of directors, so I was on my own for lunch. Which was just the excuse I needed to trot over to the park for a Sabrett's hot dog dripping with mustard and sauerkraut. A Sabrett's hot dog is not Adrian's idea of a proper lunch.

My idea of a proper lunch is whatever I happen to be jonesing for at the moment. And at that moment it was a Sabrett's. I handed the hot dog–cart guy my three bucks for the delicacy itself and one extra for standing out there in all weathers under his yellow-and-red umbrella just so people like me could get their fix. Also, he always gave me extra paper napkins.

The chill of autumn had finally well and truly arrived. Huddled on a bench facing the fountain, I wolfed down my lunch in record time. I was tossing my condiment-smeared napkins into one of the park's green-slatted trash cans, when my cell phone rang. The number was unfamiliar, and as a general rule, I don't answer unknown callers. But for some reason—maybe because of the sheer boredom of almost three days of a safe, sane, sensible life—that time I did.

"Tory?"

I recognized the voice immediately. Detective Mendez-Cruz. It took a second, though, before I could choke out, "Detective Mendez-Cruz?"

"Sebastian, yes."

There was another pause while I absorbed the fact that Detective Mendez-Cruz *wanted me to call him Sebastian.* It wasn't Seb, but I would take it.

"Can you hear me, Tory?"

I shook my head to clear it. "Yes, um, Sebastian, I can hear you now." I mean, what was I going to say? *"I'm sorry for the delay but I'd been temporarily struck dumb?"*

"Good. I hope you don't mind my calling. I got your number from your cousin. I was hoping we could meet to discuss the Sailor Savoie case."

Sebastian wants to meet with you, Tory, to discuss the Sailor Savoie case.

"Did I lose you again?"

"Ah, no, um, I'm here, but I'm in the park so maybe the reception isn't the best." *Way to start a relationship, Tory. With a sort-of lie.*

Well, as it turns out we weren't starting a relationship. *Sebastian* didn't actually want to meet with me. Well, not with me exclusively. He was hoping I could arrange what he called a "meeting to discuss further developments in the case."

Now, I'd learned enough from watching reruns of *Law & Order* with Nic to know that the police are perfectly entitled to talk about an ongoing investigation with those outside the enquiry if the detective in charge expects to garner some information pertinent to the case. So this was worthy of note. I was pretty sure, then, that he wasn't suggesting a meeting in order to share *his* inside information with *us*; he was hoping we would share *our* inside information with *him*—inside information about the worlds of old money and new, of Broadway and Hollywood, of socialites and social wannabes. He needed our impressions, our expertise, our access to those worlds to help his investigation make sense. Well, he was welcome to them. Not to mention to our actual new evidence.

"Of course," I said. "We had some thoughts that we wanted to share with you, anyway. Especially the fact that Rachel knew about arsenic in emerald green covers." I went through the whole Rachel-being-in-the-room-when-I-warned-Howard-about-the-*Angel-Whispers* thing.

"That's very helpful to know," Sebastian said. "We should discuss that more when we meet. And I'd like to have your friend Mrs. Mallowan there, if possible."

I didn't ask him why because the why was obvious. The woman was brilliant. Probably crazy. But brilliant. And he didn't know about the *probably crazy* part.

"She's going to be at the library again on Monday after work. Is that okay for you?"

"Monday is fine. And maybe you could ask Mr. Gooding if he's available. I appreciate his objectivity." *So that's what you call it.*

"I'll ask him," I said, even though I knew that nothing short of a 40 percent–off sale at Mr Porter could keep Adrian away.

"And your cousin, of course," he added all casual like. "She needs to be kept in the loop."

"Can do," I said. Idiotically. *Who says "can do" these days?*

"Good. I appreciate your help."

And then he was gone.

Tucking the phone into my coat pocket, I walked back across the street in a storm of conflicting emotions. Why call me and not Nic? Well, that was easy. Mendez-Cruz, that is, *Sebastian*, was no dope. Nic had many strengths but arranging a last-minute meeting between five busy adults including a woman on holiday from . . . from wherever . . . was not one of them. Instead, ask the boring, *efficient* cousin to call the first official board meeting of what I was now, thanks to Mairead, thinking of as Agatha Inc.

Seventeen

◇◇◇◇◇◇◇◇◇◇◇◇◇◇◇◇

"Real evidence is usually vague and unsatisfactory. It has to be examined—sifted."

—Hercule Poirot, *The Mysterious Affair at Styles*

IT WAS ALL I COULD DO NOT TO POUND A GAVEL AND SAY, "I hereby call this meeting to order." Which would have done exactly nothing. There was no way I was going to call that meeting to order. Most of the people there didn't even seem to know it *was* a meeting. They clearly thought it was a cocktail party.

It had been easier than I'd thought to gather the usual suspects. Mairead, of course, was not to be put off. Adrian had indeed been thrilled to know that the hot detective valued his objectivity even though I told him that it just meant that he knew he could count on Adrian to be snarky. And Nic, of course, was delighted at the idea of a party, any party.

I was a little late upstairs, having been absorbed in putting the library's disbound copy of Ngaio Marsh's first Roderick Alleyn mystery, *A Man Lay Dead*, back together into a functional volume. When I finally arrived, there was Mrs. Christie doling out something called a Monkey's Gland that Nic and Adrian had apparently found in the Vermeire and insisted on making. I had to admit it was, despite the horrible name, super tasty. Mairead got a Shirley Temple, complete with paper parasol and maraschino cherry. Tony got a dog biscuit. And Sebastian, in a dull grey suit that looked like he'd slept in it, was drinking club soda. Click, click, click.

Once everybody was standing around with their tipple of choice, it was Mrs. Christie, of course, who took charge. Seating herself on her gold velvet throne, she set her glass aside and pulled what looked like—*yes, it was*—an embroidery hoop from her capacious handbag.

Needlework in hand, she said firmly, "Mr. Gooding, perhaps you could pull up two chairs for yourself and Miss Nicola." Apparently, in Mrs. Christie's world, as in the world of the Van Dynes, ladies did not pull up their own chairs if a man was available.

Adrian, wearing a navy velvet blazer that made Sebastian's suit look even worse than it actually was, winked at Nic and did the honors obediently. Nic winked back at him as she took her seat, carefully smoothing her black silk Jason Wu miniskirt over her slim thighs like the lady she wasn't.

I was not envious of Nic's black silk Jason Wu miniskirt. I was not envious because *I* was wearing a vintage 1992 Versace Couture pencil skirt that I'd never had the nerve to sport before. It wasn't a mini, but it fit me like a dream, and I fully intended to smooth it over *my* slim thighs once Mrs. Christie told me where she intended me to sit.

Where she intended me to sit, as it turned out, was on the couch next to Sebastian.

This was both bad and good. Bad because all I could think about was his long legs literally within inches of my own. *Those legs.* Well, that was better than being distracted by *those eyes.* Or *that mouth*. Which was smiling at me. Which meant I completely forgot about smoothing my skirt over my thighs. Not that it would have made any difference. My seatmate had other things on his mind. He had pulled a battered black notebook and a Bic pen out of the sagging pocket of his suit jacket and was busy getting ready to take notes.

I nudged him inelegantly with an elbow. "No need," I said, cocking my head over to Mairead, already seated with her laptop at the reading table.

"Is she here every Monday?" he asked.

"Pretty much," I said. "We have a sort of mentoring thing happening on Mondays. And quite frankly, her dog is a big draw for Mrs., um, M."

Sebastian nodded and tucked the notebook away. "Okay then. Her minutes from the last meeting were really helpful."

He turned to smile at the girl, and suddenly I was jealous of an eleven-year-old kid. *You are pathetic, Tory Van Dyne. You really are.*

"Anyway, it's your meeting," I reminded him, maybe a little sharply. "So you might want to call it to order."

"Oh, right," Sebastian said, and suddenly he was a different man. He leaned forward and looked at each person in the room one by one, saying nothing. Click, click, click. The room went silent.

"Thank you all for coming tonight. I appreciated your thoughts the last time we met. As I understand it, you *already* know from Ms. Savoie's sister . . ." And, it was clear, he'd been none too pleased to hear it. ". . . that I did follow up with the Mexican police. Who, I should add, were already treating the death as suspicious and following accepted protocol in their forensic toxicology. But without our suggestion, they wouldn't have tested for arsenic. And, as I *also* understand you *already* know . . ." Again with the heavy disapproval. ". . . the tests did reveal arsenic. So we should be pleased with that result."

Everyone in the room looked like they'd personally won the Nobel Prize for Solving a Murder. Everyone except Mrs. Christie, who merely glanced up from embroidering what looked, oddly, like a parrot in a rosebush and smiled complacently.

"I think," Sebastian continued, "I owe you a rundown on the case as it now stands."

I didn't believe that for a minute. This was an official homicide investigation now, and he didn't owe us anything except maybe thanks for our contribution. I'd been right about his motivation. He wanted something, something more, from us. And we owed it to him—and Sailor.

"But I must stress," Sebastian added firmly, "that what we say here tonight *cannot* leave this room. And the file with the meeting minutes will be shared only with me."

He looked sternly at Mairead, who all but saluted him. In my opinion, he would have done better to look sternly at Nic, who was well into her second Monkey's Gland. Adrian nodded matter-of-factly, though Mrs. Christie promised nothing, merely saying, "A wise precaution." *God knows*, I thought before I could stop myself, *what she's planning to report back to the Eternity.*

"And I *also* understand," Sebastian went on, the irritation now very clear in his voice, "that you *already* know from Ms. Savoie's sister that the delivery receipt showed that the bottle of tequila was sent by Rachel Featherstonhaugh."

"I can never remember that girl's name," Nic said to nobody.

Sebastian continued as if she hadn't said anything, which with Nic is usually the right approach. "I have asked Ms. Savoie's sister to refrain from discussing the case further with you." Here he all but glared at Nic, who smiled back beatifically.

"Also, you all should know that yesterday Ms. Featherston-haugh was taken in for questioning." Well, *that* was interesting.

"Surely she didn't deny sending the bottle?" Mairead asked.

"No," Sebastian said. "She could hardly do that. It had her fingerprints all over it."

"Yessss!" Adrian said. "I knew it was her."

Sebastian cut his celebration short with a raised hand. "But she claims she sent the bottle at Mr. Calhoun's request."

Blank silence at this. I shook my head, as if maybe there was something wrong with my hearing. "But that's ridiculous," I said. "Howard had been dead for a week when Rachel sent that bottle."

"True," Sebastian acknowledged. "But she is adamant that she was just following his instructions. According to her, about a week after he got back from India, he'd sent her out to buy the tequila and put it on his account at . . ." Here he paused to pull the battered black notebook back out and flipped a few pages. ". . . Teterbaum's Fine Wines and Liquors. Which we checked and which indeed happened. She says it then sat on her desk in the utility room with a Post-it reading 'SS birthday' until the Friday morning when her boss was leaving for the Hamptons. When she arrived that morning, she says he told her to send a card saying 'Happy birthday, Sailor. Too special to share.' and to FedEx the bottle and the card that afternoon to Sailor's resort with a note to hold it for her birthday the following weekend."

"Which Rachel didn't do because she ended up in the emergency room that day," I put in.

"Exactly," Sebastian said. "And she says she was too busy on Monday taking care of Bertram to send it. And then, of course, Howard Calhoun was killed the next day. But she says that after his death the cousin asked her to 'tie up any loose ends,' so she went ahead and sent it 'just to get it off her desk.'"

Adrian sighed. "So the long and short of it is, she's going to stick to her story that sending the bottle was all her boss's idea."

"Well, easy for her to say," Nic put in. "Howard's not around to say she's lying."

"But am I wrong that Mr. Calhoun was fond of sending expensive gifts to young women he hoped to represent in the theater world?" Mrs. Christie asked mildly.

"Well, he certainly bought this expensive gift," Sebastian said, "or at least it was bought on his account."

"Yes, but that's just it," Nic said. "Sure, it was just like Howard to give Sailor a fancy bottle of giggle juice for her birthday. But why would he put arsenic in it? He told me the day he, well, died that she was going to sign on with him now that she was getting into movies and all and she would need an agent because, you know, she's a big frog in a little pond on Broadway but Hollywood is a whole different kettle of fish." Nic was not one to be satisfied with a single metaphor when two could be mixed.

"So probably not a good idea to kill the goose that might lay a really, really golden egg," I added. "Especially given that Howard was practically bankrupt."

Mrs. Christie nodded. "We would do well to remember that Mr. Calhoun's financial situation does seem to have governed his actions." Which, oddly, sounded more like a caution than a confirmation.

"So," Adrian said, much encouraged by Nic's news, "if it wasn't Howard, it must have been Rachel who leached out the poison and added it to the tequila. She knew about emerald green, she could have made the reduction. Did you ask her about that?"

"Once I'd heard from Tory about it, yes," Sebastian acknowledged. "She dismissed the idea flatly, which is kind of her go-to defense. All she said was, 'So you think I switched out the tequila in that bottle for a bunch of poisoned water? And that Sailor Savoie would *drink* that? That's just stupid.'"

"And Rachel isn't the only possible suspect," Mairead broke in. "How about that theater director bloke who hates the movie producer bloke? How better to sabotage his movie than to kill off his big-name star?"

Well, I had to admit, the kid had a point. Everyone knew about Schifrin's high dudgeon at being frozen out of Neuman's film. I thought about Nic's assessment at the memorial service about Schifrin's antipathy toward Wren: *"He hates her just for being in it."* Maybe he hated Sailor just for being in it, too. So maybe it had been easy, then, to try to scuttle Neuman's ship by killing her.

Mendez-Cruz nodded. "You're right, Mairead. Jonathan Schifrin definitely had a motive."

Mairead gave a satisfied smile. "And he probably had opportunity," she said. "After all, that tequila was sitting out for a week where anyone visiting could have tampered with it. Maybe this Schifrin had been there."

"That's where the theory falls down, I'm afraid," Mendez-Cruz responded gently. "He has an unshakable alibi." Mairead's smile faded. "Based on certain, let's call it, information received, we confirmed today that for the past six weeks he's been in an alcohol rehabilitation facility upstate, leaving only to come in for Howard Calhoun's memorial service."

"Hey," Nic broke in, "that 'information received'—air quotes here—"you received from *moi*. You were listening in to me gossiping with Tory at the memorial service!"

And, I realized, had immediately followed up on said information. Why was I surprised? Why did I keep forgetting that this was the man's *job*?

"Guilty as charged," Sebastian admitted with a grin. "More

significant, during his visit, he was accompanied at all times by a male nurse from the facility."

"Ah," Nic said thoughtfully. "The beefcake guy. I sure got that one wrong."

"So we're back to Rachel," Adrian said, sounding positively cheerful.

"Except we don't have any motive there at all," Sebastian pointed out.

Almost shamefaced, I put forth my Rachel-hated-Sailor-for-almost-killing-Bertram theory. "I must be right that Howard told her that Sailor had deliberately tried to slip Bertram an oxy. She was furious at the idea of anyone trying to hurt that dog. She really loves him."

Mairead could contain herself no longer. "So Rachel thought that Sailor had deliberately poisoned Bertram. And how better to take revenge on a poisoner than by poison! I'm telling you, it's right out of Agatha Christie."

Mrs. Christie looked modestly down at her gaudy parrot in its rosebush and smiled complacently, but Sebastian looked less than convinced.

"Well, it's a motive of a kind, I suppose," he said doubtfully.

Mairead then jumped in with a second possibility. "Or else Sailor knew some guilty secret of Rachel's and had to be silenced. That's how it works in Agatha Christie's mysteries." She cocked her head and then added thoughtfully, "Kind of predictable, actually."

Well, *that* got a much different reaction from Mrs. Christie. "That is often how it works, but not in every case," she said waspishly. "And it is *never* predictable."

Mendez-Cruz again seemed dubious. "Well, both of those are possible motives. But quite frankly, all of our theories around means, opportunity and motive are circumstantial rather than evidential. We can't even prove where the arsenic came from. We, of course, did search for the book you mentioned, Tory, *Angel Whispers*."

"You remembered the name of the book?" I asked, amazed. Then, recalling once again that it was the detective's job to remember details like that, felt a complete fool.

"Hard to forget that title," Sebastian said with a smile, and I felt much better. "But the point is, it's not on his bookshelves."

"So someone must have used it to make the arsenic reduction!" Mairead broke in excitedly.

"Well, either that or Mr. Calhoun decided to get rid of it . . ."

"Ach, yes," the girl admitted. "As one might, given it was made with arsenic."

"And the forensics team made a thorough examination of both his and Ms. Featherstonhaugh's apartments, including swabbing all their pots and pans, and found no trace of arsenic. And without that, we can't eliminate either of them from our inquiry."

The man had been way ahead of us. He'd thought of everything.

"Look," he said. "I agree that if what Nic's told us is true, there's no reason Howard Calhoun would want Sailor Savoie dead. Quite the opposite, in fact. And I also agree that something is very off with Rachel Featherstonhaugh. But unless we get some proof that: one, she was acting on her own initiative; two, could have made the arsenic reduction; and three, wanted Sailor Savoie dead because she thought she'd given a dog a party drug, I can't hold her. But you know the players, you know their personalities, how they live their lives. So if anyone has any thoughts, can think of any small detail we might have missed that would give us the proof we need to find Sailor Savoie's killer, I need to know about it sooner rather than later."

Think, Tory, *think*. This is your chance to impress the hot detective. You're the one who came up with the arsenic-reduction lead. Time for a new one. Or, I suddenly thought, *a more complete one.*

"Did you by any chance check to see if Rachel has a cooking strainer?"

Mendez-Cruz looked at me blankly. *Okay, so not much of a cook.*

"It's a metal fine-mesh sieve. I used a horsehair sieve to strain my book cloth reduction to get rid of the dirt and small particles of cloth that were muddying it. But Rachel could have done the same thing with a kitchen sieve. And if she did, and even if she rinsed it out, you might still find some microscopic bits of book cloth in it. Sieves are hard to clean completely."

"OMG," Nic squealed, "this is *so* like an episode of *Law & Order.*"

Mendez-Cruz gave her an indulgent smile. "I'm glad you think so. And it's something that we will definitely investigate. But even if we find that physical evidence, I'd be a lot happier if we had a stronger motive for murder than Sailor hurt a dog that wasn't even Rachel's or that she knew something about Rachel that would be worth killing for. And that's going to be tough. There's just no obvious reason why she, or in fact, anyone would want Sailor Savoie dead."

Mrs. Christie looked up from her embroidery and quoted—almost, it seemed, without stopping to think—the words of the great Belgian detective in *Five Little Pigs*. "My dear sir, the why must never be obvious. That is the whole point."

Eighteen

◇◇◇◇◇◇◇◇◇◇◇◇

It is clear that the books owned the shop rather than the other
way about. Everywhere they had run wild and taken possession
of their habitat, breeding and multiplying, and clearly lacking
any strong hand to keep them down.
—The Clocks

IT WAS A MEASURE OF HOW UNSETTLED MY LIFE HAD BECOME
when, the next morning, I overslept. I couldn't remember the last
time I'd slept in. Maybe never. I have the kind of internal alarm
clock that mentally pinches you awake at the appointed hour. But
that morning, no pinch. That morning, the alarm clock had taken
a much deserved break, and it wasn't until the unconscionable hour
of nine o'clock that I wandered downstairs to the library proper.
Where I found Adrian waiting impatiently for me in the hallway.

It occurred to me that Adrian had been waiting impatiently for
me a lot in recent weeks. He hardly ever even started the conversation with fashion commentary anymore. Which was disappointing, because that day I was sporting one of my faves—a navy
short-sleeved sweater tucked into a pair of tan 1940s-style high-
waisted, pleated trousers.

But, no, instead of the hoped-for "very Kate Hepburn," he just
said flatly, "We need to talk." *Uh-oh.*

"Is this about Mrs. Christie?" I asked nervously.

"Not really," he said, surprising me. "I'm not gonna go there. I like the woman, I really do. She's not Agatha Christie come from the Eternity or whatever she calls it, but she's smart and knowledgeable and somehow incredibly soothing. I have a hard time believing she's crazy. So, whoever she is, she has a reason for claiming to be Agatha Christie, which at some point she'll tell us. I'm in no rush there."

"Me, neither," I said, somewhat surprised at myself. Sometimes we need a best friend to tell us what we're really thinking.

"She can take all the time she needs as far as I'm concerned," Adrian said, then added, "That's not what I'm worried about."

Uh-oh again.

Adrian turned, led me back to his office and pointed to that morning's *New York Post* lying on his desk. "This ain't gonna make the hot detective happy."

What wasn't going to make the hot detective happy was the front-page headline, ARSENIC AND OLD MONEY. Well, it was kind of clever. But Adrian was right. It really wasn't going to make the hot detective happy. Not with the subhead "Savoie Heiress Poisoned?"

"Really, Adrian?" I said. "You read the *Post*? I thought you were a *Times* kinda guy."

"I read the front-page headline when I go past the newsstand," Adrian said. "Everybody does." Which is true. The *Post*'s banner headlines, which take up the entire front page, are the best. Nobody wants to miss the next HEADLESS BODY IN TOPLESS BAR.

I reached for the tabloid and flipped a few pages to the actual story. It was extremely vague and seemed to rely primarily on an interview with the chambermaid at Sailor's resort in Mexico.

Nonetheless, the reporter had managed to dig up the fact that the police "were talking to a person of interest." This person they identified—rather sloppily, I thought—as Rachel Featherstone. This was accompanied by a rather foggy photo of Rachel lifted from what looked to be an old college yearbook.

"The story's not so bad," I commented. "There's no mention of any motive, so clearly the leak didn't come from one of us." I began to close the paper.

"Wait a minute," Adrian said, frowning a little. He flipped the page back again and squinted at the grainy head shot of Rachel. "That picture. I didn't look at it very closely before. Is that really your Rachel Whatshername?"

I squinched my eyes and took another look. Thin pale face, thin pale hair. "Yup. Younger, but it's her all right. Why?"

"I've seen her before," he said. "In the Strand. Maybe six months ago. She was in the Rare Book Room looking for a first edition of *The Sun Also Rises*, but one without the errata, including the three-*p* 'stoppped' misprint, for her boss. She never said his name and at the time, I thought it made sense because a first edition without the errata only costs six grand, not eighty. But now it seems weird. Didn't you tell me once that Howard had a first edition *with* the errata?"

"Yeah," I said. "He bought it maybe three years ago. I remember him bragging about it. I never actually saw it, though, because it didn't need any work. The only really pricey book in his collection with a misprint that I worked on was a first edition, first printing of *Harry Potter and the Philosopher's Stone*."

I stopped short. There'd been something I'd heard at Howard's memorial service, something that had seemed a bit off at the time but I'd forgotten about completely when Nic hit me with the bombshell about Sailor's death. But now it came back to me.

Graham had said the Harry Potter book in Howard's collection was *not* the pricey version with the misprint.

"You're right, Adrian," I said. "This is all getting a little weird. Maybe I should check with Graham again."

GETTING TO THE ATHENEUM BOOK STORE ENTAILED AGAIN taking the M1—also known as the world's slowest bus—up Madison Avenue to midtown. Usually, I enjoyed riding the M1. I enjoyed its leisurely pace and its leisured riders and, once past 42nd Street, I enjoyed looking out at Madison's extremely expensive shops featuring extremely expensive clothing tastefully displayed in the windows. Though this was a world to which I no longer belonged or wished to belong, it was still very entertaining. But not that day. That day I was *in a hurry.*

And so, of course, the driver stopped literally every two blocks to pick up Upper East Side ladies dripping with shopping bags. Which encumbrances made getting a credit card or their phone out of their purse to tap the reader a really big time-wasting production. I swore to myself that I would try taking the subway again one of these days. Which immediately made my heart pound, so I put the notion away. Better to think about my mission at the Atheneum.

I love love love the Atheneum. Family-owned for three generations, the emporium occupies all six floors of the midtown town house that shelters it, offering more than sixty thousand not necessarily rare but often out-of-print books ranging from fiction to biography to art and architecture to poetry, even to philosophy. It is a bibliophile's dream.

To fill my time on the bus—and, I admit, to avoid overthinking the suspicion that had been growing in my mind ever since

Adrian had told me about Rachel at the Strand—I made a list in my head of some out-of-print mysteries I might try to find once I'd finished my business with Graham. Adrian and I had been looking forever to fill a gaping hole in the library's collection of Ellis Peters's Brother Cadfael mysteries. I'd love to be able to bring back the eleventh, *An Excellent Mystery*, and complete the set.

At long last, the bus made it to 58th Street, where I hopped off and walked east a few blocks to where the brownstone that was home to the Atheneum sat proudly, completely ignoring the high-rises crowding around it. They, it seemed to say, were merely new-comers. The Atheneum was forever.

I pushed through the plate glass doors into the bookstore's main floor and had to steel myself against the terrible temptation of shelves and tables spilling over with books, books and more books. "Get thee away, Satan," I muttered as I made my way past all these treasures and headed upstairs to the First Editions department.

There I found Graham bent over his ancient oak desk entirely absorbed in some book's copyright page, always a first stop in deciphering a volume's printing history. I sat down on the equally ancient leather chair facing him, and he looked up, pushing his wire-frame reading glasses onto his forehead.

Without bothering with the niceties, he immediately started in on the bookseller's complaint. "You know, if all publishers had agreed, as they most definitely should have, on one code for printing history, my professional life would be far more leisurely."

"Yes," I said, "but you'd also have far fewer clients if everybody and their uncle could spot a first edition. I mean how many people know that Harper Brothers used a unique two-letter code between 1912 and 1922 to indicate the month and year of publication? I only know it because you told me."

Graham looked modestly gratified at that. "Your words are true," he said. I love love love Graham's positively Dickensian syntax. "And what wisdom, Victoria, am I able to impart today?"

"You sold a copy of *The Sun Also Rises* with the three-*p* misprint to Howard Calhoun a few years ago, right?"

"I did indeed," Graham said. "He purchased the volume with great enthusiasm. And, if I do say so myself as ought not, it is the crown of his collection."

"Did he ever talk about getting a non-errata first edition as well?"

Graham looked positively shocked at the idea. "Certainly not. That would be akin to acquiring a Picasso oil and then looking for a print of the same piece."

His words confirmed a suspicion that had been growing in my mind ever since Adrian had mentioned Rachel's visit to the Strand.

"I know you're arranging the sale of Howard's collection for his cousin," I said. "Are you confident that the volume with that misprint is the one that's in the collection now?"

Graham looked at me sadly, as one would gaze at a madwoman who needed to be gently but firmly disabused of her fancies. I wondered briefly if that was how I looked at Mrs. Christie, and if it offended her.

"My dear Victoria, not only am I confident that it is the volume with the errata, I have it here. I've only just started going through Mr. Calhoun's library, but I wished to start there. Perhaps we should glance at page 181, line 26 to reassure you."

So saying, Graham pulled a key from the pocket of his ancient tweed jacket, unlocked one of the desk's heavy oak drawers and pulled out an absolutely pristine edition of *The Sun Also Rises*, complete with its original gold, black and tan dust cover. I got up and moved to stand next to him as he gently opened the book to page

181. His finger moved down the page, and I looked over his shoulder as he got to line 26.

Which read "She had not stopped looking at Pedro Romero."

Graham looked up at me, his usually ruddy cheeks pale.

"This is most definitely *not* the volume with the errata," he almost whispered. "*Where* is the volume with the errata?" Like *I* was the one who had absconded with it. "Did he sell it? And if he did, why substitute it with this, this *fake*?" Well, hardly a fake, I thought. I was fairly sure that what we were looking at was the very nice first edition that Rachel Featherstonhaugh had been searching for at the Strand. The first edition *without* the misprint.

"It's complicated, Graham," I said carefully, not wanting to reveal anything that might compromise Sebastian's investigation. "But I think someone else might have substituted this edition for the more valuable one and then sold the first one on."

"That's appalling," Graham said, clearly, well, appalled. "Who would do such a thing?"

"That's up to the police to find out," I said. "I'm in touch with them on another matter, but I'll let them know about this. In the meantime, do you think you could quietly ask around, see if there's been any talk about a first edition *with* the misprint coming on the market?"

"Of course," Graham agreed. "Though, since the stolen volume would have to be sold without provenance, the talk will necessarily be in whispers. But I shall do my best."

"I know you will, Graham," I said. I got up to leave, then stopped. "What about Howard's Harry Potter, the one with the misprint in the shopping list?"

"That one I've checked," Graham said. "It is a fine first edition, first printing. But it is *not* one with the misprint."

"Which is odd," I said. "Because I restored the spine ends on Howard's copy when he first got it, and the book I worked on *was* one with the misprint."

Graham stared at me. "What on earth is going on here?"

It was a good question. I tried to clarify my thoughts about Rachel's possible book scam. How simple it would have been for her to buy the externally identical first edition of the Hemingway without the errata, expensive as it was, and switch it with the much more valuable edition. A $6,000 investment with a $72,000 payoff was a pretty sweet deal.

And there were definitely book collectors out there who would find it easy to look the other way in terms of provenance when a rare prize like the Hemingway with the three p's came along. Or the Harry Potter with the two wands on the shopping list. Or, probably, any number of other books in Howard's collection.

If Rachel knew nothing about Howard's impending bankruptcy, she could have been planning to systematically plunder his shelves like that for months, even years, swapping in visually identical volumes for the pricier editions. Clearly she'd already pulled off her little scam with the Potter. Howard would never have noticed. For him it was all about the chase, not the book. Once a prize was safely ensconced in the glass-fronted bookcase housing his collection, he simply turned to the next prize. Rachel would have thought she was onto a gold mine.

If she didn't know about his bankruptcy.

"Graham, you mentioned at Howard's memorial service that he had engaged you for a confidential sale of his collection," I said. "Did you tell Howard's assistant, Rachel, or *anyone else* about that at the time?"

Graham looked, if it was possible, even more shocked than

before. "Certainly not," he said. "If, as I suspected, Mr. Calhoun was in financial difficulties, to let that be known would be to significantly reduce our negotiating power with potential buyers."

"I never really thought you had," I assured him. "I just needed to confirm it."

Graham looked somewhat mollified, but no less bewildered by all he'd just learned.

"Graham," I added, "believe me when I say you have my sincere apologies for bringing you this unhappy news." Good lord, it was catching. I was beginning to sound positively Dickensian myself.

I SPENT MOST OF THE BUS RIDE HOME TRYING TO UNDERSTAND the implications of said unhappy news. Sebastian was looking for a possible motive for Sailor's murder. Was this it? Had Sailor somehow found out about Rachel's swindle and confronted her? Sailor definitely had that cat-playing-with-a-mouse tendency. Would Rachel kill to protect her secret? Had Rachel killed her tormentor?

Nineteen

◇◇◇◇◇◇◇◇◇◇◇◇◇

"Where do one's fears come from? Where do they shape
themselves? Where do they hide before coming out into the open?"
—Jerry Burton, *The Moving Finger*

IT WAS JUST CLOSING TIME WHEN I GOT BACK TO THE LIBRARY.
And once again Adrian was waiting impatiently for me in the hallway, where a gaggle of crime fiction buffs were making their very
slow way out the door as they argued about the critically important
question of whether Nero Wolfe ever actually physically left his
townhouse at 922 West 35th Street.

"Where have you been?" Adrian demanded as he pulled me
into the relative quiet of the now-empty main reading room.

"I was at the Atheneum," I said. "Where I *told* you I was going."

"Oh, right," he said. "Did you find the eleventh Cadfael?"

For a quick moment, I was dismayed. I'd completely forgotten
to look for the Cadfael. Then I remembered my real mission. "No,
I did not find the Cadfael, Adrian. I did not even look for the
Cadfael. But I did get the dirt on that Hemingway from Graham."

"Well, save it for the hot detective. He's in the Hammett
Room."

I wasn't expecting *that*. Not in a million years.

"Sebastian Mendez-Cruz is in the Dashiell Hammett Room?"

"His choice," Adrian said. "It appears he's a fan." He allowed himself a smile. "And it seemed an appropriate venue for our very own Sam Spade."

"As I recall, Hammett describes Spade as looking like a 'blond Satan.'" *Not a dark angel*, I didn't add.

"And a Bacardi drinker," Adrian said, "which, it appears, our hot detective is not. Though he was perfectly willing to accept a few fingers of Hammett's scotch while he waited—and continues to wait—for you."

Oh lord, I'd been so happy playing Hammett trivia that I'd kept the hot detective waiting.

I turned and dashed up the stairs to the second floor, then paused for a few not-at-all-calming breaths before opening the heavy mahogany door to the Hammett Room.

I had to admit, Sebastian looked remarkably right sitting there in the library's reproduction of Hammett's padded rocker sipping a glass of scotch and doing exactly nothing.

When I'm nervous, I tend to forget the social niceties. "What are you doing?" I demanded.

"Thinking," he said. "Care to join me?"

He raised his glass in invitation and tilted his head a bit toward the bottle of scotch next to him on a twin of the table on which Hammett most likely wrote *The Maltese Falcon*. I realized he might be just a little, well, tipsy. It was kind of cute.

"Not for me, thanks," I said. I needed my wits about me.

I settled myself on the couch facing him and waited. Yes, I had news for him, but he wouldn't be here if he didn't have news for me.

"Why the alarm clock?" he asked.

I looked at him blankly. He gestured at the table with its Remington typewriter and alarm clock perched on a copy of Duke's *Celebrated Criminal Cases of America.*

"Why an alarm clock on a desk?"

"Oh," I said, finally catching up. "This room is a replica of the studio apartment where Hammett lived in San Francisco. In the original there was a Murphy bed that folded down from the wall next to the writing table. We don't have the bed here." *Obviously.* "The alarm clock was for, well, waking up." *Brilliantly explicated, Tory.*

Sebastian nodded. "Good to know. I don't have much info on the guy even though I've read everything he's ever written."

I blinked at him. "Everything?"

"Not the short stories," he admitted. "But the novels, yeah."

"Somehow you don't seem the Sam Spade type," I said.

"We all have our demons," he said quietly. "Some of us hide them better than others."

I had no idea how to respond to that. Fortunately, he didn't give me a chance.

"I wanted to talk to you about that sieve idea of yours," he said, suddenly all sober. Well, it had been fun while it lasted.

"Okay," I said. My news could wait.

"We searched Rachel's place for a strainer and it's a no go."

I wasn't ready to give up so easily. "She could have tossed it."

"She could have. But I doubt she and Calhoun were *both* cooking up some arsenic in their kitchens."

It took me a minute. "You're saying you found a sieve with traces of arsenic in *Howard's* kitchen?"

Sebastian nodded. "Just like you said, there were a few microscopic bits of cloth left in the strainer. And, yeah, they tested positive for arsenic. It looks like Calhoun was the one making poison soup for Sailor's birthday tequila, not Rachel."

For a moment I was confused. "And in between him poisoning the bottle and Rachel sending it off to Sailor, somebody killed him? Why? Wasn't he just on the wrong subway platform at the wrong time?"

"Well, yes," Sebastian admitted, "that's the likeliest scenario. There's nothing so far to suggest any connection between the two events. As far as we know, nobody involved in all this had it in for him or benefited from his death."

"How about the cousin?" I suggested. "She was his only living family. She didn't know she wouldn't benefit from his death. And she definitely had expectations. Maybe she got tired of waiting for her imagined inheritance."

He shook his head. "First of all, if that was the case, then, like I said, there's no connection to Sailor's murder."

I had to admit, the man had a point.

"And second," he added, not without a little self-satisfaction, "the cousin's got a cast-iron alibi for the time of Calhoun's death."

I sighed. "Do tell."

"She was sitting in a dentist's chair having a rear molar pulled."

"Ah," I said, grinning in spite of myself. "That does make complicity in Howard's demise rather unlikely."

"Rather," Sebastian said with an answering—and totally disarming—grin in return.

"So," I said, recalling myself back to the problem at hand, "if the choice is between Howard and Rachel as the one who made the arsenic reduction, my money's still on Rachel."

"And why is that?"

"Look," I said, "you asked us for any information that might give you a window into what happened. Well, I can tell you that Rachel had full access to Howard's apartment. Most days when he was off doing whatever it was Howard did, she was there alone."

"That's good to know," Sebastian acknowledged. "But it's not enough. Everything points to Calhoun being Sailor Savoie's killer."

It was interesting, I thought, that Detective Mendez-Clark no longer referred politely to his now-primary suspect as Mr. Calhoun or even Howard Calhoun. Just Calhoun.

"The poison was made in his apartment. The bottle was sent at his instruction. The card was sent at his instruction."

"Howard would never kill Sailor," I protested. "He was about to sign her as a client."

Rather than argue the point, the detective just said mildly, "Well, that's as may be but there's no motive for Rachel to kill Sailor, either. Unless you subscribe to Mairead's Guilty Secret theory."

"But that's just it!" I said, leaning forward. "I do. I mean, there is one. A guilty secret, that is. Not a theory. A real guilty secret."

Are you never going to be able to talk to this man in complete sentences, Tory?

"You're saying Rachel was hiding something? Something that she might kill to cover up?"

I nodded madly. "Exactly! I think that Rachel has been systematically replacing very valuable rare books in Howard's collection with much less valuable copies and then selling the rare volumes to unscrupulous collectors." There. If that wasn't a full sentence, then I didn't know what was.

I proceeded to fill him in on everything I'd learned from Graham and what I knew myself about Howard's collection.

"So," I concluded triumphantly, "if Sailor somehow found out about Rachel's little gig and threatened to expose her, Rachel absolutely had a motive to kill her. She hated Sailor anyway because she thought she'd tried to kill Bertram. It's literally a double motive. All we have to do is prove that Rachel was doing that book switch. And Graham's looking into that."

Sebastian stood and, taking one last swig of his scotch, said, "Tory Van Dyne, you are amazing. I could kiss you."

Which, of course, he did not. It was just a figure of speech. At least, I assumed it was just a figure of speech. Because before he could make good on it (if indeed he'd really wished to make good on it), Nic poked her beautiful head into the Dashiell Hammett Room and said brightly, "Oh, yay, you're here, Seb." *Seb.* "You ready to go?"

Mendez-Cruz, as I was suddenly determined to call him, had the good grace to look just a little bit guilty. Even if it's just a figure of speech, you don't talk about kissing one woman while you're waiting for another one to show up. Because, I now realized, the hot detective hadn't really been waiting for me. The hot detective had been talking to me while he waited for my cousin. My hot cousin.

"Nic!" he said, all flustered. "Um, sure. Where are we going?"

"Shopping," she said, as if it should have been obvious. "I called the precinct and some guy there said you were here."

So he *hadn't* been waiting for Nic. He'd come to talk to *me*. So that felt good. Not that it lasted.

"I mean," Nic continued, "if you're taking me to the Library Lions Gala on Saturday, you can't wear some crappy old suit." Not one to mince words, our Nic. "I take it you don't have a tux?"

Sebastian looked at her as if she'd asked him if he owned a Maserati. "Uh, no. I do not have a tux."

"Wait a minute," I said to him, trying to catch up. "You're taking Nic to the library gala?"

Before he could respond, Nic said, "Well, now that Howard's, um, passed and I don't have our trip to the Hamptons for that film festival as my excuse not to go, Mummy is insisting I have to show and no way am I going to sit there at that dinner with some empty plate next to me." Heaven forfend that Nic should be seen at any event on her own. "So Seb suggested he go with me. That way I get an escort and Seb can do his detective thing and look for suspects in Sailor's murder."

Yup, good idea. In between awards, Seb *can personally interrogate all 450 of the gala's attendees. Especially the Pulitzer Prize winners.*

Nic turned back to the man who, apparently, was going to be her date this Saturday. "Well, it's a shame you don't have a tux," she said. "It's too late to get one ordered, fitted and tailored."

She looked Sebastian over the way a horse breeder eyes up a promising stallion. He looked at her like a deer caught in the headlights.

"Which is why I have a plan B," she said. "I'll talk to Chase Pomeroy. You're about his height and build, and I happen to know for a fact that he got a new tux for every one of his weddings." *Chase Pomeroy has been married three times in his forty-two years. He is the poster child for serial monogamy.* "I'll borrow one of his for you and ask Daddy's tailor to make any little last-minute tweaks you need. We can pick up a tux shirt today at Bergdorf's. How about dress shoes?"

"Dress shoes?" Sebastian asked weakly.

"Yes," Nic said with a sigh. "You know, black patent oxfords, maybe black velvet loafers? Something like that, you know, that goes with black tie?"

Sebastian just stared at her. Clearly the concept of black velvet loafers had floored him completely.

"Well, you can't borrow someone else's shoes," Nic said. "That's just gross. C'mon, let's go buy you some."

And so saying, she took *Seb*'s arm and led him from the room.

"AND *THAT'S* HOW IT'S DONE."

Adrian had stuck his head into the Hammett Room mere

seconds after Nic and Sebastian (*Seb*) left for their shopping spree, which made me suspect that he'd been listening at the door and then ducked into the Golden Age Room when the happy couple came out into the hall.

I sighed. I was suddenly very tired. "You know what's *not* done, Adrian, at least in some circles? Listening at keyholes."

Adrian dismissed my scruples with an eye roll. "So you're really going to just let your cousin dress that gorgeous man up like a monkey so she can have a date for some society bash?"

"As you well know, Adrian, it's not just 'some' society bash," I countered. "*And* her mother's on the committee. *And* it's too late to get one of her pals to step in. The gala's this Saturday, and nobody's free on a Saturday night with less than two weeks' notice." By which I meant, nobody in Nic's crowd. Pretty much anyone in my crowd, if I'd had one, would definitely be free. "And again I repeat, it's not polite to listen at doors."

Adrian came into the room, made free with the scotch in a clean glass, and sat himself down in the rocker so recently vacated by a man who may or may not have been preparing to kiss me.

"Well, I listened at the door for *you*," he said. "Somebody has to protect your interests."

"And how do you intend to protect my interests, Mr. Gooding?"

"By making sure you go to the gala, too."

"Oh no no no no no," I gabbled. "I'm not going to the gala. I never go. I can't go."

Adrian's brown eyes softened. "You can, Tory," he said gently. "It's been almost eight years. And you went to Howard's memorial service. You were fine. You told me so yourself."

"But I can't go to the Lions," I said. "There will be hundreds of people there."

"All sipping cocktails in that ginormous Astor Hall before

wandering up to the even more ginormous main reading room to sit on little gilt chairs eating lobster tail while listening to the celebrity MC welcome the night's luminaries, literary and otherwise," Adrian said. "C'mon, Tory, it's not the same. Not the same at all."

Adrian was right. I knew Adrian was right. It wouldn't be the same. Not the same at all.

Ginormous is a pretty accurate description of Astor Hall, the grand foyer of one of the grandest buildings in New York City, the main branch of the New York Public Library. It stretches the whole of the library's two-city-block length, and its marble arches climb a full thirty-four feet to its vaulted ceiling. So plenty of room to breathe there, even with more than four hundred people sipping cocktails. The main reading room, where the dinner would be held, is even more impressive, at double the size of Astor Hall and with a ceiling soaring to more than fifty feet—nearly as large as the Main Concourse at Grand Central Terminal.

So, not the same. Not the same at all.

But, the screamy voice that had lived in my head for the past seven years said, *it might be.*

And for the first time another voice answered it. *Tory Van Dyne,* the other voice said calmly, *you are amazing.*

But, the screamy voice reminded me, *the doctors thought you were amazing, too.* Because I had survived when others had not.

IT WAS ONE OF THOSE HORRIFYING STORIES YOU READ ABOUT in the paper, but you know couldn't possibly happen to you. But you're wrong.

Seven years ago, only days after I'd received my master's degree from NYU's Conservation Center, I'd allowed myself to be persuaded by my bubbly roommate, Shawna, who had just completed her own master's in social work, to celebrate our freedom from academia with a visit to a very dark, cramped and crowded dance club. I am a truly terrible dancer, but for a while there I was actually having fun. I remember I was happily, if awkwardly, bopping to Katy Perry's "This Is How We Do" when it happened. Later, we learned that some idiot had lit a string of firecrackers. What I and everybody else in the club thought we heard were gunshots.

In the resulting stampede for the one ground-floor fire exit, two of the club's young patrons died. A dozen more, including me, were injured in the crush and taken to the hospital. The doctors said I was "one of the lucky ones." When I'd fallen, I'd instinctively curled myself into a protective ball. I'd suffered three broken ribs, but I could breathe. My roommate, Shawna, the doctors told me when they thought I could bear it, had not been one of the lucky ones.

I did not consider myself lucky. Yes, I had survived. Yes, I was still alive. But I lived in a fog of fear and grief and guilt. I lived with terrible nightmares, which I somehow thought I deserved. Why had I survived? The girl whose grand plan was to hide herself away in a basement laboratory with a bunch of old books? Why not brilliant, funny Shawna, who was going to devote her life to helping others?

And as if the guilt weren't punishment enough, whenever I imagined going out into the world again, a world full of crowds, of life spiraling to death in an instant, I felt myself backing away. I didn't deserve life. And I was terrified of it.

Six weeks later, on the day I was discharged from the hospital, I was met by Grandmother and Uncle Rupert's driver, Norman, husband to the redoubtable Mrs. Johnson. Tall and solidly built but quiet and unassuming, Norman had always been a reassuring presence in the lives of his "young ladies," as he invariably referred to Nic and me.

As the nurse led me, hollow-eyed and fragile, out of the hospital and I saw him wearing his regulation navy blue suit and standing by the open car door, his mere presence was a comfort. In a world that could change in an instant, some things remained unchanged.

Norman took one look at me and stepped forward to guide me gently into the rear seat of the car, where Grandmother was waiting for me. After a quick, no-nonsense peck on the cheek, she instructed Norman to take us not to the family pile but to Washington Square North.

Whatever. I didn't care. When Grandmother led me up to the top two floors she'd had renovated into a separate apartment for me while I "convalesced," I didn't care. For a long time, for weeks and weeks, I didn't care about anything. Out of politeness, I ate the delicacies that Grandmother had delivered from Zabar's, but I barely tasted them. I thanked her politely for the books she picked out for me at the Mysterious Bookshop (billed as The World's Oldest & Greatest Mystery Fiction Specialty Store) but they sat, unopened, on my bedside table. The days passed one after another, unchanging. Until the day Abraham Plum decided that enough was enough.

Dragging his aged bones, as he put it, out of his basement lair and up the three flights of stairs to what Grandmother was pleased to call my "flat," Abe knocked on my door and, when I opened it in my bathrobe and slippers, said gruffly, "Go get dressed. We have work to do."

And so I got dressed. And I did my work. After that, I got up every day and I got dressed every day and I did my work every day.

When Grandmother had moved me bodily into her house, I'd been dimly aware that she'd managed to commandeer a complete refit of the third and top floors of the house in a mere six weeks, but I was blind to this labor of love for a shamefully long time. And then one spring day, not long after Abe had taken me in hand, I woke in my cozy attic bedroom luminous with skylights and was struck by Grandmother's instinct for creating a space that was both a sanctuary and a reminder of the possibility of joy. I'd then gone down to the third floor and saw with new eyes the whitewashed open living/kitchen space and the French doors leading to the narrow wrought iron balcony overlooking the park across the quiet street below. For the first time in months, my heart lifted.

So life got better. Bit by bit. Sometimes, though, in the closer confines of our basement lab, I'd have one of my panic attacks and Abe would sit me down, saying very little except an occasional Zen-like "This too shall pass." Which was somehow enormously comforting. Finally, at Abe's insistence, I found Dr. Cynthia. Though the fear of crowded spaces persisted, gradually the nightmares and panic attacks grew less frequent. Life had color and interest again.

Grandmother had saved me. Abe had saved me.

And now maybe, just maybe, Adrian—Adrian, who was insisting I go to the Library Lions Gala—was saving me. I smiled at him. "But, Adrian," I said, "I can't go to the gala. I have nothing to wear."

This was my feeble attempt at a joke. Going to the gala would present a number of challenges, but the least of them was having nothing to wear. Quite the opposite. Both my grandmother and her mother before her had been fashion mad. And both had had the wherewithal to indulge their passion. I had inherited their love of beautiful clothes, but sadly lacked the wherewithal to indulge it. So I suppose I shouldn't have been surprised when I found that after her death Grandmother left me a carefully curated selection of their favorite pieces spanning half a century of vintage couture. It was her final gift to me.

That afternoon, Adrian and I spent at least an hour rifling through the finery I'd inherited. In the end, the choice came down to two. One was an Elizabeth Hawes "Styx" gown, a column of iridescent blue taffeta presented by the American designer in Paris in 1931 and immediately snapped up by Great-Grandmother Victoria. The Styx had always been a favorite of hers. (Second only to her 1947 Dior "New Look" Chérie dinner dress with its impossibly narrow waist and a skirt so voluminous that when, at her request, she was buried in it, an extra-wide casket was ordered to accommodate it.) My other choice for the evening was a 1959 Jacques Heim deep pink ballerina-skirted evening dress that had formed part of the designer's famed Cecil Beaton Collection, a gown my grandmother had worn to that year's April in Paris Ball at the Waldorf. Where she'd danced with then-senator John F. Kennedy, whom she'd pronounced "charming."

I ended up going for the Styx. Not only because of its truly sexy halter neckline atop a waterfall of oceanic blue and green silk, but because Elizabeth Hawes was a fashion rebel who thought the average American woman actually deserved handsome, well-made clothes and had once written a wonderful book entitled *Fashion Is Spinach*. A dress made by this redoubtable woman, I thought, would be my armor against whatever lay ahead.

Twenty

◇◇◇◇◇◇◇◇◇◇◇◇

"By Jove, Poirot," I exclaimed, "did you see that young goddess?"
—Arthur Hastings, *The Murder on the*
Links

AND FINALLY, TERRIFYINGLY, THE NIGHT OF THE GALA ARRIVED.

Adrian and I looked solemnly at the woman in the mirror.

"Dahling," he said, "you look mahvelous."

"Billy Crystal said it better," I commented, dodging the compliment. Grandmother had instructed me more than once that the only proper response to a compliment is a simple thank-you, but I had never gotten the hang of it. "And I gotta say," I added, "I'm not feeling so mahvelous."

Adrian gave me a little twirl so that the gown floated out around me in a silken billow and allowed a glimpse of my very beautiful, very high Jimmy Choo heels before I wobbled and he had to right me. It had been a long time since I'd worn heels like that. Almost impossible to walk in but also almost impossible to resist.

"Well, to further quote Mr. Crystal," Adrian said, "'Don't be a schnook. It's not how you *feel* but how you *look*.'"

He was trying to keep things light, bless his heart. And a gay

Black librarian channeling Billy Crystal channeling a Spanish playboy would normally have had me rolling on the floor. But tonight was the big night. And not only was I not feeling particularly mahvelous, I was, in fact, almost frozen with dread. Even an emergency session with Dr. Cynthia had not fully prepared me for what I knew—or thought I knew—lay ahead.

Nic, on finding out my plans from Aunt Bunny (who had no trouble adding me to what she seemed to view as *her* guest list), had happily suggested that I "tag along" with her and Seb. *Seb.* I declined her kind offer—and it was a kind offer, I knew—as gently as possible. If I had to do this, I would rather do it solo.

Dr. Cynthia had disagreed with that decision, encouraging me to "accept the support system of others." What she didn't know—because I had somehow neglected to tell her—was that this particular support system consisted of a cousin I loved on the arm of a man I, let's just say, liked way more than I should.

So, no, I wasn't feeling particularly mahvelous.

"Now, now," Adrian said, seeing the clouds gathering. "Let's just tidy up that hair a bit and go down to the Christie Room for a little liquid courage."

The woman in the mirror smiled wanly, smoothed her hair—which had seen the ministrations of a professional that morning and did indeed look mahvelous—and took a deep calming breath. *Some day that would work.* I picked up my evening bag and wrap—a hooded cape by Givenchy in pale blue silk virtually identical to the one worn by Audrey Hepburn in *Sabrina*—and turned to Adrian. "Okay," I said. "Let's go hit the Christie Room."

I SHOULD HAVE KNOWN SHE'D BE THERE. EVEN IF IT WASN'T A Monday.

Just seeing her in her usual armchair, gaudy embroidery in hand, worked better than a hundred deep calming breaths. *This* was the support system I needed. A support system dressed in a boxy red wool suit and, on her grey curls, a rather alarming mink disc that I took to be a hat. I gave Adrian a silent *Was this your do-ing?* look, but he shook his head. He was as clueless as I.

"Miss Van Dyne," Mrs. Christie said, with a smile that lit her face, "what a stunning gown. And how lovely you yourself look. You are positively glowing."

"I wish you would call me Tory," I said, meaning it but also once again deftly dodging a compliment. Nonetheless, I was pleased. I had spent what felt like hours struggling to bring my makeup up to the standard set by the professional updo. Finally, I decided to channel Nic and—amazingly—found that blush, blush and more blush did wonders for one's cheekbones and three layers of mascara were, indeed, eyelash magic.

"Tory it is," Mrs. Christie said, nodding graciously. She turned to Adrian, dressed impeccably in a slim black suit, white shirt and brilliant scarlet tie. "And you, Mr. Gooding, are a worthy escort to this beautiful young lady."

"Thank you," Adrian said easily, "but I'm afraid I have another engagement." Adrian was on his way to the all-important third date with the Man You Don't Keep Waiting, which is why he looked almost as beautiful as I did. "Tory is flying solo tonight."

"I'm going to a fund-raising gala for the New York Public Library," I sort of explained. "My aunt is the chair of the committee."

"I see," Mrs. Christie said. "And will that nice Detective Mendez-Cruz also be at this gathering?"

What was she, psychic?

"Well, in a way," I hedged. "He will be there, but with Nic, of course."

"I see no 'of course' about it," Mrs. Christie said pointedly.

Adrian murmured a quiet "Hear, hear," and I glared at him.

"Can I get anyone a cocktail?" he deflected smoothly.

All voted aye, and the moment passed.

While Adrian did the honors ("Campari and soda tonight, I think. One doesn't want to show up snookered in front of the likes of Zadie Smith or, in my case, Mr. Gorgeous."), I took the opportunity to catch Mrs. Christie up on my Hammett Room conversation with Detective Mendez-Cruz (as I insisted on calling him, as if to deny any personal involvement) as well as what I'd discovered about Rachel's presumed book scam.

"Very well done, Tory, my dear," she said. "You are a most remarkable sleuth."

That remark did me more good than any number of Campari and sodas.

"All thanks to Adrian," I said. "He was the one who recognized Rachel as the woman he saw at the Strand and had the wit to wonder about her book choice."

Adrian blew me a kiss and then, checking what he liked to call his "chronoscope" and we mere mortals call a "watch," threw down what remained of his drink and made his goodbyes, first to Mrs. Christie and then to me.

As he air-kissed my cheek, he whispered in my ear, "You can do this."

The door shut behind him, and Mrs. Christie did one of those conversational swerves that always knocked me a little off-balance. "Surely it was not necessary for Detective Mendez-Cruz to come to the house the other day to talk to you about his investigations," she pointed out. "A telephone call would have sufficed."

"Well, he lives and works close by," I said, "and, like Nic said, I'm always here."

"But tonight you will not be here," Mrs. Christie pointed out mildly. "Tonight you will be at a gala affair. Which Detective Mendez-Cruz will also be attending."

"Detective Mendez-Cruz is not the reason I'm going," I said, maybe a tad defensively.

"Of course not," Mrs. Christie said. "You have your own reasons." Her eyes softened. "Important personal ones, I think?"

And so I told her.

I told her everything, including terrible details I had never revealed to anyone, not even Dr. Cynthia. I don't know why I told her. There was something about the way she almost never looked directly at me, just sat quietly working on her embroidery, occasionally murmuring an "I see" or "How very dreadful for you."

"And so," I concluded lamely, "I feel, well, I mean, Adrian feels, and now I think *I* actually feel, like I can do this. He's right, seven years is a long time. And bit by bit, I've been able to go to a restaurant or a book fair or even, lately, a memorial service. But I swear I couldn't have done what I'm trying to do tonight until now. Dr. Cynthia thinks I need a support system, but I'm weird, I feel like I have to do it alone, or mostly alone, if you know what I mean . . ."

I was babbling, but Mrs. Christie seemed to be following me. "I do know, my dear Tory," she said at last, looking up from a particularly violently colored rose. "There are those lucky people who gain confidence in themselves from the assurances of their friends and loved ones. And then there are those of us who can only find that confidence by reaching deep within ourselves. It is much the harder path, and difficult for others to comprehend, but it can be done."

I was stunned. Here was someone who understood that for some of us, healing happens slowly and privately. We, the quiet, interior ones, know that we can't rejoin the world until we are almost whole once more. With all the best intentions in the world, our friends try to help and then are hurt when we turn them aside.

As if she'd read my mind, Mrs. Christie added, "Nonetheless, it is wise to allow our friends to walk with us at least partly down that path. Friendship is a rare and valuable gift."

As she had just proved by example.

I stood and draped the silk cape around my shoulders. Norman would be waiting for me outside by now with Uncle Rupert's car, sent by Aunt Bunny to make sure I had no excuse not to make it to the gala.

"Thank you, Mrs. Christie," I said, "Nic is right. You are *the best.*"

YOU'D THINK AFTER THAT LITTLE PEP TALK, I'D GO SWEEPING UP the massive stone steps of the main branch all Kate Hepburn–esque and self-confident. But you'd be wrong. Norman, who of course knew my history, must have noticed my hesitancy. After he handed me out of the car, he said quietly, "I'll be right here out front, miss, should you wish to leave." And then he stood for a moment, still holding the door open as if to give me an immediate escape route if I needed one. And honestly, I think I would have climbed right back in if it hadn't been for Patience and Fortitude.

Patience and Fortitude are the massive crouching marble lions that have welcomed visitors to the New York Public Library from their pedestals in front of their majestic home on Fifth Avenue and 42nd Street ever since the main branch was dedicated more than a hundred years ago. It would be hard to find a New Yorker who doesn't claim a personal affection for them. But as a child, their names had been a mystery to me. Who needed patience and fortitude to read a book? But tonight was different. Tonight the lions seemed to whisper to me as I looked up at them, trying to decide if I could really do this.

"Patience," said one. "Fortitude," said the other.

Tonight the names made sense.

I turned back to Norman, still standing by the open car door. "Thank you, Norman," I said. "I think I can take it from here."

When the ancient Romans built their enormous public baths, they employed techniques to amplify a sense of space, no matter how crowded the rooms might be. And Roman baths were *crowded*. So the vast rooms had very high vaulted ceilings that made the space seem to extend indefinitely. The halls, no matter how crowded, were somehow airy. This approach was used to very good effect in later great public buildings in Europe and America, including the main branch of the New York Public Library. For which I will be forever grateful. Because as I walked in through the library's massive front doors, Astor Hall was packed.

The space was teeming with men and women in their finest regalia, clutching glasses of warm champagne and chatting to each other at the tops of their lungs. I tried to breathe deeply. That didn't work. I tried looking up at the soaring columns and great domed ceiling. That worked a little, but not enough. I almost turned back and probably would have if a volunteer greeter-cum-coat-check-girl hadn't put out a hand to my panicky self and said, "Why don't I take your lovely wrap, ma'am?"

Old habits die hard. Staff politely instruct you, and you do as they suggest. Almost automatically, I was saying "Thank you" and untying the blue ribbons at my neck and handing over the cape. The next few minutes were spent scrabbling in my clutch to find a tip to give my rescuer and wishing desperately that one of the milling waitstaff would bring me a lovely glass of warm champagne.

"Patience and fortitude," I murmured to myself.

"You know," a low, familiar voice said behind me, "Mayor Fiorello La Guardia gave them those names in the 1930s after the qualities he believed New Yorkers most needed to get through the Great Depression."

I turned to face whatever long-unseen friend had found me in the crowd. It was not a long-unseen friend. It was Detective Sebastian Mendez-Cruz. But Detective Sebastian Mendez-Cruz as I had never seen him before. He was resplendent. If this was what happened when Nic dressed a man like a monkey, then have at it, Nic. He looked like James Bond, as if he'd been born wearing a perfectly tailored tux and holding a dry martini—or in this case a glass of champagne—in his hand. In lieu of black velvet loafers, he'd opted for simple black dress shoes. Thank god.

I stared at him. He stared at me.

"You look like a goddess."

What do you say when you are literally breathless and witless after James Bond calls you a goddess?

"Thank you," I said. *There, Tory. Was that so hard?*

Then we stared at each other a little longer.

I don't know where the conversation would have gone at that point ("And you look like a god"?) if we hadn't been firmly hijacked by Brooke Sinclair, swathed in acres of black tulle and enveloped by a cloud of Chanel No. 5.

"Darling Tory," she exclaimed in ringing blue-blood tones as she swept in. "How absolutely wonderful to see you here. And looking so chic." She turned toward Sebastian, who, I realized, had been her quarry all along. "Don't you agree, Mr. um . . ."

As if she didn't know. Sebastian had been at Howard's memorial service, and I was sure that Brooke had made it her business to find out who the stranger in the untidy brown suit was. I was

equally sure she had decided then and there that it would be un-
seemly to acknowledge this, this *policeman*, at her celebration of
Howard's life. It would have come a little too close to recognizing
the gritty reality of Howard's death. But this polished man in the
smashing tuxedo? He was definitely worth recognizing.

I obligingly chimed in. "Brooke, this is Sebastian Mendez-
Cruz. Sebastian, Brooke Sinclair."

"Ah, yes, *Detective* Mendez-Cruz, am I right?" Brooke said,
nodding graciously.

"Yes, ma'am," Sebastian said.

"Brooke, please."

Sebastian merely smiled politely.

The conversation seemed to have come to a standstill, and I was
wondering how best to extricate Sebastian and myself when
Brooke was engulfed by the same little group of friends who had,
let's say, supported her at Howard's memorial service.

"Brooke, darling, the girls and I are having just the teeniest
little argument," the woman I remembered as Candice said. "There
is talk that your Howard actually *proposed* to you after you came
back from India. And that you refused his offer."

Wait, what? Howard had *proposed* to Brooke Sinclair?

"Well, yes, Candice," Brooke admitted modestly. "It's true, the
dear man did propose. But I felt that, for his sake, I couldn't accept."

Two of the ladies standing next to Brooke sniggered quietly
behind their hands in a most unladylike manner at that, but Brooke
was oblivious. "You see, there was the difference in our, shall we
say, financial circumstances. As my companion, Howard was in-
dependent. His money was his own, mine was my own. But as my
husband? Well, he would have been nothing more than a kept
man. I simply could not do that to him."

Wow, I thought, *as a justification for keeping a firm hand on your bankbook in the face of a gold digger, that was pretty darn good.*

"Howard understood this," Brooke added. "Howard was a giver, not a taker."

She broke off to bury her sorrow in her champagne glass while her audience waited, enthralled by her performance.

"At least *I* always had Howard's best interest at heart," she said when she came up for air. "Not like *some* I could name."

She didn't have to name them. I turned to follow the eye daggers she was throwing over my shoulder at none other than cousin Nic, bearing down on me, all breathless and beautiful.

"Tory! You made it!" she squealed, enveloping me in a Nic hug so enthusiastic I feared for my updo. "I told Seb to keep an eye out for you!" Ah, so he hadn't been looking for me on his own account, but under orders from Nic. Of course.

"Are you okay?" she then whispered in my ear.

Was I okay? I considered the question. I thought maybe I was. Certainly, for that brief moment in time with Sebastian, my mind had been on other, better things than the fact that I was in an enclosed space with literally hundreds of other people, all of whom could, at a moment's notice, stampede screaming toward nonexistent exits.

I waited for the panic to set in. I was nervous, yes. My heart was pounding, yes. But, with my cousin beside me, I could breathe. I didn't want to sink to my knees and weep. I was, in fact, okay. Turns out, Dr. Cynthia and Mrs. Christie were right. I could do this, but not alone. I needed, and needed to accept, the support of the people who cared about me.

I smiled at my cousin. "Thanks," I said. "I'm fine."

"Great! I knew you would be," Nic said happily, and proceeded to hold me away with both hands on my shoulders, the better to review my dress.

"You wore the Styx!" she exclaimed with delight. "It's perfect for you! You're, like, the sexiest girl here!" This from a woman wearing gold stiletto sandals and a jet-black Christian Siriano strapless gown slit up one side almost to the top of her hip.

I tried to channel Grandmother. "Thank you," I said. I was getting good at this.

Nic was suddenly aware of Brooke standing next to us, listening intently.

"Brooke!" she said. "Wow. I didn't expect you here after, well, after Howard . . ."

"One does what one must," Brooke said, all noble and all. "I couldn't let your mother or the committee down. They so rely on me."

"Of course they do," Nic lied. "It was good of you to come."

Lady Bountiful smiled graciously and wandered away.

I couldn't wait to tell Nic my gossip. I hardly ever had any gossip. "Guess what? Turns out, Howard proposed to Brooke after they got back from India, and she said no."

But Nic, it appeared, had lost interest. She had turned slightly to smile, starry-eyed, across the crowd at a very well-polished forty-something fellow, in a blue velvet tux that Adrian would have killed for, who was smiling right back at her.

"Oh my god, you guys," she said, turning back to Sebastian and me. "I forgot to tell you who I met. You'll never guess who that is." She did not wait for us to guess. "Grant Neuman!"

Mendez-Cruz looked at her blankly.

"The producer of that movie Nic is hoping for a part in," I explained. "Surely she's mentioned it once or twice."

"Ah, yes," he said. "I think I did hear something about that."

And then he winked at me. Well, not a wink so much as a subtle eyelid flutter, but I knew what it was and, pathetically, my heart lifted again.

"C'mon," Nic said, grabbing each of us by the arm and towing us right out into the middle of the glittering throng. I didn't even have time to prepare myself. Which was probably a good thing, because it meant I wasn't all crazy eyes by the time she managed to steer us into the orbit of Grant Neuman himself.

Twenty-One

◇◇◇◇◇◇◇◇◇◇◇◇◇◇◇◇◇◇◇◇

"The different parts came together—and made a pattern."
—Miss Jane Marple, *A Murder Is*
Announced

NIC'S CELEBRITY RADAR, I THOUGHT NOT FOR THE FIRST TIME, was a wonder. Somehow in what was probably a half an hour since she'd arrived, she'd managed to find the producer and succeeded in attaching him to her. Not that Grant Neuman, in his navy velvet tux and as blond and buffed and polished as a male model, would be difficult to spot. Nor did he look unhappy to be attached to Nic. Men seldom were.

"Grant," Nic said, "this is my cousin, Tory Van Dyne."

We shook hands and murmured the standard greetings.

"And this," Nic said, pushing her date forward, "is Sebastian Mendez-Cruz. Seb is a real live detective with the NYPD. Seb, this is Grant Neuman. Grant is producing the movie version of *BB*." Nic, too, had learned her social protocol from Grandmother. When introducing two strangers, give them at least one interesting piece of information about each other to encourage easy conversation.

But as it turned out, Nic wasn't actually all that interested in encouraging easy conversation between Grant and Seb. Nic was interested in encouraging easy conversation between Grant and Nic.

"So, Grant," she said, "I asked my friend Seb to come with me tonight, you know, because Howard and I were supposed to be out in the Hamptons but, well, he's not, you know, with us, so I decided to come to the gala instead because I'm a little sad." She took a little sad sip of champagne from her glass.

Grant, to give him credit, didn't go all sentimental in response. "Yeah, that was a rotten thing to happen."

"Anyway," Nic said, bringing the conversation back where it belonged, "for sure Howard would have hounded you about me, Grant, if he was here . . ."

Again Grant surprised me with his straightforwardness. "Yeah, the guy was a terrier, not to say a royal pain in the ass. Wouldn't stop, even after I told him that Mrs. Potts wasn't for you. You're way too, um, young . . ." I was pretty sure he'd been about to say "clueless" but thought better of it. ". . . for that role. You're a very specific type, a great type—wide-eyed, enthusiastic, ditzy but smart, like Reese Witherspoon, you know, in *Legally Blonde*, but not a Mrs.-Potts-the-therapist type. And definitely not a Beast."

None of this was news to Nic, and if it hurt her to hear it all again you wouldn't have known from her understanding nods as Grant talked.

"I told Calhoun that back in September," the producer continued, "as soon as he got back from India."

"Really?" Nic said, puzzled. "Because he didn't tell me until, like, weeks later. I remember because it was the same day he was . . ."

She stopped cold but Grant was oblivious. "Yeah, well, I told him that when I told him that you would have been great as Belle if it weren't for Wren. Because Wren is the next Barbra Streisand, you know?" *Boy, this guy really didn't pull any punches.*

"Oh yes," Nic agreed, recovering nicely. "He did tell me that. And you're right. Wren is amazing."

"And then, of course, he tries to tell me that Wren is a risk given her little nose-candy habit, so I tell him that's not a problem because my plan was always for Sailor to take over as Belle if Wren ended up in rehab or whatever."

"Oh," Nic almost whispered. And that one small quiet word said it all.

She'd never had a chance. First she'd missed out on playing Belle to Wren. A decision she'd understood. And she'd never been in the running for Beast. Which she also understood. Then she'd been nixed as Mrs. Potts, which had clearly hurt. And now to find out that Sailor had been Grant's choice for Belle if Wren was out of the picture—because, as we all knew, Sailor was a Savoie.

My heart ached for my cousin. I looked closely at her to see how she was going to take this news. This is how Nic looked: Nic looked like she needed a drink.

As if she'd read my mind, she plunked her empty champagne glass on the tray of a passing server and asked plaintively, "Could someone get me a *real* drink at the bar? Like, maybe a martini?"

Before Grant could respond, Sebastian jumped in. "I'll get it," he said. "How about you, Tory? Anything I can bring you?"

"Not unless it's your heart," I wanted to say. What I said was, "No thanks, I'm fine."

He nodded and began to wend his way toward the bar at the far end of the hall, now besieged by attendees desperate to avoid another glass of warm champagne. Nic was going to have to wait a long time for that martini.

When I could no longer see Sebastian through the crowd, I turned back to Nic and Grant.

"I'm giving Beast to that girl, Diana," Grant was saying. "The one who understudied all of you in the play."

"She'll be a great Beast," Nic said gamely. "She's a born Goth."

"Exactly," Grant agreed. "So it's all under control. Actually, Wren and I were planning to meet here and quietly start letting people know that, even though we've lost Sailor, we've got it all in hand."

A little alarm went off in my head but was almost immediately drowned out by Nic saying brightly, "Of course you have it all in hand. That's what makes you so good at your job. So tell me, Grant, what else are you working on? Anything for the next Reese Witherspoon?"

I was impressed. The girl was a total professional.

The two of them chattered on, but I wasn't listening. Something was bothering me, something that Grant had said . . .

Were. Had Grant said that he and Wren *were* planning to go to the gala?

"Were?" I said, grabbing Grant's arm. "You said you and Wren *were* planning to come to the gala. Wren's not here?" I couldn't believe Wren had bailed on her widowed mother, let alone her producer.

Grant looked just a little pissed off. "Yeah, well, no. I mean, she's not here. I was just getting into my Uber earlier tonight when she called me. We were going to have a drink at hers before heading over to the main branch. She has a little place nearby, you know?"

I nodded. I'd been to Wren's "little place," a stunning two-bedroom, two-bath condo about five blocks away from the main branch in very upscale Murray Hill. With a terrace no less. After an in-unit washer and dryer, a terrace is every New Yorker's dream.

"But then," Grant continued, now really getting into his stride, "she calls me literally at the last minute to tell me she has to cancel because she's been coming down with the flu or something all day and now she's all coughing and wheezy and thinks she has a fever, too."

Again with the alarm bells in my head.

But he wasn't done yet. When it came to run-on sentences, Grant Neuman was up there with Nic.

"So I was annoyed, mostly because I really wanted to get the word out here tonight that the movie was still good to go ahead even without the Savoie girl."

"That was understandable," I said, trying desperately to stay calm and channel my inner Mrs. Christie. "But why 'mostly'? Why else were you annoyed?"

Grant looked around to check if anyone nearby could hear us. *As if.* In that din, *I* could barely hear him. Nic appeared to be following the conversation, but you could never be sure with Nic. I smiled at Grant encouragingly.

"Well, she admitted she'd done a little pre-party coke that some friend of hers had sent her for her birthday. She said it wasn't a lot and she wasn't supposed to share it. Like I wanted any. I don't like drugs. They're bad for business. Anyway, she thought maybe it had made her flu or cold or whatever worse. I was pissed off, but what can you do? The girl's got the flu. At least she's high. Not like me, drinking crap wine."

But I had stopped listening to Grant's whining at "wasn't supposed to share it."

"*Who* gave it to her?" I demanded, giving his arm a shake. "*Who* said not to share it?"

Grant looked at me like I'd grown fangs. "Um, I don't know," he stammered. "*She* didn't even know. She said it came by messenger from one of those ring-and-bring dealers, you know?"

Yes, I did know. Ring-and-bring dealers were essentially the pizza-delivery system of the drug world. Or so I'd heard from, yes, Wren Madison. You texted a number, you placed your order, their delivery guy is at your door in under thirty minutes. Which is faster than pizza delivery, actually.

"There was a message or something like 'Happy birthday, don't share,'" Grant added. "I can't remember exactly."

"Maybe 'too special to share'?" I asked. *Please god, let him say no.*

"Yeah, that was it," Grant said.

Oh no no no. *Was it possible to lace cocaine with arsenic?*

And then I heard a precise, fluting voice in my head. "Inhaled abrin presents with difficulty breathing, fever and sweating . . ." *Not arsenic. Abrin.*

I hadn't realized I'd said it aloud until I saw Grant looking to Nic for help with this crazy cousin of hers. But Nic seemed as confused by the direction the conversation had taken as he was and just shrugged her shoulders at him.

"We need to call her, Nic," I said, beginning to panic. "You have her on speed dial. Call her. Now."

"Okay," she said. "Whatever." She pulled her cell out of her evening bag, punched in a number and held the phone out to me.

I put it to my ear and, very attractively, stuck a finger in my other ear to shut out the noise around me. I needn't have bothered. The phone rang. And rang. And rang. And when I got the tinny "Hi, you've reached Wren . . ." I hung up and gave the phone back to Nic.

"Keep trying," I demanded. "Leave a message, tell her the cocaine's bad, tell her to call you back. I need to find Sebastian."

Nic nodded and I looked around wildly, hoping I would see Sebastian coming back from the bar. But if he was, he was invisible in a sea of tuxedos. For one brief, irrational moment I thought, *I could find him if he was wearing one of those horrible brown suits of his.*

But he wasn't, and I couldn't see him, and I had to do *something*.

What I did was whip off my very beautiful, very high Jimmy Choo heels and shove them in my bewildered cousin's hand. I couldn't afford any wobbling now.

"Hold these," I ordered. "I'm going to go check on Wren. When Sebastian comes back, tell him where I am. Tell him I think Wren's been poisoned. And find Mrs. Madison, but don't alarm her yet. Wren must have called her, told her she wasn't feeling well, so just say I've gone to check on her, see how she's feeling. I'll get back to you as soon as I can."

Nic seemed finally to understand what was happening. "Got it. You go. I'll call Wren. I'll find Seb. I'll talk to Mrs. Madison." She set off briskly through the crowd, my shoes dangling from one hand, the other holding the phone to her ear.

I turned to leave. And froze.

I could see the library's huge double doors, still open for any late arrivals, across the crowd. A chattering, laughing, happy crowd. *But all that,* the screamy voice pointed out, *could change in an instant.* I felt the familiar shudder begin, the one that would send me to my knees.

And then the other voice. *"Tory Van Dyne, you are amazing."*

And suddenly I was furious. *Well, not amazing, maybe,* I thought. *But stronger than some stupid voice in my head that wants to cripple me for the rest of my life.* A voice that would rather let Wren Madison die than me face my own stupid fear. Well, *that* wasn't gonna happen.

The shuddering stopped. With both hands I lifted the hem of my gown above my ankles and ran across the room in my bare feet, elbowing away any guest foolish enough to stand in my way and dashing through the doors and down the library's broad marble steps like some kind of demented Cinderella.

There was no time to try to find an empty cab in midtown on a Saturday night. My plan, such as it was, was to run the five blocks to Wren's apartment. But I'd forgotten about Norman.

Just like in the fairy tale, my coach and driver were waiting for me. Except this time the coach was a Mercedes S-Class sedan double-parked in front of the library and the driver was Norman. Who, the moment he saw me charging down the library steps, stepped out and opened the rear door for his young lady. Who, ignoring this invitation, opened the *front* passenger-side door herself and literally threw herself in, all the while shouting, "Drive, drive drive," like some kind of deranged action-film character.

This was unprecedented. No one ever sat up front with Norman. But Norman, unfazed, briskly stepped forward to tuck the folds of my gown into the car after me and, with a murmured "Excuse me, miss," leaned over to snap my seat belt around me before shutting the car door. If Norman was going to *drive, drive, drive*, he was going to make sure his young lady was safe. He then, equally briskly, stepped around to the driver's seat and, adjusting his own seat belt, asked, "Uptown or downtown, miss?"

"Downtown," I gasped. "Wren's apartment, 38th between Park and Madison."

"I know the place," he said calmly, adding as he pulled out smoothly into the downtown traffic, "I take it this is an emergency?"

"I think she's done some bad coke," I said, a little calmer myself now that Norman was in charge. "I can't get her on the phone."

"Not to worry, miss," Norman said steadily. "We'll get you there in double time."

It had never occurred to me before that Norman, being a professionally trained chauffer for a very rich man, had almost certainly been schooled in driving under high-stress and high-speed conditions. A cab, even if I could have found one, would have taken fifteen, maybe twenty minutes to fight its way to Wren's address. We were there in fewer than seven. I know because I was obsessively checking the car's dashboard clock the whole way. Down Fifth to 38th, then across town for another two-and-a-half blocks as Norman wove through traffic at twice the speed limit, timing the lights almost instinctively, running the yellows at will and, when he could see that the coast was relatively clear, sometimes even the reds, horn blaring.

Under any other circumstances this might have been exhilarating. Under the current circumstances it was terrifying. What if, despite Norman's assurances, we were too late? Mrs. Christie's litany about the fatal effects of inhaled abrin began to pound in my brain: "... *and with a full dose, fluid buildup in the lungs leading to low blood pressure and respiratory failure.*"

And then Norman was pulling up with a screech of brakes in front of Wren's building. I tumbled out of the car before he'd even had a chance to put it in park. "I'll be right here, miss, if you need me," he shouted to my departing back.

What does a well-trained Midtown doorman do when a madwoman in a ball gown and bare feet careens into his building and demands that he call up to Miss Madison's apartment immediately? Well, he calls Miss Madison's apartment immediately. And when Miss Madison doesn't answer, he promptly obeys the madwoman's command to take her upstairs and use his passkey to open the apartment because Miss Madison is *very, very ill*. Good manners weren't the only thing Grandmother taught me. Grandmother, who had volunteered for the WAVES after Pearl Harbor and served in Naval Intelligence as a code breaker, had also taught me that in an emergency, someone must take charge.

The elevator ride up to Wren's apartment seemed to take forever. When the doorman insisted on first knocking politely on Miss Madison's door, I wanted to knock him politely on the head. Instead I grabbed the passkey from him and used it myself to open the door to the apartment.

Where Wren was sitting calmly on the living room couch.

No, I realized. Not sitting calmly on the couch. Sitting unconscious on the couch.

I ran over to her, calling her name gently, but there was no response. I put a trembling hand on her forehead. The skin was hot, burning hot and wet with sweat. Which was good, I told myself. She wouldn't still have a fever if she was, well, dead. Putting my ear close to her mouth, I could hear that she was still breathing, though with shallow, wheezing gasps that seemed to catch in her throat.

I turned to the doorman, standing horrified behind me. "Call 911. Tell them we have a woman here who's been poisoned, maybe with bad cocaine." Wren took another gasping breath. "And tell them she's having a hard time breathing."

"Yes, ma'am," he said, all but saluting. "My phone's at the front desk. I'll take the stairs down. It'll be faster." And with that he was gone. And I was alone with a dying girl.

NOT THAT I WAS ALONE FOR LONG. IN SHORT ORDER, THE room was filled with a kind of mad, chaotic efficiency, as EMTs and paramedics rushed in, followed by two uniformed cops, who stood by taking notes while the medics hammered me with questions as they examined Wren, moved her to a stretcher and started administering oxygen.

I gave them all the information I could—that I thought she'd recently used cocaine laced with something else, most likely a poison called abrin. They, in turn, looked at me like I was crazy—which I completely understood. You'd have to be a fool to think the coke was cut with anything other than the latest and most deadly cocaine additive, fentanyl. You only had to watch the evening news to know that. So the EMTs were perfectly correct in immediately administering the fentanyl antidote, naloxone. But naloxone works within minutes, and even I could see that it wasn't having any effect on Wren's breathing. If anything, her breaths were getting shallower.

That careful, fluting voice sounded in my head again. *"There is no antidote, although rapid administration of oxygen and treatment of the pulmonary edema can be effective in preventing death."*

In my work I've had more than my fair share of laypersons trying to tell me how to do my job, so I'm a great believer in letting professionals do what they've been trained to do. But not in this case. I needed, at the risk of sounding like an interfering layperson, to step up.

I walked over to the paramedic standing by Wren's gurney, a tall Black woman with a kind of quiet, no-nonsense efficiency that immediately inspired confidence. The name embroidered on her green twill jacket read "Angela."

"Angela," I said, "I really don't think we're dealing with fentanyl here. I think the coke was laced with that poison I mentioned. It's called abrin."

To give Angela credit, she did not dismiss me outright. "Okay," she said. "Then what's the antidote?"

"There isn't one," I began. Irritation flashed across Angela's face. "But what you're doing, administering oxygen, I think that's a good first step," I said quickly. "But I'm afraid things are going to go downhill fast."

"Downhill how?" Angela fired back.

"I don't know," I admitted. "But I think things are only going to get worse. Including something called severe pulmonary edema." Whatever that was.

"Oh shit," Angela said. She turned to the two EMTs strapping Wren onto the stretcher before moving her. "We need to get this girl into the rig *now*."

Within minutes, they had rushed Wren into the building's freight elevator and out to the ambulance parked in front of the building. Norman, of course, was double-parked just behind it, engine running. The EMTs loaded the gurney into the ambulance, locked it into place and took their positions next to Wren's inert body. Nobody paid any attention whatsoever to me, so I waved Norman away and took it upon myself to slide into the vehicle's cab as if I had every right to be there.

And then the door was yanked back open and a man was leaning into the cab. A man in a tuxedo. A tuxedo with a gold-and-blue detective's shield pinned to its satin lapel. In a voice of quiet authority, he asked the driver, "What hospital are you taking her to?"

"NYU Langone," the driver said.

"Got it," Detective Sebastian Mendez-Cruz said, and looked at me. "Nic told me what was going on. I'll catch up with you when I'm done here." *Of course.* His business would be with the two uniforms at the crime scene, if a crime scene it was. I barely had time to nod before he was slamming the door shut and the driver—with a terse "Fasten your seat belt" to me—was pulling out into the crosstown traffic, siren wailing and lights flashing. I checked the side mirror and saw Norman following closely on our tail.

Within seconds we were speeding across 38th, then whipping down Park to 34th before heading east again toward Second Avenue and NYU's Langone hospital. I clung to the edge of my seat at every curve and did my version of prayer—a desperate *please please please*—that stopped only when we lurched into the hospital's admitting dock.

Within seconds the paramedics had the gurney out of the ambulance and were running with it into the emergency room, me following close behind. The ER was a hive of men and women in blue scrubs sitting at desks cluttered with blinking screens or walking with controlled purpose to and from the curtained patient cubicles arranged around the sides of the space. Wren's paramedics, however, were heading at speed toward a pair of green swinging doors with a clearly stenciled sign that read NO ADMITTANCE, HOSPITAL PERSONNEL ONLY. Which I ignored. I needed to be nearby to explain to the doctors about abrin. Until then I wasn't letting Wren out of my sight.

Or so I thought.

Just as I was pushing through the doors, a blue-clad arm grabbed my elbow from behind. "Whoa! Whoa, there!"

I was so shocked I actually whoa'd. I turned to see who was keeping me from my self-appointed task. The arm was attached to a formidable, grey-haired woman wearing blue scrubs and a name tag identifying her as Susan Tulliver, RN. Nurse Tulliver apparently had been compelled to step out from behind what I now realized was the admitting desk when she saw me heading toward the green doors. I looked at her frantically and then, equally frantically, at the doors swinging closed behind the EMTs.

"Not to worry," the nurse said, relenting slightly. "She'll be well taken care of. But right now you need to fill this out." She handed me a clipboard with what looked like a thousand-page form.

Tory, I said to myself firmly, *now is not the time to act like a madwoman.* Even though, I realized, that was exactly what I looked like. Bare feet, my updo now mostly a down-do, my goddess gown hemmed with grime. *What would Grandmother do in this situation?*

I thought about the many desperate husbands, wives and friends that Nurse Tulliver had to face every night. Their anxious demands that something be done *right now.* But Grandmother had also said, "In a crisis, when all the calls are to go faster, slow down. More mistakes are made in haste than deliberation." I felt sure Nurse Tulliver would agree. So I slowed down.

"I'm happy to fill out these forms," I said, and I thought I saw the nurse relax slightly. "The patient's name is Wren Madison, and I have reason to believe she's inhaled a toxin mixed with cocaine."

Nurse Tulliver simply said, "A toxin."

I nodded. "I gave the EMTs the information and they are acting on it. But I do think it's important to talk to a doctor about this specific toxin."

Nurse Tulliver nodded, clearly relieved that she was not talking to a madwoman. "Of course," she said. "Tell me more."

I forced myself to slow down again. "Wren was brought in as a result of what appeared to be a severe reaction to cocaine laced with some other substance, most likely, in the opinion of the paramedics, fentanyl."

Nurse Tulliver again nodded her understanding.

"But naloxone had no effect on her symptoms, which are worsening rapidly," I explained. "I have reason to believe that my friend was given cocaine laced with a drug called abrin."

At which Nurse Tulliver looked blank.

"It is related to ricin."

At which Nurse Tulliver looked panicked.

Truth be told, I was pretty close to panic myself. I could hear the minutes ticking by in my head like some kind of enormous, threatening alarm clock. The nurse did another one of those iron-arm grabs but this time snagging a nurse's aide who looked barely old enough to drive.

"Get Dr. Levinson," she barked. "*Now.*"

The aide rushed off, and Nurse Tulliver turned back to me. "He's tonight's attending," she said. "He's good."

Dr. Levinson was indeed good. Though he hardly looked older than the nurse's aide who brought him to us, he had, miraculously, heard of abrin poisoning.

"I'm from Florida," he explained after I'd given him the details of the situation. "Rosary pea grows there. Most kids know to avoid it."

"Then you know that there's no antidote to inhaled abrin and without immediate treatment for the edema, respiratory failure can quickly be fatal," I said.

But Dr. Levinson was way ahead of me. In fact, Dr. Levinson was moving toward those swinging green doors at top speed. I was glad. The time to go slow was past.

Twenty-Two

◇◇◇◇◇◇◇◇◇◇◇◇◇◇◇◇◇◇◇◇◇

She gave me the impression of one who has been afraid—but has not dared to show fear—and who knows the occasion for fear is now over.

—Hugh Norreys, *The Rose and the Yew Tree* (written under the pen name Mary Westmacott)

IN CONTRAST TO THE CLARITY OF MY THINKING EARLIER, THE rest of that night was a blur. The nurse's aide guided me to a chair in the ER waiting room, a remarkably comfortable space separate from the controlled chaos of the ER proper, clean and well-lit and somehow soothing in its quiet. In order not to disturb the others waiting for news of their loved ones, I moved out to the hallway to call Nic. When I pulled my phone out, I was amazed to see that, including the twenty minutes I'd spent in the ER proper, it had been only slightly more than an hour since my mad dash down the library steps. So short a time for so much to change.

Before I could speed dial Nic's cell, the phone buzzed in my hand. The incoming call number looked vaguely familiar. But if this was spam, somebody was about to get an earful.

"Yes," I snapped.

"Tory, it's Sebastian."

Thank you, Universe.

"Sebastian," I said, my voice suddenly shaky.

"How are you doing?" His voice was soft, and I was afraid that I'd simply fall apart if I wasn't very careful.

"I'm okay," I lied, and cursed myself silently for the little catch in my breath.

"Good," he said evenly, though I thought I heard a little wobble there, too. He cleared his throat. "And Wren? Any word?" His voice now was official, competent, immediately steadying.

"Not yet," I said. "I'm in the ER waiting room. They're treating her for suspected abrin poisoning." I gave him the same rundown I'd shared with Dr. Levinson.

"Great," he said. "Good job on your part."

I knew I had done a good job, but I told myself, there wasn't anything wrong with being inordinately pleased that Sebastian recognized it, too.

"But tell me why you were so sure it was abrin," he added.

I gave him a brief outline of my suspicions, particularly Wren's symptoms and Neuman's recollection of the words Wren had used about it being a birthday present and too special to share. Sebastian, of course, immediately recognized the similarity to the card sent with Sailor's tequila.

"Okay," he said. "Here's what we're going to do. I've designated Wren's apartment as a crime scene. I'm heading down to the hospital as soon as I can. I'll meet you at the ER. In the meantime, could you call Nic and let her and Mrs. Madison know what's happened?"

"Absolutely," I said. "I was just about to do that."

"And could you keep in touch with me as to . . . Wren's condition?"

For a moment I couldn't speak at all. "Okay," I finally managed to croak.

"Hey, Tory," he said, his voice suddenly gentle, "everything's going to be all right." He paused, then repeated it. "Everything is going to be all right, Tory."

And for the first time that night I almost believed that somehow everything might, in fact, be all right. It was an amazing feeling to be on the other side of that verbal hug. I tried to remember if anyone had ever, even during the worst of my personal crisis, said those exact words to me. I didn't think they had. Mostly it had been "How awful for you" and "Here's a pill that should help." No, that wasn't true. Abe had said them, more or less. "This too shall pass," he'd said. Abe would have liked Sebastian, I thought.

"Thanks," I said. "Really, that helps."

"Good," he said. "I'll let you call Nic now."

I said goodbye, steeled myself and hit Nic's speed dial.

She picked up almost immediately. "Hey, babe," she said, "I'm here with Wren's mom. Let me put her on speaker." Her speech was unnaturally bright even for Nic, and I realized she was doing what she could to keep things upbeat. As if that was even possible. But I did my best to match her tone.

"Hi, Mrs. Madison," I said, trying to think how to tell her the truth without frightening her or giving her false hope. "Everything's under control. Wren was pretty sick, so we went to the ER. The doctor knows what the problem is, so she's in good hands."

"Oh my god," Mrs. Madison said, her voice breaking. "Thank you, Tory. Thank you for everything." My heart ached for her. First her husband, now her daughter? It didn't bear thinking about.

I heard a muffled exchange between Mrs. Madison and Nic and then my cousin came back on the line. "Tory, we've gotta go. Mrs. Madison's driver is bringing her car around and we should be at the ER in fifteen or twenty minutes, depending on traffic."

"Good," I said. "Maybe I'll know more by then."

BUT OF COURSE I DIDN'T KNOW MORE BY THEN.

There was a bit of a stir in the waiting room when Nic arrived, Mrs. Madison in tow. My fellow travelers in ER purgatory had quickly accepted me, the bedraggled Cinderella in their midst, because in a New York hospital waiting room all are created equal. All pain is shared pain. All humanity is shared humanity. But for a moment, when two more women in formal evening gowns arrived, this time not at all bedraggled and one carrying a pair of high-heeled Jimmy Choos dangling from one elegantly manicured hand, the others in the waiting room were nudged out of their misery long enough to wonder at the spectacle. But then they decently averted their eyes as the three of us hugged each other and Wren's mother asked, tears leaking down her face, "Is there any news?"

I shook my head. "Not yet."

"But what happened?" she asked. "We were supposed to meet at the gala, but she called me just as I got there, said she had the flu. Told me to stay, have a good time. But it's not the flu?"

Oh god oh god oh god, how to explain? I settled on keeping it simple.

"No," I said. "It looks like somebody gave her some tainted cocaine."

Mrs. Madison didn't even pretend to be surprised that her daughter did cocaine. "I've warned her about that, begged her not to play around with drugs. But she always said it was just for fun, never anything serious."

"I'm sure that's all it ever was," I said, trying to give the woman some comfort. "And the doctor is pretty confident about what the additive was . . ." Now was not the time to go into my part in that. ". . . so they know how to treat it. We just have to wait now."

Mrs. Madison nodded, and the three of us simply sat there, holding each other's hands, dread and hope warring in our hearts.

Time, as we all know, is elastic. Hours can seem like minutes; minutes can seem like hours. By that second calculation, when Sebastian Mendez-Cruz finally walked into the ER waiting room, we had been sitting trapped in our thoughts for at least two days. Nonetheless, another quick glance at my phone told me that the wait time had been under an hour.

Oddly, Sebastian came not from the outside world but from out of the emergency room itself, accompanied by Dr. Levinson. I couldn't quite figure that one out until I realized that this was the kind of access that a man with a detective's shield pinned to the lapel of his tux was clearly entitled to.

The three of us stood up and Mrs. Madison looked uncertainly from the doctor to me, hardly daring to hope.

I nodded. "Mrs. Madison, this is Dr. Levinson. Dr. Levinson, this is Wren's mother." I stepped back and stood quietly next to Nic. This was no longer my story.

Dr. Levinson, bless him, was quick to assure Mrs. Madison that Wren was in stable, though critical, condition. "She's in the ICU, intubated for the time being until we can be sure that the edema is under control. But all signs point to her pulling through."

The relief was too much for Wren's mother, and, grabbing the doctor's hand, she wrung it between both of hers, saying, "I cannot thank you enough, doctor, for saving her life."

"I didn't save her life," the doctor said firmly. "The emergency team saved her life. But without the information passed on by her friend here"—he nodded toward me—"they and we would have been at a great disadvantage in treating her appropriately."

At which point Mrs. Madison looked at me in amazement and began to wring *my* hand. Which was embarrassing.

"I told you Tory would know what to do," Nic said to her. "Tory *always* knows what to do." And started in on me with one of her Nic hugs.

This was all getting to be a bit much for Yours Truly. I'm as fond of public displays of affection as the next girl. Well, actually, that's not true. Unlike the next girl, I'm not really fond of PDAs at all. And we'd already had one hug. A second was going way over the top.

Dr. Levinson came to my rescue by suggesting that we all move to his office, and Mrs. Madison dazedly allowed herself to be led away by the good doctor and Nic.

Sebastian and I were, for the moment, left alone. He stood looking down quizzically at the Jimmy Choos Nic had left behind on her plastic chair, then at my grimy, bare toes peeking out from under the grimy hem of my dress. And without a word, he knelt down and slid the shoes onto my feet. I nodded my thanks because suddenly I couldn't speak.

"We should go, too," he said, standing.

I nodded again and we trailed behind the others through a maze of olive green corridors that would presumably lead to the doctor's inner sanctum. While we walked, Sebastian asked if I'd seen anything like a note or card in the apartment that might have come with the doctored coke.

"I didn't even think of it," I admitted. "Mostly I just looked at Wren, willing her to keep breathing, you know?"

Sebastian nodded and put a hand on my bare shoulder in brief sympathy.

That touch, the perfect warmth of it, changed everything. Both of us knew it, and neither of us knew what to do about it. Or what to say. The silence as we walked down the cold hall was not an easy one. Finally, I could stand it no longer.

I stopped and nodded toward the shield pinned to his tux.
"Nice lapel brooch," I said. "Adrian tells me they're all the rage."

"I worried that it might be a tad too much," he said, grinning.
"But I've been told it's quite . . . arresting."

And just like that, everything really was all right.

THE CONFAB IN DR. LEVINSON'S OFFICE WAS BRIEF, AT LEAST
for those of us who were not members of law enforcement or the
medical profession. Mrs. Madison announced that she would be
staying at her daughter's side until she regained consciousness, and
recognizing the immovable object that is a mother keeping watch
over her child, Dr. Levinson gave in and handed her over to a passing nurse. Sebastian asked me to come to the station on Monday
morning when someone would take my official statement. He then
suggested—well, insisted—that Nic and I "go home and get some
sleep." Granted, by this point it was two o'clock in the morning,
but I understood this to mean "Let the professionals do their job."
Because his, I knew, was only just beginning.

Accordingly, I led my cousin out to the hospital parking lot to
Norman, who had now been waiting for hours in the car and yet
somehow seemed as fresh as a daisy. Nic and I, on the other hand,
were as limp as week-old tulips. Norman handed us into the back
seat, pausing only to ask, "And Miss Madison? Is she . . . ?"

"She's going to be okay," I assured him. "In large part due to
you. You got us there in time."

"Just doing my job, miss," he said, his voice studiously neutral.
But I noticed his shoulders squaring, his chin going up just a bit
higher, and I thought he was pleased.

Nic, whose usual resiliency seemed to have deserted her
altogether, elected to come home with me. We dragged ourselves

upstairs, and I steered her toward the guest bedroom usually commandeered by my mother on her rare visits to the city but that also served as a crash pad for Nic after the occasional late-night clubbing downtown. So she knew exactly where to head.

"I'm never going to get to sleep," she muttered before falling facedown on the bed—Siriano and all—practically in midsnore. I took off her golden sandals, pulled the goose-down duvet from the foot of the bed over her and trudged upstairs to my own room.

It was all I could do to slide my dress down over my hips to the floor, where it puddled around my ankles like a dirty aquamarine cloud. I looked in dismay at my bare feet, still begrimed with god knows what nastiness I'd managed to pick up on my mad dash across Astor Hall and down all those—what? two dozen?—steps to the—*shudder*—sidewalk. Not to mention standing around in the—oh lord—*emergency room.*

These kinds of circumstances are exactly why God invented showers. I don't know how long I spent in that white-tiled cocoon, soaping every inch of my body and leaning into the hot, cleansing spray and crying tears of remembered fear, of relief and, finally, of gratitude, until I had no tears left.

Twenty-Three

"Listen, darling, are we investigating a crime or are we match-making?"

—Lucy Eyelesbarrow to Miss Jane
Marple, *4.50 from Paddington*

"YOU KNOW, WE'RE GOING TO BE LATE FOR SUNDAY DINNER."
I stared at my cousin. It was noon the next day, and we were seated at my kitchen table, hands wrapped around mugs of coffee. Nic had already called Mrs. Madison to check on Wren and received the happy news that her friend was on the mend. But both of us were absolutely beat, even after ten hours of sleep. Nic was still in her somewhat-worse-for-wear Siriano, her hair every whichaway, looking like a first-class lady passenger in one of the *Titanic*'s lifeboats. I, in my now-thoroughly-deflated updo, was sporting my favorite ratty but super comfy bathrobe and looked, no doubt, like I'd fallen down a well two days ago and had only just been rescued.

Neither of us had said much to each other besides "Do you want some coffee" (me) and "Yeah" (Nic). That is until it occurred to Nic that today was Sunday. And Sunday, of course, meant Sunday dinner. With the whole famdamnily. And, as she rightly pointed out, we were going to be late.

"I'm not going," I said flatly.

Nic nodded. "Me neither."

This was heresy on both our parts, and we knew it. No doubt Norman would have told his wife, the redoubtable Mrs. Johnson, about last night's drama and she in turn would have relayed it to Aunt Bunny. But there was no reason to suppose that our collective relatives would consider our possible fatigue from the night's events sufficient excuse to miss Sunday dinner.

"Maybe we should call," Nic suggested halfheartedly. "They might be worried about us."

But when I tried to imagine any real concern on the part of the family, nothing came to me.

"No, they aren't," I said, surprised at this revelation.

Nic raised her eyebrows in equal wonder. "You're right," she said.

"All they'll want to do is talk about how to keep our names out of the paper," I added.

"Yup."

"So we're not going," I said.

"Nope," Nic said.

And we clicked our coffee mugs in quiet celebration.

"Instead maybe we could talk to Mrs. M about it tomorrow?" Nic asked hopefully.

"God willing," I said.

Like Nic, I very much hoped that Mrs. Mallowan/Christie would make it her business to appear the next night for cocktails. I'd long since given up trying to figure out how and when the woman decided to grace us with her presence, but Mondays seemed to be her preference. Probably because she knew that was when Mairead would be there. And where Mairead was, the dog Tony followed.

That being said, I did call Mairead's father later that afternoon to explain what had happened the night before in case he thought the ensuing conversation on Monday might not be appropriate for an eleven-year-old girl. Because I really, really thought it wasn't. But not Cormac Butler.

"It would be more than my life is worth to try and stop the lass," he said, chuckling.

"You do understand, though," I said, still worried, "that there have been three attempts on the lives of people connected to my cousin, two of them successful. I don't think Mairead is in any danger herself, of course, but . . ."

"I do understand," he said. "But seriously, Tory, my daughter is, for the first time in the two years since her mother's death, truly engaged. She loves learning from you about book conservation. It means more to her than you will ever know. And she feels important, valuable in her role as secretary to your team discussions."

"She is, actually," I said. "Even the detective in charge of the case has said so."

"And as long as your good detective is present, surely there is no need for concern," Cormac pointed out.

I didn't actually know if my good detective would be present, but decided at that point that he better be. "He'll be there," I said with much more conviction than I really felt.

I needed Sebastian to be there so that Mairead could be there. I needed Mairead to be there so that Tony could be there. And I needed Tony to be there so that Mrs. Christie would be there. That, I told myself, in a truly unprecedented example of circular thinking, was why I needed Sebastian to be there.

And maybe, just maybe, I wanted to see Sebastian again for personal reasons. Okay, partly for personal reasons, but just partly. And I admit that my heart lifted when he responded immediately to my text about coming by on Monday with an admittedly not hugely romantic "OK." But also—and quite frankly, more important—I wanted to see him because I very much needed to know what conclusions he'd drawn about recent events.

Because I had my own, and I did not like them at all.

MY FIRST ORDER OF BUSINESS ON MONDAY MORNING WAS TO collar Adrian and get him up to speed on the gala that wasn't. Once we'd gone through the whole is-Wren-okay-are-you-okay-yes-I'm-okay routine, Adrian announced his intention of joining us at that evening's meeting because, he said, "Things are getting way too real, and I'm the only one who has the guts to point a finger."

"Yes," I agreed. "Because you're a meany."

"Because I'm *objective*," he corrected me. "*And* a meany."

That afternoon, we gathered the troops (except for Sebastian, who had texted me a super romantic "running late") downstairs shortly before the appointed hour. I wanted to give Mrs. Christie every opportunity of apparating—however it was that she did that—away from prying eyes. I did not want the lady scared off.

As I hoped—well, prayed, if an SOS to the Universe can be considered a prayer—Mrs. Christie did somehow see her way to the Christie Room that night. When I peered around the door, there she was in her gold velvet armchair, embroidery in hand and wearing the same squashy hat and boxy suit she'd chosen for her first visit. When she saw me, she put the needlework aside and smiled a welcome.

"Tory," she said. "Do come in." I would never get over the way the woman assumed the role of hostess in what *was not her home.* Oh well, she was there, and that was the important thing.

Before I could do more than smile back at her, Nic had the poor woman in one of her usual clinches. "Oh, Mrs. M, am I ever glad to see you!" she exclaimed. "You won't believe what poor Tory went through this weekend!"

She then released our hostess to turn toward the bar cart, where the copy of the Vermeire still rested, left over from our last meeting.

"Oh, goody! I love this book!" She held the volume out to Adrian. "You choose."

"But first," Mrs. Christie interrupted, standing and tucking the embroidery hoop into her handbag, "perhaps Mr. Gooding would be so kind as to place a few chairs around the coffee table for ease of conversation. I believe . . ." And here she stopped to inspect my outfit for the occasion, a late '60s figure-hugging red jersey shift by Geoffrey Beene. ". . . we will be six."

Did the woman really deduce from my choice of frock that Sebastian would be coming? I wouldn't put it past her.

"In which case," she continued, "I would be grateful, Mr. Gooding, if you would pull my armchair"—*her* armchair?—"a bit closer to the sofa and place the two others across from it as before. Mairead, of course, as secretary, will be at the desk." Mairead positively glowed at this recognition of her exalted position.

Adrian gave a little bow in Mrs. Christie's direction and did as he was bid. Mrs. Christie thanked him politely and regained her throne, closely followed by Tony, who could smell those dog biscuits right through that Launer handbag.

Nic began making a beeline for the couch, but Mrs. Christie was too fast for her, gently redirecting her to the chair closest to the bar cart. "We require someone near the refreshments," she explained with a smile, "should our glasses need to be refilled." Nic was quick to see the wisdom of the suggestion.

Mrs. Christie then decreed that I would be most comfortable on the couch, and I obediently took my place.

And so, while Adrian and Nic consulted on that night's ambrosia,

Mairead set herself up for note-taking and Tony munched happily on his hardtack, Mrs. Christie leaned toward me and began her discreet interrogation.

"And now, my dear Tory, do tell me what's happened."

And so I told her everything about Saturday night, from the glittering crowd at the gala ("how very glamorous") to the various bits of gossip I'd gathered, including the news that Brooke had turned down Howard's marriage proposal ("which explains a great deal") to Nic finally finding out that Sailor, not Nic, had been slated for the role of Belle should Wren fail to come through, and that Howard had known that for weeks and never told her ("my, my, that *is* interesting").

I then moved on to my realization that someone had sent Wren cocaine tainted with abrin ("very skillfully deduced") to Norman's speed-demon drive to Wren's apartment ("there is simply nothing like a fast automobile") and finally to bossing around the paramedics and ER staff ("you can be rather formidable, my dear"). I loved that last one. I did not know that about myself. I had never in my entire life been told I was formidable.

What I didn't cover were my little "moments" with Sebastian. The last thing I needed was Mrs. Christie murmuring something like "how very delusional."

When I'd finished, Mrs. Christie looked at me with something, I thought, very like respect. "You were very, very brave, my dear," she said. "I congratulate you."

I knew, of course, what she was talking about.

"No," I said, deflecting madly. "It was like I was someone else. Especially running across Astor Hall. A brave someone else. Because, really, I'm not brave at all."

"Well, my dear, that might have once been true, but recent events suggest you might wish to revise that estimation."

That made me laugh, and me laughing made Mrs. Christie laugh, and that is why when Sebastian Mendez-Cruz came into the Christie Room, the detective found us giggling together like two schoolgirls. Gentleman that he was, he pretended not to notice Mrs. Christie's lapse from her usual dignity and simply stood by until she had regained her composure. Once herself, Mrs. Christie suggested that Detective Mendez-Cruz sit next to "Miss Van Dyne" (apparently, I was only Tory in our private tête-à-têtes) in the event that we should want "to confer."

Which is when, as the British say, the penny dropped. *Mrs. Christie was determined to throw Sebastian and me together.* Once again, I was the one, not Nic, who would be sitting next to Sebastian on the cozy couch. We could easily have *conferred* from separate chairs. I certainly wouldn't have plumped myself down next to Sebastian as a matter of course. Heaven forfend that Tory Van Dyne should assume any kind of claim on a man with whom she had exchanged a couple of significant glances and a laugh or two. In retrospect, *"Everything is going to be all right"* was hardly a declaration of love. But if Mrs. Christie wanted to play matchmaker, I would take it. I certainly wasn't going to make much headway romantically on my own feeble efforts.

So I was inordinately pleased when Sebastian played along with her little game.

"Of course," he said, looking not at Mrs. Christie, but directly at Yours Truly. "I always enjoy *conferring* with Miss Van Dyne."

AGATHA INCORPORATED MEETING MINUTES
MONDAY, OCTOBER 28

Topic: The attempted murder of Wren Madison

Members present: Mrs. Mallowan (Mrs. M), Tory Van Dyne (Tory), Nicola Van Dyne (Nic), Adrian Gooding

(Mr. G), Detective Sebastian Mendez-Cruz (Det. M-C), Mairead Butler (MB), Secretary

First order of business: Bamboo Cocktails all round (Shirley Temple for MB)

Second order of business: Update on Wren Madison (hereafter W)

Nic: W still in the hospital but out of ICU and doctors say should make full recovery. But was a near thing. Tory saved her life. (begins to cry loudly)

Tory: (embarrassed) Give it a rest, Nic. If anyone saved Wren's life, it was Mrs., um, Mallowan, who told us about abrin. (begins to cry quietly)

Mrs. M (embarrassed): Nonsense.

Det. M-C and Mr. G offer handkerchiefs all round.

Third order of business: Update from NYPD

Det. M-C: W told police the cocaine arrived by a ring-and-bring messenger wearing a helmet that afternoon. No idea who'd sent it, but messenger said was already paid for and told her the message was "happy birthday, too special to share." Which explains no card found in Wren's apartment.

Mr. G: (interrupting): Why would she take that risk? Taking coke from a stranger.

Nic: Whoever sent it knew it was her birthday so she would have figured it was from a friend.

Det. M-C: W says began feeling sicker after first hit, but thought it was just the cocaine making her flu symptoms worse. Flushed the bag with what was left down the toilet. Called Neuman and her mother, told mother to stay at the gala. By then so tired thought

she'd just watch some TV. Doesn't remember anything
after that. Good news is team did find small poly bag
like type used by drug dealers in U-bend of toilet. No
fingerprints recoverable. Bag had twisted shut when
flushed down toilet and when examined was found to
contain some cocaine residue. And, when tested, abrin.

Mr. G: So the coke had abrin in it.

Det. M-C: Yes. Wren Madison was poisoned with abrin-
laced cocaine.

At this point in the proceedings, all pretense of an actual meeting was abandoned. In the ensuing cacophony, Mairead totally
gave up on taking minutes. Mostly because, I suspected, she had
her own theories to put forward and couldn't talk and type at the
same time.

"Meeting adjourned," Mairead concluded diplomatically, "in
favor of roundtable discussion."

The discussion, such as it was, centered on the now-familiar
means/motive/opportunity trope, leading, of course, to the all-
important who.

The means was obvious. Poison. First arsenic, then abrin.

Mairead, jumping right into the fray, pointed out that poison
"is, of course, a woman's weapon. Hercule Poirot always said so."

"I vote with Poirot," Adrian said.

Mrs. Christie smiled at that, but felt compelled to add, "Actually, of the twenty-nine novels in that canon with poison as a
weapon, seventeen of the murderers were men and only twelve
women."

Let's not go there, I thought. "And we're not talking about an
Agatha Christie novel here, Mairead."

As soon as I said it, I felt like a grumpus and wished I hadn't. But Mairead just smiled at me innocently. "But does it not sometimes feel as though we are?"

Before I had a chance to process *that*, Sebastian chimed in with, "Actually, women are still seven times more likely than men to choose poison as a murder weapon."

I gave up. "I stand corrected," I said, and took a large sip of my Bamboo Cocktail in consolation.

"Also," Sebastian added, "if Rachel Featherstonhaugh was the perpetrator of the attack on Sailor Savoie . . ."

"OMG," Nic put in. "*Perpetrator.* You talk, like, right out of *Law & Order.*"

Sebastian ignored Nic politely, repeating, "If Rachel Featherstonhaugh was the perpetrator of the attack on Sailor Savoie, which only circumstantial evidence suggests, as well as the attempt on Wren Madison, for which there is no evidence whatsoever, we have to admit that motive is still a sticking point. What would her motive be?"

To which I posited my by-now-familiar book-scam theory. Which Sebastian promptly wrote off.

"It's great that you figured out the scam. And we'll be following up with your contact at the Atheneum on that. But until we get some proof that she's actually sold those books, we're not playing that card with her yet. She'll only claim, like she did at the Strand, that she was doing it on behalf of her boss."

"Which, once again, she knows he's conveniently not around to dispute," Adrian pointed out. "Am I the only one who thinks that maybe Rachel had something to do with *Calhoun's* death?"

"Not at all," Sebastian answered. "That's been an avenue of inquiry, of course."

Of course it had been. Why was I surprised? How many times did I have to remind myself that the detective was under no obligation to share the details of an ongoing investigation? Quite the opposite, in fact. Which explained why he told us only as much as we needed to know in order for him to get the information he needed from us.

"But we would need some actual evidence linking her to that crime, which we don't have, and a convincing motive, which is a stretch. I mean, nobody, including Rachel Featherstonhaugh, was aware that Howard was planning to liquidate his collection except for Tory's friend at the Atheneum. As far as Rachel knew, Howard dead would mean no more access to his collection."

Adrian nodded glumly. "I see your point."

Sebastian turned to me. "And even if your friend does come through, we have no indication that Sailor Savoie knew about the scam or, if she did, was somehow and for some reason holding it over Rachel Featherstonhaugh."

Well, that took the wind out of our sails. And there was more discouraging news to come.

"What we *do* know," Sebastian continued, "is that Wren Madison was not aware of the book scam. In fact, she says she can't think of any reason why Rachel would want to kill her. Says she's barely exchanged ten words with her. You know these people. Can any of you think of any reason why Rachel would have an animus against her?"

Silence again while we all came up with exactly nothing. Growing bored (and probably not sure what "animus" meant), Nic escaped "to take a pee," raising quite an eyebrow from Mrs. Christie. In the meantime, since coming up with an animus against Wren was such a dud, Mairead had another question.

"Why two different poisons? Especially since Rachel only knew about arsenic."

"Good point," I said. "Howard, at least from what I gathered from Rachel at the memorial service, never told her that abrin was probably what made Bertram so sick."

"So *she* says," Adrian put in. "I mean, how could she have known if Howard didn't tell her? Nobody else knew about abrin except you and Nic. And Nic was afraid to even mention poison when she called to tell her about Bertram on Sunday morning."

At that point Nic came back into the room wearing what looked like fresh lip stain, fresh blush and maybe even another lick or two of mascara. So much for just taking a pee.

"You know," she said, "I just had a thought in there. I mean, why change the poisons?"

"Keep up, Nic," I said. "That's what we're talking about."

Nic took no offense. "Good. I mean, it wasn't like anyone would suspect arsenic unless they were supersmart like Mrs. Mallowan or something. So why not just use it again?"

I glanced over to see how Sebastian was taking being told he wasn't supersmart like Mrs. Mallowan. Here's how Sebastian was taking it: Sebastian was nodding.

"And then I thought," Nic was continuing, "maybe because it would be, like, so much easier to get Wren to *sniff* poison, especially mixed in with a little nose candy, than to *drink* it in tequila, like Sailor. Tequila was nothing special for Wren. She could take it or leave it."

"So the killer chose the poison according to the victim's appetites!" Mairead announced with more relish than was perhaps appropriate for an eleven-year-old.

We all looked to Sebastian, who, through all of this had been notably silent, taking it in, looking from face to face as each of us spoke. Click, click, click. For a brief, very uncomfortable moment,

I wondered if every adult in that room was more than a potential source of information crucial to his investigation. Maybe we were all potential suspects.

Finally, he spoke. "Nic and Mairead may be right about the choice of toxin and its administration being dependent on the intended victim."

Nic looked a tad confused at that, so I leaned across the coffee table to her and said in a quiet aside, "Different strokes for different folks."

Nic grimaced. "Why didn't he just say that then?"

"But in the case of the adulterated tequila," Sebastian went on, "Rachel Featherstonhaugh says flatly that she's guilty of nothing more than sending the bottle at Howard Calhoun's instruction, which we have no way of refuting. And, in the case of the cocaine sent to Wren Madison, we have *nothing* that points to her involvement."

Sebastian paused here, looking distinctly uncomfortable. Which was odd. I'd never seen him look uncomfortable. He cleared his throat and turned to Mrs. Christie. "I recall you once saying that any coincidence is always worth noticing and that it can be thrown away later if it is only a coincidence. Quite aside from the question of who might be the perpetrator, would you say that the poisoning of two of the three women who starred in the play *BB* is simply a coincidence?"

Mrs. Christie took a moment to consider the question. She finally began by paraphrasing Miss Jane Marple in *Sleeping Murder*. "If it is a coincidence, it is a very remarkable one, and remarkable coincidences do happen." She paused, then added, "But no, Detective Mendez-Cruz, I do not believe that it is simple coincidence."

Her voice was heavy with warning.

Now even Mairead looked properly frightened. I looked at Nic to see what she was making of this, but my cousin simply looked confused.

Why was I the one who had to say it out loud?

"Are you telling us that you think Nic will be the killer's next target?"

Twenty-Four

◇◇◇◇◇◇◇◇◇◇◇◇◇◇◇◇◇◇◇◇◇◇◇

"The supernatural is only the natural of which the laws are not yet understood."

—Dr. Rose, "The Hound of Death,"
The Hound of Death and Other Stories

"WELL, THIS ONE FOR SURE AIN'T GONNA MAKE THE HOT DE-tective happy."

It was like some weird replay of that morning last week (*Really? Only a week ago?*) when Adrian had shown me that day's *Post* headline. Once again Adrian lying in wait for me as I came downstairs. Once again Adrian, dressed impeccably and ignoring my own carefully chosen outfit (that day, in deference to my grey mood, a grey Ralph Lauren sweater dress from my favorite resale boutique, the RealReal). Once again Adrian steering me into a chair in his office and pointing to the front page of that morning's *Post*.

What was different this time, though, was the headline: ARE THE BELLES OF BROADWAY CURSED?

Which was disturbing, not least because after last night's little meeting at which Nic had discovered she might well be the next target of a homicidal maniac, she had declared she wasn't moving from my place until Seb caught said maniac.

"I'm not kidding, Tory," she'd said. "I'm sticking with you until we know I'm not going to be the next *Post* headline. Or at least the next sad *Post* headline. I'm fine with the old 'Private Heiress in Public Fountain' kind of headline."

Today's banner was *so* the wrong kind of headline.

What was also different this time was the photo accompanying the story—actually, the same photo that had accompanied the Private Heiress-Public Fountain headline. Once again the public was being treated to that paparazzi shot of Sailor, Wren and Nic dancing in their skivvies in Central Park's *Three Dancing Maidens* fountain. There they were, circling joyfully in the spray, dripping wet and laughing with the sheer joy of being young and alive. Except they weren't all young and alive anymore. Not Sailor anyway. And almost not Wren. I couldn't bear to think what the paper's logical inference would be.

I forced myself to read the story. Mostly it was a rehash of Sailor's death and whatever the reporter had managed to glean about Wren's close call, which was that she appeared to have used cocaine with a toxic additive, the obvious inference being fentanyl. There was at least no outright suggestion of foul play, though the paper had felt compelled to ask, "Will actress and socialite Nicola Van Dyne be the next Belle to succumb to the curse?"

I pushed the paper aside and looked at Adrian, stricken. "They're making the same connection we did," I whispered shakily. "They think Nic is next in line."

Adrian was immediately contrite. "I'm sorry," he said. "I shouldn't have sprung it on you like that. Sometimes I get carried away with my own cleverness. It's a kind of defense against real emotion, I suppose."

I had never known Adrian to apologize before. Or to admit a

vulnerability. It made me love him even more. "That's okay," I said. "It just came as a shock on top of last night."

"Yeah," Adrian said, moving to the seat behind his desk. "I have to admit, until Sebastian and Mrs. Christie suggested in their sideways fashion that Nic might be in danger, I'd totally missed it."

I opted not to tell him that I hadn't missed it. No need to rub salt in the wound. "I bet you did notice, though," I said, "that Sebastian wasn't surprised by my question."

Which was true. What Sebastian had said in response to my desperate query was, "We are, of course, considering that possibility."

Considering that possibility? I wanted to scream. *When were you planning to tell Nic about that possibility?*

And then it became clear to me. Sebastian taking Nic home after Howard's murder. Had he suspected even then that Nic, not Howard, had been the hooded killer's intended victim? Had Howard stepped forward unexpectedly and received a push intended for my cousin?

I thought about Sebastian at Howard's memorial service. Not just looking for suspects. Watching over Nic. Click, click, click.

And then, after Sailor's death, Sebastian accompanying Nic to the gala. Not as her date for the evening. As her bodyguard. Just in case. No wonder he had insisted on being the one to fetch her drink. The girl wasn't getting poisoned on his watch.

And finally the attack on Wren confirming his worst fears. Someone was indeed after the Belles of Broadway. That, I was sure, had been the reason for last night's meeting. It was time for Nic to know that she was in danger.

"Yeah, I noticed," Adrian said. "The hot detective is always two steps ahead of us."

"Well, he's a detective. He's *supposed* to be two steps ahead of us."

"That doesn't explain why your Mrs. Christie is *also* always two steps ahead of us. I mean, yeah, I was the one who said we don't need to be sure who or what she really is, but she's almost like our very own Harley Quin, you know?"

I did indeed know. Harley Quin was, by Agatha Christie's own admission, her favorite character. Probably, I'd always thought, because she wrote the short stories featuring him only when she, not some irritating publisher, felt like it. The mysterious Mr. Quin usually appears to his friend Satterthwaite in a flash of harlequin-colored lights just in time to guide the sleuth toward the correct answer to the story's puzzle, usually with some apparently random but actually very pointed observation.

"Yeah, there's a lot of Harley Quin in her," I said. "But, Adrian, she's not *my* Mrs. Christie. She's *our* Mrs. Christie. And do we really want to know why the woman's always two steps ahead of us? Are we really going to try to explain that?"

I could hear my voice getting shrill with emotion. I hate getting shrill with emotion. I don't like getting shrill. And I don't like emotion. (Well, most of the time.) But somehow I couldn't stop. "Are we really going to try to find out how a brilliant loon with an encyclopedic knowledge of Agatha Christie's work is sneaking into the Mystery Guild Library at will and drinking our booze to no noticeable effect except to always ask the right question? After all this time, are we going to, you know, knock on walls looking for secret passageways? Or set up hidden cameras to catch her coming and going through the back alley?"

Adrian said nothing. Actually, I didn't give him time to answer. I was on a roll. "Conversely, are we going to try to prove to ourselves that Mrs. Christie really is some kind of otherworldly manifestation of the Queen of Crime on holiday from the Eternity here to drink our booze to no noticeable effect except to always ask the right questions to help us find a killer? Are we going to call in a ghost hunter? Join some paranormal fan club?"

Again no response from Adrian.

"Are we really going to try to prove either of these possibilities?"

I sat back, exhausted by my little diatribe, and waited for Adrian's response.

Adrian shook his head. "No, we are not," he said firmly. "We are not, for the simple reason that if we tried to prove either of these possibilities, our heads would explode."

I BROUGHT THE *POST* UPSTAIRS TO SHARE WITH NIC, FIGURING it was better coming from me than hearing about it from her friends online, which in Nic's world would take about a nano-second. Much to my surprise, she was already up and sitting at the kitchen table in my second-favorite bathrobe, bleary-eyed and clutching a cup of coffee from the pot I'd made earlier that morning. I poured myself a cup, handed the paper to her and watched her read it, dreading her response.

I should have known better. Because Nic in my experience had never been anything if not optimistic. Nic had never been anything if not brave. Because Nic often, shall we say, thought outside of the box.

"I have a plan."

Uh-oh.

"You have a plan," I repeated dully.

"Yeah," she said, tossing the paper aside. "I thought about it a lot last night, and you know how we talked about how somebody, maybe even Rachel, wants to kill me, too?" She said this the way someone else, someone not as incurably sunny as my cousin, might say "wants to sell me a raffle ticket." Like it's an annoyance but nothing that can't be avoided.

"Yeah, I know," I said carefully, "but that's just a theory. We can't be sure . . ." I trailed off and then nodded. There was no use pretending. "But yeah, I know."

"Then what are we going to do about it?"

"*Do* about it?" I asked, incredulous. "*We* aren't going to do anything about it. *We* are going to let the police do something about it."

"Weren't you listening last night?" Nic said with exaggerated patience. "If it is Rachel, Seb already told us he can't hold her for Sailor's murder until he gets some proof that she did the dirty with those books and that Sailor knew about it. And even if she did, that's not why she tried to kill Wren. He needs some reason why she wanted to kill both of them."

"I get it, Nic," I said finally. "But we just have to wait until he has more to go on."

"Yeah, but can we wait that long? I mean, what if before your book guy gets the proof Seb needs or Seb figures out some other reason she hates us all, what if before all that *Rachel tries to kill me*?"

"Well, that's an awful thought," I said in my most measured tone, trying to turn down the temperature despite my own growing fear that she was right. "But there's nothing we can do about it."

"Yes, there is," Nic said triumphantly. "I figured it all out last night. Maybe Rachel just hates all of us because she's, I don't know, jealous of us. Maybe she just needed an excuse, like to . . . what do you call it . . ." She searched for the right word. ". . . to justify it. That's it! To *justify* to herself why Sailor should die, why Wren should die. Maybe we'll never know what her excuses were but we *can* give her an excuse for killing me. We can make Rachel *want* to kill me and then actually *try* to kill me. That's my plan!"

I stared at her. "That's not a plan, Nic. Waiting for Rachel Featherstonhaugh to try to kill you is *not* a plan."

Nic shook her head, frustrated at my slowness. "We're not gonna *wait* for her to try to kill me. We're gonna make it *easy* for her to try to kill me. Like today. Like, right now I invite her to meet me for coffee, and when she gets there, I say I have proof about her little book scam."

"Which you don't."

"Of course I don't. It's a lie, dummy. But she'll believe it because she knows she did it. So now she has a reason to shut me up."

"But what if the book scam wasn't her motive, even for Sailor? And, by the way, how are you going to get her to meet you in the first place? I can't imagine Rachel rushing out to have coffee with you."

"That's the best part," Nic said. "Who does Rachel love?"

"No idea."

Nic rolled her eyes. "Bertram. She loves the dog Bertram. So I bet you anything if I told her that I needed to talk to her about Bertram, she'd totally meet me."

I considered that. "Yeah, that might work. But what's the rest of the plan, Nic? You tell her you've got the goods on her and then we spend the next week looking over our shoulder waiting for her to poison you?" *Because*, I did not say, *you are not cohabitating with me for a week.*

"Of course not. Use your head, Tory."

"I'm trying, Nic." I sighed. "I'm really trying."

"And *then*," she continued with exaggerated patience, "I bring out something that looks like cocaine and tell her it's the leftover poison coke that Wren took and I say I need to go to the ladies' room and then I walk away and you'll be watching from another table while she puts the pretend poisoned cocaine in my coffee."

"Wait, wait, wait." It took me a minute to break that incredible sentence into its component parts. "You want to *trap* Rachel into trying to poison you?"

"Why not? She's done it twice before."

"Well, if she did, it was only after a lot of planning," I pointed out. "What makes you think you can get her riled up enough to try to poison you *in a coffee shop?*"

Nic heaved a sigh. "Keep up, Tor. I already told you that. *Bertram.* Nothing gets Rachel riled up like Bertram. I tell her that after our little talk, like *soon*, I'm going to blab the whole thing to Brooke Sinclair. All I have to do is say that when I tell Brooke, she'll take that doggy back in, like, a minute. And then she'll *give Bertram to me.* I guarantee you, the thought of that dog going to me will drive Rachel right over the edge. Then I say I'm going to the ladies' and I leave my purse behind on the table, like, by accident with the fake poisoned coke poking out of it and she'll pour it into my coffee while I'm gone and you'll video the whole thing with your cell phone."

"But presumably I'll be sitting far enough away that Rachel doesn't notice me, which means that I won't be able to *hear* your conversation. And even if I take a video of her pouring the fake cocaine in your coffee, she could just say she thought it was sweetener or something."

"Not if I secretly record our conversation on my phone," Nic said promptly.

"That's got to be illegal," I protested.

"Nope," Nic said. "I checked it out online." She tapped her phone and read aloud, "'New York is a one-party consent state. It requires that only one party consent to the recording of a conversation. It is legal for an individual to secretly record an in-person or phone conversation as long as that individual takes part in it.'"

Nic talking like a lawyer was mind-blowing. All I could do was stare at her.

"Okay," I finally conceded. "That might work. But where are you going to get the fake cocaine?"

Nic pulled a little see-through poly bag, maybe an inch-and-a-half square, out of the pocket of her—*my*—bathrobe. "This had a pair of these really cute earrings in it that I bought from one of those street vendors when I went home yesterday. It looks just like the bags dealers use, and, see, it has a teeny tiny ziplock top." She passed the mini baggie to me and I nodded. It did indeed have a teeny tiny ziplock top. "Now," she continued, "all we have to do is fill it with something that looks like cocaine, I don't know, like confectioner's sugar or something."

"You are devious, Nic," I said, impressed in spite of myself.

"I totally am," she said with great pride, adding, "I can do this, Tory. I can make her believe me. I'm a good actor."

"Yes, you are," I admitted.

"But first you have to explain that book-scammy thing to me again."

"I can do that," I said.

"So you're in?"

I thought about the scheme. The upside was that if all went according to plan, Rachel would give herself away and the nightmare would be over. The downside was that Rachel would *not* give herself away and all Nic would have succeeded in doing was putting a nice big bull's-eye on her back.

On the other hand, if Rachel was out to get Nic for some reason that we still didn't understand, that bull's-eye was already there, and there was little Sebastian could do about it short of twenty-four-hour protection. Which, if my admittedly limited knowledge of police procedure from *Law & Order* was correct, would require more justification than that Nic *might* be in danger from someone who *might* have killed two of her friends and who *might* not like her, either. So, yes, I admitted to myself, maybe the plan was risky, but no riskier than waiting for Rachel to act. At least this way, we'd be in control of the narrative—the where, the how, the why. At least this way, Nic would be in a public place. At least this way, she'd be safe from an outright physical attack. And at least this way, we might actually get some answers.

I briefly considered whether we should let Sebastian know what Nic was planning, but decided that, for his sake, it was better not to. I was pretty sure that law enforcement frowned upon cops who used civilians to try to trap killers. Better in this case, I decided, to ask for forgiveness later than permission now.

"Okay," I said, "I'm in."

Nic jumped up from the table and smothered me in a Nic hug. "Tory, I'm telling you, you won't regret it."

And despite every rational bone in my body telling me not to, I believed her.

THE PLAN TO LURE RACHEL INTO THE OPEN WENT, WELL, AC-cording to plan. A quick text from Nic asking to meet "because I'm worried about Bertram" worked like a charm. Within seconds, Rachel was texting back, trying to get more information. But Nic hung tough with further ominous texts like "better to talk in person" and "only care about Bertram's happiness."

Ultimately, Rachel agreed to meet Nic at ten for breakfast at Veselka. Nic and I had decided on the legendary East Village

Ukrainian restaurant/diner because (1) it was halfway between Washington Square and Rachel's apartment on Avenue A, and (2) I was enough of a regular there that I could sit on a stool at the lunch counter nursing a coffee while spying on Nic and Rachel without being rushed along. Also, it seemed Nic was "jonesing" for their challah French toast. Which was fair. Veselka's challah French toast is to die for.

Veselka is a Lower East Side institution. For generations, New Yorkers have been trekking to the eatery to nosh on its handmade pierogi, spoon up its borscht and savor tall glasses of sweet honey ice tea or heavy cups of the restaurant's secret (and highly guarded) blend of coffee. Nic and I had first started coming there for lunch on the occasional Saturday in our teens, where we would perch at the counter on high stools with black vinyl seats, chowing down on the restaurant's version of a Reuben made with their own sliced Krakovska ham. Heaven. As was, yes, the challah French toast.

We had almost two hours before meeting Rachel, which Nic insisted was plenty of time to prep for her role, as she put it. I outlined a combination of questions, threats and outright lies that I thought might, just might, goad Rachel into action. Nic, for her part, proved what I'd always known about her. She was the consummate professional, learning her dialogue within minutes and improvising on the spot when I, playing Rachel, threw curveballs her way.

When we felt confident that she was as prepared as she could be, I scrounged around the kitchen cabinets until I found an old box of confectioner's sugar that I'd once bought for no reason that I could now imagine.

"Will this do for the fake cocaine?" I asked.

"Perfect!" Nic said. She dumped a spoonful into the little poly bag, sealed it, and tucked it into her shoulder bag.

She then proceeded to take a lengthy shower in *my* bathroom, apply *my* blusher and mascara ("Really, Tory? *Drugstore* cosmetics?") and make free with *my* undies and *my* closet ("What? I'm going to wear my disgusting *yesterday* clothes?"). All I could think was *God help you, Tory Van Dyne, if this roommate situation goes on for much longer.*

I, in turn, pulled on an old tan raincoat, my sunglasses and a New York Yankees baseball cap that I found in the library's lost and found, in which outfit I hoped to be even more invisible than I usually was. Then I checked myself out in the mirror and was dismayed by how well the disguise worked.

Once Nic was resplendent and I was negligible, we trotted over to Second and 9th to get to the restaurant before Rachel. Peering through the storefront's plate glass window, we could see that there were only a handful of customers at the counter. So that was good. Still plenty of stools for me to choose from. The tables, too, looked to be only half-filled.

"I'll take the stool closest to the door," I said, then pointed to a small table for two far enough away that Rachel probably wouldn't notice me but close enough for an unobstructed sightline for my hopefully incriminating video. "You take that table and grab the chair facing the counter so Rachel has to sit with her back to me."

We pushed through the door. I slid onto my chosen stool, my back to the door, and the guy behind the counter looked up from topping off a customer's coffee long enough to give me a little nod of recognition. If he thought it was strange that I took a counter seat while my friend headed for a two-top, he didn't say anything. New Yorkers mind their own business.

"Breakfast?" he asked, holding out a plastic laminated menu.

"No, thanks," I said. "Just coffee."

"Gotcha," he said, tucking the menu away and plunking a

Veselka coffee mug in front of me with one hand and filling it with the other. The move was a thing of beauty. I took a sip and waited for that first hit. As always, wow. I put the mug down and tested out my barstool. It twirled me obediently toward Nic's table. Perfect. I swiveled back and placed my cell phone on the counter next to me, its camera already set at video just in case Rachel did indeed attempt to poison my cousin. I then applied myself to my coffee, all the while sneaking glances at the door.

Nic, in the meantime, had taken possession of her appointed table. She was dithering charmingly with the waiter over the blintzes with raspberry sauce versus the challah French toast when Rachel came into the restaurant.

She was, as usual, all beige. Hair, face, coat. All beige. Only her eyes, guarded, watchful, held any life. She spotted Nic, and I watched as suspicion hardened her usually expressionless face. Well, I thought, she's right to be suspicious.

Nic waved to Rachel with one hand and tapped her phone quickly with the other to start the recording. As Rachel headed toward her, she casually dropped a paper napkin over the phone.

It was time to catch us a killer.

Twenty-Five

◇◇◇◇◇◇◇◇◇◇◇◇◇◇◇◇◇◇

"Conversations are always dangerous, if you have something to hide."

—Miss Jane Marple, *A Caribbean Mystery*

**TRANSCRIPT OF CONVERSATION BETWEEN
NIC VAN DYNE AND RACHEL FEATHERSTONHAUGH.
[EDITORIAL COMMENTS COURTESY OF TORY VAN DYNE.]**

Nic: Rach! Rachel, over here.

Rachel [flatly]: I see you.

[sound of chair scraping]

Nic: I'm having the amazeballs challah French toast. What do you want?

Rachel: Nothing. I thought we were here to talk.

Nic: I talk better when I eat. How about a cup of coffee? You want a cup of coffee? I'm having some. It's delicious.

Rachel: Whatever.

Nic [to waiter]: Could you be a doll and bring us both some coffee?

[silence except for background hum of quiet conversation at

other tables and clink of plates and cutlery when server
brings coffee and the challah French toast]

Nic: Thank you. You're a doll.

[silence]

Nic [mouth full]: OMG this challah. I swoon.

Rachel: You wanted to talk to me about Bertie.

Nic: I did! How's he doing? I heard from Brooke Sinclair that
you're fostering him.

Rachel [heatedly, for her]: Not fostering. He's my dog now.

Nic: Well, yeah, maybe it seems like that. Except on paper he
still belongs to Brooke. I know 'cause she told me so. She
told me she's probably gonna want to take him back and
breed him at some point. And I'm not so sure Brooke would
want her dog living with a crook.

Rachel [maybe alarmed, but hard to tell]: What do you mean, a
crook?

Nic: I mean a crook. You know. Like somebody who steals a
superexpensive book by that Hemingway guy from the man
she works for and switches in a regular copy and then sells
the stolen book for pots of money? That kind of crook.

[silence from Rachel]

Nic: Wouldn't you call someone who did that a crook?

Rachel [faintly]: I didn't do that.

Nic: Yeah, you did.

Rachel: Who says I did?

Nic [lying]: Sailor Savoie said you did.

Rachel [clearly confused]: How would she know anything about
it? [Catches herself] I mean, I didn't do it, but even if I did,
how would she know?

Nic [a little confused on this point herself]: Well, um, she did.
And she told me. [lie]

Rachel: Anyway, she's dead.

Nic: And I bet you're glad of that. In fact [going way off script], I bet *you* were the one who put arsenic in her tequila.

Rachel [flatly]: No, I did not put arsenic in her tequila. If anyone did that, it was Howard. I told the police that.

Nic [still ad-libbing]: Yeah, right. And maybe it was *Howard*, who was *dead* at the time, who put that abrin stuff in the cocaine that sent Wren Madison to the hospital.

Rachel [clearly surprised]: Abrin?

Nic: Yeah. From that bead you ground up.

Rachel [shaking her head]: Not *me*. *I* didn't grind up any bead.

Nic [still ad-libbing madly]: Okay, maybe not you, but somebody did and put it in Wren's cocaine.

Rachel [again clearly surprised]: Why would he want to do that?

Nic [flummoxed again]: I dunno. [getting herself back on script] Anyway, I was with Wren the night she OD'd. The police don't know that and I'm not gonna tell them because my family would kill me if I got involved in that mess. Wren took a hit, but then she told me just to take the rest since she wasn't feeling so good. So I put it in my pocket and left. [takes bag of fake cocaine from her purse and puts it on the table] I still have it. [as if to herself] I should get rid of this . . .

Rachel [still puzzled]: First arsenic and then abrin?

Nic [giving it one last try]: Yeah, that you gave them.

Rachel [all flat again]: No, I didn't. I didn't have any reason to want to kill those girls.

Nic: Except that maybe they knew about your book scam. Or maybe because Sailor was the one who poisoned your dog. I mean we can't be *certain* how that happened.

Rachel [surprisingly calm]: No, she didn't. You must know that. [voice begins to shake] But you're right. Anyone who wanted to kill Bertie deserved to die.

[Brief moment while Nic tries to recover from that little statement]

Nic [finally]: Well, whatever. Anyway, I mean I get it. Feeling like that makes sense. [lie] I mean, you love that pooch. I do, too. [lie] He's the best. [lie]

Rachel [hopelessly]: He is. He loves me. He's the only friend I have.

Nic: And you're not going to have him for long.

Rachel [almost inaudible]: You aren't going to tell the police about the book, right? [catching herself] I mean, that I supposedly stole.

Nic [moving on]: No. I haven't told anybody. Nobody even knows I'm talking to you. And I'm for sure not getting mixed up with the police. [ha ha ha] I don't care about the book or who poisoned Sailor and Wren. [big lie, but completely convincing] Like I said in my text, I'm here about Bertie.

Rachel [fearfully]: What about Bertie?

Nic: Well, I love that doggie. That night when he was so sick and I held him in my arms, I knew we were meant to be together. [somehow said with a straight face] And, like I said, Brooke gets to decide who he lives with, right? Even if nobody can prove you stole any stupid old book, I'm telling Brooke about it. You know, everybody says she's the one who bought that Hemingway for Howard. [lie] So you stole a book that belonged to her.

[Rachel moans softly]

Nic: So, yeah, I'm not telling the police because they're gonna want proof and all, which, let's face it, there isn't any. Nope, I'm just telling Brooke, who will totally believe me, and she'll take that dog of hers away from you so fast it'll make your head spin. She won't keep him herself, of course. She's all gaga about that stupid new Pomeranian. But she really doesn't like other people claiming what she thinks is her stuff.

Rachel [distracted for a moment]: Yeah. That stupid, greedy bitch. You know, she's actually coming by on Thursday to steal back some painting of Howard's that she gave him on one of his birthdays, because now she figures it's hers and that [air quotes here] "very unattractive cousin couldn't possibly appreciate it."

Nic: Yeah, that sounds about right. So she's not going to give Bertram up. But she'll always need somebody to hold him for her. And once you're out of the picture, I'm first in line. She doesn't like you. Not even a little. But she likes me.

Rachel [voice tight with rage]: No, she doesn't like you. Don't forget, I was around a lot when she was hanging out with Howard at One Fifth. She was so jealous of you and your stupid friends. She hated that Howard called you his "sweethearts." That stupid old bitch didn't even know for the longest time that the only sweetheart Howard had was himself. Which is probably why she blew him off in the end. And I heard her after that memorial service talking to one of her so-called friends. She called Sailor and Wren hypocrites. She said they used Howard's dinner parties to network even though they were never going to let him be their agent. But she's no fan of yours, either. She said you were no better than them, taking expensive presents and

booze and drugs from him even though you're all rich and
he had to work for a living. She called you "entitled."

Nic [stunned by this diatribe and reverting to the playground]:
Yeah, well, at least I'm not a crook, so I win. I'll get the dog.

[silence while Rachel takes this in]

Rachel: Why are you telling me all this?

Nic [back on script]: 'Cause I'm a nice person, Rach. I'm no fan
of Brooke's, either, you know. At least this way, you're
prepared. I don't want to give her the satisfaction of seeing
you cry.

Rachel: I don't cry. Ever.

Nic [startled]: Well, gee, that's not very healthy.

[silence from Rachel]

Nic [getting up from her chair]: Well, listen, Rach. I've gotta use
the ladies'. Don't let the guy clear my coffee, okay? I've got a
long day ahead of me and I'm gonna need the caffeine."

[Nic unobtrusively slides phone into her shoulder bag and,
leaving fake cocaine baggie on the table, heads for the
ladies' room.]

This of course was my cue. I picked up my phone, turned
around on my stool and pretended to be a super boring tourist
making a super boring video of one of New York's landmark eater-
ies to post on my super boring Instagram feed, pausing only when
I got to Nic and Rachel's table.

Rachel sat there immobile, staring down at the little bag of
faux poisoned coke in front of her. I had to admit, I felt sorry for
the girl. I hadn't been able to hear the conversation at the time, of
course, but I'd seen the pain and shock on her face as Nic took her
punches. And now she was just sitting there, alone. As always.

Nobody was paying any attention to her. Nobody, as far as she was aware, knew that Nic was meeting with her. And nobody, as far as she was aware, knew what Nic knew. But Nic, as far as she was aware, would tell Brooke and Brooke would take Bertram away from Rachel and give him to Nic. All Rachel had to do to stop this from happening was tip some white powder from that little baggie into Nic's coffee. Just tip it into Nic's coffee and walk out.

And if she didn't? What next? What if our whole carefully worked-out plan was a bust?

Twenty-Six

◇◇◇◇◇◇◇◇◇◇◇◇◇◇◇◇◇◇◇

"I do not argue with obstinate men. I act in spite of them."
—Hercule Poirot, *The Mystery of the Blue
Train*

NIC CLICKED OFF THE RECORDING AND PUT HER PHONE DOWN
on the Christie Room coffee table. "Like I said, a total bust."

Because Rachel hadn't tipped that little bag of powdered sugar
into Nic's coffee. What Rachel had done was just sit there, rigid
and white-faced with suppressed emotion, whether rage or fear or
something else altogether was impossible to know. When she saw
Nic coming out of the ladies' room, she'd seemed to wake from her
trance. She stood and silently placed four one-dollar bills under her
untouched cup of coffee and left the restaurant.

A bust. A total bust. It was the Thursday after the total bust, and
Nic and I had effectively been summoned to the Principal's Office
(otherwise known as the Christie Room) by none other than Detective Sebastian Mendez-Cruz. Nic, once again preferring a foolish disclosure to a sensible reticence, had called him after her
meeting with Rachel to tell him about our little failed plan. The

detective's response had been a cold anger. And not with Nic. With Yours Truly. In fact, he'd demanded that Nic pass her phone to me so that he could give me his "take." His take seemed to be that I was my cousin's keeper and that I, in allowing Nic to put herself in harm's way *and* directly interfere in a police investigation, had acted "with surprising irresponsibility."

That's when it hit me. He was right. I had acted irresponsibly. And I had enjoyed it. It had felt wonderful to do something ill-conceived, foolish, maybe risky, probably even marginally illegal. For a brief time I had felt young.

Not that I said anything like that to Detective Sebastian Mendez-Cruz. Mostly because he wasn't done telling me off. Apparently, I had also deliberately gone against his "orders." Well, *that* got my dander up. Like I worked for the guy. He also demanded that I email him an MP3 file of the recorded conversation and that Nic and I come to the Sixth Precinct to discuss the issue "stat."

Now, I have a problem with the word "stat." It makes me not like the person who says it. And it makes me want to go very, very slowly. I informed Detective Mendez-Cruz that I was currently quite busy with work, but I would of course ask *Nic* to email him a copy of *her* recorded conversation as soon as possible. I also advised him that we would endeavor to be available the following evening if *he* would care to come discuss his concerns. He advised me that he would be there.

I confess my reasoning behind the delay was twofold. First, to show him he wasn't the boss of me. Second, because Detective Sebastian Mendez-Cruz was pretty scary when he got all cold and official and I needed time to talk Adrian into being there to act as a kind of buffer. Also, I was planning multiple pleas to the Universe to send me Mrs. Christie as well. Even if it was a Thursday. I mean, what was she going to miss? Harp lessons?

However, once I'd gone through the story with Adrian, it took me about five seconds to realize that he wasn't going to play along.

"Are you insane?" he'd said, leaning across his desk toward me. "I mean, I know Nic's insane, but *you*? What if that Rachel girl had had a gun? I mean, she could have shot Nic right there. She could have shot you!"

Which was ridiculous. "In Veselka?" I said. "In front of a half dozen people eating bagels with a schmear?"

Adrian had had to laugh, and the moment passed. But I knew that in the coming showdown with Detective Sebastian Mendez-Cruz, Adrian would definitely be on the scary detective's side.

So before the coming showdown, I grabbed Nic and Adrian for a last-ditch advance confab in Adrian's office. We'd hardly begun when the din of the doorbell interrupted. I went to explain that the library was closed, only to find Mairead, Tony in tow, grinning up at me and dressed, oddly, in what appeared to be some kind of clown outfit. What was she doing at my door on a Thursday evening? She opened her mouth to say something, but I really didn't care what important engagement her da had that evening. She was here, and I would have to make the best of it. Before she could get a word in, I said, "Okay, come in, and I'll catch you up."

This clearly hadn't been what she was expecting, but Mairead was not one to look a gift horse in the mouth. "Sure and I'll just text my da to pick me up later," she said, already tapping away on her phone.

Nic and I had been getting her up to speed in Adrian's office on what she called, awestruck, our "grand adventure," when at precisely six p.m. the doorbell announced the arrival of Detective Sebastian Mendez-Cruz. I opened the door and, after one look at his face, said nothing more than, "Come on in."

The five of us had then trooped silently upstairs, where (*thank you,*

thank you, thank you) Mrs. Christie was waiting for us in her favorite armchair. Nobody suggested drinks. Mairead took her usual
place at the table behind the couch, despite not having her laptop
with her. Adrian pulled Mrs. Christie's chair and one for himself
up to the coffee table and Nic and I sat very close together on the
couch as if our combined body heat might defend against the cold
front that was Mendez-Cruz sitting opposite us on the chair that,
in a brief moment of rebellion, I hoped was twice as uncomfortable
as it looked.

The detective had looked at us stony-faced. Well, not at everybody. Mostly at Nic and me. Well, mostly at me. Then he'd asked
Nic to explain her "plan" and to play the tape for the assembled
company. After which she'd made her "total bust" comment.

Mrs. Christie looked up from the transcript that I'd also provided and which she had been reading along with the audio. Her
face looked troubled, deeply troubled, but her words were mild. "I
am not so sure, Miss Nicola, that I would term your, ahem, conversation with Miss Featherstonhaugh, 'a total bust.'"

No, I thought, Mrs. Christie would never use so crude a phrase.
She would be much more likely to term it something like "an unmitigated disaster." But I was wrong. Instead she said, "There is
much to be learned here."

So Mrs. Christie didn't think it was an unmitigated disaster.
What had she heard that mitigated it? And why did she look so
concerned?

But Mrs. Christie wasn't ready for the big reveal, at least not
yet. "First, I believe Detective Mendez-Cruz has something he
wishes to say." Well, duh, you only had to look at his face to know
Detective Mendez-Cruz had something he wished to say.

In fact, he had a lot he wished to say. None of it pleasant.

"I'd like to speak openly with you today," he said, all quiet and cold, "but I seem to recall that the last time we met I made it very clear that what we discussed was not to leave this room. Why would I trust you now?"

"Because I lied to Rachel," Nic said proudly. "I lied about that book scam. I said you guys didn't know anything about it."

"You also told her Wren Madison was poisoned with abrin."

Well, yes, Nic had definitely gone off script with that one.

"Yeah, you got me there," Nic said. "I might have gotten a little carried away."

"The point is," the detective continued, staring directly at me while ostensibly chiding my cousin, "it was irresponsible and dangerous to confront a suspect in an ongoing homicide investigation."

If I'd hoped for some defense from Mrs. Christie, I hoped in vain. Apparently, she still wasn't ready to reveal why all of this wasn't an unmitigated disaster.

"I would agree with Detective Mendez-Cruz," she said, "about the very real risks involved in the meeting with Miss Featherston-haugh. I confess, I am deeply troubled myself. However, what is done is done, and I think we must move forward." *Yes, please.* "Detective, is there new information—which I am quite sure will be held in strictest confidence—which you feel would be helpful to your investigation to share with us at this juncture?"

I don't think it was my imagination that Mrs. Christie was somehow emphasizing the fact that the detective was the one who had controlled the flow of information in this case all along. That he decided what to share with us and when, only giving us as much as *we* needed to provide *him* with the background and details that might help him. Which meant he bore some responsibility if Nic and I had gone too far to give him that help.

Nor do I think it was my imagination that Sebastian, at that moment, understood exactly what she was saying.

"Well," he said formally, "I'm open to listening to questions any of you may have, but any new information will only be forthcoming if it does not in any way jeopardize the ongoing investigation."

Fine. If we were going to talk new information, I knew what I wanted to hear about. Without actually looking at the detective, I asked, "Were you able to confirm anything with the Strand or from Graham about the book swindle?"

Apparently, the detective had decided that this was something he could share, because he had a lot to say on that subject. Yes, the Strand had confirmed the sale to a Rachel Featherstonhaugh of a first edition of the Hemingway without the errata. And, yes, Graham had managed to follow the rumor trail to a certain slightly shady rare-book dealer, whose name the detective did not share, who had indeed been approached by a young woman who had preferred to remain anonymous. The young woman had a copy of the Hemingway *with* the errata (but without provenance) that she wished to sell for cash. When presented by the police with photos of several young women, the dealer unhesitatingly identified Rachel. Of course, the dealer was shocked, *shocked*, that the book was stolen goods.

"So there's your proof that the scam was real," I said. "Somehow Sailor knew about the scam and Rachel wanted to shut her up."

And, apparently, the detective wasn't averse to our usual team approach to speculation, especially if he thought you were on the wrong track.

"No," he corrected me, "what we have is proof that Rachel was working the book scam. And that's a step forward. But how would Sailor have figured it out? After all, Tory, you're in the rare-book business and you're smart, and it still took you some real thought and real digging." *Well, thanks for that at least.* "And once again I have to ask, does anyone here know why Sailor Savoie, even if by some remote chance she did stumble upon Rachel's secret, would want to hold it over her?" *Aha, so now we're back to our roles as expert witnesses.*

"Well, not me," Nic said. "I mean, even when Rachel asked me that same question, I couldn't come up with diddly. It was embarrassing, actually."

"So maybe Rachel had some other reason for wanting to kill Sailor," Adrian posited, clearly loath to give up his favorite suspect.

"For instance?" I asked.

"Well, I don't know. Jealousy? Maybe Rachel was jealous. Maybe she was secretly in love with Howard and jealous of his attention to Sailor. After all, Sailor was everything Rachel is not—beautiful, rich, easy to like. And that jealousy could apply to Wren and . . ." He trailed off. Even Adrian the Objective could not say "Nic."

Nic shook her head definitively on that one. "You heard Rachel. She wasn't jealous of anybody. She knew Howard only loved Howard."

Mrs. Christie voiced a little "ahem" to catch our attention. "Miss Nicola makes a good point. It is important to listen carefully to how and what Miss Featherstonhaugh actually says, and, of course, to what she does not say." She paused to let us absorb what I thought was a pretty enigmatic statement. "Because in the long run," she continued, "either through a lie, or through truth, people are bound to give themselves away."

Adrian looked at me, quickly mouthed, "Poirot in *After the Funeral*," and then turned his attention back to our leader.

"And I believe," she continued, "that thanks to Miss Nicola's deft management of their dialogue, Miss Featherstonhaugh has given herself away through both."

It probably isn't to my credit that I was a little hurt by not being given any recognition for whatever upside it was Mrs. Christie had discovered. Trust Nic to fix that omission, though.

"I didn't manage anything," she said. "Tory came up with the Q and A. All I had to do was learn my lines. Even though I did ad-lib a little." Bless her big heart. I thanked her with a little namaste hands gesture.

But Adrian, impatient with the mutual-admiration society, waved his copy of the typescript impatiently. "Yeah, well, how about we just skip to whatever it is Mrs., um, Mallowan sees in here as giving something away through a truth or a lie."

"I think I know," Mairead said quietly.

Truthfully, I think we'd all forgotten she was there. She had been, in fact, very, very quiet, reading and rereading the transcript, a worried frown on her usually clear brow.

"How very interesting, Mairead," Mrs. Christie said, nodding at her to go on.

"I think she gave away something about herself through the truth. I think she *didn't* kill Sailor Savoie. Or try to kill Wren Madison."

There was silence in the room as we all took this in. *Out of the mouth of babes*, I thought.

Mrs. Christie nodded at Mairead again, this time like a teacher ever so pleased with a star pupil. "Do go on, my dear."

"Well, can you not see that it's no bother to her when Nic accuses her of poisoning them? She just says she didn't do it. All quiet-like. Like Nic is being silly. She's not really irked a'tall."

"She's probably a sociopath," Adrian pointed out. "Sociopaths are often affectless." It would be well to mention here that Adrian's senior thesis at Vassar had been "The Mind of the Murderer in the Works of Ngaio Marsh as seen Through the Lens of Modern

Criminal Psychology." Ever since, Adrian had used the word "sociopath" whenever he detected an opening.

But I couldn't agree with him on this one. "No," I said. "Rachel's not always affectless. Just listen to her when she talks about Bertram. She's intensely emotional when it comes to that dog. Just not when it comes to Sailor or Wren."

"Which seems odd," Mrs. Christie put in, "since you mentioned that at the memorial service she was . . . livid, I believe was the word . . . yes, livid . . . at the idea that Miss Savoie might have been responsible for the dog's illness."

I thought back. "Actually, she just said trying to kill a defenseless little dog was wicked."

"She didn't mention Miss Savoie by name?"

I thought back. "No. Never by name. I guess I just assumed Howard had told her his preferred version of Bertram's near escape, which was that Sailor had deliberately given him an oxy."

I turned to the detective. "What do you think?"

He suddenly looked very tired, and despite everything, my heart went out to him. "I don't know what I think," he said carefully. "Mairead could be right. From this recording and from my own conversations with Rachel, I have to agree that she doesn't seem to have any strong feelings about Sailor *or* Wren. And she doesn't seem to have that urge to show off that we usually see in people who've plotted elaborate murders. They can't help giving themselves away, bragging just a little, saying things like, 'Wow, that's a pretty brilliant story you've come up with, but of course I didn't do it.' Rachel just says, 'I didn't do it.' But, as Adrian points out, that could be sociopathy. That being said, I have a strong feeling she's hiding something. And I also have a strong feeling that that young woman is dangerous."

Here's the thing. When you're scared—and now I was *really*

scared—your blood doesn't run cold. It runs like electric fire through your veins. It was hard to believe that Nic, only inches away, couldn't feel the heat coming off me in waves. But she sat there, seemingly unperturbed. "Well, she had her chance right there in Veselka and she didn't take it," she pointed out.

Which was true. The fire in my veins subsided a bit.

Sebastian sighed and seemed to concede the point. "Anyway, what I *feel* doesn't matter. It's only what we can *prove* that matters."

"No, Detective Mendez-Cruz," Mrs. Christie said, leaning toward him in her chair and, unusually for her, looking directly into his eyes. "I would not be so quick to discard your intuition. I would imagine that in your line of work what you call your *feeling* is really an impression based on logical deduction or experience. Almost without realizing it, you've noticed a host of small signs and details, and the result is the definite impression that something is wrong. But it is not a *guess*, it is an impression *based on experience*."

It wasn't until much later that I realized how cleverly she'd borrowed from Hercule Poirot in *The A.B.C. Murders*. At the time I was too taken up by trying to understand what the woman was clearly saying to Sebastian without actually saying it out loud. My feeling (ah, that word again) was that Mrs. Christie was speaking not in general but very specifically about one feature of the case in particular—and that Sebastian knew exactly which one. His eyes never left hers as she spoke, and when she had finished, he said nothing, simply nodded, as if they had come to some unspoken understanding.

But this silent dialogue, I thought, needed to be shared with the rest of us. Particularly with Nic. And I wasn't going to put Sebastian in the uncomfortable position of risking his professional integrity again by pushing him to say what at this point was only supposition. But maybe Mrs. Christie could and would. "What do *you* think?" I asked, turning to her. "Do you think Rachel is dangerous?"

Mrs. Christie seemed surprised that I needed to ask. "Oh yes, my dear," she said. "I now have no doubt that Ms. Featherstonhaugh is very dangerous indeed."

And with that coda, it seemed we were dismissed. Or at least most of us were dismissed. When Sebastian stood to take his leave, Mrs. Christie said quietly, "Detective, I wonder if I might have a word?" The detective nodded and sat down again while the rest of us filed out.

Twenty-Seven

◇◇◇◇◇◇◇◇◇◇◇◇◇◇◇◇◇◇◇◇◇◇

"The human face, after all, is nothing more nor less than a mask."
—Dr. Peter Lord, *Sad Cypress*

"DO YOU NEED ME TO WALK YOU HOME?" I ASKED MAIREAD AS the team headed downstairs.

"No bother," the girl said. "I've texted my da and he's coming by to take me over."

I didn't ask over to where. I was just too tired to care. Then the doorbell rang, and she said excitedly, "That'll be him now, no doubt." By this point I had plunked myself wearily on the bench by the door, so Nic obligingly opened it to The Man Who Could Be Mistaken for Colin Farrell—if he hadn't been wearing a red spongy ball on his nose. Which, when he saw Nic, he whipped off in double time.

"Well, hello," Nic said, brightening considerably. "You must be darling Mairead's wonderful father." *Darling* Mairead's *wonderful* father?

"And you must be the famous actress." The *famous* actress?

This ridiculous exchange of flattery went on for what seemed like hours but was probably only a few minutes. At a certain point, darling Mairead lost patience, stepped outside and pulled her father away by the hand. "We'll be sayin' goodbye now," she announced firmly and literally shut the door in the famous actress's face.

Adrian left shortly after the Irish contingent, and Nic and I sat in silence waiting for Sebastian—me rehashing in my mind the evening's disturbing possibilities and Nic, I was pretty sure, enjoying the afterglow of her little flirtation. Sebastian came downstairs after another fifteen minutes or so, and we saw him out, but only after Nic and I solemnly promised we would "stay put" for the time being.

Since it appeared we were under house arrest, I suggested we call out for food. But Nic found two frozen macaroni-and-cheese dinners hiding in the freezer, and we decided it was easier to nuke them than decide between Chinese or Turkish.

"Odd coincidence," Nic said around a mouthful of mushy macaroni. "Odd coincidence" is one of Nic's favorite games. For instance, it was an odd coincidence that Nic shared a birthday with Arnold Schwarzenneger. Or at least she thought it was an odd coincidence. I once tried to explain to her that there are only 365 days on which a person can have a birthday. This means that within a random group of twenty-three people, there is about a 50 percent chance that two of them will have the same birthday. Nic didn't care. "It's still an odd coincidence," she maintained. "I mean, that it's Arnold Schwarzenegger."

I wasn't really interested in today's odd coincidence, but just to be polite I asked, "What is?"

"That you and Rachel both like these frozen macaroni-and-cheese dinners."

I stared at her blankly. "And you know this how?"

"I've seen them in Howard's freezer. She keeps, I mean kept them there for lunch. I asked her about them once. Same lunch every day. She said that's what she usually ate at home for dinner, too. Said food didn't mean much to her."

"That's just sad," I said.

"Or just weird," Nic said matter-of-factly.

"Or sad and weird."

Nic nodded. "Like Rachel."

And suddenly, looking down at our sad, weird dinner, we both wished we'd gone with takeout.

Scraping our half-empty plates into the garbage, I announced that, as the night was still young, I was going down to my lab to catch up on some work. What I was really catching up on was a much anticipated trial run of my new Peachey English-style leather paring knife.

"Fine," Nic said in the tone of voice that I knew from long experience meant *not fine*. Nic requires pretty much constant entertainment.

"I think the new season of *Only Murders in the Building* starts tonight," I offered. At this, Nic perked up considerably and wandered off happily to the living room for a streaming binge.

If I'd thought that things were finally going to calm down a bit, I was sorely mistaken. I'd barely had time to don my lab coat and begin that first delicate shaving operation when Nic shouted down the stairs to the basement, "*Only Murders* doesn't drop until Sunday, so I'm going uptown to pick up some decent clothes. Back soon!"

For a moment, I was too stunned to respond. Not that responding would have made a difference. Nic was on the move, and Nic on the move was like a boulder bounding downhill. Unstoppable. But that didn't mean I wasn't going to try. *What was she thinking?*

What part of the word "dangerous" didn't she understand? Granted, it was highly unlikely that Rachel would find a way to poison Nic on her way uptown, but still . . . One thing was for certain, though—I wasn't going to give Sebastian Mendez-Cruz any more reason to accuse me of failing in my apparent duty as Nic's keeper.

But my mind's little feud with the detective, I realized, was simply my way of denying what was, in fact, a very real fear. Maybe the fear was irrational, maybe it was just a feeling. But Mrs. Christie had said to trust feelings, that they were intuition based on some kind of reality. And I could do worse than follow Mrs. Christie's advice. Plus, I really, really did not want Detective Mendez-Cruz all up in my face again. Not when I was just beginning to know him as Sebastian.

Within seconds I was up the stairs from the basement and out the front door. From the top of the front steps, I peered up the street for a glimpse of Nic in her hooded red vegan leather cape. I did not see my cousin in her hooded red vegan leather cape. What I saw was a zombie apocalypse.

To be more precise, what I saw were two dozen zombies lurching down the street and laughing like the demons from hell they were. Or were pretending to be. They were no more zombies than the half-dozen killer clowns in smeared red lipstick dancing up behind them were malevolent circus performers. Not zombies. Not killer clowns. Halloween revelers. I'd forgotten. I'd forgotten it was the 31st of October. Which meant that tonight was Halloween. Which explained Mairead's getup and her da's noseball. And the hordes of carousers. Because here's the thing about Halloween in New York City's Greenwich Village: Halloween in Greenwich Village means the Village Halloween Parade.

Which means thousands of wildly, often hilariously, costumed participants marching, dancing and just generally having the time of their lives as the parade wends its way up Sixth Avenue—a mere one block west. Thousands more, most of them also in costume, line the parade route to cheer them on, to point in wonder at the giant twenty-foot puppets (many of them articulated skeletons) dancing above their handlers and to dance to the tunes of marching bands ranging from New Orleans's Young Fellaz Brass Band to Brooklyn's all-female Brass Queens. It is the most bouncing, joyful, surreal Halloween party in the world. And my cousin had just stepped out into the thick of it.

Well, not quite the thick of it. The thick of it would be when the parade winding its way up Sixth hit our neck of the woods, in about—I checked my watch—a half hour. But until then there would be a steady river of costumed merrymakers pouring in from all over the city to watch the extravaganza.

Already literally hundreds were streaming west in front of me along Washington Square North, which, I now realized, had been blocked off to cars in anticipation of the crowds. My chances of finding Nic in that bobbing sea of Jokers, witches and mummies, even from my perch at the top of my front steps, were very slim.

And then I saw it. A red swirl at the end of the block, a red swirl just about to turn onto lower Fifth. *Of course.* Nic had realized there was no way she was going to get an Uber or a taxi in this mob scene. Instead, she'd decided to walk a half block east to Fifth and then head up to the Union Square subway station at 14th Street. *By herself.* I slammed the door shut behind me and raced down the steps and out the front gate, barely aware that I was wearing nothing warmer than my white lab coat.

I frantically elbowed my way against the tide of merrymakers heading west toward the parade route on Sixth, but the going was very slow. When I finally managed the half block and turned onto Fifth Avenue, the upstream swim was even worse. Fifth was still open to vehicles, which meant that the throng heading toward me had no choice but to jam the sidewalk. Granted, traffic was light, but this had only encouraged the regular Fifth Avenue buses to barrel down the avenue before turning left onto 8th Street toward Broadway at top speed. Nobody wanted to take a chance walking in the street with those behemoths zooming by.

I stood on tiptoe and tried to scan the crowd for a bright red hood, but there was no sign of Nic up ahead. Nonetheless, I pushed hard against the scrum. After what seemed like hours but was probably just a minute or two, I'd covered only the half block up to the Washington Mews, a private gated lane running east-west between Fifth Avenue and University Place. The mews is bordered on its south side by NYU's Irish-studies building, in front of which I stopped for a moment to try to catch my breath, and on its north side by the Art Deco magnificence of One Fifth Avenue, erstwhile home to Howard Calhoun.

I began to despair. I was never going to catch up with Nic at this rate. Not with people like those two women over there standing under One Fifth's green entrance canopy having a nice little chat right in the middle of the sidewalk, completely indifferent to those forced to circle around them. *My people*, I thought to myself, *how very proud I am of them.*

So it came as a bit of a shock when I realized that at least one of the women was, in fact, one of my people. She was, in fact, my cousin. She'd pushed back the hood of her cape, which explained how I'd missed her before.

I stood there staring, now myself completely indifferent to the inconvenience I was causing to those forced to circle around me. Who was that woman, her back to me, Nic was talking to? The woman with the helmet of perfect ash-blond hair and what looked like—could it be?—a small, framed painting under one arm. Rachel's words came back to me: *"She's actually coming by on Thursday to steal back some painting of Howard's."* Brooke Sinclair. Nic was talking to Brooke Sinclair. Who had, it seemed, followed through on her intention to lay claim to anything she could conceivably justify as belonging to her.

I shook my head in exasperation. Why was Brooke *always* in our business?

Obviously Nic had run into the woman on her way to the subway and had, ever polite, stopped to chat. Did I want to chat with Brooke Sinclair? No, I did not. I was only a half block away from them, but decided to wait until Nic was able to extricate herself from the social niceties, at which point I would dash over to my cousin and firmly guide her back to safety. Finally realizing that I was getting a lot of muttered "Stand in the middle of the sidewalk why don't you" from those forced to circle around me, I scooched back into the doorway of Ireland House, where I was out of the way of foot traffic but still had a clear sightline to Nic and Brooke, standing maybe fifty yards away.

I saw Brooke point up the avenue with her free hand, as if to say she would walk the few blocks with Nic to Union Square. I very much doubted that Brooke was headed for the subway so could only assume that she was off to one of her favorite haunts, the very staid and very pricey Restaurant Dominique between Fifth and Sixth on 11th Street. So the odds were they'd just walk three more blocks north and Nic would be free of her. I could easily follow them without Brooke noticing me. She probably wouldn't recognize me in my lab coat anyway. People see a lab coat and all they see is generic "doctor."

Brooke had moved on to showing Nic her (actually, I reminded myself, Howard's) painting. This was going to take a while. To pass the time, I began mentally awarding points to the costumed carousers streaming past me. I was just giving ten out of ten to a trio of drag artists costumed as circa-1960 stewardesses, none of them under six feet tall in their impossibly high-heeled pumps and equally sky-high beehive hairdos. I was admiring their sky-blue suits, jaunty pillbox hats and matching Pan Am flight bags when I saw it.

A slight but somehow malevolent figure in black sweats and one of those cowled *Scream* masks that look like a melting ghost face. The creature would not have stood out in the crowd except for the fact that it was standing stock-still not ten feet from the two women under the awning and staring—if a mask can be said to be staring—straight at them. Not moving. Just staring.

I started pushing forward through the crowd just as Brooke stashed the painting back under her arm and she and Nic began walking up Fifth.

Followed by the figure in the *Scream* mask.

Suddenly, the half block between us felt like a half mile. Hopefully the light at the corner of 8th and Fifth would be against them and I could catch up. I began to zigzag my way through the crush, calling out to Nic, but my cry of alarm was instantly absorbed by the hubbub of the crowd.

Desperate, I pushed through the ersatz flight attendants, shouting "Move, move, move! It's an emergency."

And suddenly the seas parted.

It took a moment for me to realize that the trio had essentially formed a flying wedge in front of me and were shoving people out of my way, shouting, "Let the doctor through!" Such is the power of a white lab coat.

Within a minute—which can seem like a very long time when your cousin is about to be attacked by a maniac—we were almost at the corner of 8th and Fifth. As we got closer, I could see that the light was indeed against Nic and Brooke. For a moment I was afraid they'd do that New York thing of crossing against the light and I'd be cut off. But, no, they were waiting obediently at the curb, probably because they'd noticed the M1 bus flying down Fifth and about to make its turn in front of them onto 8th. I was going to make it. Only a few more feet to go.

That's when I saw the creature reaching out with both hands. Reaching out to push my cousin in front of the M1 bus as it careened around the corner. *My cousin.*

And then somehow I was doing a flying tackle, screaming Nic's name. My hand found one vegan leather–covered arm and the next thing I knew, we were rolling together on the sidewalk. The relief was indescribable. Nic was safe from the creature with the melted face. The danger was over.

That was when I heard Brooke scream.

I looked up from the pavement, my hand still clutching Nic's arm, and saw the creature's true goal. Not Nic but Brooke. Brooke teetering dangerously on the edge of the curb, still clutching the painting and struggling in the grasp of a creature determined to pitch her in front of the bus as it made its turn. I tried to scramble to my feet to help her, but I knew I was too late. Everything had moved too quickly. The crowd around us, at a loss to understand what was happening, stood frozen.

Except for the stewardesses. The stewardesses were having none of it. Stewardess No. 1 leaped forward and grabbed for the sweatshirt's hood hanging down the creature's back and, with what appeared to me to be remarkable strength, used it to yank the creature off its feet. Stewardess No. 2 simultaneously snatched Brooke away from the curb, away from the bus zooming by just where she would have fallen. The creature, meanwhile, was twisting free from Stewardess No. 1 and might well have escaped if

Stewardess No. 3 hadn't taken one mighty swing at its head with her Pan Am flight bag and knocked the sucker senseless. In that way that the mind has of focusing on the ridiculous during the dangerous, my first thought was *What on earth does she have in that flight bag?*

My second and no less idiotic thought, as Stewardess No. 1 pulled the rubber scream mask off Brooke Sinclair's attacker, was, *What is Rachel Featherstonhaugh doing at the Village Halloween Parade?*

Twenty-Eight

◇◇◇◇◇◇◇◇◇◇◇◇◇◇◇◇◇◇◇◇◇◇◇

"Use that fluff of yours you call a brain."

—Miss Hinchcliffe to Miss Murgatroyd,

A Murder Is Announced

WHAT STEWARDESS NO. 3, AKA EDWINNA, HAD IN THAT FLIGHT bag was about twenty pounds of makeup.

I found this out while Nic and I were waiting at the Sixth Precinct to sign our witness statements, which had been taken by a very nice police officer while an ominously silent Detective Mendez-Cruz—called, of course, by Nic—stood by. The wait was mind-numbingly boring, except for one very uncomfortable moment when the police led a handcuffed Rachel, minus, thank god, the horrible mask, down the hall not three feet from us.

It was a relief when the stewardesses joined us to wait for their statements. Granted, it was probably weird that my first question to Stewardess No. 3 was about the flight bag that had delivered the knockout blow, but let's face it, the whole night had been weird.

"It's no joke getting ready for drag," she said in answer to my query. "It's an art, and it requires specialized tools. I was doing all three of us, so that's like three different foundations, three eye-shadow palettes, two kinds of hairspray for the wigs, you get the idea. And we were going to a parade after-party so I brought it all along with me for touch-ups."

"That makes sense," Nic said. "I always carry a complete makeup kit for touch-ups."

I, as someone who barely remembers to carry a lipstick and never remembers to do a touch-up, just nodded and asked my second most pressing question. "The way you handled yourselves," I said. "What was that? I mean, that was a coordinated response."

All three stewardesses, whose parade names I'd found out were Thomasina, Roberta and Edwinna, respectively, nodded in tandem.

"It's part of our day job," Edwinna explained. "Tom, Bob and I are flight attendants. We're trained in handling emergencies and, let's just say, obstreperous and in some cases dangerous passengers."

"You're trained to smack people on the head with a flight bag?" Nic asked in all seriousness.

"No, silly," Edwinna said. "That was just instinct."

"Yeah," Nic said, nodding sagely. "I've done it myself."

I decided not to ask Nic when she'd done it herself. Sometimes it's better not to know. Instead I said to our heroes, "You do realize that you three saved Brooke Sinclair's life."

"That's her name?" Thomasina asked.

"The woman with the helmet hair?" Roberta asked.

"The one dressed up as Margaret Thatcher?" Edwinna asked.

Before I could explain that that was no costume, another very nice police officer came to take the stewardesses back into the bowels of the station to sign their statements. After an exchange of hugs all around, our new friends were gone.

Nic turned to me. "It's, like, after midnight. They took our statements hours ago. Why don't they tell *us* we can leave?"

That familiar, quiet voice of authority sounded from behind us. "Because I told them not to."

Uh-oh.

THE WALK BACK TO WASHINGTON SQUARE WAS A SILENT ONE. It was well past midnight, and only the occasional Halloweener was still out. Even Nic was too nervous to talk. You only had to look at Detective Mendez-Cruz's face to know that there was going to be no easy way out of this. And I couldn't blame him this time. Tonight had been a textbook illustration of unintended consequences. Somehow Nic and I had put Brooke Sinclair in the path of a killer. The fact that when I'd weighed the pros and cons of Nic's plan to use Bertram to force Rachel into action, I'd never imagined that Rachel would use physical violence—let alone on Brooke Sinclair—was no excuse.

Nor was the fact that we—or, rather, Roberta, Edwinna and Thomasina—had prevented a sure tragedy going to cut much ice with Detective Mendez-Cruz. Not that it should. Our original "ill-conceived, dangerous and irresponsible" plan had been just that. I no longer felt young. I felt about a hundred years old and very, very tired.

"Do you want to come in?" I asked the scary detective when, after about two hundred years, we finally made it to our front gate. *Please say no.*

"Yes."

Uh-oh.

I unlocked the front door and the three of us filed upstairs in silence. I couldn't imagine taking him into my apartment, my safe space, so by mutual unspoken agreement we went into the Christie

Room. *Please let her be here,* I pleaded to the Universe before flicking on the light.

But Mrs. Christie was not there. The room was empty and cold and—for the first time in my experience—unwelcoming.

Nic and I sat on the blue couch facing the detective. For a long moment, nobody said anything.

"I'm not going to ask what you were thinking," he finally began. *Why do people always say that just before they* do *ask what you were thinking?* "I'm not going to ask why Nic thought it was a good idea to go out after she'd promised to stay here *for her own safety.*"

Nic opened her mouth to explain, and I shook my head at her. I mean, what was she going to say? *I wanted to get some decent clothes because Tory's are soooo boring? I thought Rachel was a poisoner, not a mugger?*

Now the cold dark eyes were turned on me. "Did it really not occur to you that someone who maybe poisons people and hates your cousin might try to maybe push her under a bus?"

Well, obviously I hadn't thought exactly that, *but I had been worried about* something *happening.* But I didn't say it. Because what was the point? Every step of the way, I'd failed to keep my cousin safe. I just shrugged and hung my head. Nic, realizing that this was probably the best approach to the situation, followed suit. So we just sat there, silent, like a pair of broken bobblehead dolls.

Detective Mendez-Cruz, still all frozen and official, said, "Going forward, both of you will take no further action in regard to Rachel Featherstonhaugh. She is in custody, so any danger is no longer immediate. I will tell you that she has been charged with the attempted murder of Brooke Sinclair and Brooke Sinclair only. Any evidence of her involvement in the death of Sailor Savoie or the attempt on Wren Madison is, at this point, purely circumstantial.

That may change as our discussions with her continue, but that is not, I repeat, *not* your concern."

Not our concern? I wanted to protest. *Of course it's our concern. What if it's not Rachel killing off the Belles of Broadway? What if it's somebody else out there? Have you thought of that?*

And then I realized that of course the detective had thought of that. And so I said nothing. Nic and I nodded silently in miserable unison.

"Good," Detective Sebastian Mendez-Cruz said, standing up to leave. "I'm glad we had this little talk."

Twenty-Nine

◇◇◇◇◇◇◇◇◇◇◇◇◇◇◇◇◇◇◇◇

"To get at the cause for a thing, we must study the effect."

—Mr. Satterthwaite to Harley Quin,

"At the Bell and Motley,"

The Mysterious Mr. Quin

IT IS A SHOCKING FACT OF LIFE THAT IT JUST GOES ON. NO MATter how dreadful any event is—how frightening—life just goes on. I already knew that, and yet I was somehow surprised when, the next day, life just went on. I woke and numbly chose something to wear, though to this day I do not know what it was. Something beige, I think.

I checked online and there was nothing in that day's *Post* or any other media outlet. No doubt to the bystanders of our near tragedy, the incident had just looked like a fracas that got out of hand, but no harm done. I mean, what was the paper going to say? "Nobody Hurt When Bus Fails to Run Over Rich Lady"?

I went down to the lab at eight a.m. and resumed my project with the new Peachey knife. It worked fine. I heard Adrian arrive at eight thirty and Susie jabbering away at nine. At nine fifteen I could hear Derek vacuuming the main reading room, and at ten footsteps overhead told me the library's first patrons of the day had arrived. I cleared my workspace at twelve thirty and trudged upstairs where I knew Adrian would be expecting me to join him for lunch.

And there he was, just outside his office door. He took one look at my face and held his arms out. I fell into them, buried my face into his chest and wept. Still holding me, he danced us backward into his office and shut the door behind us with one foot.

"What is it?" he asked. "What's happened?"

"I thought she was going to kill Nic," I sobbed.

Adrian stepped back, took me by the shoulders and sat me down gently in my usual chair. "Slow down, child," he said, his usually tamped-down island lilt coming through in his concern. "Slow down and tell me what's happened. Is Nic okay?"

I nodded.

"Good," he said. "That's good. And you, you're okay?"

I nodded again.

"Well, then, that's all that matters," he said gently. "You and Nic are okay."

BIT BY BIT, HE GOT THE STORY OUT OF ME. HE WAS ALMOST AS good a listener as Mrs. Christie, but without the embroidery hoop, and instead of murmuring "How very dreadful for you," was prone to whispering "You poor stupid kid." And somehow that was enormously comforting. It struck me that I was getting used to accepting a little help from my friends. I realized that talking about what had happened actually helped to exorcise the memory. *Who knew?* Well, obviously Dr. Cynthia knew. Poor Dr. Cynthia. If only I'd given her half a chance to do her job.

When I'd cried and talked it all out, Adrian passed me a nice clean handkerchief. (Were Adrian Gooding and Sebastian

Mendez-Cruz the last men in New York City to carry nice clean handkerchiefs?) "Here," he said. "Blow. You're all snotty and disgusting."

Which made me laugh.

"So what happens next?" he asked, when I'd finished mopping up the mess that was my face.

"You got me," I said, shrugging hopelessly. "He told us he'd be in touch, but I don't believe him. I think he's had it with me. Nic and me, I mean. Well, actually me. He's had it with me."

"You do understand that you had nothing to do with what happened last night, right? Nic was the one who went running off against orders. And if it hadn't been for you alerting the nurse drag queens . . ."

"They were stewardesses," I corrected him primly. "And the preferred term is 'drag artists.'"

Adrian nodded. "Duly noted. If it hadn't been for you alerting the *drag artist stewardesses*, Brooke Sinclair would probably be, well, dead."

"I guess so," I admitted reluctantly. "But what I still don't understand is why Rachel went for Brooke instead of Nic."

"That's easy," Adrian said matter-of-factly. "I think Rachel had been following Nic ever since they'd met at Veselka. So she knew Nic was staying with you. She also knew that Nic used the subway to get around town. So she figures all she has to do is wait until Nic comes out and follow her to the subway. The first day, that Wednesday, she takes up her post but Nic never comes out. But Thursday is different. First of all it's Halloween, so Rachel could wear a mask without standing out in the crowd. And better yet, Nic comes out, looks like she's heading for the subway. Rachel follows her, sees her meet Brooke. And, looking at the two of them standing there in front of One Fifth, Rachel figures out that *Nic* isn't the threat. Brooke Sinclair is. Nic actually said that to Rachel, remember? She said that Brooke could always find someone to take Bertram for her. So what would be the point of getting rid of Nic? She was just one in a long list of possibilities for taking on Bertram. So Brooke is the one who has to go."

"Oh lord," I whispered. "This really was all our fault."

"Oh yeah," he said. Just because he'd talked me off the ledge didn't mean he was going to sugarcoat the truth. Adrian was constitutionally incapable of sugarcoating anything. But he could offer some consolation. "Not that you were to know that a downtown bus was going to be Rachel's weapon of choice this time."

I thought about that. "It makes sense, though. Rachel wasn't going to get many opportunities to slip some arsenic in Brooke's tea or something. And even if she did, she's smart enough to know she'd be the first person *he* would suspect if Brooke keeled over after sipping her Lapsang souchong."

"What, you're never going to say *his* name again?"

I didn't pretend to misunderstand him. "I don't know what to call him. I can't call him Sebastian. He was Sebastian when we were, um, friends."

"Almost more than friends."

"Okay, maybe almost more than friends. But whatever we were, we're not that now. And I can't call him Detective Mendez-Cruz, like I only know him in some official capacity. And just Mendez-Cruz sounds, I don't know, like I'm mad at him or something."

"How about you just go back to 'Sebastian,'" Adrian suggested. "Or failing that, 'hot detective.'"

At which I laughed so hard I got the hiccups and Adrian had to go get me some water and tried to get me to drink from the opposite rim of the glass, which never works, and the water went all over his desk and we both laughed so hard we both got the hiccups. It was wonderful.

"So now we just wait, do nothing?" Adrian asked, wiping up his desk with yet another clean handkerchief, this one from his top right-hand desk drawer. I'd always wondered what he kept there. Women keep under-eye concealer and other necessities in their top right-hand desk drawer. That's the law. I didn't know what the law was for men. Generally not clean handkerchiefs, I suspected. Probably half-eaten Snickers bars.

"We could talk to Mrs. Christie," I offered, rationalizing that when the hot detective said no sharing, he certainly hadn't meant Mrs. Christie. "Let her know what's happened."

"You don't think she already knows?" This was probably as close as Adrian was ever going to get to admitting the possibility that Mrs. Christie might be, shall we say, omniscient.

I shook my head no. "She told me from the very beginning that she doesn't know anything more than we do."

"And what we tell her."

"And what we tell her."

"Okay, then, we'd better tell her."

Lacking any method of communication with the Eternity (*or whatever*) other than my usual secret plea to the Universe, Adrian and I decided to wait a few days for the next regularly scheduled Monday gathering. In the meantime I called my mom and then Mairead's da to update them on the continuing saga of dangerous missteps by the Van Dyne girls. Both surprised me by their response. My mother had been rather gratifyingly impressed by my failed heroics. And Cormac listened avidly, only to respond by saying, "Ach, but the lass will be disappointed to have missed all the excitement." As usual he seemed to find no problem with his daughter attending the upcoming chapter meeting of Agatha Inc. When I warned that things might go on well past the usual time, he assured me that he'd use that as an excuse not to cook dinner himself.

"Just have her text me when you're done, and I'll come by and take her over to Bleecker for a slice of John's." Yum, a slice from John's pizzeria, still the best slice in New York after almost a century.

THAT SATURDAY, MRS. MADISON CALLED ME WITH THE HAPPY news that Wren had been discharged from the hospital, apparently none the worse for her ordeal and suitably chastened as to recreational drug use.

"She says she can't even look at a can of Diet Coke these days," she announced happily.

As I suspected, there was no communication over the weekend from the hot detective to either Nic or me.

"I can understand him ghosting *me*," I said to Nic with maybe just the teeny tiniest bit of bitterness. "But not *you*."

Nic looked at me with infinite pity. "Tor, I get that you're clueless about stuff like this," she said. For a moment I didn't follow. I wasn't used to Nic calling me clueless. "But I'm not interested in Seb. I mean, yeah, I asked him out to dinner, but it took, like, five minutes and I could tell that he was, too, I don't know, *serious* for me and in, like, ten minutes that he wasn't interested in me anyway. He was interested in *you*. He's *still* interested in *you*. That's why he gets so, like, frozen when he has to tell you off. He hates doing that so he goes all policeman on you so it's not really him, Seb, I mean, being tough on you, it's Detective Mendez-Cruz."

I stared at my cousin, my cousin who had always been shrewd

about matters of the heart, as opposed to Yours Truly, who had always been, yes, clueless on that score.

"So you're saying he's the boy sitting behind you in school who pulls your braids because he likes you?"

"Got it in one, girl."

Despite Nic's assurances that Sebastian's occasional coldness was simply proof of his "interest" in me, I found I simply couldn't bring myself to invite him to join us on Monday and have him go all policeman on me again. It hurt too much.

So that evening Adrian, Nic, Mairead, Tony and I climbed upstairs to the Christie Room, where Mrs. Christie was just coming out of the kitchenette with an ice bucket in one hand and a bowl of cut limes in the other. *Of course.*

Adrian rushed over to take the offerings from her and placed them on the bar cart.

"Thank you, Mr. Gooding," she said. "You are ever the gentleman."

I swear to god Adrian gave her just the tiniest of bows, like some kind of Regency courtier to royalty. *Well, she is the Queen of Crime*, I thought before I could stop myself.

"I think tonight," Mrs. Christie announced, "the simple pleasure of gin and tonics."

While Adrian obediently did the honors, I caught Mrs. Christie up on the events of All Hallows' Eve, as she called it. Having gone through my story twice by this time—once to the police and once to Adrian—I found it almost easy to tell it again. *Lesson learned, Tory.*

Mairead, who had apparently given up on her secretarial duties given the absence of the hot detective, plunked herself down crosslegged on the floor next to Mrs. Christie and listened avidly to my tale. Tony found the whole thing boring and snored in Mairead's lap.

Nic briefly slipped out of the room toward the end of my spiel, but returned shortly to sit, miserable, next to me on the couch, limiting her contribution to, "It was all my stupid fault. Tory was the one who was scared something might happen, who tried to catch up with stupid me, who saw Rachel in that horrible mask and that Prada hoodie watching Brooke and stupid me, Tory who thought I was going to get killed. Stupid me was totally clueless."

I'd never seen Nic in self-flagellation mode before. I didn't like it at all. Neither, it appeared, did Mrs. Christie.

"I do think your self-reproach is misplaced, my dear," she said tactfully. "*No one*"—and here she looked directly at me—"is to be blamed for a crime except the person who committed it. In this case, Miss Featherstonhaugh."

There is nothing like the lifting of the burden of guilt. Nic was right in there with "Mrs. M, you're the best." I started to add my own thanks for her absolution, but only got as far as "Thank you so . . ." when I was distracted by Adrian, who'd been sitting quietly on the other side of the coffee table from me, clearing his throat theatrically. Catching my eye, he stared pointedly over my shoulder at the door to the Christie Room. I turned my head, and there he was, standing quietly just inside the doorway. Click, click, click.

The words died in my mouth. At this, Mairead looked up from playing with Tony, and Mrs. Christie turned to see what, or in this case who, had stopped me in my verbal tracks.

"Isn't that so, Detective Mendez-Cruz?" she said pointedly.

"Absolutely," he replied. "And I need to remember it."

I suppose I should have basked a bit in the glow of this almost apology on the part of Detective Mendez-Cruz—*Sebastian*, I reminded myself—but I was too dumbfounded by his arrival to enjoy the moment. Plus, my heart was racing. All the man had to do was walk in the room and my heart was racing. Even more humiliating, I could feel the blood rushing to my face. To hide my confusion—or whatever it was—I decided to get angry at him for his *uninvited* appearance *in my house*. Which was, after all, rather rude.

"What are you doing here?" I demanded.

"I was invited," Sebastian said.

But I wasn't done being prickly. "By who?"

"Oh, that was me, my dear," Mrs. Christie said, as if it should have been obvious. "I had a few questions for Detective Mendez-Cruz after our gathering last week and suggested that he follow up with us tonight."

I was about to go into a this-is-*my*-house routine when I remembered that Mrs. Christie felt the same way about the Christie Room. And this was not the time to argue that point.

"And I let him in," Nic added helpfully.

"You knew he was coming?" Now I really was annoyed. *Why did everybody know what was going on except me?*

"Of course not. I would have told you if I did," Nic said. "I just got a text saying he was almost here and would I come down and let him in since he couldn't reach you."

Uh-oh.

I took out my phone. Yup. Muted. As it pretty much always was when I was working. And I'd forgotten to turn the sound back on, as I pretty much always did.

Okay. Mystery solved. Let's get back to how Detective Mendez-Cruz should not be blaming the victims.

But no, Mrs. Christie had other plans. "Won't you come take a seat, Detective? And perhaps update us on your research, if you feel it is now appropriate."

"Of course," he said, taking a seat on the hopefully more-comfortable-than-it-looked wooden chair and pulling the battered notebook out of an equally battered pocket of an equally battered mud-brown tweed suit. *Hopeless*, I thought to myself, *the man is hopeless when it comes to clothes*. And my heart melted.

"First, I want to update you on Featherstonhaugh's justification for the attack on Mrs. Sinclair." Was it significant that Sebastian was no longer calling Rachel "Ms. Featherstonhaugh"?

"This I gotta hear," Adrian muttered.

"I'm only sharing this because Nic may be called upon to confirm her defense."

"Whatever it is, I won't," Nic said stoutly.

"You may not have a choice," Sebastian responded. "She says she was only trying to stop Mrs. Sinclair from stealing a painting from Calhoun's apartment. They struggled for it and Mrs. Sinclair tripped and started to fall."

We should have been prepared for this admittedly very clever pivot from the truth.

"It's credible," I said, almost against my will. "It's a lie, but it's credible. I suppose that's how she'll justify wearing that horrible mask. She'll say she didn't want Brooke to know she was the one who took the painting back from her."

Sebastian nodded. "Exactly. She says she was planning to return it to Calhoun's cousin anonymously."

"So she's going to wriggle out of this attack, just like she wriggled out of the attacks on Sailor Savoie and Wren Madison," Adrian said.

For a moment, Sebastian looked like he was going to counter the assumption of Rachel's guilt in those attacks, but then seemed to catch himself.

"No one's wriggling out of anything," he said quietly. "Not if I can help it."

Why was it that when the man was at his quietest, he was also at his scariest? For a moment I almost felt sorry for Rachel if she did turn out to be the poisoner. I wouldn't want this guy coming after me.

Adrian, despite his clear preference for Rachel as the perpetrator, could not help but be objective.

"Actually," he pointed out, "what about Brooke Sinclair? *She's* a dark horse. We know that she resented Calhoun's attentions to Sailor and was no fan of Wren's, either. Also, by all accounts, she was in and out of his flat at her own whim. Maybe she saw that bottle of tequila sitting around with the note about Sailor's birthday. Maybe Calhoun told her about emerald green. Maybe she was the one who cooked down the arsenic in his kitchen and added it to the bottle. *And* she was with Calhoun in India when he bought that jewelry. She might have known about rosary peas."

I had to admit, Adrian had worked it out thoroughly. I thought about all the times that Brooke seemed to pop up in the case. I even wondered wildly if she had been planning to push Nic under that bus before Rachel so rudely interrupted her. And it certainly explained something that had bothered me at the memorial service.

"And there was that line of Brooke's at Howard's memorial," I added, "about those who didn't give Howard the credit he deserved in his lifetime now having a lifetime of their own to pay that debt. Maybe she literally meant a *life* of their own. Maybe she meant Sailor's and Wren's lives."

I should have known. I should have known that Detective Sebastian Mendez-Cruz had already been down that road.

"It's a credible theory," he acknowledged, "but after talking with Mrs. Sinclair, we're convinced that she had nothing to do with the poisonings of Sailor Savoie and Wren Madison."

This amazed me. "How do you get away with questioning a

society matron who has just escaped death by crazy about her possible involvement in another case?"

Sebastian looked shocked. "You don't, of course. Not without a warrant. That information was *volunteered* by Mrs. Sinclair."

"Well, I'm glad to hear it," I said.

"Which doesn't mean that I didn't encourage our conversation to be, let's say, wide-ranging," Sebastian admitted. "Even to the extent that at one point, Mrs. Sinclair, after some initial embarrassment, confirmed Nic's *information received* that during the two weeks between Calhoun buying the tequila and Featherstonhaugh sending it to Sailor Savoie, she was recovering at her house in the Hamptons from something called 'lasering' on her face. She says, and her housekeeper confirms, that she never left her beach house until the day of the memorial service."

Nic nodded sagely. "Yeah, it takes about two weeks for those scabs to fall off. That lady wasn't going anywhere looking like that. Not even to kill somebody."

"To state the obvious," Sebastian concluded, "Brooke Sinclair had no opportunity to tamper with that bottle. So she is in the clear in terms of Sailor Savoie's death." He paused significantly.

"But not the attack on Wren?" I prompted.

"Oh yes," he said, "she's in the clear on that one, as well."

Quite frankly, I had to admit it strained credulity to imagine Brooke Sinclair in conversation with a drug dealer. "Oh, my dear, your blow is simply divine." Nope. Didn't work. But before I could ask how Sebastian knew Brooke was in the clear—*which, of course, he wouldn't answer anyway*—Adrian was galloping ahead.

"Which means we're back to Rachel," he said with some satisfaction. "It doesn't matter if we haven't come up with a motive. There's no other suspect left."

"Oh no, Mr. Gooding," Mrs. Christie put in so mildly that I

was immediately suspicious. "Of course there's another suspect. And the motive, in their case, would arguably point to them as the killer."

Even Adrian didn't know what to say to that.

I looked to Sebastian, willing him to give me some sense that he knew where this was going. But his face revealed nothing. Click, click, click.

Mrs. Christie looked around at the rest of us as if expecting that we would announce as one who the real killer might be. When it became clear that that wasn't going to happen, she gave up. "You remember, of course, the essential question—Who benefits?"

The question was rhetorical but we all nodded anyway.

"Well, clearly," Mrs. Christie said, as if the rest of us should have recognized this ages ago, "if all had gone according to plan, the person who, first and foremost, would benefit from the death of Miss Savoie and Miss Madison would be Miss Nicola Van Dyne."

Thirty

◇◇◇◇◇◇◇◇◇◇

"It's lucky it's not in a book. They don't really like the young and beautiful girl to have done it."

—Ariadne Oliver, *Cards on the Table*

IT WAS LIKE SOME HORRIBLE ECHO OF GREAT-AUNT DORIS AT Sunday dinner. *"I never liked how that Savoie girl always got all the best parts. So it's very good news for you, Nicola dear."* Except this wasn't Great-Aunt Doris talking. This was Mrs. Christie talking. Who'd been right *every time.*

While the rest of us were trying to manage our shock, Mairead took barely a second to react. "Aye, she's the least likely," she said. I kept forgetting she was only a kid.

That brought at least one of us out of our trance.

"You bet I'm the least likely," Nic said, her face a thundercloud. "I'm the least likely because all the *benefit* I got out of Sailor dying was a dead friend. And all the *benefit* I would have gotten from Wren dying was *another* dead friend."

At which point she burst into tears, and I did what I always do. I wrapped my arms around her and murmured, "It's all right, Nic.

Everything's going to be all right." Which I did not believe for a minute.

This seemed to bring the reality of the situation home to the youngest member of the team. Her forehead creasing with concern, she looked to Mrs. Christie for an explanation. "But sure you're having us on, Mrs. Mallowan?"

"Oh, my dear Mairead, murder isn't a game," Mrs. Christie admonished her sadly. It was only much later that I realized she was channeling Miss Marple from *A Murder Is Announced*. At the moment my brain was in no condition to search my catalogue of great Agatha Christie quotes. At the moment my brain was just shouting *No no no*.

I looked around me. Judging by the stunned look on Adrian's face, he was similarly staggered. Sebastian, of course, was unreadable. Click, click, click.

"But you have misunderstood me," Mrs. Christie continued. "You've heard what you *feared*, not what was actually said." *Oh, thank god.* "What I said was Miss Nicola *first and foremost* would have benefited from the death of Miss Savoie and . . ."

"How?" Nic interrupted angrily. "How? How would I have benefitted from Sailor's death? You tell me that."

A trace of annoyance, perhaps at being interrupted yet again, could now be heard in Mrs. Christie's voice. Rather than try to explain how we had misunderstood her, she decided, rather tetchily I thought, to counter Nic's defense point by point. "Why, Miss Nicola, the answer is obvious. With Miss Savoie out of the way, wouldn't you be that much closer to a role in Mr. Neuman's film?"

"*No*," Nic said. "Because I didn't *want* Sailor's role. I didn't want Beast and I always knew I wasn't going to get it because I would stink at it and Grant Neuman knew that."

Mrs. Christie beamed at Nic as if she'd said exactly the right thing—which I could see was confusing for Nic, as she hardly ever says exactly the right thing. "And didn't Mr. Neuman tell Mr. Calhoun that you'd be very good as Belle, if it were not for your friend Wren? Who is, I gather, quite exceptional."

I was beginning to see where this was going. "Nic," I began, "she's not saying . . ."

But before I could finish, my cousin was taking her next big swing. "Well, sure, Mrs. M. I told you that already. So why kill Sailor? Why not just kill Wren?"

"Because," Mrs. Christie explained patiently, "as I believe Mr. Neuman *also* explained to Mr. Calhoun, if Miss Madison for some reason could not continue in the role of Belle, he would simply replace her with Miss Savoie."

"But Nic didn't know that," I protested. "She didn't know it until the gala, when Grant told us."

"Yeah," Nic said, and then added, distracted from her own defense, "and even if I did . . ." *Oh, great, Nic.* ". . . and I didn't, why kill Sailor first and then Wren? Your way is all out of order."

Well, Mairead knew the answer to that one. "Because if Sailor is killed first," she piped up, "it appears there's no motive because you didn't want her part as Beast and knew you wouldn't get it and have witnesses to prove that. So, then, when Wren dies, Sailor is already out of the way and it just looks like you got lucky."

Nic stared at the girl as if she had snakes instead of curls on her head. "You can't believe I'd do that."

"Ach, not a'tall," Mairead said, adding with the ruthless honesty of childhood, "For sure, anyone who knows you would never believe you could have worked out that plan. I mean no offense, but Tom Ripley you are not."

Nic, fortunately, took no offense at being compared to and

found wanting against Patricia Highsmith's antihero, since Nic had no idea who Tom Ripley was. But she had definitely caught Mairead's gist. "So you don't think I could have done it."

"Not half," Mairead said dismissively, earning a full-blast Nic smile as a reward. Never had an insult been so well received.

Nic now turned back to her BFF-turned-tormentor. "Then why did *you* say I killed Sailor and tried to kill Wren, Mrs. Mallowan?"

"Oh no, my dear," Mrs. Christie hastened to explain before she could be cut short yet again, "I did not say you killed Miss Savoie and tried to kill Miss Madison."

"That's sure what it sounded like," Nic muttered.

Adrian, who had been remarkably silent through all this back-and-forth, could no longer hold back. "It's Rachel," he announced, triumphant in his conviction that we were again bearing down on his number one suspect.

He turned to Mairead, adding, "It's a good theory of yours, but overly complicated. I mean really, who goes first, who goes second. It's crazy. But with Rachel it's simple. Hated them both. Took the opportunity when it presented itself."

He paused and looked significantly at Mrs. Christie. "And it's like Hercule Poirot always says, the simplest explanation is always the most likely."

Mrs. Christie smiled at Adrian benignly, which I knew from experience was a bad sign. I thought back to the first time Adrian had posited Rachel as the killer. Mrs. Christie, it now seemed to me, had had reservations even then about that conclusion. *It is always wise to suspect everybody until you can prove logically, and to your own satisfaction, that they are innocent.*

"And yet, my dear Mr. Gooding," she said, "Monsieur Poirot was also a great believer in the *psychology* of a killer. As he says in *Murder on the Orient Express*, it is not the mere act of killing, it is what lies behind it that appeals to the expert." *Oh, nice one*, I thought. She hardly needed to add, *And you are no expert.* "Though I always felt as you did, that under certain circumstances Miss Featherstonhaugh had it in her to kill, I also agree with Detective Mendez-Cruz that she does not have the psychological makeup for this type of crime. She is quiet, almost dull, but when truly roused reacts strongly and almost completely in the moment. As she did when she attacked Mrs. Sinclair."

"'It's like all those quiet people,'" I felt compelled to put in, à la Megan Barnard in *The A.B.C. Murders.* "'When they do lose their tempers they lose them with a vengeance.'"

Mrs. Christie favored me with a smile. "Exactly." Adrian favored me with a glare, which I chose to ignore.

"'And this is a crime . . . '" I said, continuing the Poirot quote (I mean how many chances do you have to show off what is admittedly a pretty esoteric little hobby?), "'. . . very carefully planned and staged. It is a far-sighted, long-headed crime. It is a crime that shows traces of a cool, resourceful, deliberate brain.'"

"Well said, Miss Van Dyne," Mrs. Christie said with that smile of hers that makes you feel like you've been accepted as a member of a very exclusive club.

Adrian snorted. "Whose side are you on, anyway?" he asked me.

"I'm on the side that says Nic didn't do it," I shot back.

"Yeah, well, Mrs. Mallowan says I *did* do it," Nic muttered.

Mrs. Christie heaved a great sigh. "Miss Van Dyne, I have repeatedly tried to explain that I did *not* say that. What I said was that you *first and foremost* would have benefited from the deaths of those two young women. What you have repeatedly prevented me from saying is that you are not the *only* person who would have benefited. There was another who would *also* have benefited, *secondly but still significantly*, from your change in fortune. Another person who *did* know that both women would have to die to ensure that the role of Belle came to you."

She paused for a moment. Nobody said a word. Honest to god the woman really knew how to hold an audience.

"No, my dear, I did not say you killed Miss Savoie and tried to kill Miss Madison. I'm afraid that distinction goes to your agent, Mr. Howard Calhoun."

Thirty-One

◇◇◇◇◇◇◇◇◇◇◇◇◇◇◇◇

*"That's your business. It's the business of the police. What do we
pay rates and taxes for, I should like to know?"*

—Mrs. Price Ridley to Chief Constable
Melchett, *The Murder at the Vicarage*

"BUT HOWARD WAS DEAD BEFORE ANY OF THIS EVEN HAP-
pened!" Nic cried. "And he didn't need me. He had Sailor. She was
going to be his ticket out of bankruptcy. He told me that!"

I despaired of my cousin, who somehow didn't know to shut up
and take the gift of not being accused of poisoning her two best
friends. No, Nic decides she needs to state the obvious flaws in
Mrs. M's argument. She was maybe still just a little pissed off at
Mrs. M.

"Oh, my dear, you should never believe anything anyone says
without first checking it," Mrs. Christie said, appropriating one of
the Belgian detective's "first axioms" from *Third Girl*. "As I'm sure
Detective Mendez-Cruz would agree." Mrs. Christie then modestly ceded the floor to Sebastian with a nod and a smile.

And looking at him smiling back at her, I understood why he'd
been so quiet, so poker-faced through the whole did-Nic-kill-
Sailor-and-Wren-or-was-it-Rachel-or-surprise!-it-was-Howard

discussion. He wasn't trying to hide his surprise because he wasn't surprised. Ever since Mrs. Christie had pulled him aside for "a word" at our last little get-together—which no doubt had been the theory she'd just presented to the team—he'd been coordinating the good, solid police work needed to prove or disprove her thesis and his own intuition right. Much like Poirot and Miss Marple, Mrs. Christie had been reluctant to share her conclusions until she was very sure of her case.

His first words confirmed my assumption. "When Mrs. Mallowan and I talked after the last meeting, she asked me a few questions she thought I could help answer. The first was, of course, did Sailor Savoie really intend to take on Calhoun as her agent?"

"Good question," Mairead said admiringly.

Sebastian smiled at her. "I agree. So I talked to Grant Neuman, and he said, and I quote, 'Not unless she was lying to me when she told me she was signing with that hotshot Grace Chan at William Morris.'"

"Ooh, Grace Chan," Nic breathed, lost in momentary envy. "She's the best." Then, coming back to the matter at hand, she asked, "So why did Howard say Sailor was signing with him?" Which I thought was a good question.

And then the light dawned. "So that," I said, "in the remote chance that Sailor's death was seen as suspicious, everyone would think that he had no motive for killing her." I was very pleased to see Mrs. Christie inclining her head in agreement.

"Oh yeah," Nic said. "Like we all did."

"Like we all did," I admitted. I looked sharply at Sebastian. "But you weren't so sure. I remember when that came up, you said, 'We need to look into that.' And you already were looking into it, weren't you, even before Mrs. Chr . . . um . . . Mallowan asked you to?"

"I was," Sebastian said. "But I have to admit it was because of something Mrs. Mallowan once said that was nagging at me. She said, 'We would do well to remember that Mr. Calhoun's financial situation does seem to have governed his actions.'"

"I remember that," I said. "I remember because at the time it sounded more like a caution against, rather than confirmation for, the argument that Calhoun needed Sailor alive."

"Exactly. So I decided to find out if Sailor Savoie was, in fact, going to save Calhoun's financial ass." He stopped abruptly and colored, looking shamefaced at Mrs. Christie. "If you'll excuse my French."

Mrs. Christie nodded regally. "Of course, Detective. Think nothing of it."

"Thank you," he said. "And when I complained that there was no obvious reason why *anyone* would want to kill Sailor Savoie, you said the why must never be obvious, that that was the whole point."

Mrs. Christie nodded. "Because, of course, somebody was making very sure that the why was *not* obvious. And I found it difficult to imagine that that somebody was Ms. Featherstonhaugh, who by all accounts was making a terrible hash of hiding her dislike of Miss Savoie. Whereas Mr. Calhoun, if he was lying about Miss Savoie becoming his client, was doing a masterful job of seeming to have no motive—of, in fact, hiding the why." Here she paused and then said with a mischievous glance at the detective, "The why, of course, being to save—through Miss Nicola, *not* Miss Savoie—his financial ass."

It took some time after that to call the meeting back to order. I was doing my usual embarrassing laughy/snorty thing, Nic was literally falling sideways laughing, and Mairead was giggling madly. Even Adrian was grinning. Sebastian and Mrs. Christie simply sat there soaking in the audience reaction to their partners-in-crime-fighting comedy routine.

"But it's true," Nic said once she'd righted herself. "I'd get, like, seven figures for that role, so Howard's twenty percent would be like . . ." She paused, and then gave up. "Like a lot. And once I was a big movie star, the money would just keep coming." For a moment, I had a vision of Nic lying by the pool at the Bel-Air while producers rained hundred-dollar bills on her.

It was Adrian the Objective, of course, who brought us back to reality. "Okay, so Calhoun lied about Sailor becoming his client. That doesn't prove he's the killer. It just makes him a blowhard. The only real evidence we have in this case is still Rachel's fingerprints on the poisoned tequila bottle. If it was Calhoun, don't we need some real evidence against him?"

I looked to see what Sebastian was making of this challenge, but he merely smiled and said equably, "I think I can help you with that. It's true that Rachel's fingerprints on the bottle are the only solid evidence we have, although it's going to be hard to disprove her statement that she sent the bottle at Calhoun's request. And there's nothing to indicate she was the one who put the arsenic in it."

"But she did know about the arsenic in the book cover," I pointed out.

"She did. But do you remember how, when I told her we knew the cover had been boiled down to a reduction, she said, 'So you think I switched out the tequila in that bottle for *a bunch of poisoned water*.' She clearly had no idea what a reduction was."

"I can believe it," Nic said. "She's no cook. The girl lives on frozen dinners."

"And she thought the tequila had been *replaced* by this bunch of poisoned water," Sebastian said. "So all that was significant, though not proof of her innocence. But it was enough to make me look hard at Calhoun. The onus was on my team to find direct evidence against him."

He flipped back a few pages in his notebook. "Let's look at the timeline. On Monday, September 16, he gets back from India. The following Friday, September 20, Grant Neuman tells him that Nic is not getting the role of Mrs. Potts. Not only that, he says that if Wren Madison doesn't come through as Belle, the role will go to Sailor Savoie."

I nodded. "That sounds about right. Grant told us that at the gala." And, I suddenly remembered, when I'd relayed that bit of news to Mrs. Christie, she had said, 'My, my, that *is* interesting.'" *Sigh. Missed another one, Tory.*

"And Howard never told me," Nic added bitterly.

"No, of course he didn't," Sebastian said. "All he told you was that lie about Sailor. Because clearly almost immediately after talking to Neuman he knew what he was going to do."

"Which was curious," Mrs. Christie murmured to herself. *Aha.* Maybe I'd finally caught one. I made a mental note. *Come back to that, Tory.*

"We know this," Sebastian continued as if she hadn't spoken, "because when Mrs. Mallowan and I talked last week, she asked if I could find out if Mr. Calhoun had researched poisons, particularly arsenic."

"I was thinking, of course," Mrs. Christie explained, "of books on poison which Mr. Calhoun might have owned or borrowed. Detective Mendez-Cruz advised me that such research can now easily be done on a computer, which," she added wonderingly, "it seems everyone now has in their homes, not just exceptionally bright young people like Miss Butler." At which Mairead beamed but also looked a bit perplexed. "Moreover, it appears the computer retains a record of these researches."

This inexperience with computers made sense to me because when the real Agatha Christie died in 1976, personal computers were just in their infancy. I looked around to see if our Mrs. Christie's anachronistic techo-ignorance had struck anyone aside from Mairead, but they were all too interested in how the net was tightening around Howard.

"So," Sebastian said, "we went back to Calhoun's laptop and checked out his search history, and yes, he did, in fact, research arsenic the day after Grant Neuman talked to him. And most of the sites he hit pointed out that arsenic is almost never considered in forensic toxicology except in cases of industrial pollution because your average Joe can't get his hands on any. But Howard thought he knew how he could get his hands on some."

"His copy of *Angel Whispers*," I said.

"Exactly. And, as a pretty sophisticated cook, he figured it would be easy enough to extract the arsenic from the cover by boiling it down into a reduction. Which, I should add, probably never would have occurred to any of us if it hadn't been for you, Tory." Was I wrong to want to jump up and kiss him for that acknowledgment? "And at that point his thinking is—and remember, he doesn't yet know about abrin—he could kill both Sailor Savoie and Wren Madison with a poison so archaic nobody would think of it, let alone test for it."

"Boy, that's really cold," Nic said.

"Yeah," said Adrian, looking rather shocked himself. "He makes Lucrezia Borgia look all warm and fuzzy."

"Not a good guy," Sebastian agreed. "Plus, for his purposes the timing of the two birthdays couldn't have been better. In a few weeks, it would be Sailor's thirtieth. And he knew she planned to spend it alone in Mexico."

"Yeah, he did," Nic confirmed. "He was on that group email she sent out."

Sebastian nodded. "He was. We checked." *Of course he had.* "It was preferable to take out Sailor first, since if there were any questions, he would appear to have no motive. And then when Wren dies on her birthday a few weeks later, it will just look like Nic, and by extension Calhoun, were the innocent recipients of a terrible tragedy."

Nic snorted again. "Innocent. Me maybe, but not that, that piece of . . ." She stopped herself and, unlike Sebastian, remembered she was in polite company. "Poo," she ended lamely. Which set us all off again.

"So," Sebastian said firmly, "to get back to business . . ." As if he hadn't managed a smile or two himself. Which, I had to admit, had been a lovely window into what the man might be like if only you could get him away from murder and mayhem for a while. ". . . that weekend, Calhoun makes the reduction. On Monday, the 23rd, he sends Rachel out to buy a very specific bottle of tequila, one in a ceramic bottle. Later that day while she's out, maybe walking the dog . . ."

"For sure she was," Nic put in. "There's a strict walkies schedule with Bertram. Eight in the morning, twelve noon, four in the afternoon and eight at night. After that, it's pee pads all the way."

"Good to know," Sebastian lied politely. "So, probably during the noon walk, Howard removes the clear plastic security tape around the bottle's stopper, adds the arsenic reduction and tapes the stopper back in place. He puts it on Rachel's desk with a sticky note saying 'SS birthday.' The following Friday, the 27th, just before he leaves for the weekend, Calhoun tells her what to write on the card and to FedEx the bottle that afternoon to the resort in Mexico to hold for Sailor's birthday the *following* Friday. When, once again, he'll be conveniently away in the Hamptons."

"Or, as it happened, conveniently dead," I didn't say. Either way, the alibi had worked.

Suddenly Adrian saw it all. "He set Rachel up as suspect number one in case there was any chance that Sailor's death was considered suspicious. And I fell for it. Jeez, the guy really had it all planned out."

"And all of it simply as a precaution," Sebastian said. "After all, the chances that her death would be considered anything other than food poisoning were, he thought, pretty slim. And even if there were suspicions, who would think of testing for an old-fashioned poison like arsenic in this day and age?"

Mrs. Christie, never one to toot her own horn, simply managed a small "ahem," which of course was enough for Sebastian to smile at her apologetically and add, "Except for you, of course."

"And then he was going to do the same thing with Wren?" Adrian asked.

Sebastian nodded. "Probably added to something to eat like chocolates, so the coincidence wouldn't be so obvious."

Nic shook her head. "Caviar," she said definitively. "One of those expensive little tins of caviar. Wren loves caviar."

"Okay," Sebastian said. "Let's say it was going to be caviar. Caviar to be bought and sent by Rachel to Wren on her birthday because, once again, Howard would be away in the Hamptons."

"With me," Nic supplied. "He was supposed to take me except he didn't. Go to the Hamptons, I mean, or take me. I mean obviously because, you know, he was dead and so he didn't send her caviar."

"Correct," Mrs. Christie finally put in. "He did not send caviar because I gave him a better idea. I gave him abrin."

Thirty-Two

"They are never really dead, these super criminals."

—Tommy Beresford in imitation of

Hercule Poirot, *Partners in Crime*

"YOU CAN'T BE BLAMING YOURSELF," I PROTESTED. "A MOMENT ago you were warning us against just that kind of thinking. I mean, am I responsible because I told Howard about arsenic in old book covers?" *Yikes. I didn't even know I'd been thinking that.* "*We* told Howard about Bertram inhaling abrin because it was the *truth.* What he chose to do with that truth was *his* doing, not yours, not ours, not anyone's but Howard Calhoun's."

Mrs. Christie gave me a grateful smile. "Of course you're right, my dear," she said. "Isn't it odd how easy it is to give others advice and how difficult it is to accept that same counsel oneself?"

"And besides," Nic put in, "*he* was the one who brought that poison jewelry back. And even if we'd never told him about abrin, he was going to get Wren with arsenic anyway. I mean the guy was, what do you call it? Ruthless?" She rolled the word around on her tongue and found it good. "Yeah, that's it, the guy was *ruthless.*"

"Oh, I've no doubt of it," Mrs. Christie said. "And I'm sure Detective Mendez-Cruz is correct that Mr. Calhoun originally intended to kill both young women with arsenic. "But then, of course, *we*"—here she shot me a significant look—"gave him abrin."

"But once he knew about abrin on that Sunday," Adrian put in, "why not use it—a completely undetectable poison—for both?"

"Because it was too late," Mrs. Christie explained. "Or at least he thought it was. Remember, he'd doctored the bottle and instructed Miss Featherstonhaugh to send it off on Friday. Then he left for the weekend. But Miss Featherstonhaugh didn't send the bottle off on Friday, because shortly after her employer left for the weekend, she was in hospital, and the bottle remained on her desk in the utility room. But, of course, Mr. Calhoun did not know that and when he arrived back on the Sunday and learned about abrin, he assumed that . . ."

"The plan was already afoot!" Mairead interrupted excitedly.

Mrs. Christie smiled at her. "Indeed. He assumed that the bottle containing the arsenic reduction had already been sent to Ms. Savoie. Am I right, Miss Nicola, that Mr. Calhoun was not a frequent visitor to the utility room that held Miss Featherstonhaugh's desk?"

"Like, only when he had to," Nic said, wrinkling her nose, "on account of the stinky pee pads and all."

Mrs. Christie nodded her understanding. "Thus he assumed it was too late to use abrin on Miss Savoie, but not too late for the attempt on Miss Madison."

"How do you know all this, though?" I asked.

"An excellent question," Mrs. Christie said. "I don't. But certain aspects of our conversation with Mr. Calhoun that Sunday lead directly to that conclusion." *Oh lord, what had I missed? Again.*

"What aspects?" I asked despairingly.

"Well, tell me, do you recall Mr. Calhoun's reaction when Miss Nicola told him about Bertram's narrow escape?"

I thought back. "Well, at first, he was fine with it. He was inclined to blame Rachel, but when Nic defended her, he just said, 'Dogs get sick, it's nobody's fault.' But then, when Nic felt obliged to say it hadn't been Sailor's fault, either, he became really, I don't know, disturbed."

"That's right," Nic chimed in. "He kind of went grey the minute Sailor's name came up." I could almost see her replaying the scene in her mind. "But when I explained that I *didn't* think she'd slipped Bertram an oxy . . ."

"All of a sudden he was intrigued," I broke in.

It was true. *"You're saying Sailor gave Bertram oxy?"* Howard hadn't been appalled by the idea, he'd been interested in it.

"And just before he left," I said, thinking back, "he was almost, I don't know, *pushing* the idea of Sailor and the oxy."

"You're right," Nic added. "He said if anything made Bertram sick it was some kind of party drug of Sailor's."

I looked at Mrs. Christie uncertainly. "But maybe that's just hindsight?"

"Oh no, my dear," Mrs. Christie said. "I noticed the same thing." *Of course you did. You notice everything.* "No doubt, Mr. Calhoun's first, rather panicked, reaction was that, in the event of Miss Savoie's death being investigated, a rumor that she had poisoned his dog might be construed by some as a motive on his part to kill her. But on second thought, he realized that what would seem perhaps a weak motive in his case—anger over an attempt to kill a dog that he'd clearly never cared for—was quite a strong one in the case of Miss Featherstonhaugh, who everyone knew cared deeply about the dog."

"So later, when he told Rachel that Sailor had poisoned Bertram, it was to set Rachel up with a motive *just in case*?" I asked, appalled.

"Oh yes, I'm quite sure that became his intent. After all, he'd been very careful from the beginning, as Mr. Gooding has pointed out, that should the finger of suspicion be pointed at anyone, it would be Miss Featherstonhaugh. What a gift to be given a motive as well."

But now something else was bothering me. "There was something going on with Howard, though, even before he started blaming Sailor for everything," I said. "It was after Nic told him about crushing the rosary pea and explained about abrin . . ."

"Which you will recall," Mrs. Christie noted, "she described as untraceable."

"I did," Nic said proudly. "It took me a second to think of the word but then it came to me."

"Okay," I said, "which she described as untraceable. But the point is, he stopped and thought about that for a minute before getting all patronizing and dismissing the whole idea."

"That's right!" Nic said. "He tried to make us feel small and he called you an old lady, Mrs. M, and said the whole thing was some fairy tale you made up. I didn't like that at all."

"And you defended me nobly, Miss Nicola," Mrs. Christie said with a fond smile.

Nic beamed, and I knew that any previous misunderstanding with Mrs. M had been wiped from the books. "Well, it made me mad," she said. "And I didn't like the way he said all snooty-like, 'Well, I'm sure Bertram did not almost die from a *seed*.' Nic's impersonation of Howard at his most pompous was spot on, and I had to smother a laugh. "He thought it was stupid."

"Not at all," Mrs. Christie corrected her. "He thought it brilliant. He merely wanted us to *think* he'd dismissed the idea. But, as your cousin points out, he listened very carefully to what we had to say about abrin and then was for a brief time quite silent. I'm sure that was when he realized that abrin was a better method to effect Miss Madison's demise than arsenic."

"I think you're right," I said. "At first it was almost like his interest was caught. It was only later when Nic defended you that he went ballistic."

"Yeah, well, Howard never liked being told he was wrong," Nic said.

"True," I said, "but it wasn't just that." I had a glimmer of an idea. "What did you actually say, Nic, do you remember?" I wasn't sure I recalled the exact words, but then I wasn't an actor trained to retain dialogue.

"*Of course* I do," Nic said. "I said, 'She's a smart lady, and if she says it's poison, I believe her.'"

"Did you ever actually use the word 'poison' before then?" I asked.

I could almost see Nic running through the whole scene in her head. "Nope," she announced finally. "That was the very first time I used that word."

I turned, triumphant, to Mrs. Christie. "And *that's* when he went ballistic. 'This *poison* talk is ridiculous,' he said."

"Yeah," Nic confirmed. "And then he kept repeating it. He said, 'You keep quiet about this poison bullshit.'" She turned to Mrs. Christie. "I'm sorry, his words, not mine."

"Of course, my dear," Mrs. Christie said. "Think nothing of it."

I turned to Mrs. Christie. "At the time, I thought he was afraid that Brooke would blame him," I said. "But now that I think back I remember you weren't convinced. When I said he was worried Brooke would be angry with him, you just said 'perhaps.'"

Which was true. When was I going to learn to *pay attention* to the least little utterance by this woman? *Especially* to the least little utterance.

Mrs. Christie nodded. "It did seem to me to be an overreaction. But I couldn't be sure. And I try never to be too sure, to be able to admit that I do not know." To paraphrase Hercule Poirot in *Curtain*.

"But now we know that by that point Brooke had already rejected his marriage proposal," I added. "So why would he care if she was angry with him? If anything, he was probably already looking for another rich widow."

"Indeed. When you relayed that information after the gala, it seemed to me to put a very different complexion on the matter."

I remembered then her quiet *"Which explains a great deal"* when I'd told her about it. *Once again Tory Van Dyne fails to pay attention.*

"So, it was the word 'poison' that set him off, not concern about Brooke," I said.

"Yes, that would be my conclusion as well," Mrs. Christie agreed. "And, of course, it makes perfect sense. The man was already planning the use of a second poison. The less that word was used, the better."

Nic was still trying to catch up. "Are you telling me he came up with how to use a rosary pea on Wren while he was standing right there in front of us that day?"

"Oh yes, I've no doubt of it. He knew cocaine was Miss Madison's weakness. I'm sure he immediately recognized the advantages of cocaine mixed with a virtually unknown and untraceable poison over caviar dosed with arsenic. Not to mention that the circumstances of the second attack—seemingly tainted drug use—would have the additional advantage of being quite dissimilar from what was seemingly a common foodborne illness in the case of Miss Savoie."

"Like when in a book the killer uses a knife the first time and a gun the second," Mairead put in excitedly. "It confuses things, makes the killings look unrelated. It hides the murderer!"

Mrs. Christie liked this observation. In fact she liked it so much that she felt compelled to quote Hercule Poirot on this very topic from *The A.B.C. Murders*, but with her own particular emphasis. "It is very true," she said, "that sometimes it seemed as though there were two intelligences at work. But crime is terribly revealing. Try and vary your methods as you will, your tastes, your habits, your attitude of mind and your *soul* is revealed by your actions." She paused. "And I'm afraid Mr. Calhoun's soul was, to quote Miss Featherstonhaugh, quite, quite wicked."

But Adrian the Clear-Eyed Observer had an objection. "This all sounds good on paper, but there are still some questions that need answers. I mean, first of all, how do you crush something that hard? We don't all wear ten pounds of platform boots on our feet like Nic. And how do you grind it into powder without inhaling it yourself? We aren't all almost six feet tall like Nic. Howard was a short guy with what, a hammer?"

"No," I said. "A mortar and pestle."

"Ah, of course," Adrian said with heavy irony. "What else. A mortar and pestle."

"Look," I said. "Howard was a foodie. When he ground spices, he didn't take the easy way out, like an electric spice grinder, before he added them to his chicken masala or whatever."

"Ooh, I remember that chicken masala," Nic said. "It was *fire*."

"It was," I agreed. "And do you remember how Howard bored us all to tears telling us how he used a special granite mortar and pestle to pound and grind his peppercorns and suchlike?"

"Well, no," Nic admitted. "I was kind of too busy eating."

"The point is," I said, "pounding a rosary pea open and then grinding the insides to a powder in a mortar and pestle would be nothing to Howard."

Here Adrian raised his hand, but I beat him to it. "The tricky part, of course, is not breathing it in yourself. So I ask you, how many of us have an extra N95 mask left over from the pandemic tucked away in some bathroom cabinet 'just in case'? I know I do."

Adrian had to give me that one. "I do, too," he admitted.

"Me, too," Nic said.

Mairead and Mrs. Christie somehow knew this poll wasn't for them, but Sebastian nodded.

"Okay," Adrian conceded. "That makes sense. But where's the proof?"

Ah, the $20,000 question. To which, amazingly, I thought I had the answer.

"Probably still in the mortar. I'm sure he wiped it out carefully, but that granite is rough, unpolished, with lots of nooks and crannies to give the pestle something to grind against."

I looked over to Sebastian. "Your team was looking for evidence of an arsenic reduction, so probably didn't consider the mortar and pestle in their testing. Not to mention that Howard kept it as a kind of decorative piece on the sideboard in his living room, so they wouldn't have considered it as a kitchen item. But I bet they could get something out of it. I mean, obviously, it hasn't been used since Howard, um, died."

Sebastian nodded. "We'll take a look."

"Okay," Adrian said. "Let's take it as a given that *someone* grinds the abrin and adds it to some cocaine that Wren gets on her birthday. But if it's Howard, how do you get around the fact that Howard was *dead* when he sent it to her? I mean, how does a dead man buy cocaine, add poison to it and then send it to someone else?"

"I think," Sebastian broke in, "that I can answer that."

"Glad to hear it," Adrian said. Sincerely, I might add. Adrian the Snarky had long since left the room.

"Quite frankly," Sebastian admitted, "we didn't know how Calhoun could have safely ground the abrin fine enough that it wasn't an obvious add. So Tory's explanation helps a lot there. But we do know this—Calhoun was the one who sent the coke to Wren Madison. And we know how he did it, even though as you put it, he was dead."

"Oh, well done, Detective," Mrs. Christie said.

Sebastian nodded to her. "All credit to you."

Turning back to the rest of us, he explained, "Mrs. Mallowan's second question to me last week was a lot like Adrian's. How do you arrange a delivery of poison cocaine when, one, you're the guy who has the poison, not the guy who has the cocaine, and, two, you're a pile of ashes."

Mrs. Christie looked a little startled at this freestyle version of her words. "Actually, Detective Mendez-Cruz, what I asked was, Is there any possibility that Mr. Calhoun could have poisoned that cocaine and arranged *before* he was killed to have it delivered on Miss Madison's birthday?" Which was, I thought, more like an elegant solution than an actual question. "And if that could have been done, was there any way to prove it?"

"So your second and third questions, actually," Mairead pointed out.

"Exactly, my dear," Mrs. Christie said with a crisp nod. At least *someone* was sticking to the script.

"I take it the answer to both questions was yes?" Adrian asked.

Sebastian nodded. "With Featherstonehaugh in custody, we were able to get a warrant to check her phone history. Which got us nothing except some texts to Calhoun about work. No takeout pizza, no friends, certainly no cocaine orders."

"That's kind of sad," Nic said. "I mean, not about the cocaine but the, like, no friends part." Sometimes I just loved loved loved my cousin.

Sebastian then added the kicker. "Not like the texts on Calhoun's phone."

Of course. Of course they'd checked Howard's phone. Somebody had pushed the man in front of a subway. It might be a good idea to check if he'd gotten threatening texts. There was only one problem that I could see.

"His phone was, um, accessible? Not, I mean . . ." *What, Tory? Not crushed beneath the wheels of the No. 6 train, like its owner?*

"It took some, um, work," Sebastian said delicately, "but yes, within a week or so we were able to recover his recent history. But back then we were looking for any threatening incoming communications, not buy texts to dealers along the lines of 'one gram.'"

"So you looked again for orders like that on his phone?" The questioner was Mairead and suddenly I realized that we were *talking about how to order cocaine from drug dealers in front of an eleven-year-old girl.* Maybe it was time to send her home.

"Mairead . . ." I began. But the girl knew exactly where I was going.

"Oh, not to be fussed," she said airily. "There's nothing you can tell me about drugs that I haven't already learned at school." I must have looked a bit shocked, so she added, "I mean through the Courage to Speak program, y'know, where they tell us what to say and do if we're approached to buy drugs in the park and other such nonsense."

I realized the girl probably knew more about street drugs than I did, which was, as Nic would say, kind of sad.

"Okay," I said to Sebastian. "Carry on."

"We found lots of texts on his phone for pizza." *Ah, so Howard wasn't always the food snob he claimed to be.* "And for cocaine."

"Doesn't surprise me," Nic said. "I think Howard considered coke a business expense, something to give as a little giftie to people he wanted to impress or add as a client."

"People like Wren," Adrian said.

Nic nodded. "Exactly like Wren. He loved giving her a little bump before a dinner party. Then he'd try to talk her into dumping her agent for him, which she was, like, never gonna do because her agent is her cousin."

Why was nobody asking the obvious question?

"When was Howard's last order?" I asked Sebastian.

"I'm glad you asked," he said, smiling at me like I was his favorite person in the world. I wanted that smile for the rest of my life. "His last order, for a smallish one gram, was sent at ten forty-seven a.m. on Monday, September 30."

"The morning of the day he died."

"Exactly. The morning of the day he died."

"But we don't know if that was the coke that was eventually sent to Wren."

"Ah, there you are wrong," Sebastian said, for all the world like some kind of Golden Age detective. I was surprised he didn't exhort me to use my little grey cells. "Let's consider the timeline."

This was clearly going to take a while, so we all settled in to listening mode.

"On Sunday, Howard learns about abrin. On Monday morning, he texts the number of a known ring-and-bring dealer for delivery of one gram of cocaine. We know the number because dealers tend to hang on to the burner phones they use for taking orders longer than they should, mostly because it's a pain to have to let their regular customers know when the number has changed."

We all nodded as if we could perfectly understand this business concern.

"But what we really needed to know was what happened to the cocaine once it was delivered to Calhoun. And for that we needed to find the delivery guy. My theory was Calhoun takes the delivery and arranges a little side deal with the guy. He says he's going to be out of town for a while, so he wants the guy to hold on to the coke for a couple of weeks and then deliver it to a friend on her birthday while he's gone. He offers him a hundred under the table that day and another two hundred when he gets back."

"The way you tell it, that doesn't sound like a theory," I said. "That sounds like you know that's what actually happened."

"Well, it was the theory, but you're right," Sebastian said, not even trying to keep the satisfaction out of his voice. "That's what happened. Once the delivery kid agreed to his plan, Calhoun said he'd just nip up to his apartment with that little baggie of coke and put it in an envelope with the birthday girl's info on it and what the guy was supposed to say when she came down to take delivery. 'Happy birthday, too special to share.'"

"How do you know all this?" Mairead asked, her eyes wide.

"Our guys on the street tracked the delivery guy down. It wasn't hard. He'd bragged about his side gig to his buddies, including one of our regular informers. So they pulled the kid aside and when they told him they weren't after him, just some info on a client, he was happy to talk. First of all, most of these small-timers think if you do the cops a favor, maybe they'll do you one at some point, and our guys on the street don't actively discourage that kind of thinking. Second, he was ticked off because he never got his second payment."

"Because Howard was dead," I said.

"Because Howard was dead."

"But is any of this delivery guy's information admissible?" Adrian asked. A reasonable question, I thought.

"Almost none of it," Sebastian admitted. "It was all off the record."

"So Calhoun thought of everything."

"Not everything," Sebastian said, smiling once more. "He wiped his prints off the packet but assumed the guy would toss the instructions. But here's the thing. Apparently, this kid got a big fine last year for littering. He claims the ticket was just harassment by the cops, but he's real careful now. He never throws stuff on the street. He just crams it into his saddlebag."

"And the envelope with the address and what he was supposed to say was still in there?" I asked. Well, squeaked. I mean, this was *exciting.*

"Oh yeah," Sebastian said, giving me that favorite-person-in-the-world, to-die-for smile. "With Calhoun's prints all over it."

"We've got him!" Mairead cried gleefully. *We,* I thought. *You gotta love this kid.*

"Yeah," Adrian the Wet Blanket said gloomily. "Except the guy's still dead. So we can't really *get* him if you know what I mean." Adrian has a kind of Old Testament sense of justice that I really like.

Nic leaned into me and half whispered, "Does this mean, like, if Howard wanted me alive, you know, for his cut, then he isn't going to poison me from, like, beyond the grave like he did Sailor and Wren?" Her voice broke. "Does this mean I'm safe, Tor?"

I realized then how desperately she'd been trying to keep up a brave front in the face of a terrifying uncertainty. "Yes," I said, my voice only a little wobbly. "Yes, that's exactly what it means, Nic."

At which point Nic promptly burst into tears.

I scooched over and put my arm around her. "It's all right, Nic," I said. "Everything's all right."

Because, for once, I knew it was.

It seemed to me that it was time to call this particular meeting of Agatha Inc. to a close. If nobody else was exhausted, I certainly was. It's not every day that you find out that the life of the flibber-tigibbet cousin you love like a sister is no longer in danger.

Of course, rather than admit any such emotional vulnerability (heaven forfend), I simply used Mairead as my excuse to bow out. Looking pointedly at my watch, I said, "Good lord, it's past eight! Mairead, your da will be wondering what's become of you."

Mairead looked at me like I was crazy. "No, he won't. He knows I'll text him when we're done here."

"Well, then," I said, looking to the others for support, "wouldn't you all agree that we're done here?"

"Certainly," Mrs. Christie said. "For the time being."

Nic was all in. "Who wants to go out for a celebratory drink on me?"

"I've never been known to pass up a free drink," Adrian said with a grin.

Sebastian, who suddenly looked as tired and drawn as I'd ever seen him, simply said, "I'll pass," and I realized that for Detective Mendez-Cruz, all this had been work—weeks of painstaking, grueling police work. None of the relief I was now feeling could have, would have, happened without him.

"Thank you, Sebastian," I said. "Thank you for everything."

His dark eyes grew soft. "You're welcome, Tory." He was speaking to me and only to me. It was as if we were the only two people in the room. "You are so very welcome."

Thirty-Three

◇◇◇◇◇◇◇◇◇◇◇◇◇◇◇◇◇◇◇◇◇◇◇◇

"Everybody always knows something," said Adam, "even if it's something they don't know they know."

—Special Branch Operative Adam
Goodman, *Cat Among the Pigeons*

I WAS BORED.

It had been a week since the last meeting of Agatha Inc., and I was hideously bored. Even choosing my daily outfit had become a bore. Today's was particularly uninspired—a black tunic top over black leggings. Snore. Not even work relieved the boredom, mostly because I was finally getting around to attending to that most boring of all conservator tasks, board (pun fully intended) slotting. Board slotting is the repair of a leather-bound book in which the cover boards have, through overuse, detached from the book's spine. I'd been ignoring about a dozen or so of the library's saddest cases for too long, and so here I was using my handy-dandy board slotting machine to cut a slot into each cover board just wide enough to accept the replacement textile flange that attaches the spine to the board. And, yes, it is just as tedious as it sounds. I had to remind myself that they wouldn't have called it "work" if it was fun. If that were the case, they would have called it "fun."

And maybe my feelings were just a little hurt. A full week and *not one word* from Sebastian. Had I imagined that moment of connection?

And, to top it all off, yesterday's Sunday dinner with the whole famdamnily had been quite the affair, what with Nic doing all the parts in the Tory-thought-Nic-was-going-to-be-pushed-under-a-bus-because-the-killer-was-watching-her-only-it-turned-out-the-killer-was-actually-after-Brooke-Sinclair drama and Great-Aunt Doris saying things like, "This comes as no surprise to me. Once a shark has tracked down its prey, it stalks it before going in for the kill."

What did come as a surprise, though, was Nic's other piece of news.

"And, oh yeah," she'd added, almost as an aside, "I'm taking the dog."

Aunt Bunny sat up very straight at that. "Dog? What dog? In this house? We can't have a dog in this house!" It was as if Nic had suggested bringing in an orangutan.

I knew about Aunt Bunny's "pet allergies." We all did. We all also knew they were not so much a reaction to pet dander as to what she perceived as pet chaos. The jumping up on furniture, the giving of slobbery kisses, not to mention, *shudder*, the occasional "mistake." And, if the dog Nic was talking about was the one I thought it was, then Aunt Bunny was about to suffer a very rude shock indeed.

It was, of course. It was Bertram.

"I mean, what choice did I have?" Nic pointed out when she shared this unhappy news. "I'm practically the one who got Rachel thrown in jail." *Well, no, that honor lies with Mrs. Christie and Sebastian, but okay.* "Bertram is back with Brooke and she, Rachel that is, knows Brooke is going to give Bertram away to somebody and she, Rachel that is, says I'm the only one she trusts with him because he actually likes me and because I told her I loved him when we were at Veselka—which was maybe a little exaggerated, but I do *like* the pooch—and could I tell Brooke I'd take him."

"You have been speaking with that, that . . ." Aunt Bunny couldn't bring herself to say the word "killer" or "murderer." It literally wasn't in her lexicon. ". . . that *awful girl?*"

"Of course not," Nic said. "Her lawyer called me. It made me sad."

"So you're doing this as a favor to that, that . . ." Finally, Aunt Bunny found the word. ". . . that *felon?*"

"Well, no," Nic said. "It's really a favor to Brooke on account of because I called her after he, the lawyer, I mean, called me and I said I'd be happy to take care of Bertram and she said she would be . . ." Air quotes here. ". . . 'forever grateful' if we 'took the poor doggy in.'"

Oh, well played with the "we," I thought. How could Aunt Bunny resist having Brooke Sinclair forever in her social debt?

"Well, I suppose it's the right thing to do," Aunt Bunny said nobly, before adding, "but we can't have the animal here."

Nic didn't skip a beat. "Yeah, I've been thinking about that. I mean, if I'm going to start acting like a grown-up, you know, like taking responsibility and doing the right thing and all, maybe I should start living like a grown-up, too. Like having a place of my own." *Game, set and match to Nicola Van Dyne,* I thought.

And I was right. Aunt Bunny turned to her husband, who, in a vain attempt to ignore the whole controversy, had been busy forking in roast chicken as if he didn't know where his next meal was coming from. "Rupert," she said, "I do think it's past time for Nicola to have her own place. Please arrange it."

And with that, the problem was solved. Nic gave me an enormous wink, and said demurely, "Whatever you say, Mummy."

AND NOW IT WAS MONDAY, AND THE ONLY THING I COULD look forward to was maybe seeing Mrs. Christie after I finished all my mind-numbing work.

"Maybe" being the operative word. Because I thought there was every possibility that I would *not* be seeing Mrs. Christie as usual because there was every possibility that Mrs. Christie—having finished her appointed task of helping me (or at least her crime-fighting partner Detective Sebastian Mendez-Cruz) solve a murder—might have been, let's say, recalled to the Eternity or wherever it was she habitually resided.

Adrian, on the other hand, was convinced she'd be with us, if only because of her rather cryptic response at last week's meeting to my "Wouldn't you all agree that we're done here?"

"Certainly," she'd said, then added, "for the time being."

I hadn't really paid much attention to it at the time, but when Adrian brought it up a few days later, I thought maybe he was right. Maybe there had been a hint of some unfinished business there. Or maybe Mrs. Christie was just saying "so long" until the next murder mystery came along for her to help me solve. The likelihood of which was practically nil.

Oh well. No sense in fretting. I turned back to my boredom, which was only relieved when Mairead came by with Tony after school for our usual session. She was thrilled when I let her handle the slotting machine.

Things also picked up a bit at quitting time, when Nic showed up because she'd been looking at loft apartments in Tribeca all afternoon and really, really needed a drink. We met Adrian in the hall and he was all in, too. I wondered if Sebastian might possibly, just possibly, show up to give us some kind of update, though what that could be I had no idea.

And then the doorbell rang, and there was Sebastian at my front door. As if I'd somehow *manifested* him. Now, Adrian and I agree that this manifesting nonsense is just that. Nonsense. But the fact remains that when the doorbell rang and I opened it, Sebastian was standing at my front door. As if I had willed it. And all I could think was, *Why did you choose this incredibly boring outfit, Tory?*

"Oh, it's you," I said. Idiotically.

"Um, yeah, it's me," he said. Equally idiotically. "You look nice," he added, barely glancing, thank goodness, at my incredibly boring outfit.

"So do you," I said, barely glancing at his truly ugly brown suit.

Then we just stood there, staring into each other's eyes like dumbstruck teenagers.

Thank goodness Adrian was standing by to guide the kids through this terribly awkward encounter.

"Come on in, Sebastian," he said, elbowing me out of the way and holding the door wide. He then hissed in my ear, "Here's where you ask him to join us for a drink."

"Would you like to join us for a drink?" I asked woodenly.

"Yes," Sebastian replied woodenly.

Adrian heaved a deep sigh. "Good. Because obviously we all need one."

There was much rejoicing by Terrier Tony at the sight of his friend Sebastian, which helped to break the ice. And then Nic took over with the Drama of Bertram as we went up the stairs to the second floor, so that when we arrived at the Christie Room, Sebastian and I had almost moved out of zombie mode.

She was there, of course. Wearing a silk dress in a surprisingly gay print of red circles of various sizes against a dark blue background. It was almost as if she had dressed for a party. My heart sank. Maybe a going-away party?

Tonight's special, Nic and Adrian decreed, was something called a Houla-Houla Cocktail, which necessitated me running upstairs for orange juice from my fridge but was well worth the trip. Once we were all settled in our usual places (which meant, it appeared, Sebastian sitting next to me on the couch), Adrian could contain his curiosity no longer.

Turning to Mrs. Christie, he said, "You mentioned something at our last meeting that seemed odd at the time."

Mrs. Christie smiled. "I say many odd things, Mr. Gooding."

"But they only *seem* odd at the time," he noted. "In retrospect, they make perfect sense. Brilliant sense, even."

"Thank you," she said simply. *You see how it's done, Tory?* "And what did I say that you feel needs explaining?"

"You said that we were done *for the time being*. As if there was more to discuss."

"Well, of course there is," Mrs. Christie said as if it should have been obvious.

"But we'd solved the case," Adrian persisted, and then corrected himself. "Or, rather, you and Sebastian had."

"Oh, Mr. Gooding," Mrs. Christie said in her best Miss Marple voice. "Have you forgotten about the murder of Howard Calhoun?"

The murder of Howard Calhoun. The murder that Mrs. Christie had ostensibly been sent by the Eternity to help me solve.

"I thought Howard got pushed under the No. 6 train by some nutter," Adrian said, and looked to Sebastian for confirmation.

"That was one hypothesis," Sebastian said evasively.

Adrian looked sharply at Mrs. Christie. "Are you saying you know who pushed Calhoun under that train?"

"Oh no, Mr. Gooding. That determination, of course, will be made by Detective Mendez-Cruz. You see, until very recently, I, too, believed Mr. Calhoun had met his death randomly at the hands of some poor demented soul."

She turned to Sebastian. "But I don't think you, Detective Mendez-Cruz, ever truly believed that. If you had, there would have been no reason for you to attend Mr. Calhoun's memorial service. Though, I confess, that did not occur to me at the time." *Take a bow, Tory. It* did *occur to you at the time.*

"It's true," Sebastian said. "In these kinds of crimes, people tend to assume the perpetrator is a man, because, let's face it, it usually is. Even Nic called Howard's killer 'a guy.' But what if that big baggy hoodie was deliberately chosen because it *was* big and baggy? What if it was chosen to hide more than just the killer's face? What if the person who pushed Calhoun under that train was a woman, a woman trying to conceal that fact? If that was the case, then the attack might not be random at all. So I figured the memorial service would be a chance to learn more about the people, especially the women, closest to Calhoun."

"And then after the attack on Mrs. Sinclair," Mrs. Christie said, "am I correct that you began considering Miss Featherstonhaugh as a prime suspect in Mr. Calhoun's death?"

Sebastian nodded. "It seemed like too much of a coincidence that both the attack on Calhoun and Mrs. Sinclair were the same MO and in both cases the perpetrator was wearing a mask and an oversize black hoodie. But we can't be sure. A lot of people wear black hoodies, so really nothing to go on there.

"Nothing to go on there." I'd heard those words before. Where? And then I remembered Sebastian's description of Howard's subway attacker. *"The clothes are all black, so nothing to go on there."* More to the point, I remembered noticing Nic's briefly perplexed look when he'd said it. Why hadn't I jumped on it then? *Because you were all wrapped up in listening to the hot detective, Tory.*

"Ah, yes," Mrs. Christie said, and turned to Nic. "Now, Miss Nicola," she said, "do you recall how you described the . . ." She paused as if she was still having trouble getting her head around the word. ". . . the *hoodie* worn by the person who pushed Mr. Calhoun to his death?"

Nic creased her brow for a moment and then said, "Yeah. I do. I said they were wearing one of those black designer hoodies with a scarf tied around the neck."

"A designer hoodie," Mrs. Christie repeated. "Am I to understand that hoodies are now in the domain of couture?" There was just a little tinge of dismay in her voice.

"Well, no, not couture exactly," Nic said, "But yeah, once streetwear got cool some of the big-name designers like Prada and Cucinelli started offering hoodies in their bridge lines but with their logo so people would know that it cost, like, thousands of dollars."

Mrs. Christie nodded her understanding. "Tell me, why did you assume that the hoodie worn by Mr. Calhoun's killer was a designer item?"

"I have no idea," Nic said wonderingly. "But something must have made me think that."

"Perhaps there was a particular logo that identified it as such?" Mrs. Christie prompted.

Nic closed her eyes, thought for a moment and opened them again. "Not really. One end of the scarf was hanging over where the logo would be. But now that I think about it, I'm sure there was something that made me think it was a Prada."

Sebastian sat up straight at that and leaned toward Nic intently. "What made you think that?" he asked sharply. "Can you see it in your mind's eye?"

Nic shut her eyes again, then opened them wide. "Yes!" she said excitedly. "It was the aglets, of course." As if that should have been obvious.

"The aglets," Sebastian repeated tonelessly. "Help me out here, Nic."

"You know, those little thingummies they wrap around the ends of drawstrings to keep them from unraveling? Like on shoe-laces?" Sebastian nodded, although I thought Mrs. Christie looked a bit lost. "Usually they're just like tiny plastic sleeves but I'd seen this model before and it has, like, silver aglets with the name Prada printed on them in teeny, tiny letters."

"And that day in the subway you noticed these little, um, aglets with Prada printed on them?" Sebastian asked.

"I couldn't see the writing, but, yeah, the silver really stood out against the black."

"You never mentioned them at the time," Sebastian pointed out.

"Well, *at the time*," Nic pointed out in return, "I was trying *not* to remember what I saw. I mean, I always automatically notice style stuff like that, but I didn't actually *remember* it until Mrs. Mallowan started asking me all these questions."

"Fair enough," Sebastian conceded. He nodded to Mrs. Christie to continue.

"Thank you," Mrs. Christie said. "Now, Miss Nicola, to explain your assumption that the hoodie was by Prada, you concluded that you must have come across one before. Where was that?"

Nic thought for a moment, then gave up. "No idea," she said.

But I thought I knew.

"Nic," I said, "What about the one that Howard tried to push on you at Fashion Week?"

"I can't believe you remembered that. I mean, it was, like, five years ago," Nic said, looking at me like I was some kind of witch. Nic tends to forget things after five minutes. On the other hand, Mrs. Christie was looking at me like I had just handed her the key to the castle.

"Tell me about that, Miss Nicola," she said.

"Well, Howard had one that he got as a promo from Prada, like, years ago when they wanted me to wear it to their New York Fashion Week show and post about it on my Insta feed because back then there was that, like, fad for girls wearing guy stuff and he said sure he would get me to wear it but I never did because I accidently spilled some nail polish on one cuff, so it wasn't, like, pristine. So I wore one of their structured silk blazers instead. I still have that."

"But not the hoodie?"

"No," Nic said, "I don't know where that went. I know Howard didn't want it. He said it made him look fat and he was right, I mean, he was way too short to carry off that bulk, so he asked if I wanted it and I said no way so, I don't know, he probably just pawned it off on somebody who doesn't know anything about clothes."

"I see," Mrs. Christie said thoughtfully. "One more question, then. Can you remember how you described Miss Featherston-haugh when she attacked Mrs. Sinclair?"

This one, being so recent, was easy. "I said she was wearing that horrible mask and . . ." Her eyes widened. ". . . *that Prada hoodie.*"

"Just so. And how did you know that this hoodie was a Prada?"

"Well, because this time there was nothing covering the logo . . ." She hesitated for a moment.

"And?" Mrs. Christie prompted.

Nic took a deep breath. "And because of the aglets."

Thirty-Four

◇◇◇◇◇◇◇◇◇◇◇◇◇◇◇◇◇◇◇◇◇◇

"Oh dear, I never realized what a terrible lot of explaining one has to do in a murder!"

—Clarissa Hailsham-Brown, *Spider's Web*

"YES, OF COURSE. THE AGLETS." MRS. CHRISTIE PAUSED FOR A moment to let this sink in. "I assume, Detective Mendez-Cruz, that the garment Miss Featherstonhaugh was wearing when she attacked Mrs. Sinclair is now in the possession of the New York City Police Department."

"It is," Sebastian said. "And, based on the details that Nic's just given us, we'll digitally enhance that subway surveillance video of the attack on Calhoun to bring up those . . ." He looked at Nic again for help.

"Aglets," she said patiently.

". . . those aglets to see if we've got the same jacket."

"Check out the cuff, too," Nic suggested, "for a big old dollop of green gel lacquer."

Sebastian looked confused again, so she raised her hand and waved her neon-green manicure at him in illustration.

"Great," he said. "That ought to clinch it."

And then he said to Mrs. Christie with the kind of smile that made me, at least, want to kiss him all over his face, "As always, you got it in one."

Mrs. Christie, it appeared, wasn't immune to that smile, either. Coloring a little, she said modestly, "Actually it wasn't until I considered what Miss Nicola had said about a 'designer hoodie' in the first instance and a 'Prada hoodie' in the second that I realized my error. I, of course, recognized the Prada name, as I once possessed a House of Prada handbag." She paused, fondly remembering what I knew must have been a lovely piece back in 1935 when Prada was a premier purveyor of luxury leather goods. "And with this additional knowledge," she continued, "I had to pocket my pride and readjust my idea." To borrow from Monsieur Fournier in *Death in the Clouds*. "However, it wasn't until Miss Van Dyne recalled where her cousin might have seen that item before and thus knew it was by Prada, that the connection between the two murders made sense." *Well, good on you, Miss Van Dyne.*

"And now, Detective Mendez-Cruz," she said pointedly, "I firmly believe that *we* are correct about Miss Featherstonhaugh's part in Mr. Calhoun's death."

Adrian could hardly contain himself at the turn the conversation had taken.

"I knew it!" he crowed in a kind of verbal fist pump. "I should have been a detective. I was *sure* that girl was a killer."

Mrs. Christie was prepared to give him that. "So you were, Mr. Gooding," she said, and Adrian beamed. "Though you were perhaps too quick to cling to your theory that her intended victims were Miss Savoie and Miss Madison."

Adrian nodded glumly, and Mrs. Christie added gently, "It is so very difficult to wipe out your false starts and begin again."

I knew the reference at once—Colonel Race in *Death on the Nile*. I glanced at Adrian to see if he'd caught it. He did me one better. In his very best British colonel accent, he deftly completed the exchange. "'It often seems to me that's all detective work is— wiping out your false starts and beginning again.'"

Mrs. Christie laughed delightedly, nodded her recognition, and added, "But without you, Mr. Gooding, we would not have known where to look for the source of the arsenic that killed Miss Savoie. It was *you* who brought the dangers of emerald green book cloth to our attention."

Now it was my turn to be chagrined. I waited for her to say it, to say "and certainly not Miss Van Dyne." Because what I had thought at the time was, *We are not here to provide this woman with another murder to solve.*

Had that really been me? A young woman so afraid of any threat to the carefully constructed walls around her life that she had been willing to ignore the possibility of *murder*? Who was that woman? I certainly didn't know her now. Which, it suddenly occurred to me, was also Mrs. Christie's doing. Perhaps she hadn't come from the Eternity (*or wherever*) solely to help me find a murderer (or in this case, two murderers). Perhaps she had also come to help me find myself.

But that was not what Mrs. Christie said. What Mrs. Christie said was, "And we would not be where we are now had it not been for Miss Van Dyne's brilliant . . ." *Brilliant*. ". . . work on how the arsenic was extracted and the abrin ground."

Here Sebastian felt obliged to add, "And how to find evidence of that process."

Did he mean what I thought he meant? "You *found* the mortar?" I asked. "Why didn't you *tell* us?"

"That's why I'm here tonight," Sebastian protested. "To tell you that you were absolutely right about Calhoun's mortar-and-pestle routine."

"I *knew* it," Nic squealed.

"Brilliant!" Mairead chimed in.

Even Adrian went so far as to give me a thumbs-up.

I confess I took a moment to bask in their regard and to wonder how it was that, in the space of two months, I appeared to have finally actually found my people.

It took an eleven-year-old to bring me back from these philosophical musings.

"But what about *motive*," Mairead was saying. "Why would Rachel kill Mr. Calhoun? She was making a profit on books that he would never miss. She didn't know he was bankrupt. According to Tory's friend at that bookstore, nobody knew. So she thought she was onto a fine thing."

"Ah, my dear," Mrs. Christie said. "That is a good point. But greed is not the only motivation for murder."

I'd heard those words before. I thought back. Yes, when Mrs. Christie had cautioned Sebastian not an hour after Howard's death. *"Greed is often the motivation for murder,"* she'd said, *"but not, of course, the only one."* And now here she was, all ready to present us with what that other motivation might have been.

"Though we may never be able to prove it," she said, "I am convinced she killed Mr. Calhoun for the same reason that she tried to kill Mrs. Sinclair. And I am convinced it was, as Miss Nicola so perspicaciously noted, 'all about Bertram.'"

Nic didn't have to know what "perspicaciously" meant to know she was being complimented. Nic could recognize a compliment a mile off.

"Well, thanks, Mrs. M, but I don't get it," Nic said. "I mean, Howard wasn't any threat to Bertram."

And then it came to me.

"But," I said, "maybe Rachel thought he was."

"Exactly," Mrs. Christie said, nodding firmly. "Though perhaps you could clarify why she would think such a thing."

"Of course," I said. "It makes sense when you think about it. Early Monday morning Howard puts on an N95 and grinds himself some abrin in the kitchen. Rachel lets herself into the apartment with the recuperating Bertram in her arms. To get to the utility room where the dog sleeps, she has to pass the kitchen. She glances in and sees Howard at the kitchen counter, but doesn't say anything and he doesn't notice her, focused as he is on grinding something in a mortar and pestle and wearing, of all things, an N95. So that's odd, but she's not that curious. He's making one of his usual concoctions, maybe doesn't like the smell, whatever. She's focused on getting Bertram comfortable, not on whatever Howard's making for lunch. She doesn't say anything, just goes about her business."

"And then what?" Mairead prodded.

"Then, once she's got Bertram settled, she comes back into the kitchen. The mortar and pestle are nowhere to be seen, probably back on the shelf in the living room, and Howard is mask-free. They talk about Bertram's narrow escape, and Howard tells her it was because Sailor gave the pup an oxy. I think she believed him at that point, but not for much longer. Not once she found out that abrin was probably what almost killed Bertram."

I took a deep calming breath. (I will never learn.)

"But Rachel didn't *know* about abrin," Mairead pointed out. "When Nic called her on Sunday to tell her about Bertram, Nic didn't know about abrin yet, so obviously she couldn't have told Rachel about it."

Nic frowned a bit at that, which I thought was significant, and I noticed that Mrs. Christie gave her a sharp look, which was also encouraging.

I paused here, trying to marshal my argument. I thought again about what Rachel had said to Nic at Veselka in response to Nic's halfhearted suggestion that Sailor had poisoned Bertram. *"No, she didn't,"* Rachel had said. *"You must know that."*

"You did talk to Rachel about abrin, didn't you, Nic?"

"Well, yeah, of course I did," Nic replied, as if that was somehow obvious. She looked around at our blank faces. "Didn't I tell you that? Was it important?"

No, of course she hadn't told us that, not even at that meeting in the Christie Room when Adrian had posited that Howard might have told Rachel about the abrin. And why hadn't Nic said something then? Because Nic had been out of the room *taking a pee.*

"No, Nic," I said as calmly as I could. "You didn't tell us that. But it explains why Rachel didn't even ask you what abrin was when you mentioned it at Veselka. If she didn't know what it was, she would have said, 'What's abrin?' She was clearly surprised, but only by the news that it was abrin that had been added to Wren's cocaine."

Mrs. Christie gave me an admiring glance, as if I'd passed some kind of test. It felt good. "Yes," she noted. "One thought at the time that that was an odd omission."

Well, it hadn't struck *this* one as odd then, which made me feel pretty stupid. But at least it did now. And thank you, Mrs. Christie, for once again giving me the confidence to put myself out there.

"When did you tell her about abrin, Nic?" I asked. "And what exactly?"

"Well, I mean, Mairead's right. Like, I didn't tell her on Sunday morning when I called her because, I mean, obviously, I didn't know about it. But after I learned about it from Mrs. M on Sunday night, I called her, Rachel that is, again the *next* day, later on Monday morning, you know, to check on Bertram and let her know about abrin so she could take a mop to the bathroom floor just in case there was any smushed seed left. Of course, I just said it was a *possibility* that abrin made Bertram so sick because I really didn't want her bringing it up with Howard and him getting all bent out of shape again, but I did tell her it was, like, a next-level poison."

So I'd been right. Which meant maybe I was right about what had happened next. Nonetheless, my sneaking suspicion was a reach. I might have abandoned it right then if Mrs. Christie hadn't taken it upon herself to read my mind.

"This might explain what Miss Featherstonhaugh said when you, Miss Nicola, accused her of grinding a rosary pea to add to Miss Madison's cocaine. Do you recall what she said, and, more significantly, *how* she said it?"

For Nic that was an easy one. "Sure, I do. She said . . ." And here Nic did that actor thing she does, where she becomes the other person. ". . . 'Not *me*. *I* didn't grind up any bead.'"

It was like Rachel was in the room with us. It creeped me out, but Mrs. Christie just nodded and said, "As if not she but *someone else* had done so." *Yessss.*

"And she had a pretty good idea," I added with new confidence, "who that someone else was."

"Indeed," Mrs. Christie said, nodding. She knew where I was going with this.

"And," Mairead broke in, "she knew it was a man. Don't you remember, when Nic said that somebody had put abrin in Wren's cocaine, Rachel said, 'Why would *he* want to do that?' So who was *he*?"

Thank you, Mairead, for setting it all up so perfectly. *"He* was Howard," I said. "Ever since Nic's call, she'd known exactly what she'd seen Howard doing in that kitchen."

"Interesting," Mrs. Christie mused. "Tell us, Miss Nicola, what was Miss Featherstonhaugh's reaction when you told her about abrin on that telephone call?"

I knew where she was going. We were definitely both on the same road.

"Well," Nic said, thinking back to the call, "she was pretty upset because you know how she is about Bertram. She asked if Howard knew about the crushed rosary pea possibility and I said yes and she said 'Well, that's not good, he never told me that.'"

"So clearly," I said, "Howard only told her Sailor gave Bertram a pill or something."

I paused for a moment, exhausted by my recitation. I looked at Mrs. Christie. "I don't know how you do this," I said. "All this explanation, getting everything in the right order."

"Well, it *is* my profession," she pointed out.

Uh-oh.

Before she could start on how she loved working things out in her little exercise books, I rushed in to resume my reconstruction. "So, after that phone call with Nic on Monday, Rachel now believes that for some reason, Howard doesn't want her to know about abrin."

"And she's not stupid!" Mairead broke in. "She puts it all together. She realizes what she saw him doing in that kitchen. That's why, when Nic told her that Howard knew about abrin, she said, 'Well, that's not good.'"

"Exactly," I said. "But who would Rachel think it's not good for?"

"No doubt whoever Howard is planning to poison."

"In hindsight, yes," I said. "But what would *Rachel's* logical conclusion be *at the time*? Think about Rachel. She's very aware now that Howard knows about abrin and how it is made. She's equally aware that for some reason he doesn't want her to know about it and, even more suspicious, doesn't want her to know that he knows." Good lord, this was beginning to sound like a Nic "explanation," but it was the best I could do. "Why? Because, she reasons, he was planning to *use* it. But use it on a *person*? Why would she think that? In the general run of things, people don't poison other people. And quite frankly, I can't imagine Rachel caring much if they did.

"But she knows that people do poison dogs, especially if they don't like them. And Howard doesn't like or even need Bertram anymore. Remember what Rachel said at Veselka, that Brooke 'blew him off in the end.' She knows that Howard's got nothing to lose now with Brooke, so why wouldn't he get rid of *Bertram*? It might seem like a leap to us, but for Rachel—lonely, obsessive Rachel whose emotional life is entirely wrapped up in Bertram—it would be a real and terrifying possibility."

"And then," Mairead broke in, eyes shining, "she takes her earliest opportunity to push the villain under a subway before he can carry out his evil plan!"

"Well, that's not exactly the way I would have put it, but yes, that's what I think," I said, finally willing to admit that this was all speculation. "When she realized, or thought she realized, what Howard was planning, I think she put on that hoodie—which I'm guessing Howard let her take when nobody else wanted it—and a leftover surgical mask as a disguise and set out to do exactly what she did. She knew his schedule, she knew he was going uptown for drinks. I think she waited outside One Fifth and when she saw him come out with Nic and head toward the subway, she followed them."

Nic paled. "Was she planning to kill me, too?"

"I doubt it. She knew Howard as well as you did. She knew he'd push to the front. And I don't think she was angry with you. You'd been nice. You'd called to check on Bertram. And with that hood pulled down and the mask on, there wasn't much chance you'd recognize her."

I looked toward Mrs. Christie for some sign that I was on the right track. She indulged me beyond expectations.

"It would certainly explain another of Miss Featherstonhaugh's comments at Mr. Calhoun's memorial service. You told me that she said, 'It would be such a wicked thing to do. To try to kill a defenseless little dog. Wicked, wicked, wicked.'"

"Yes," I said, impressed at Mrs. Christie's recall. "She said precisely that. I don't know how you remembered it so exactly."

"Well, you see, the phrasing struck me at the time as peculiar. She didn't use the past tense. She didn't say, 'It *was* a wicked thing to do.' She wasn't claiming someone *had* poisoned Bertram. She said, 'It *would be* such a wicked thing to do.' She was pronouncing on someone's *intention* to do so."

"Oh god oh god oh god," Nic suddenly broke in. "And how about what she said to me at Veselka?"

Mrs. Christie knew exactly what she meant. "Yes, Miss Nicola. Do you remember her exact words?"

Nic nodded. "She said, 'Anyone who wanted to kill Bertie deserved to die.'"

"Again, a curious use of tense," Mrs. Christie said "Not '*deserves* to die' but '*deserved* to die.' As if the someone had, in fact, already died. For just that reason."

"Howard Calhoun," Adrian said, but with no relish this time. "Howard Calhoun had already died at the hands of Rachel Featherstonhaugh because she was convinced he was going to poison Bertram."

Thirty-Five

◇◇◇◇◇◇◇◇◇◇◇◇◇◇◇◇◇◇

"Murder can sometimes seem justified, but it is murder all the same."

—Hercule Poirot, *Murder in the Mews*

THERE SHOULD HAVE BEEN SOME SATISFACTION IN FINALLY seeing the whole picture. In understanding what had driven Rachel to kill. But even Adrian, whose instinct about her had finally been proved sound, looked miserable. The rest of us were no different. But it took a child to express what we couldn't.

"I feel sorry for Rachel," Mairead said into the silence. "I mean, she thought she had to kill Mr. Calhoun to keep him from killing a dog that she loved. Sure and I know it was wrong, but I can almost understand why she did what she did." She pulled Tony into her lap and buried her face into his scruffy fur.

"And that, my dear Mairead," Mrs. Christie responded, "is your great strength. One forgets how human murderers are." *Until a child reminds us.* (Or because we've read *A Murder Is Announced*.)

Mairead persisted, her face a picture of worry. "Does that mean *anybody* could become a murderer? Because t'other day at school some fool boy asked me if my mam was really dead or did she just run away because I was so ugly." Her face crumpled at the memory, and she hugged Tony even more tightly. "I truly wanted to kill that boy."

And so, at that moment, did every adult in the room.

"You mustn't let that worry you," Mrs. Christie reassured the girl. And then, quoting Hercule Poirot in *Curtain*, added with her usual clear-eyed honesty, "You will find as you grow older that in everyone there arises from time to time the wish to kill—though not"—she paused for emphasis—"the *will* to kill. That will, my dear, is very rare and, in your case, simply not possible."

She spoke with the voice of authority, and you could almost hear Mairead thinking, *Well, she's been right all along about everything else, so she must be right about this.*

The girl, now reassured, pushed on. "But Rachel was very wrong to try to kill that Mrs. Sinclair. For sure, the woman might take the dog Bertram away from her, but that is not a'tall the same thing as *harming* him."

"Indeed," Mrs. Christie agreed. "But I'm afraid that she had discovered with the success of her attack on Mr. Calhoun that it's so dreadfully easy—killing people. And you begin to feel that it doesn't matter. That it's only you that matters! It's dangerous—that." As Jacqueline de Bellefort explains so calmly to M. Poirot in *Death on the Nile*.

Mairead nodded her understanding. "She wanted to kill Mrs. Sinclair for her *own* sake, not for Bertram's."

"Precisely," Mrs. Christie said. "Though neither attack was justifiable, of course. Murder never is. Not even of a man like Howard Calhoun."

And then I couldn't help but play an ace. "Because, although you agree that Howard was not nice, he was alive and now he is dead, and you have a bourgeois attitude to murder. You disapprove of it."

Mrs. Christie smiled knowingly at me. I smiled knowingly back.

Then we recited in tandem, "As Hercule Poirot says in *Cards on the Table*."

"WHO IS SHE?" SEBASTIAN ASKED ME.

We—that is, Sebastian, Nic, Adrian, Mairead, Tony and I—had been heading downstairs while Mrs. Christie "tidied up." Which meant leaving the glasses for me to wash, I knew, but I forgave her.

Sebastian and I had been lagging behind the others, who were now waiting for us in the hall below, their easy chatter in marked contrast to the once again awkward silence between the two of us. I'd begun to despair that we two odd ducks—Sebastian with his disorienting swings from warmly personal to coolly professional, myself still undecided between my once safe, sane, sensible life and the dizzying, terrifying possibilities of the new one that might lie ahead—were ever going to find an easy space as, let's just say, more than friends.

Then he'd stopped suddenly halfway down the staircase. He'd turned to me, and I was disconcertingly aware of his closeness. I flashed back to when I'd first seen this man, to my instinctive reaction to those long legs and slim hips, to those dark eyes, to *that mouth* . . .

"Who is she?" he asked.

His eyes were warm, his voice gentle, undemanding, even a little unsure. Unsure of himself? Or merely unsure of the answer? Or worse still, unsure of me? I searched his face, his eyes, those warm dark eyes that could go cold in an instant. Did I trust this man? If I told him everything that had happened since Mrs. Christie had first confided her childhood fondness for the quiet refuge of the water closet would he simply see it as proof of her instability? Or, worse still, of mine?

"It's a complicated story," I hedged. "And it would take a long time to explain it."

"That's okay," he said, his eyes still warm, his voice still gentle. "We have a long time, don't we?"

"Yes," I half whispered. "Yes, we do."

I HAVE NO IDEA HOW LONG WE STOOD THERE, SIMPLY LOOK-ing at each other. It took a while—maybe years, maybe just minutes, who knew? who cared?—but eventually the shouts of "Get a move on" and "We don't have all night" from the audience below penetrated our little bliss bubble.

"I've got to walk the wee one home to Mac," Nic was calling up to me. *Mac.* The girl had met Cormac Butler exactly once and she was calling him *Mac.* Sometimes I just love love love my cousin. Well, at least I now knew that, for Nic, automatically giving a man a nickname did not necessarily mean a desire for a romantic relationship. Although, I thought, she could do worse than the dreamy Cormac Butler.

Adrian, standing next to Nic at the open front door, tapped his chronometer with one impatient finger. "Are you guys coming with us?" he asked.

Sebastian and I looked at each other, then both shook our heads no.

"Okay," Nic said, "then we're off."

And suddenly we were alone again in our little bubble of happiness, just looking at each other.

Sebastian recovered first. "I, um, need to get back to the precinct," he said reluctantly.

"And I've got to get back to *her*," I said, equally reluctantly. "She asked for 'a word' as we were leaving. I should find out what that's about." Actually, I had a sinking feeling that I already knew what that was about.

"You know," Sebastian said as I was preparing myself to turn away and go back upstairs, "she said a very odd thing to me as I was leaving."

I stopped short. *Uh-oh.* I'd learned by now that when Mrs. Christie said something odd, it was time to *pay attention.*

"She suggested that I might want to look into the death of Calhoun's wife."

I *knew* there was something. Something I'd vowed to come back to. And, of course, had promptly forgotten. It was when Sebastian had noted that Howard must have come up with his plan to poison both Sailor and Wren "almost immediately" after learning that the part of Belle would never be Nic's. And Mrs. Christie had said, "Which was curious."

Which it was, I now realized, because poisoning people who are making life difficult for you isn't generally the first solution that springs to one's mind. Unless, of course, one has had success with that solution before.

"She thinks poisoning Sailor and Wren wasn't Howard's first rodeo," I said.

"Tory Van Dyne, beautiful and brilliant," Sebastian said with that smile. *That smile.*

It was all I could do to say firmly, "And rude. I'm being rude. She's waiting for me."

"Go," Sebastian said with that smile again. "Tomorrow, we will *confer.*"

Thirty-Six

◇◇◇◇◇◇◇◇◇◇◇◇◇◇◇◇◇

*"Never mind. Console yourself, my friend. We may hunt together
again, who knows?"*

—Hercule Poirot, *The Mysterious Affair at
Styles*

WHEN MRS. CHRISTIE HAD ASKED ME FOR A WORD, I'D HAD A
terrible feeling I knew what that word was going to be. I'd had a
terrible feeling it was "goodbye."

After all, she'd done what she'd set out to do—she'd helped me
solve a murder mystery. Several murder mysteries, actually. Her
"holiday" from the Eternity (*or wherever*) was over. I tried to feel
gratitude for all that she'd done for me, for Nic, for Sebastian, for
Mairead, even for Adrian, who, I suspected, was actually beginning to believe in *something*. Maybe just the power of friendship.
But it was a start.

So I tried to feel gratitude. But all I felt was bereft. She couldn't
be leaving.

But she was.

I knew it the minute I stepped back into the room because the
Launer handbag was no longer in its usual place on the floor beside

her. It was now in her lap in that kind of anticipatory grasp that means someone is preparing to leave.

She took one look at my face and knew that I knew.

"You do realize, my dear Tory," she said gently, "that it's time I was getting back."

I nodded. I nodded because I didn't have the words. The words that would express how much I valued and admired her. And then it came to me.

"Mrs. Christie," I said, "if I were at any time to set out on a career of deceit, it would be of you that I should be afraid."

And then that musical laugh, that laugh like clear water over brook stones. "In the immortal phrasing," Mrs. Christie said, "of the Reverend Leonard Clement to Miss Jane Marple in *The Murder at the Vicarage.*"

Immortal. Was it my imagination that she'd placed some subtle emphasis on the word? Well, even I wasn't quite ready to go there yet.

"I want to thank you," I said. "Thank you for what you've done for all of us, but particularly for what you've done for me."

"Well, I only did what I promised, my dear Tory. I helped you solve a mystery," Mrs. Christie pointed out.

Oh no. I wasn't going to let her get away with just that. "You have done much, much more, Mrs. Christie. I've spent the last seven years of my life making sure I was the kind of person that nothing ever happens to. And when you arrived, you changed everything."

"Nonsense, my dear," Mrs. Christie said briskly. "I changed nothing. The moment I met you, I said to myself, life will not pass her by. Strange and exciting events will surround her. You've only got to look at her to know it." Which, I happened to know, was what Dr. Lloyd's companion had said about the tango dancer in Agatha Christie's short story "The Companion."

I had a brief vision of Yours Truly in vintage couture dancing the tango with Sebastian Mendez-Cruz in one of his awful suits and burst out laughing. "I have never danced the tango in my life."

To which Mrs. Christie responded, her eyes sparkling, "But your time will come, my dear. Your time will come."

Overwhelmed by her kindness, I asked—well, whined—"Will I see you again?"

"Oh, my dear, I cannot see the future," she said gently. "I told you that when we first met."

"But," I said, ever hopeful, "that's not necessarily a no."

She nodded. "That is not necessarily a no."

And then she did something rather odd. Opening the Launer, she pulled out her embroidery hoop with its wonderful gaudy parrot and laid it carefully on the table beside her. It was only half-finished.

She stood and said gently, "And now, my dear Tory, I must go."

It was goodbye.

I nodded, moved toward the door and then looked back at her.

"But what will I tell the others?" I asked, keeping my voice as steady as I could. "Where will I tell them you've gone?"

"Tell them this," Mrs. Christie said. "Tell them that I've taken the Road of Dreams."

Epilogue

◇◇◇◇◇◇◇◇◇◇◇◇◇

THE ROAD OF DREAMS

The Road of Dreams leads up the Hill

So straight and white

And bordered wide

With almond trees on either side

In rosy flush of Spring's delight!

Against the frown

Of branches brown

The blossoms laugh and gleam,

Within my dream . . .

—Agatha Christie, from *The Road of Dreams*,
the author's first volume of poems,
published at her own expense by British
publisher Geoffrey Bles in 1925

Author's Note

◇◇◇◇◇◇◇◇◇◇◇◇◇◇◇◇◇◇◇◇◇◇◇◇◇

MY GRANDMOTHER MARGARET JANE PERSHING WAS A NOTED Emily Dickinson collector—but with a twist. Quite aside from assembling an invaluable collection of Dickinson's works (most of which were never published in the poet's lifetime), Margaret Jane also searched out copies of books in Dickinson's personal library in an effort—as she explained it to teenage me—"to understand the poet's mind." As a girl with a very overactive imagination, I pictured my grandmother actually sitting down for a little chitchat with Emily Dickinson, surrounded by the books once treasured by the poet. It made sense to me.

I've been reading mysteries all my life, particularly the Golden Age classics like those by Agatha Christie. And, oddly, when I turned my hand to writing "detective stories" (as Agatha Christie herself called them), that image of Margaret Jane and Emily Dickinson in conversation kept coming back to me. I thought, "What

if someone were to re-create Agatha Christie's personal library—
even to the furnishings and architecture—and unwittingly opened
a portal through which the Queen of Crime came visiting? Or at
least attracted a person *claiming* to be the Queen of Crime?" That,
I thought, would be a book worth writing.

AS A DEDICATED AGATHA CHRISTIE FANGIRL (BEFORE FAN-
girls were even a thing), I'd already read pretty much every one of
the Queen of Crime's sixty-six mystery novels, many of them more
than once, well before I decided to put pen to paper. But for the
book that I was contemplating, more research, *much* more research,
was required.

Getting to know Agatha Christie herself was the great joy of
my investigations. (Though I confess to being quite disappointed
to discover that she denied ownership of the pithy quote so often
attributed to her: "It is ridiculous to set a detective story in New
York City. New York City is itself a detective story.") I read the best
of the Christie biographies, and of those I heartily recommend
Lucy Worsley's excellent *Agatha Christie: An Elusive Woman*. And
I devoured *Agatha Christie's Secret Notebooks: Fifty Years of Mysteries
in the Making*, compiled by the indefatigable John Curran and a
veritable crash course in how to write a mystery novel (of which I
took full advantage!). Most exciting of all, after watching the few
extant television interviews with Mrs. Christie and reading her
own delightful autobiography, I imagined I could almost hear her
voice in my head as I began to write—a bit reserved but warm,
quietly confident and often very, very funny.

Fiction began to grow from fact, and my Mrs. Christie (whoever and whatever she might be) began to come to life in my head,
my heart and on the page.

THE STICKING POINT OF MY PREMISE WAS, OF COURSE, THAT
Agatha Christie's actual library still exists in her holiday home,
Greenway House, now preserved as a living museum by Britain's
National Trust. Wouldn't that be the most likely landing zone for
my heroine? But based on what I'd learned in my reading, I thought
for the purposes of my story it wouldn't work. Agatha Christie had
been quite a shy person. It seemed to me that Greenway House,
with its many daily visitors wandering the halls, would be far too
peopled for her comfort. There would be too much chance of discovery. The real Queen of Crime had learned the perils of unwelcome publicity, much to her cost after her infamous disappearance
in 1926. I doubted very much that in any story I penned, her
earthly (or otherwise) manifestation would welcome that kind of
exposure again. My Agatha Christie would need a quieter, more
private portal.

Also I decided that we needed a credible *reason* for my Mrs.
Christie's sudden urge to return to the living. But what would in-
duce her to do so? I tried to imagine Agatha Christie—with her
fertile imagination, her love of carefully working out whodunits—
lounging around in the Great Hereafter where *everything is known*.
And all I could think was, *"The woman would be bored to death."* (If
you will forgive the pun.) But what if her fertile imagination was
needed, say, in New York, the original home of her American father
and a city she'd visited several times over the course of her life and
very much enjoyed? Might that not be enough incentive to take a
short holiday on Earth? Especially if we gave her a quiet, entirely
familiar room—essentially her Greenway library re-created—in a
small private library (there are several such in New York) devoted to crime fiction? A room where, after hours, she could help

a carefully chosen few—maybe a reclusive book conservator? An NYPD detective with the face of a sad saint? A lonely, tech-savvy little girl? A librarian who believes in nothing?—in solving a mystery. Perhaps even a murder mystery.

How could she resist?

And thus, *Mrs. Christie at the Mystery Guild Library* was born.

need just the *tiniest little bit* of rethinking—and he's pretty much always right. Also, he's really handsome.

Finally, there are the many dear friends who have cheered me on in my "lonely" work. I can't list you all here, but you know who you are. I do, though, want to send a special thank-you to Ronald Mendez, Ada Cruz and Pilar Mendez-Cruz, for allowing me to name the "hot detective" after them!

ACKNOWLEDGMENTS

Someone once said that any author who claims they don't write in their bathrobe is a damn liar. As a writer who can easily spend an entire day scribbling in her bathrobe, I couldn't agree more. I am also suspicious of any author who says book writing is a lonely business. In my experience, the job is crowded with wonderful professionals there to help you with your work. Granted, they may only be in your email or on your phone, but they are *there* nonetheless, and I couldn't have written this book without them.

It all starts, of course, with my amazing agent, Sandy Harding, who is with me every step of the way—from tossing around book ideas to reading the first draft (and second draft, and third draft) to finding the exact right editor (more on that later) to celebrating the final result. I simply couldn't do it without you, my friend.

And as to that "exact right editor . . ." Well, you just couldn't find an editor more exactly right for me (and Mrs. Christie) than Berkley's Michelle Vega. Warm, funny and very, very smart, this is an editor with a talent for reading a manuscript as the *reader* would, and my work is much the better for it. Also, she loves exclamation points!!!

And in my case, there's also family—near and far—cheering me on. The nearest and dearest, of course, is my wonderful husband, who reads every word I write and somehow never doubts me, even when I doubt myself. A brilliant first reader, he has an amazing ability to very diplomatically point out where something might